Stage Four

A work of Fiction

By John C. Payne

Apr 25, 2014

To: Jessica

Enjoy the read !!!

PAGE PUBLISHING, INC.
New York, NY

First originally published by Page Publishing, Inc. 2014

ISBN 978-1-62838-464-2 (pbk)
ISBN 978-1-62838-465-9 (digital)

Printed in the United States of America

PRAISE FOR STAGE FOUR

This book proves Payne's talent as an immensely creative writer. Sharp, page turning plot. Raw visuals. Characters that spring from the page through crisp dialogue. A real hold-onto-your-seat read.

–Karen Casey Fitzjerrell. Author of **Forgiving Effie Beck** (July 2013) and **The Dividing Season,** 2013 EPIC Award Winner.

Wow John Payne is great! He is a fun read. I like this book because it always throws me off just when I thought I had it figured out. That's Mystery-Thriller a "Thai Mall Queen" can get into. It's hard-boiled macho with a spice of animal friendly. What more could a girl want?

–Nancy Oakley – Author of **The Quest for Serendipity** - Star of Mall Queen Reality TV.

John Payne writes a good story and readers can count on being surprised by his clever plot twists. If you're into pets and how they can mysteriously guide your well-being, be links to higher callings and as well invoke justice – then you will really dig this inventive tome. It's Murder She Wrote – Pet Cemetery Style.

–Eric Dreyer Smith – Author of **No One Blames San Antonio for the Civil War.**

ACKNOWLEDGMENTS

ONE SPECIAL PERSON IN MY life, my loving wife, Carol, encouraged me to continue writing. She also contributed in the editorial process. Thanks to Dr. Wally Fredrick, author of the popular novel *The Sea of the Morning Sun* for both his clinical insight and knowledge of watercraft.

Dr. Gordon Rainey provided valuable insight regarding the treatment of melanoma. Jack Selby, a long-time friend and professional associate, helped in the edit. Favre Sparks, another San Antonio author and friend, contributed to the review. Bill Yunker suggested some of the weaponry described in the book.

Thom Somes, The Pet Safety Guy, www.PetTech.net, was persistent in suggesting the need for clarification of the morphing process and several other key issues.

Wikipedia, the free Internet encyclopedia, was consulted for descriptive information about the animals portrayed in the novel.

I am grateful to all of these persons for their time and consideration in making this new book an exciting read.

AUTHOR'S NOTES

THIS STORY IS MY OWN take on the fantasy/paranormal field after careful deliberation and discussion with other readers and friends. I avoided writing about the vampire, zombie, and werewolf characters because their stories remain abundant in the book stores.

Animals play a major role in the story. Three household pets react with their masters in a unique way and under unusual circumstances. Birds, chimps, and the great white shark lend an interesting component to the story.

Thom Somes, The Pet Safety Guy comments, "If you are a pet parent, then you must read this book. Imagine taking that special bond you have with your dog, bird, or even a snake cranking it up 1,000 percent. It is a great read that takes you on an unexpected and imaginatively fun and thrilling ride!"

Enjoy the read.

SOMALIA

THE EXTRACTION V-22 OSPREY with its powerful Rolls-Royce engines took on sporadic rounds from late arriving enemy reinforcements. The pilots maneuvered the chopper away from the exchange of fire with minimal damage to the cockpit. The swirling cross winds and the tree-hugging escape route challenged the pilots, but they stabilized the aircraft and sped to safety. It was a bumpy two-hour hop back to the USS *San Antonio*, the Combined Task Force amphibious flagship.

Blood seeped out of Sergeant First Class Jamie Richard's upper right arm near the shoulder joint. It ached like hell. The compression bandage applied earlier served as a temporary fix. The bullet wound was severe, a through-and-through hot missile missing the humerus bone yet ripping apart a mass of soft flesh.

"I think you'll live to fight again, Richards. Our good doc will stitch up that arm soon as we land," Denis Sweeny said as he spit a wad of tobacco into a "juice cup" on the chopper floor. Jamie shrugged at the rugged and hardened Navy SEAL serving as the team leader. He towered over the six foot, two-hundred-pound Richards.

Grimacing in pain, Jamie flashed him a *V* for victory hand signal with his left hand.

"I bet you can't wait to get back to the States and rejoin your unit, huh, pal?" Denis said, trying to steer his friend's mind from the combat injury. His glass eye was off-center, and to Jamie, it appeared to be twice the size of his one good eye.

"You bet your sweet ass," Jamie said with conviction. "Routine training maneuvers are not as violent and unpredictable as this god-forsaken rat's nest. Shouldn't have volunteered for this last mission. Ninety days and a wakeup call, and I kiss the army good-bye."

Damned if this big lug Sweeny doesn't remind me of the Cyclops in Greek mythology with that weird eye, but thank God it's not in the middle of his forehead. That would be awesome.

"Those *bastards* deserved it," Denis said. "These rogues from hell hijacked the wrong ship. We had no recourse but to blow them away. That'll teach them to stop targeting US flagged vessels on the high seas."

Jamie shrugged. "They claim they're defending their native waters from the illegal dumping of toxic materials intended to wipe out their fishing industry. What a pile of bullshit!"

"Yeah, right," the SEAL responded coyly. "Maybe true, maybe not, but how do they explain to the world the killing, kidnapping, raping of innocents and multiple violations of nautical protocol?"

"No way can they justify their actions to the civilized world," Jamie snarled, his cropped blond hair failing to hide the jagged two-inch scar creeping downward behind his left ear to the chin. He hated the permanent memento from a Taliban sniper in Afghanistan, but there wasn't much he could do about it unless he wore a lengthy mop of curly hair. He hated that hairstyle, too civilian.

"You got a real set of stones, Richards. I was shell-shocked watching the way you wiped out two of the guards with those meat hooks. What a killer you are, a true warrior!"

"If you had the time to witness the action, why the hell didn't you warn me about that fat pirate straddling over his buddy's dead body drawing a bead on me with his AK47?"

"Look, *be all you can be*, army man. The shit was hitting the fan. My hands were full with other problems," Sweeny uttered with a slight grin. "I got a glimpse of you slicing off their ears with that gigantic combat knife. Wasn't it enough that you gutted them like pork farmers butcher their hogs? You turned around hoping that nobody would see you slicing them up. You're some kind of nutcase, Richards, that's for sure."

Jamie stared back at his comrade whose glass eye had repositioned itself in the socket. *I guess he didn't see me lick the blood off the blade. I'm addicted to the taste of the red elixir of the gods. He's jealous of my Yarborough knife awarded to me after I finished the Special Forces Qualification Course. Too bad, I sleep with that baby strapped to my leg. He cared less how I cut them up and tossed some of their body parts to the growling guard dogs to quiet them.*

"Who me, Sweeny? Just finishing up the job. Got to warn the rest of these high-water crooks they can't screw with anything labeled US. For your information, I wanted to cut their tongues out, but they swallowed the slippery devils when I crushed their windpipes. My grandpa Rod told me that some of his troops collected Cong ears as souvenirs during the Vietnam War. Some kind of human bounty, so to speak."

"While you were playing surgeon, why the hell didn't you carve the gold fillings out of their teeth? I'm sure they're more valuable than those sun-burned, shriveled-up pork rinds hanging out your back pocket. By the way, what do you plan to do with them?"

Jamie took a pass on the question, smirked, and changed the subject. "My hat's off to Naval Intelligence for locating the pirates. The Arabian Sea with irregular shorelines off the Gulf of Aden offered the Somali pirates strategic hiding places. Who would have guessed they'd hole up in that exposed cove so far inland? Sounds like a good hiding place to me."

"Not me," Sweeny exhorted. "Doesn't matter. Our team's mission was to search, destroy, and even annihilate. This encounter was a punitive strike and not a hostage rescue mission like most of them. We accomplished that this morning, killing twenty of those no good pirating bastards."

"Hooah!" Jamie shouted, pounding his chest with a single closed fist, still favoring his wounded arm.

Denis Sweeny rubbed his glass eye. It was bothering him. The ocular muscles in the bad eye were never the same. "One bar brawl too many," Sweeny would tell his friends. "I wouldn't encourage any SEAL tough guy to jump in and try to break up a fight featuring four hard core bikers and a young US Marine in a seedy bar south of San Diego."

The assault on the pirates had caused debris and funnel clouds of sand and dirt to fly in every direction. Jamie wondered if the big Irish lug was going to pop the prosthesis out of the eye socket and toss it into his mouth giving it a good washing. He saw it happen in an Errol Flynn pirate movie years ago.

"By the way, why were you invited to our raiding party? Some of my SEAL team buddies questioned the wisdom of an army *grunt* joining our esteemed group for such an ambitious and dangerous mission."

"I guess you weren't briefed about me. Want me to fill you in?"

"Yeah, better late than ever," Sweeny said. "Hold on a minute, you're twitching. Your right sleeve is sucking more blood out of the bullet hole. Stick your arm out and let me tighten that tourniquet. We wouldn't want an army guy to bleed out on one of our missions. Bad for the SEAL reputation."

Jamie swore under his breath and complied. He began his spiel. "I'm sure you've guessed that I was a member of Delta Force, the Army's First Special Forces Operational Detachment before I was assigned to Fort Hood, Texas. Two years ago, I lead a mission to Somalia to *snatch and grab* Ahmad Makkman, one of their renowned bad guys. He was a feared maniac and secular warlord secretly sup-ported by our government. He waged fierce battles against Islamic groups for control of Mogadishu. We liked that. Somewhere along the line he soured and turned on us. I'm sure he wanted more dough."

"Did they order you to take him out alive?"

"Yes, Delta insisted. We were told they needed intelligence about other warlords in terms of unit operational capabilities, stra-tegic plans, and how they recruit. They wanted to know their entire organizational structure. My team spent a month planning the raid. It was a mandate that we not only had to study but also memorize every acre of topography within a five-mile radius of his known posi-tion. The jungle training in preparation for the mission was grueling, no doubt as physical and demanding as Navy SEAL training."

"Not possible," Sweeny grunted, his grim face turned scarlet red and his good eye rolled up, crossing in the direction of his bulbous nose.

"What do you mean?"

"If you believe that bullshit theory about your training com-pared to our standards, you're not well-informed. Get to the bottom line. What the hell happened in the pursuit of your warlord?"

"We located Makkman's headquarters and neutralized his outer security perimeter. Not making a sound and without the enemy fir-ing a weapon, we killed seven of his other soldiers. One of our team members heard some screaming and traced the noise to a wooden structure on the far edge of the encampment. He found Makkman sexually brutalizing a young native girl. We stopped it."

"Any more tidbits? That's the whole story?"

"Yes, for now. Later, I'll tell you why I was awarded the Bronze Star. We were safely extracted. Later, we heard in a debriefing that Ahmad Makkman sung like a canary and spilled his guts out to our interrogators. I'm sure they water boarded him. Soon after that mis-sion, my stint with the Delta Force was finished, and I was reassigned to Fort Hood."

"I still don't get it."

"Get what?"

"How did you get dumped in our midst? I'm not being sarcastic here, but as far as I know, this arrangement has never happened before. Our leadership prides itself on the ferociousness and integrity of all SEAL teams. Outsiders are not allowed in this *hallowed* setting."

Jamie laughed, even though his arm began to throb more. He squinted several times. The pain was screaming for help, anything to make it disappear. He grabbed hard at his shoulder and the SEAL reacted by loosening the tourniquet. Jamie had been wounded before in the line of duty, but this penetration hurt more than the others. *Maybe I should have the medically trained SEAL give me a shot of morphine.*

"I can read your mind, Richards, but we're nearing the San Antonio. Let's wait a few minutes before we do anything further to your body. Doc will check you out before you know it. Get to the point, why did you join our team?"

Jamie squirmed and considered how much he should tell the SEAL. As far as he knew, it wasn't classified, so he began. "I learned early on in my Delta Force orientation our leadership was always in touch with every other *like* agency, foreign and domestic. Your navy component, the Naval Special Warfare Development Group, was interested in my earlier mission to Somalia. The brass found out that I burned the coastal geography of Somalia indelibly in my mind. I was a valuable asset for future operations because of it."

Denis whistled.

Jamie continued, "Somalia has the longest coastline in the continent. Thus, hiding places are abundant for the pirates. Our intelligence folks narrowed down the five most probable locations the pirates would opt to spend their down time. We zeroed in on the most obvious site to penetrate."

"Come in for a landing, Richards. We're making our final approach to the vessel."

"Got it. The brass wanted me to lead you guys into the jungle and find this particular group of high sea gangsters. They boasted internationally of their heroics capturing an American-sponsored ship, duly inflated of course for propaganda purposes."

Sweeny squinted and said, "Why didn't the navy secretly pilot us in on one of their high-speed watercraft? Makes more sense to me."

"Too risky," Jamie said. "They wanted an overland assault. I was familiar with this stretch of real estate. As you recall, I guided you around environmental obstacles not called out by your point man and some ambush sites that I thought were strategically located to wipe us out. We succeeded. The mission was accomplished, and a group of seafaring criminals were sent to their beloved Allah."

"Thank you, army man, my team thinks the world of you and your Delta buddies."

The V-22 Osprey landed hard on deck. Jamie Richards was stitched up by the ship's doctor. They had to knock him out because remnants of his frayed jungle fatigue jacket were absorbed inside the wound requiring major debridement. After the procedure, the doc gave him a tetanus shot and added a mild sedative that allowed him to rest.

"Report to your base hospital when you get back, Richards," the doctor ordered. "You need to get those stitches removed in ten days and get a final check on that arm."

"Aye, aye, sir, and thanks for taking care of me."

He spent the remaining time on deck with Sweeny. He liked the big ogre even though the goof ball never shut up, always telling jokes that made no sense, but he laughed anyway. Three days later, his SEAL team was transferred to another navy ship heading back to port for debriefing. Jamie bid farewell to them, and after partying all night with Sweeny and his fellow warriors, they exchanged e-mail addresses.

"Let me know what you're going to do after you get your grimy ass tossed from the army, Richards. I plan to hire on as a state cop after I retire. Perhaps I'll find a way to wiggle into the FBI or even the CIA. My glass eye shouldn't be a problem. The navy allowed me to stay in, decided I was too damn good to be medically boarded and thrown to the barking civilian dogs. Maybe we can hook up in the future, even conduct another joint operation together. Wouldn't that be a hoot?"

"I'd be honored, Denis Sweeny. Keep the faith, big man."

En route to the States, he pondered what he would discover when he arrived home. *Will that sweet thing from the billeting office be waiting for me back in my apartment? After messing around with nasty Arabian Sea pirates, I'm in dire need of different strokes. One last all-nighter with her would be a great Christmas present. Ah, shit, I forgot to lug back the four pirate ears. She'd go off big time if I came in toting them on a necklace.*

He cogitated about his future after leaving the army. Would he venture off as a private investigator like his grandpa? Did he have the requisite skills to become a professional football scout like dad?

Maybe I'll hire out as a mercenary and return overseas and kill people. I'm excellent at that and relish the hunt. There is money to be made for my kind of sick soul, tons of it.

Five days later, Jamie was back in the familiar confines of Fort Hood, Texas.

CHAPTER 1

DATELINE

San Francisco—Christmas, 2011

K AT KURBELL LOVED THE DRIZZLE swirling around her head walking down Sansome Street to her law office in the Transamerica Pyramid building. It didn't matter that her thick brown-rimmed glasses got fogged up in this funky weather. She didn't need glasses, but she wore a pair to look more scholarly. Her father thought it would help her appearance because she wasn't good looking. Growing up on a farm in Iowa, Kat was considered a tomboy. She loved to hunt and fish with her father. She was short and now twenty pounds over her ideal weight but vowed every January to lose the extra poundage. She always wore her long strawberry-blond hair in a tight bun. Her main objective after graduating from Yale Law School was occupying an office in the highest skyscraper in San Francisco. Kat had fallen in love with *the city* on an earlier visit with her parents. She was bright and lucky to have reached her objective landing a job there.

Christmas was approaching. Yesterday, she wrapped up a murder trial that seemed to drag on forever. She was physically and mentally drained. She had no idea why the constant fatigue and loss of appetite persisted. Finding the cause would top her list of New Year's resolutions. Today, she planned to sneak off and begin Christmas shopping, a chore she always put off until the last minute. She went home at noon and collected her gift lists.

"Good-bye, Stryker. Don't get in any trouble while I'm gone."

The big bird screeched in acknowledgement. She loved her pet, a pygmy peregrine falcon. It had to be specially ordered from a pet shop in Oakland. She paid dearly for him. Exotic pet shops were becoming popular in the Bay Area. She remembered the conversation she had with the gruff owner of the pet store where she bought Stryker.

"What do you know about falcons? Ladies shy away from birds of prey."

"Not me, I know plenty. My oldest cousin was a registered falconer in Iowa. When I was young, he took me to an organized excursion in Fort Dodge and later taught me the finer points of training the bird to hunt. It sought out starlings and flickers, but one time, it downed a pigeon. For some unknown reason, his falcon seemed to accept me as a member of the clan, so to speak. The falcon even gave me a loving peck on the arm whenever I came by. I fell in love with that wonderful specimen and swore I'd own one when I grew up."

"I see your point but have my doubts that a falcon would adapt to living in a confined environment."

"Why? I'll exercise and train him for hunts."

"These birds can be dangerous. They are renowned for their speed, often reaching at least two hundred miles per hour stalking and killing prey. Most scientists agree that the falcon is the fastest member of the animal kingdom. Not only that, falcons have exceptional powers of vision. The visual acuity of one species has been measured at more than twice that of a normal human. To protect their eyes, the falcons use their third eyelids to spread tears and clear debris from their eyes while maintaining vision."

"I knew all that. They are a rare breed."

"Lady, are you sure you want to buy him?"

"Yes. What do you suggest I feed him?" she asked, hoping for a simple reply but didn't get one.

"Unlike other animals of prey, they rarely hunt mammals but will on occasion go after smaller species such as rats, voles, shrews, and mice. Coastal populations of larger subspecies feed almost exclusively on different species of seabirds."

"Thanks for the review. Where can I purchase such, um, food for my guy?"

"Here is a this list of pet specialty food stores in the area. I'm sure they are stocked with what you need to keep your pet healthy and happy. Good luck."

"Where to, ma'am?" the turbaned taxi driver asked while snuffing out a rolled cigarette.

"Macy's, Union Square and step on it."

"What's the big hurry? They're open late tonight. Crazy last-minute shoppers. I hate all of them…too pushy."

"You should find another job, you hypocrite," she snapped.

"Oh, oh, I be velly sorry. Long day, wife and baby sick. Make no money today."

She disregarded the cabbie's comment and shifted to the other side of the seat. He wouldn't see her face unless he adjusted the rearview mirror. A quick pain shot through her gut, and she gasped aloud. Excess gas and bouts of nausea were everyday occurrences. She cancelled a visit to the stupid doctor who told her she should see a dermatologist for her leg rash. She hated doctors, especially the chauvinistic male creeps who dominated her HMO plan.

As they approached Union Square, the taxi swerved to a sudden stop. Kat bounced off the front seat headrest. The heavy wooden ponytail holder anchoring her long reddish hair whisked around and slapped her smartly above her right eye. It knocked her glasses off and brought tears to both eyes.

"Let me out of here, you idiot," she demanded as she massaged the sore spot.

"Are you all right?" he asked, not really caring either way.

"Get some glasses and take a remedial driving class, or you'll be hauled to court one day."

"Solly about that," he said meekly. "Ten bucks, lady, and I are out of your life."

She tossed him a ten spot and shimmied out of the back seat. Her right platform shoe wedged in a sidewalk crack, and she almost fell. Righting herself, she was interrupted by the cell phone demanding her immediate attention.

"Hey, you irresistible creature, it's Barry. What's happening?"

"Not much, I feel like shit."

"Same-same on my end. You wouldn't believe it. All hell broke loose last evening."

Barry Gregg was a prosecuting attorney from Oakland. He played tight end at Cal during his college days and still worked out every day. She had met him while defending her first manslaughter case and was excited by his movements from judge to jury and back across to her. He was calm and moved like a big cat stalking an antelope. Barry annihilated her. The thug she represented was mandated to prison for thirty big ones. Gregg tried to maneuver her out to dinner after the devastating defeat, but she declined. He continued to pursue her, and she caved. They became lovers but held that fact close to their professional vests. No more boyfriends du jour for her. She wanted to keep the relationship personal and not public. He agreed.

"What happened?"

"Man, I'm nursing a big time headache. I barely made it home last night from the office Christmas party, and it hit me. I tossed so many cookies, I began searching for body parts. Felt like my insides were deserting me."

"And did you find any?"

"I think I saw my rectum swirling around before the pot gobbled it up." He laughed. "Never again. I'm getting too old for the party animal bit."

"I told you last year that you play too hard," she scolded him.

"I remember. By the way, not assaulting my body was the second New Year's resolution I scribbled on the fridge note-taker."

"You mean after trying to manipulate me to the altar." She laughed and grabbed at her stomach. "Hey, Barry, got to run. Call me tomorrow."

She liked him a ton and would even consider becoming his wife. Her first need was to grow her reputation in the competitive circle of defense lawyers and catch up with Barry's success. As she crossed Sutter Street, she ran into one of the law clerks from the office.

"Hello, Kat, where ya headed in such a big rush?"

"Macy's, I need to run down to the lower level and grab something to eat from one of the food shops. I'm famished. Haven't eaten a thing all day. Care to join me?"

"Yes, I could use a midday boost. Kat, are you losing weight? I'm jealous."

"Maybe. The headaches I've been having lately are severe enough that I've skipped meals. Regardless of the discomfort, I've been hitting the gym hard every third day when not in court. I think that helps to keep the pounds off."

"Are you still living in the tanning booth salon?" the law clerk asked with emphasis on the word *living*. She knew Kat spent at least an hour a week getting her white skin *tropicalized*.

"Nope, I'm taking a hiatus from that damned booth. It's like undergoing an MRI test, and I'm becoming more and more claustrophobic. I shake every time they roll me in. It's like crawling into a tomb. Don't you think I'm tan enough now?"

"Of course." The law clerk chuckled. She was sincere, but in reality, she thought Kat was overdoing it. *Being black has its advantages. No tanning booths for this big body of mine. Nature took care of that and made us beautiful enough without having to buy our way in like my white friends.*

Union Square was abuzz with activity. Christmas time was the happiest time of the year for most people. Bright and colorful decorations adorned most landmarks in the city. Kat observed that the Salvation Army uniformed workers were not as aggressive as in the past. Across the street, crowds were gawking in delight at all the Macy's window decorations.

"Don't you relish the Christmas season, Kat?"

She was a step behind the law clerk. Not hearing a response from her lawyer friend, she turned around to witness Kat falling to the concrete surface of Union Square. Her head faced skyward staring up at the graceful figure adorning the Admiral Dewey Victory statue. Blood began to pool on the floor behind her left ear.

"Hey Kat… Kat, wake up. What happened?" She began to shake her.

"Don't do that," a passerby yelled at her. "She's drunk."

"Someone call an ambulance," a nearby tour guide urged.

Ten minutes later, the EMTs arrived.

Paris—Christmas, 2011

"GOOD MORNING, MONSIEUR DUVAIR. would you like your coffee and croissants now, or shall I bring them when you get dressed? The patisserie delivered the goodies five minutes ago, and they are still warm." Andre waited for an answer as he shuffled back toward the door.

"No, not yet, please. I have a bellyache and need some Alka-Seltzer or whatever you can find for me to settle down my tummy.

Please come here and help me with my robe," Pierre spoke with a middle-class Parisian accent.

"Yes, sir," the butler said with a wink. Andre had fought with the French Resistance during the Second World War and walked with a limp. He was captured by the Vichy regime and tortured. Both legs were broken and shattered, yet they strapped him to the deplorable rack and stretched his body daily. They pumped him for information, but he prevailed. The bruised and beaten Andre had executed a daring escape when he was barely able to crawl.

Andre placed the silk robe on the bed stand. He was taller than his master. Pierre Duvair thought the butler reminded him of a gangly General Charles De Gaulle who he despised. The butler never married. He feared that no French woman would ever accept a "crip" for her husband even though he was decorated for valor.

He left the room with his usual pomp and circumstance which Pierre hated. He was aware of the less than honorable discharge Duvair received from the French Foreign Legion after the 1973 Paris Peace Accords ended the Vietnam War. Pierre had been in Vietnam on a secret mission orchestrated by the French government before the war ended. Rumor had it that he was found naked in bed with a male Vietnamese magistrate. The facts surrounding his departure from the esteemed Legionnaires were purged from the official war records.

"Hurry up, Andre!" he shouted impatiently with tears streaming down his face.

"Hold on, master, my head is buried in the medicine cabinet."

Pierre was a blue-eyed blond of average weight for his five-feet-four-inch height. His face was pox-marked from a childhood disease. He tried every publicized anecdote from dermabrasion to plastic surgery to improve his appearance. Nothing worked and he remained self-conscious about his face. Pierre's mother was of Spanish heritage. Her parents forced her to marry his flamboyant father three months into the difficult pregnancy with her son. His biological father took off the day Pierre came into the world.

"Aha! found what I'm looking for, sir. Be there in a second."

Last year, Pierre retired as the senior banker from the Banque de France. He proudly reminded everybody who would listen that Napoleon Bonaparte granted great powers to the beginnings of his respected financial institution. He lived, breathed, and relished his association with the bank. Nobody knew that he set aside bank funds to augment the retirement "pittance" he received after forty years of dedicated service. It was safely stashed with his male lover. Duvair was secretive about his wealth. Nobody cared. Most people avoided the demanding Frenchman.

The butler came back to the bedroom suite, this time using a cane to steady his slow gait. "Here you go, sir, I procured just what you need for your bowels. I might add that if you'd lose some of that despicable midriff, you'd feel better. Bottoms up, they say."

Pierre gulped the huge glass of yellowish liquid down without taking a breath.

"Good job, master."

Duvair knew that he wasn't well. His disdain for Parisian doctors and their superior attitude forced him to look elsewhere. He loved the tiny pharmacy down the Champs-Elysees and the withered but eclectic pharmacist who owned the place. He had all of the solutions for whatever ailed Pierre in the past. He would consult him again about the constant gnawing in his rear end.

"Summon my driver, Andre. I'm off to exchange some of the ghastly Christmas presents I received. It should have been obvious to my dearest friends that I have been losing weight." He planned to see the pharmacist before picking up his *special* friend. Andre let out a slight cough at the mention of weight loss.

"By the way, before I forget to mention it to you, make sure you take Louie for an extra long walk this afternoon. He gets obnoxious and passes so much gas to annoy me when I only take him on short strolls."

"The relief of gaseous contents is normal and quite healthy for a dog, sir."

Pierre enjoyed his fawn-colored, flat-eared, flat-faced miniature French bulldog even though the species originated from the "ghastly" English bulldog family years ago. Louie's neck was thick and well arched, with loose skin at throat. His forelegs were short, stout, straight and muscular, and set wide apart. In his research for a pet dog, he remembered that in his youth, his father took him to one of the local art museums. He was held spellbound by the paintings of two famous artists, Degas and Toulouse-Lautrec. Their use of the French bulldog in their paintings of Parisian social life fascinated him. Prostitutes loved the breed for some unknown reason. Pierre was fond of artists but despised the slovenly ladies of the street.

"*Bonjour*, Pierre," the pharmacist greeted him as he shuffled in. One older lady was at the counter paying for a prescription. She looked at Pierre with an air of discontent and left the pharmacy with her nose still up in the air.

"Sorry about the countess. She left her manners at home. What can I do for you today?" the pharmacist asked with a tight smile.

Duvair walked straight at the pharmacist, kissing him on both cheeks and said, "Give me something to settle my stomach and soothe my posterior. You wouldn't believe how awful my intestines are acting up. I can't hold down any food and spend half the day on the bidet in my toilette."

"Aha, I have just the thing for you. It's a different elixir that I've prepared for you in the past. You should feel much better in a few hours. Give me a minute to mix it up."

"All right, but make it snappy," Pierre ordered. "I have some other pressing chores to attend to and it's getting late."

The pharmacist hustled off to the back room and took several bottles of powders and liquids from the shelf. He worked up a mixture of baking soda, sugar, a dash of salt, and some water. He went to a locked cabinet and withdrew two ampoules of a banned halluci-nate. Whistling "Jingle Bells," he worked the drug into the prepared substance.

"Here you go, Pierre. I've printed the instructions on the bottle. Wait until you get finished with your errands before you start the medication in case you need to be near the toilette. Call me in two days and let me know how you're feeling."

Pierre grabbed the bottle with his stubby fingers. "You are a dear friend. How much do I owe you?"

The pharmacist bowed his head and said, "Nothing. It's a Christmas present for you. *Au revoir.*"

Pierre ordered his driver to pick up his best friend who lived in the Montmartre section of Paris. The driver hated the weekly jaunts to the friend's house during the busy rush hour traffic. This was his driver's scheduled day off, but that meant nothing to Pierre. He was paid to serve the master; everything else was deemed a personal inconvenience.

Hugues Chaban was dressed in artist attire when Pierre let him-self in with the key Hugues gave him after their first date. Chaban always acted surprised when his main man came unannounced through the front door. He and Pierre had been lovers for years, sep-arated for brief periods of jealous spats.

They'd met at the L'Hotel National des Invalides, the burial site of Napoleon. It happened in summer when throngs of tourists visited the tomb. The crowds tossed them into each other's arms while they were maneuvering for a closer view. He was much taller and thinner than Pierre but well-proportioned, just the way Pierre liked his men. A real "Jack in the Beanstalk," Pierre always kidded him. Chaban's long black hair was arranged in a tightened ponytail. A red beret was clinging perilously close to the back side of his head, positioning itself to leap to the ground.

"*Bonjour,* Pierre. Did you bring me any gifts today?" Hugues remembered that in past Christmases, Pierre always made a grand entrance like the three magi trekking in from the East bearing gifts but in his case, only gold. Gold rings, gold necklace chains, and even once, a gold belly-button ring. He wore all of the gold except the belly adornment much to Pierre's disappointment.

"No, not this time, Hugues."

"Ah, I'm disappointed."

"I'm returning a few of my own packages today. Come with me. Extract that cute long body of yours off the couch and let us proceed."

Hugues jumped to attention. "I can't wait to go shopping again. I love trying on the new clothes you buy me. You have such a marvelous taste for trends that are still in the embryonic stage of development. I don't know how you do it."

"I told you we're not going shopping. Are you deaf or dumb? I have to return some stupid gifts I received for Christmas. And yes, that includes the ridiculous Meerschaum pipe you bought me."

Hugues shrugged. He thought Pierre would look more like a retired banker puffing on a big pipe rather than the average retired Frenchman with a half-lit cigarette dangling from his jaws.

"Oh my gracious, I'm so dejected. You didn't like my special present." Slumping back on the couch, he gave Pierre a pained expression.

Hugues Chaban was an aspiring artist but didn't have a job. He couldn't afford to shower his special guy with expensive gifts. Pierre didn't care; he just wanted Hugues to be available for…whatever. He set him up in a cozy studio at the base of the Basilica Sacre Coeur. He seldom brought him to his extravagant apartment on the Champs-Elysees. Andre did not accept or understand his sexual orientation. If he found out, he'd kill him like the Germans did when they tried to purify the Aryan race embraced by Nazi ideology.

On their way to the first department store, Pierre got sick. His anus hurt, and he was nauseated and hot with fever. He started to moan and shake, and his faced flushed with fear.

"Take him to the nearest infirmary," Hugues ordered the driver in a quivering voice.

"No, no, take me home," Pierre begged. All of a sudden, he experienced a seizure and passed out in the back seat of the limo. Brownish red stains crept along the seat next to Hugues. Obnoxious odors filled the vehicle. The driver cursed as Hugues vomited out the window. Andre would soon absorb the brunt of his master's hideous disease.

Chicago—Christmas, 2011

METROSEXUAL BEST DEFINED SLADE GLICK. He lived in downtown Chicago, had tons of money to spend, and shopped in the best department stores that lined opulent Michigan Avenue. He had memberships to the exclusive clubs in the area and weekly frequented Jon Jon's, the highest rated hair salon in the area. Nothing daunted him. He had found within himself his own love object and beamed pleasure at his sexual preference: women and lots of them. He was insecure about not having a professional degree to further accentuate his uniqueness among men.

"My dear Slade, when are we going to Miami and sail in your boat again?" The newest of his female conquests sighed as she scratched his back.

"It's not a boat, dear heart. It's a schooner and it's in dry dock now."

They were tangled up on an oversized love seat in his Millennium condo a half block off Michigan Avenue. She never felt comfortable in his condo because of the pet he owned. She hated snakes—all snakes, poisonous or not. But it didn't matter. Serpents were all recreations of the hated Satan.

When Slade was researching for a pet, he wanted something exotic. He made it a point to be different from his few peers. Their conventional cat and dog assemblages were a complete disgrace to him. He opted for an African rock python. One of his male friends couldn't believe the pet selection. He had questioned Slade one night while they were speeding down Lake Shore Drive in his extravagant new Lexus.

"Jumping Jesus, Glickie, you must be insane to have a giant killer living with you. What prompted you to buy a python?"

"Last year, I was visiting my uncle down in the Florida Everglades. He's an outdoorsman and an avid hiker, so one day, we took a long walk around a wetland area. I witnessed the most exciting thing I had ever seen in my entire life."

"Like what?" his friend asked as Glick tromped down on the accelerator.

"We rounded a clump of bushes and, twenty yards ahead of us, stumbled upon a giant python coiled around a flailing alligator. It didn't see us. We stopped in our tracks and watched the snake squeeze the gator to death. I was so enthralled with the action my uncle had to put his hand over my babbling mouth. We retreated around the bushes but still in sight of the action. He whispered to me that African rock pythons were recently discovered in the Everglades, but this was the first time he'd seen one."

"But why attack an alligator?"

"Uncle told me that it was probably a female and had eggs nearby that the gator was trying to steal. According to him, they exhibit an unusual level of maternal care."

"Slow down, you idiot, you're going to get us both killed!"

"Sorry about that. I get this uncontrolled state of euphoria whenever I talk about the scene in the Everglades. That night, when we were asleep in my uncle's cabin, I had these dreams…dreams that confused my overactive brain cells."

"I suppose you felt sorry for the gator."

"To the contrary, I became the python. I rolled around all night, sweat moistened the cotton sheets, and I slipped off the bed. I wouldn't tell any other person about this incredulous dream, and I'll kill you if you ever repeat it…but I think I had an orgasm."

"No shit! The renowned lady killer gets his rocks off on a slimy snake."

"Yes, sir. When I returned home, I researched several periodicals claiming the African rock python is popular in the pet trade but scare people because of its large size and unpredictable temperament. Regardless of those facts, I had to have one, the rest is history."

"I think you made a great choice, Slade, fits your personality. Let's get back to your place and get drunk."

"Ouch, slow down. You're digging in too deep," Slade cautioned as he shifted back to reality. "You gotta cut those long fingernails. Do you want to draw blood or what?"

"Blood but only if you want me to," she answered with a slight chuckle. "You told me you like pain, but do you really?"

"Yes, whenever I can deliver it." He leaned further into her busy hands.

She laughed and started to softly rub the top of his head.

"Stop that, stop it right now," he ordered and shoved her hand to his thigh. He didn't want her to see, feel, or touch his new wig. His head was completely shaven, and the wig served to cover the small brown spot he discovered several months ago when Jon Jon informed him about the abnormality. He would be more content if she would massage his strong legs, the result of weekly strenuous jogs around Grant Park. She picked up the vibes and began rubbing in circular patterns.

"How long have you owned that boat down in Florida?" she asked.

"I told you, it's not a boat. It's a schooner. I've had it since my dad died twelve years ago. We'd spend our winters in Florida, actually lived part-time on *The Glickster*. Dad was in the navy at Pearl Harbor

30

during the big war and loved the water. We could afford the so-called high life because he invested wisely in past years. It didn't hurt that mom's inheritance cushioned any financial free falls that came up, bless her soul. My sister and I buried her ashes at sea three years ago."

"Where does your sister live?"

"I have no clue. She ran off with one of those Cubans down in the Keys."

"So you spent gaggles of time in that sizzling Florida sun stretched out on that luxury liner sipping dozens of piña coladas and entertaining gorgeous women."

"Well, sort of."

She stopped rubbing his thigh, thinking he should be aroused by now. She kissed him hard on the lips. He rejected her. She was stunned by his disinterest.

"And for the last damn time, it's a schooner, has nylon sails, and is not considered a luxury liner. Let's change the subject." He wasn't in a romantic mood, not with this one anyway, not right now. Last night, she showered him with enough kinky sex to bank his manly needs for a while.

"It's time that I head out to Michigan Avenue and find some bargains after the big Christmas shopping glut on the stores."

"What about breakfast? I'm famished after our marathon last night."

"I'm fasting this morning," he said curtly. "Can I give you a ride back to your apartment?"

"No, I'll call a taxi. I'm beginning to think you don't want me anymore. Go ahead. Go shopping, and have fun. By the way, are you getting something for me?"

What does this simple trollop expect after a one-night stand, especially with my foot fetish? I don't apologize to anybody like her in dire need of toe straighteners. I want to vomit when I see a lady like her with ghoulish purple glossed toe nails and golf ball-sized bunions on both huge feet. I regret I gave her what she begged for, and now she wants a gift? I don't believe it. She's history.

He didn't answer her question about the possibility of a gift. The thrice-divorced Slade ushered her out the door, glad to be rid of her. He walked back to the bathroom, removed the wig, and inspected his head. He took out a magnifying glass and studied the ugly skin disfigurement. A small globule of pus sat at the edge of the lesion. Slade didn't believe in doctors, figuring they were all quacks. He was smart enough to take care of himself.

Living as a vegan and exercising daily at the Gold Coast Gym kept him fit. His six-foot frame was adorned with well-developed muscles. He didn't have an extra ounce of body fat. Several of the women who worked out there were enamored with him. He knew it, and they knew it. He had his pick of the female gym rats. The telephone rang. It jolted him, not expecting anybody to call.

"Hello, Slade, it's Leah. Are you coming over tonight?"

"Um, no, I have to work late," he lied. He was worn out and needed a break. Slade admired this one, straight out of a Victoria's Secret catalog. Leah Malaka was a high-priced model. She was of Polynesian ancestry, born and raised in Hawaii. She had earned an advanced degree in psychology from Stanford. This beauty knew what a good time was and it cost him dearly whenever they went out.

She wanted only the best and would do anything to satisfy that pursuit. Slade could never figure out why she became an expensive escort satisfying the sexual whims of Chicago's rich and famous. Her private psychotherapy practice was thriving. He didn't care what fantasies she performed for others as long as it didn't cost him a dime.

"I understand about your work." She really didn't because Slade never discussed it. "How about tomorrow? It's Saturday, and you promised to take me to a Bull's game. I just love basketball."

"That I did, Leah. I'll pick you up at six." He coughed several minutes and said, "See you tomorrow. I can't wait to look into the whites of those big round eyes."

"You need to take care of that chronic hacking cough. You never smoked, but I suspect there's some pathology developing in those lungs. It seems to be getting worse."

"Don't worry about it, just some stupid allergy that'll be gone before you know it."

She hesitated for a few seconds then said, "*Mahalo*. Perhaps we can slip away for dinner after the game. I'll make a reservation at our favorite haunt, if that's agreeable with you."

"Go for it, Leah. Good-bye."

Slade had to procure more rats for his pet snake before hitting the department store circuit with his post-Christmas bargain wish list. Even though he was independently wealthy, he was still frugal, a trait he had learned from his military father. He didn't have a full-time job but did some *bit* acting when he wasn't modeling clothing. His claim to fame was starring in an amateur porno flick when he was only eighteen. His father almost disowned him when he'd found out about it. *To My Obvious Delight* was recently reformatted by Glick's agent and made available on YouTube.

Saturdays were usually busy days for him because he liked to mix with the common workers shopping on their days off. He wanted to buy a silk shirt for his date with Leah. He hadn't been with her for two weeks and needed his gonadal batteries recharged again. The last fling with the toed monster didn't do much for him. Leah knew all the tricks of the trade, bar none.

"How can I help you, young man?" asked the matronly female clerk with a lecherous grin.

"Show me to the men's clothing department. I would like to find some discounted shirts, maybe in the clearance bins." He stared at her ample breasts but expressed disgust at the tight-fitting clothing she wore. He never understood why women couldn't figure out that some things no longer work for an aging body.

"I'll do better than that," the clerk declared. She felt a drool forming at the corners of her mouth. She tripped rounding the counter to meet him but couldn't get there fast enough. *What a fine-looking specimen of a man. Those slanted green eyes are too much! He could "clear" my section any time he wished to. Maybe I should help him pick out some clothing and follow him to the changing room. Stop it. Stop it now. You're old enough to be his mother.*

"Please follow me," she said seductively.

As they were fighting their way through the throng of bargain-seeking shoppers, he pulled her aside and whispered, "Ma'am, please tell me where the public toilets are located. I have to take a time out from my shopping."

"Is there something I said or did that offended you?"

"No."

She pointed in the direction of the toilets in the corner of the children's section and watched while he hurried to his sudden task. Safely inside the men's toilet, Slade took five steps toward the urinals and puked on the bathroom floor. He fell underneath the opened door of a stall and began to shake uncontrollably. His wig flipped off in the process, exposing a trickle of blood from the brown spot on the top of his head. He passed out.

CHAPTER 2

FORT HOOD

JAMIE RICHARDS FULLY RECOVERED from his wounded arm although he sensed the scar was far too large for the trauma it received. He didn't mind. When he got out of the shower in the morning, he never avoided checking out his body in the mirror. He loved his scars and was littered with them, much like NFL and NBA jocks who proudly wear their ridiculous tattoos on much of their exposed flesh. He reflected back to the comments made by the navy doc on board the San Antonio about the patchwork of surgery some medic practiced on his back. "So these beauties were caused by an IED in Iraq. You're a walking advertisement for a wounded warrior, Richards. Better find another occupation, or you won't be around to serve much longer." The military clothing he wore failed to reveal the real Jamie Richards, body, heart, and soul.

"Hey, soldier, the CO wants to see you, pronto," the company clerk said softly.

"What's up?"

"Don't know, not cleared for scuttlebutt."

Jamie was concerned. He had three weeks remaining on his enlistment and had no plans to re-up. He'd had enough soldiering, and his body begged for a simpler life, maybe even a God-forbidden desk job somewhere in a lavish office.

"Sit down, Richards," the CO ordered. "Last chance to stay in the army. I'm not going to beg you, but I see a promotion for you coming down the pike and real soon. The department of the navy sent us a detailed account of your heroic actions in Somalia. Are you sure about getting out?"

"Yes, sir, I've fulfilled my military obligation." *Whew, he's not going to discipline me.*

"Got big plans for the future?"

"I sure do, sir," he said, not having the faintest idea.

Jamie had been in telephone contact with his friend, Bobby Biel, who offered to share his apartment in San Antonio with him on a temporary basis. Biel was out of work and told Jamie he didn't have the energy to look for employment. Jamie was concerned with the tone of his voice but wrote it off as disinterest, and he didn't know why. He'd find out soon enough.

"Suit yourself, soldier. You've served your country well. Good luck in civilian life."

Jamie rendered a sharp salute, did an about-face, and left the office. He wanted to visit Father Lawrence at the post chapel before leaving. Now a civil servant, Father Lawrence was formerly Corporal Lawrence, a combat infantryman who had fought in the Vietnam War. He led a daring escape from enemy captivity during the Tet Offensive carrying out a wounded GI on his bullet-riddled back. Lawrence lived a life of petty corruption after the conflict and served six months in jail for assault and battery. The prison chaplain taught him the meaning of unselfishness and the love of Jesus. After he was released from the slammer, he enrolled in the seminary. After a long, arduous struggle, he earned the starched white collar of a Catholic priest.

The chaplain knew of Richard's dangerous missions and the killing fields left behind by the Delta Force. Jamie had experienced bouts of remorse and depression. He didn't want to visit the Behavioral Health Unit on post and be labeled with PTSD. He was a warrior and in his own mind did not exhibit intense fear, helplessness, or horror on the battlefield. He remembered the healing words from Father Lawrence on his last visit to the chapel.

"I'm glad you're getting out of the army, son. You have a whole new world ahead of you to conquer, a life devoid of killing and maiming other human beings. I've given you absolution for your sins. Leave here with a clean soul and healthy conscience. Good-bye and go forth and serve the Lord to your fullest.

Jamie would perform the required five rosaries of the cross in repentance for his sins against humanity and then be ready for the next call from the Delta Force Operations Center. The cycle of "black" operations would begin again. "Yes, sir, coach, put me in. I'm beyond ready" was always his enthusiastic response.

He never confessed to the good priest his conquests of the opposite sex. Jamie was convinced those activities were a natural phenomenon that God allowed the male human being to engage in while navigating the twisting and often tumultuous road to maturity.

As a going-away gift, Father Lawrence surprised him with a pet, something he never considered owning before with his gypsy-like moving around at a moment's call. "Jamie, you'll love Victoria. When I get mad at her, I call her Vic. I think she'll change your life. She did mine."

"But, Father Lawrence, I can't—"

"Nonsense, I insist. You'll thank me every time you go to church."

"What kind of bird is she?" Jamie softened his stance when the bird whistled at him. He thought he also saw a wink from the stocky jet-black bird with bright orange-yellow patches of naked skin and fleshy wattles on the side of its head and nape.

"She's a common hill myna. I was gifted by a soldier who smuggled her in from Southeast Asia. He was at Hood for no more than six months and deployed to Afghanistan. They are hard to find in the pet shops around here and are usually purchased from breeders or importers, so take good care of Vic. She'll grow on you."

"What do I feed this feathered creature?"

"In the wild, they feed on insects and fruits but you can purchase feed at most pet shops."

"I guess they talk a lot, huh?" Jamie commented.

"Yes, in fact, they are most vocal at dawn and dusk. Vic can produce an extraordinarily wide range of loud calls—whistles, wails, screeches, and gurgles, sometimes melodious and often human-like in quality."

"My neighbor had one, and he screeched all the time." Jamie didn't like the bird.

"Not this one. I want to offer one word of advice though. Watch your mouth when you're within speaking range of her. Absolutely no foul language, or you'll live to regret it. That's all I'm going to say. Good luck, Jamie."

He left the chaplain's office with a caged Vic squawking all the way to his car. He had no idea how to manage her, but he couldn't say no to a priest that he admired, a priest who prevented him from taking his own life during a particularly bad stretch of time at Fort Hood.

The three weeks before his final out-processing went by without a hitch. Jamie hadn't seen Maria Serrano from the billeting office since his return from Somalia. She was no longer staying in his off-post apartment. Initially, he was disappointed. Either she was too busy for him, or he was too busy preparing for a smooth, unencumbered take-off from the largest military installation in the Free World.

"Where ya headed, Richards?" the company clerk asked when Jamie was signing out of his unit.

"San Antonio, Texas."

"Why there, man? I thought you were from Wisconsin."

"I lived in the frozen chosen when I entered service but have no desire to return to those long winters anymore. I have an uncle living in the Alamo City and a high school buddy who ended up there after college. I'm going to get a job and bunk in with him until I find my own apartment."

Jamie was in a hurry to finish the clearing process. He was perturbed. The company clerk never talked to him this much before. Jamie hated small talk. *No Article 15 for the clerk to prepare. Must be a slow day. The old man is probably still in a jovial Christmas mood.*

"What's your uncle do?"

"He's a child psychologist."

"Really? How neat. I'm seeing a shrink at the troop clinic. I get depressed more than the average soldier according to him. Supposedly, I have a fragile X syndrome."

"What the shit is that?" Jamie asked too quickly with a "don't care" smug look on his face.

"Doc says I suffer from anxiety because I have learning problems. I guess that's why I'm a lowly company clerk and not a famous killer like you. Do you get depressed often?"

"No," Jamie fired back. He didn't want to go there. "Let's drop the crazy talk, okay?"

"Sure, that's good. What's your friend do for a living?"

"He was a biochemist but got reengineered out of a job where he had tons of responsibility running his own laboratory. I'm not sure what his plans are now. We talked briefly the other day when he coaxed me to stay with him. He had a doctor's appointment and was quick to shut down our conversation. He didn't sound good on the phone. I heard through our high school Facebook site that he has some kind of disability. Maybe inhaling too much gas from the lab."

"Yeah." The clerk laughed. He thought that Richards was pulling his leg. "We do that all the time in the barracks."

"It's a joke, man," Jamie snapped. "We lost touch, too many deployments. He blocked for me when I was carrying the football in high school. I owe him for not getting hammered every time the ball was hiked. Some of our idiot classmates called him a nerd because he was smart. Not bad for a football player being a straight A student, wouldn't you say?"

The company clerk shrugged, not knowing how to respond. He turned his chair around, ignoring Jamie, and began typing the morning report.

He left the headquarters and on a whim, decided to go by the billeting office and see if Maria was there. The least he could do was to offer one last good-bye. After all, they shared some hot times together, but he'd written her off as a serious contender for a long-term relationship. Actually, he preferred much younger women that he could mold into his own ideal creation.

Maria Serrano was a military dependent when her father served as a command sergeant major for one of the tank units. The Hispanic stunner elected to remain at Hood when he was deployed to Iraq. She learned that his unit's primary job was to locate and disarm the treacherous land mines that maimed the NATO soldiers. Maria became a civil service employee and enjoyed her ascending government career. Normally, she didn't date GIs, but Jamie Richards was an exception. They met at a karaoke bar in Killeen, and she couldn't take her brown eyes off of him. He couldn't carry a tune to the outhouse but that didn't matter. Neither did the fact that she was at least five years older.

Maria was at the front desk scanning her emails when he walked in. Her waist-length black hair was soft and smooth. She wore it braided when they first met, but he hinted a preference for women with long flowing hair as she wore it today. There weren't any customers in sight. It was getting dark outside.

"Hi, Jamie Richards, I thought you were going to leave the Hood before saying good-bye to me. Thanks for the extra effort to stop by. I figured you were upset that I wasn't in your apartment to welcome you home from your oversea foray."

"Forget about it. That's past history."

She wouldn't and went on. "The word floating around here is that it was gory and some men got killed. If I knew you were all shot up, I would have been there for you like Florence Nightingale."

"Thanks, I survived. The rehab on the arm was tougher than hell, but that's when the tough get tougher." He laughed at his own stupid words, which sailed over her head.

She had another thought. "Jamie, if you would like to…well, you know what I mean. I could take the rest of the day off. Have tons of sick leave on the books."

"No, that's not necessary. I don't need a mercy fuck as a going-away present. I moved past it some time ago. Found out I could have a life without you."

"My, my, I wouldn't have thought that the way we carried on. You have a short memory, soldier."

"Yeah, right," he said without looking her in the eyes. "Let's face it, who in their right mind would hang with a black ops kind of guy? Here today and gone tomorrow on a wild mission. If it's acceptable with you, let's just separate as friends. Look me up if you ever visit San Antonio."

He turned and headed toward the exit and looked back at her one last time. He didn't know why. It was a big mistake. Maria with tears in her eyes looking so vulnerable. He hesitated, not sure what to say or how to say it. He hated it when a woman started crying at the drop of a hat. He reconsidered, delaying his primary task of vacating the post.

"Close up shop, honey. Take some of that sick leave, and I'll meet you back at my apartment."

She ran to him and gave him a passionate kiss that lasted so long he thought they'd need an oral surgeon to separate them. They made love the rest of the afternoon, evening and most of the next day. Ten hours of precious government sick leave went down the amorous drain. She cared less. His homecoming in San Antonio would have to wait.

"Can't you stay a few more days, Jamie?"

"No, I wish I could."

"And why not?" she pouted, hoping he'd reconsider but knowing at the same time he was too stubborn to relent.

"The manager is coming in tomorrow afternoon to clear me from the apartment. I rented a U-Haul for the remaining few pieces of beat-up furniture I'm hauling away."

Jamie left with the sweet taste of a lover he'd never forget. His delay in clearing the military complex had not been a complete waste of time. His new pet bird Victoria added multiple new words to her existing vocabulary.

CHAPTER 3

SAN ANTONIO

A LAMO PLAZA HAD THE LARGEST CHRISTMAS TREE of any municipal location downtown. Tourists often expect the "Cradle of Texas Liberty" to overshadow every other monument in town and are disappointed in the size of the Mission. The Christmas tree lights blazed unusually bright this particular evening. The skies were clear, but it was chilly. All of the city decorations, including the gargantuan tree, and the lights on the River Walk were coming down the following day.

"What do you think of her?" a tourist asked in awe with the Alamo.

Bobby Biel wasn't sure whether the tourist meant the tree or the historical structure behind it. The guy was drunk and slurred his words.

"Um, they're both beautiful," he replied and trucked on to Teddy's Tavern at the Menger for a pint of ale. The crowds had thinned downtown since he started his daily speed walk earlier in the day. The street vendors were still hawking their multi-colored iced Slurpees. Living downtown was exciting but had its limitations—tourists. He didn't care for them. They were always happy and bubbly. He got fired the week before Christmas. Being the senior research chemist at a large biochemical plant didn't matter. He recalled the conversation with his boss the week before his head got lopped off.

"Bobby, you're a damned good biochemist, the best scientist we have in the company. I don't know how many times I told you to stop conducting experiments on your own agenda and not developing the protocols your team was assigned. I guess I can find the dates in my counseling files if you ever take us to court."

"But I've made tons of money for this company," Bobby argued. *"Doesn't that mean anything to you?"*

"Of course, but that's why you're drawing the big salary we pay you. Look, I've never been personally impressed with you, Bobby, but the big boss upstairs thinks you walk on water. You must be bedding her for all I know."

"Screw you, asshole." Bobby was ready to drop the jerk with a rabbit punch to his shriveled-up neck. He hardly knew the female CEO, only talked briefly with her at the annual Christmas party. She was reportedly promiscuous, but he was never in line for any skin coming his way.

"Hold on there, mister, I have the governing board's concurrence to fire you."

"I don't believe it!" Bobby shot back, his pulse racing at record speed with both fists balled up.

"Yes, sir, I had to go over her head, but it worked. Anyway, it's a done deal. Fait accompli, as they say in the victor's trenches. I'm sure you'll land on your feet with your fancy college degrees and published papers. Pfizer or Merck will reel you in. They're always looking for research people with your credentials."

"Go to hell!" Bobby screamed at him and but left before he clobbered the guy.

As a senior executive, he was concerned about losing his extensive medical benefits package next month. Rolling his coverage over to COBRA was an option but still costly. He never trusted the government-legislated program, thinking it was inferior, cobbled together by a bunch of bureaucrats who knew nothing about the health care industry. Bobby would bear the full cost of the coverage. Because of his serious medical problem, it could drive him to bankruptcy.

"Hey, Bobby, how they hanging?" the bartender quipped as Bobby found a vacant stool at the antique English bar in Teddy's Tavern.

"High and dry."

The bartender knew him from high school and was aware that he'd lost his job. Bobby was dubbed the mad scientist in school, having an unbridled love for chemistry and physics. The coeds called him the screwy carrot-top because of his bright reddish orange hair. He was intelligent, studious, and tilted beyond the "nerdy" classification. His thick glasses overwhelmed tiny green eyes, more like peepholes. A thin mustache failed to cover his repaired cleft palate. He was occasionally referred to as Hare-lip Biel by the ignorant farm kids he grew up with before moving to San Antonio.

"Find another job yet?"

"No, not looking too hard."

The conversation stalled. Waiting for a drink order the bartender walked to some cluttered tables and began to wipe them off with a wet bar cloth. He recalled some other descriptive features about Bobby when they were together back in high school.

The guy proudly displayed an oversized pocket protector housing red, blue, and green ink pens. A protruding upper jaw added to his awkward image. He wore his long mop in a ponytail. He had one physical talent that was inconsistent with his appearance and demeanor: he had been an exceptional football player. Bobby was the team's starting center and gained All-City status by the end of his senior year. According to one of the teachers, he turned down several football scholarship offers from smaller D-2 colleges to concentrate on his studies.

Bobby broke the silence. "Gimme a pint of Samuel Adams, post haste."

"I guess you haven't gotten past the point of being fired," the barkeeper mumbled too loudly.

"Nope. By the way, how'd you know I lost my job?"

"I got a sweetheart working there. Said the employees couldn't believe they'd let you go because of all of your achievements. What are you going to do now if I may ask?"

"It's none of your goddamn business," Bobby said with a pronounced growl.

"Oops, sorry, shouldn't have gone there."

"Exactly," Biel shot back. There was a brief stand-off, but the dead silence didn't last.

"On another matter, have you heard from Jamie Richards lately? I know you guys were like…Velcroed at the hips in high school. I remember you made the jarring block that sprung Jamie loose for the touchdown that won district for us in our glorious senior year. All our classmates still talk about how you pancaked that obnoxious linebacker that gave you the bird when he expunged himself from the turf."

"Yeah, I heard from him last week."

Bobby smiled as he reflected back to those awkward days in high school. He'd met Jamie Richards halfway through their freshman year. Late one afternoon, several upperclassmen had cornered him and began bullying him and calling him dirty names. He was a real loser in their minds. One of the football players tackled him and kicked him in the groin. Jamie saw the fracas when he rounded the hallway corner and dove in to break it up. Four boys pounced on his back, but Jamie threw them off and pulled out a hunting knife he carried with him. The biggest bully in the group called his bluff and swung wildly at him. Jamie ducked and slashed the guy's right arm with the knife. Cursing and crying at the same time, the big lug took off with his friends. Jamie and Bobby became instant friends that afternoon. He was never bullied again.

"He's getting out of the army and coming to San Antonio," Bobby continued.

The bartender stared at Bobby's forehead when he put the pint of ale on the bar in front of him. Bobby's long hair was combed over and barely covered a big pinkish red spot on his lower forehead just above ear level. From what he could see, it was ugly and oozing. *Why wasn't Bobby wearing a cap and covering up the stinking mess?* He dare not ask for getting his head ripped off.

After more small talk, Bobby drained his pint of ale and headed back to his penthouse atop an apartment near the Majestic Theatre. His mind raced back to the stark events before the guillotine sliced through his neck at work. He vividly recalled the dramatic last visit to his oncologist.

"Bobby, I reviewed in detail the findings of your recent PET scan. I consulted with two other oncologists, and we came to the conclusion that your melanoma had metastasized to your bone structure. It is inoperable, incurable. You waited too long to seek treatment."

"What? How? Why?" Bobby was beyond shocked.

"You told me you were exposed to the sun when you were an adolescent living on the farm down near Laredo during your grade school years. You also reported that you and your friends lived on a small spring-fed pond during the summer. After your move to San Antonio, you performed lifeguard duties at a golf club swimming pool. You never used sun screen and blistered often."

"Yes, all that's true, Doctor, but—"

"Bobby, you have what we call an amelanotic melanoma. These melanomas tend to be more aggressive than most others."

"How long do I have?"

The doctor hesitated. He contemplated how Bobby would shoulder the bad news but answered him anyway. It was his duty.

"Your cancer is classified as a stage IV, the worse prognosis we can give you."

"What does that mean, Doctor?"

"We measure the growth of the tumor and how deep it has penetrated your skin. A patient with a stage IV means that invasion into the subcutaneous fat has developed. More than likely, it has reached the lymph nodes and transmitted to other parts of the anatomy. In your case, it has reached your bone structure."

"Sounds pretty bad."

"Yes. Bobby, you have maybe six months, give or take a few months. If I were you, I'd get my affairs in order."

"But what about the constant pain I'm in?"

"All I can do is prescribe an ample supply of pills to alleviate the pain. Some of my peers also use a form of radiation therapy to help patients cope with the continuous dull pain."

"Doctor, I don't want to be doped up like a dummy the rest of my life. Can you radiate me instead?"

"It wouldn't help in your case, Bobby. I'm sorry."

Slam bam, good-bye Sam. It was over, no punches pulled. Hitch up the meat wagon, buddy. You're on your way to meet your maker.

The telephone ring shook him out of the demoralizing trance. He jumped off the lounger, knocking off the glasses that he'd placed on his chest.

"Hey, Bobby, it's Jamie. I'm downstairs. Let me and Victoria in." I think I told him in our last telephone conversation I had a pet bird.

"It's about time you got here. Put your thumb on the small screen pad next to my address and stay on the line."

Jamie followed the instructions, and the lobby door popped open.

"Now what, Bobby?"

"Leave your luggage with the concierge. Have him keep that stupid bird down there for you. I hate talking birds. Can't shut the devils up no matter what you try. The concierge will send your suit-case up the express unit, which accesses the guest bedroom and it'll be waiting for you."

"Why can't I bring it up with me?"

"Because that's what he gets paid for. I dropped a mint to get the thumbprint ID'er and the dumb waiter installed."

"How did you get my thumb prints?"

"I hacked into the DOD personnel data base for Delta Force, found your file, and lifted them off your records. Never had the opportunity to test my brilliant system until now. Is that acceptable, military guy?"

Jamie was impressed. "Only guys like you could pull this stunt off. Who else would think of jeopardizing his life by breaking into the top secret government computers in the Pentagon?"

"Don't jerk me off, Richards. Now walk across the lobby to the elevator and repeat the process on the small screen next to the pent-house button. My front door will be open when you get up here. I'll be in the kitchen mixing a martini for us to celebrate your coming home party. If I remember correctly, you like a lemon twist. Hurry up. I got tons of things to discuss with you."

When Jamie arrived at the penthouse and saw Bobby in the kitchen, he was appalled. His friend was wearing a Texas Ranger baseball cap draped loosely above his right eye.

"You look like death warmed over, Bobby. What the hell's going on?" They hugged each other warmly and slapped each other's behind like in their high school days when breaking a huddle on the gridiron. The two friends were of equal height, but Bobby had added weight over the years until the onset of his illness. He jokingly referred to himself as the Triple F meaning fat-friendly fellow.

"Grab the martini pitcher, and I'll bring the glasses. We need to sit down and talk."

"Is it about the woman at Fort Hood that I mentioned to you on the telephone?" Jamie asked.

"Of course not, I've known you for a long time. Contrary to my non-amorous history with the opposite sex, women are attracted to you like—"

"Yeah, I know. Like flies to shit," Jamie boasted.

Bobby suddenly turned more serious and said, "Jamie Richards, I'm dying. I'll be pushing up daisies in six months."

CHAPTER 4

SAN ANTONIO

"HOLD ON A MINUTE, did I hear you correctly? You're a dead man in six months? Bullshit, Bobby, I don't believe it." Jamie was in shock. "You, the renowned Red Baron flying around the football fields with your thick black prescription goggles, tight leather helmet, and shredded jersey terrifying the piss out of the opposition."

"It's the truth, Jamie. I screwed up by not seeking help from the doctors sooner. I allowed this despicable cancer to take control of my life and dictate the terms of my death. I'm on drugs now for the excruciating pain."

"Knowing you, I'm sure you have a plan. You're not going to sit around here and wait for the Grim Reaper to reel you in, right?"

"*Mucho correcto*, good buddy, here's what we're going to do. First, walk to the desk and grab my World Atlas."

Jamie complied. "Now what?"

"Find the Mascarene Islands in the Indian Ocean east of Madagascar."

"Why?"

"We're going there. It's the last thing I want to do before I go head-to-head with Satan. Call it number one on my bucket list or whatever they refer to as the ultimate to-do list. I've always wanted to visit Reunion, one of the smaller islands in the Mascarenhas Archipelago."

"Bullshit. I ain't going there!" Jamie shouted after he reviewed the Atlas.

"Why not?"

"It's too fucking close to Somalia, and I hate that area. Full of no-good pirates and other undesirables. What the hell's going on, cancer spread to your brain?"

"Not yet, just in the bones. My geologist father visited Reunion on his way back from a consultancy in Madagascar when I was in grade school. *Mads* as dad called it, holds one of the world's largest reserves of titanium ore. He fell in love with Reunion, even though it's one of twenty-seven regions of France. Dad despised the Frogs, as he called the French, but overcame that feeling in later years. He showed us pictures of the island. The beauty was beyond one's comprehension."

"How many people live there?"

"Less than a million."

"That's all? Why truck out there and not to Hawaii, Fiji, or Samoa?" Jamie wasn't convinced that he wanted to spend his first few weeks as a *civilian* in such a faraway and remote stupid island in the Indian Ocean.

"Jamie, hear me out. The island is beyond indescribable. Not too many Americans know about it. I want to go bird watching, swim in the warm waters of the coral reefs, and mingle with the fish. If we're lucky, we can watch humpback whales play around, but it might be too early in their mating season."

"Bird-watching, are you kidding me?" Jamie couldn't believe what he'd heard. "You hate them. You wouldn't even let me bring Vic up here to your pad, you numb-nut."

"To clarify the issue for you, she's just a simple pet, one of many thousand owned by bird lovers throughout the world. From my extensive research, there is a small seabird called the white-tailed tropicbird that is exquisite and demands our attention. I like bird life in the wild, not stuck in a shitty cage in the back bedroom. Dad told me to go to Reunion if I ever had the chance. I can afford it now, even pay your way."

"You're certifiably crazy, Mr. Biel."

"Maybe so, let's get the ball rolling. You got a passport?"

"Sure, but hold on, I have other priorities."

"Like what?" Bobby looked at him tersely.

"Like find an apartment, get a job, go back to school, use my GI Bill, meet a beauty queen, and get laid, not necessarily in that order though. Any questions or clarifications?"

"Say what, Richards? I'm dying, don't you get it?" He ripped off his baseball cap and said, "Take a long look at this creeping crud!"

Jamie was stunned by the ugly mess on his friend's forehead. He was at a loss for words and didn't know what to say. He'd prefer being in jungle combat, hand-to-hand in a bayonet fight with the enemy instead of hanging around with the "walking dead."

"Can't you do your thing after I'm in the ground for Christ's sake?" Bobby implored. "I have less than six months left on this earth. Is it too much to ask you to support my dying wish? I have no family, no other friends to lean on. Please, Jamie."

"Don't be so fricking dramatic. You know I'll do it for you." After several days of calling around, Jamie found a friend to care for Vic and was now ready to travel again to parts unknown.

Two weeks later, they transited Europe and landed in Madagascar. Bobby had been in constant pain, moaning and groaning most of the trip. The mediations were slowly losing their calming effect. A short hop took them to Reunion where they landed at Roland Garros Airport. Bobby had reserved a rental car and a hotel in Saint-Pierre on the southwest side of Reunion. Jamie found a marine dive shop and rented scuba-diving gear that included a marine knife. He decided they wouldn't need wet suits because the temperature of the water didn't demand thermal protection, let alone they were a pain in the ass. He was a certified diving instructor and taught Bobby the art of diving years ago. He also had them toss in two snorkels.

Jamie noticed that the pinkish red anomaly on Bobby's forehead appeared to be getting larger by the day and constantly oozed a foul-smelling puss. He didn't share his observations with him. The poor guy had enough trouble with the constant pain in his body and being doped up half the time. He carried his cross like a seasoned trooper. Jamie stopped counting the number of pills his friend popped in his mouth every day. The following day, they prepared a picnic lunch and headed to the coral reefs on the western side of the island.

"Let's discover the most secluded stretch of this beach and try some cave diving," Bobby said.

Jamie agreed, and before long, they found an isolated harbor that met their needs. They hadn't seen another human being in several hours and hoped that would hold true for the rest of the day. True isolation was Bobby's wish. He didn't need unnecessary distractions at this point in his life.

"Frogman, did you see those conger eels down there?" Bobby asked out of breath. They'd come to the surface for a break and swam to a huge volcanic rock plateau on the shoreline.

"Naw, I was more intrigued with the sea urchins and that school of parrot fish. Didn't you see them? They circled around you several times and then took off."

They beached their cumbersome scuba gear and resumed their swim equipped simply with snorkels. Bobby swam to the far edge of the coral reef in shallow water leading back to an underwater cave. Jamie decided to pursue another route. He liked deeper water, felt more comfortable there.

Biel was amazed at the eye-catching cone snails limping along below him as though they had no care in the underwater sea world. Several of the larger ones displayed an unusual pattern on the dorsal surface of their shells. It appeared that a single angel was embedded in the red, yellow, and green color fields of the shell. The pattern was well-defined and balanced. Bobby couldn't believe it. These were supernatural spirits in nautical form.

He surfaced to signal Jamie to join him and share his discovery, but he was out of sight. Bobby swam back to take another gander. He spotted the largest cone snail moving at a slow pace across the bottom and reached down with his right hand to pick it up. He didn't see the barbed hypodermic-like harpoon darting out to sting his hand.

Yuck! How could that angelic creature of the sea be so vicious?

He didn't know this particular cone snail's venom was extremely toxic. He dropped the snail and swam back to shore. When he slipped out of the water, he inspected the hand noticing only a small welt. It continued to sting and began to turn a light red color. Bobby reentered the water and stood foot-deep rubbing his hand and arm intermittently in the soothing salt water. Every square inch of his body began to ache. Not knowing the venom's hazard, he planned to pop a few extra pain pills when he returned to the hotel and figured the episode would be history.

Jamie approached the shoreline, carrying three long conger eels he killed with the knife he had strapped to his leg. I think I see some squalls forming up," he said while pointing up to the darkened sky. Rain is eminent, We should be on our way."

"Still the armed killer, huh, Richards?" Bobby mocked when he spotted the eels.

"Yep, can't seem to get it out of my blood. We should eat these guys before the storm drives us out of here."

"Raw? That's bullshit."

"Just pulling your leg." Jamie laughed as he sliced up the eels and tossed them back into the water. "Fish food, I'm on a recycling-the-marine-creature kick. Wiggle in here, you bastardos, and eat your hearts out."

Bobby shrugged. "I think I've had enough for one day. Let's cut out." He stood watching the eel parts disappear.

Jamie noticed him wincing. "Better get your wide butt out of the water. I'm already drying off."

All of a sudden, rain and rolling thunder came crashing through the clouds. Bright rays of lightning lit up the skies encompassing a wide span of the Indian Ocean. A second clasp hit the water two feet from where Bobby was still standing. A ricochet of the powerful electrical shock wave spun him around temporarily dazing him.

"Get the hell of the water, you idiot, before you get electrocuted!" Jamie screamed.

Bobby trudged ashore as ordered, and they hurried back to the hotel before they got struck by lightning. On their return route, they looked back and witnessed the powerful force striking several trees. He elected not to tell Jamie about the snail bite. His warrior friend was covered with ugly scars on his head, both arms and his right leg. Bobby never inquired about the jagged one on the side of his head. If his friend wanted to tell war stories, it was up to him.

They spent the next several days in the hilly areas hiking and bird-watching. They never found the white-tailed tropicbird but discovered many others not found in America. Jamie met a cute-looking local in the hotel bar on their last night in Reunion. She was a tall blonde from Dallas and had fallen in love with the island on a recent visit. She decided to relocate permanently. They exchanged e-mail addresses and telephone numbers with a promise to reconnect.

On the morning of their scheduled departure, Bobby slipped into a deep coma. His friend was unable to wake him. Jamie made several frantic phone calls for medical help. The physician on call for resort emergencies, and an ambulance crew arrived an hour later.

Jamie briefed the doctor on Bobby's cancer history and the medications he was taking. After an extensive evaluation, the doctor said, "I've never seen anything like this in all my years of practicing on this island. He doesn't appear to be in any pain. Nothing I've tried revived him, yet all of his vital signs are within normal limits. Strange, this is indeed very strange."

The two EMTs with the ambulance concurred and began to pack up their gear. One of them said with a chuckle, "Once, I raced to an emergency call and found the patient in the same situation as your friend here. I tried every trick in the book to wake him but nothing worked. Three hours later, he came to and shouted, 'Bring back that sexy woman I slept with. She slipped me a Mickey.'"

"Hey, that's funny, but what are we going to do now? We're in a dilemma," Jamie said in a serious tone. "We were scheduled to leave the island today."

"Tell me what you two have been doing in Reunion since you arrived," the doctor asked.

Jamie detailed a list of their activities as though he was briefing his commander, *sans* pointer and charts. The physician didn't hear anything out of the ordinary. They were typical tourists doing what tourist do on his island.

"During my residency in Madagascar, we saw a case similar to this. The patient came out of the coma in two days and asked his wife if she'd been on a shopping spree. Never able to pin a diagnosis on him. The guy is still alive today. I get a birthday card from him every year."

"Where do we go from here?" Jamie asked again. He was paranoid listening to the stories about people in comas. Something had to be done, or he'd go berserk.

"We'll move him to the infirmary and watch him closely for twenty-four to forty-eight hours and reevaluate. I'll call immediately if anything happens. By the way, the resort will bill you for my services. The ambulance run and stay in the infirmary is on the prefecture."

At midnight of the second day, Bobby eased out of his coma. The doctor called early morning and asked Jamie to pick him up. He told him that medically, nothing was wrong with Bobby. He was fit to travel without any restrictions.

"What the living hell happened, Jamie?" Bobby asked with a puzzled look when he arrived to pick him up. I feel like I've slept for a week."

Instead of alarming his cancer-stricken friend with the truth, Jamie told him he tripped on the living room rug last night. The fall had knocked him out. Bobby bought the story and went to his room to pack. They were leaving the next day on their rescheduled itinerary.

"Ready to mount up?" Jamie asked the morning of their departure. Bobby was still in the bathroom, examining the cancer site on his forehead. It looked different and wasn't generating as much puss as when they arrived on the island. He came out of the bathroom, plopped his hat on, and said, "Let's hit the road before I stumble again and break a damn leg."

The return trip was more arduous than the initial jaunt to Reunion because of their change in plans. They had to overnight in both London and New York. Their connection from DFW to San Antonio was canceled for several hours because of a maintenance problem. They arrived in the Alamo City three days after leaving Reunion. They were both exhausted and slept for an entire day.

Bobby was the first one up. He donned his robe and sought the bathroom. He had delayed his pee call to the point that the pressure in his kidneys had ramped up for an explosion. After satisfying nature's call, he studied himself in the bathroom mirror.

I don't believe it. No way, not possible. I don't understand how the hell it happened. Very strange that I don't feel any severe pain in my body. Kinda have a numb feeling without it.

"Jamie, rise and shine. Get out of the sack and come here!" he shouted at the top of his lungs.

"You jerk-off, Biel, what's happening? I was in dreamland with the island cutie from Reunion. You remember her, the one we met in the resort bar. She was clinging to me like I was a hundred-dollar bill. We were in the sack getting ready to—"

"Shut up, you fool! Look at my head. It's gone. The cancer has disappeared. I was a dead man and have reincarnated as a superman. The pain in my body has subsided. Hallelujah!"

Jamie strolled to his friend's side to take a peek. He rubbed his eyes several times and cleared the sleep out of the corners with quick strokes of a Kleenex. He stood in awe at what he'd just witnessed. Bobby's long red hair had turned into a curly blond mop. His protruding upper jaw line had pulled back to mesh equally with the lower jaw. The tiny peephole green eyes had emerged as larger light blue orbs. He was handsome. Jamie couldn't believe the miracle that had taken place.

"Son of a bitch, Bobby, you're cured!"

CHAPTER 5

DATELINE

San Francisco—Valentine's day, 2012

Barry Gregg was hesitant to take the BART into the city to visit Kat. He'd already purchased the requisite dozen roses and a box of her favorite Ghirardelli dark chocolates. When he called her this morning, she was still in bed so he left a message. He was in the city researching police records on a serial killer. A family had hired him to represent them in the slaying of their young son. It was her special day, and he'd see to it that it would remain that way. She had called him several days ago after the embarrassing incident in Union Square and her first appointment with a dermatologist. The office visit culminated in an emergency referral to a leading city oncologist. She was devastated with the news he had given her.

"Hey, Kat, I'm in the city. Care for some company?" He waited impatiently for her response.

"Barry Gregg, I'm in bed again, called in sick today. Every time I get up, I vomit. It's getting worse. The pain, the nausea, and the depression. I've missed so much work lately, I'm thankful I still have a job. If you want to come here and play nursemaid, it's fine with me. I read the *Chronicle* and saw where you took on that high-profile case. Are you sure you have time to see me?"

"Of course, honey. Barry boy can't miss a Valentine's Day without seeing his main squeeze."

She forced a painful laugh and sobbed. "Come over right now, please, and don't stop at GO and collect the two hundred." She uttered the joke through chattering teeth. They enjoyed playing Monopoly instead of learning Mahjong. The Chinese game was now the rage of the office staff. Four Asian American lawyers introduced the game and, on occasion, stayed after hours with other workers. The enjoyed the game so much that they often played into the late evening.

Kat lived in one of the residential units that lined Union Street in swanky Pacific Heights. She had an unobstructed view of the Presidio and could even catch a glimpse of the Golden Gate Bridge from her bay window. Barry often played out the question why she never asked him to move in with her. She didn't have any religious hang-ups that would rule out such an accommodation. He would cohabit at the drop of a hat.

Barry hopped on the crowded Union Street bus with roses and chocolates in hand. Riders from Chinatown jammed the bus with all their packages and hot dinner items for the evening. He was eager to see if Kat would appreciate the goodies. She hadn't been eating enough to maintain her strength and perhaps Ghirardelli's finest would take care of that. Kat was now stick thin and had given up all of her exercise routines.

"Come on up, Barry," she said after the intercom announced his arrival. She lived on the second floor accessible by a twenty-stair climb. Two fat cats jumped off the railing as he neared the top. They belonged to the crabby widow who lived in the lower unit. The front door was ajar and he walked in and saw her lying on the couch in her pink bath robe.

As he approached her, Stryker, the pygmy falcon buzzed his head and flew back to its cage in the den. Barry was startled but knew she set him free periodically for what she termed "an extended exercise" session. He learned to accept her eccentric habits, which worsened as she approached the terminal phase of her life.

"Give me a kiss and hug me forever, Barry," she whimpered as he approached the couch.

"Gladly," he said and walked to her while placing the gifts on an end table. They caressed for several minutes, and he let her down softly and sat in the lounger facing her. The television was reporting the latest news about a homeless character breaking into city hall. He stood up and turned it off. She had a habit of taping the news programs from all the major networks so she wouldn't miss an earth-shaking event.

"When are you going back to work?" he asked her softly. "I'm sure your sick leave account has been tapped out by now."

She stared at him and was curious about which stage of his visit he would offer the roses and chocolates. He was a brilliant defense lawyer but sometimes couldn't remember when to give and when to take. He saw her eyes zero in and hold on the end table.

"Whoops, my dear Kat, I'm sorry, totally lost my train of thought when you were in my arms." He rose and presented them to her on bended knee. She hoped that he wasn't about to propose. Marriage was not an option after she had been given the six-month sentence by the devil doctor.

"Are you making any headway with your suit against the tanning booth company?" He hesitated asking the question but wanted to change the subject. She was suing them for libel due to false advertising and personal damages for not thoroughly warning their customers about the risk of ultraviolet exposure. After receiving the horrible news from her oncologist, she researched UV exposure and was alarmed that she hadn't taken any precautions or even jettisoned the habit. It could have prevented the ravaging melanoma from ever taking control of her body.

"No," she said, rubbing her throbbing left leg. "I'm not sure the suit has gained enough traction yet. The Mahjong champion lawyer in the office handling my case wants to blow it up to class action status. He's representing several other suckers who succumbed to the ill effects of UV tanning. I'll be six feet under if and when the case is settled."

"When did your folks go back to Iowa?"

"Last weekend, and frankly, their five-day visit was terrible. Mom wouldn't accept my impending death and carried on to the degree that Dad physically removed her from the room. When they left, Dad jumped me for smoking marijuana. He didn't believe it was legally prescribed for medicinal purposes. He doesn't know that we had smoked pot every weekend in my final year at Yale. I had mixed feelings when they left San Francisco."

"How's that?" Barry asked her with compassion. She started to cry and began to shake all over. He thought another seizure was coming on. He knew the drill.

"I was happy they got off my case and went back home to that stupid farm. At the same time, I knew I wouldn't see them again and that hurt. They are good people, Barry, but Father's heart is giving out. I owe them big time for ensuring that I received a superb education."

"You've paid your debt. You made them happy for your success."

Kat pulled herself up and went to the closet to retrieve her bamboo bong.

"Want some?" She took the bag of pot from the fridge and warmed it up in her small hands before adding it to the bong. Kat filled the small water reservoir and stoked up. She was addicted to pot now. The Vicodin and other pain-killing meds the oncologist prescribed only gave her short-term relief. She called on an old pot-smoking friend from college days now living in the city to space her far enough out to forget the recurring pain.

"No, thanks. Getting off the beloved cannabis was my third New Year's resolution," he said proudly and immediately regretted it.

"Want to fulfill your first resolution?" She labored getting the words out.

Barry gasped. "You mean we get married?"

"Yes, sir, consider it my final death wish."

He was stunned and at a loss for words, uncharacteristic for a big time lawyer he professed to himself. *I'm not ready for marriage, especially to a woman who'd be in the ground shortly after our honeymoon.*

"Kat, I believe the soothing effects of the pot have kicked in already. Do you realize what you just asked me?"

"I take that for a no. No to me, no to you, and no trip to the damn altar," she blurted out.

"But, Kat, think of all the adverse situations that could surface as the result of your proposal."

"Get the hell out of here, Barry Gregg!"

He tried to calm her down, but it didn't work. Barry got up and left immediately without looking back at her. He didn't see the dozen roses and box of chocolates thrown at him as the door closed. She hurried to the bathroom and puked excessive amounts of blood and mucus. When she stood up and glanced at the top suspensions of the Golden Gate Bridge, a thought raced through her pot-scrambled mind.

She called a taxi for an immediate pickup.

"Where do you want me to take you?" The cab had arrived in eight minutes, which shocked her. In the past, it took her at least a half-hour for one to respond. This day was going to be different.

"Drop me off at the Golden Gate Bridge in front of the statue of Joseph Strauss."

"Gonna walk the bridge, ma'am? That bathrobe you're wearing won't do any good up there. You'll freeze your tail off. I suggest we turn around and head back to your joint. Save the walk till the sun chases away this foggy mist."

"How much do I owe you?" she asked as she climbed out of the back door, ignoring his comments to drive her back home.

He became suspicious and said, "The ride's on me." He burned rubber on his way out of there, not wanting to be party to another crazy leaper.

Kat walked to the one-mile marker of the span and stopped. She looked out toward the Pacific Ocean and, after a short pause, pivoted in the opposite direction. Alcatraz poked up through the fog and chills raced through her body. She loved Burt Lancaster in the movie *Birdman of Alcatraz,* which she had seen five times. A packed boat was circling the popular prison ready to belch up eager tourists for one of the Park Service-led tours. She made up her mind and climbed up on the railing facing the famed prison.

"Good-bye world!" she screamed to nobody in particular and readied herself for the fatal jump.

All of a sudden, a strong hand grabbed her around one ankle and jerked her backward. She tumbled off the railing into the strong arms of Barry Gregg.

"Stop it!" she yelled at Barry, kicking him with her other foot.

"Baby, you need to settle down and think straight," he consoled with a deep pang tugging at his heart.

"Leave me alone, you big jerk. Why did you interfere? I don't want to live any longer. Your timing stinks, Gregg. How did you know I was here?"

Before he responded, he pulled her to his chest. She was cold and shivering.

"When I left your place and walked to my car, I realized how shitty I reacted to the marriage question you had posed. I sat in the car, trying to make some sense out of all that happened. I decided to return and make amends with you when I saw you jump into a taxi, still wearing your bathrobe. I followed behind the cab to see where you were headed. When you got off at the bridge, I knew what you had in mind. I barely caught up with you before you attempted the swan dive."

"I'm done with living the way I am. Can't you see that?"

"You have to stop seeing that shrink in Berkeley. I know all about him. He's a quack if ever there was one. Only in California can someone get away with the crimes he's committing. Several of my counterparts at the office discussed his advertisements regarding psychopharmacology. One of the lawyers did some research on practitioners that overmedicate patients with the slightest sign of depression. The side effects of this treatment regimen had devastating consequences according to their studies."

"Stop preaching to me, Gregg. You don't know what you're talking about."

"Maybe, maybe not, but I should have stopped you from seeing him. Quit fighting me, Kat, I'm taking you home right away."

"Over my dead body!" she sobbed and started to climb back on the railing. Barry grabbed her forcibly this time. Kat went limp as she passed out with the unbearable pain. He wrapped his trench coat around her and carried her back to his car. San Francisco General Hospital was not that far away.

Paris—Saint Valentin Day, 2012

EROTIC ASPHYIXIATION can be traced back to the early seventeenth century to find a cure for erectile dysfunction by applying a form of asphyxia during masturbation. Hugues Chaban was introduced to the practice as a young painter living in an isolated art colony south of Paris. Most of the older artists he associated with were zonked out on cocaine, and he vowed never to succumb to drugs. An older artist moved in and soon became Hughes's love interest. Weekly, they practiced the art of dominance and submission using the technique. Hugues preferred the submission role. Six months later, his lover moved to Calais. Hugues was devastated and moved back to Paris proper to begin a new life in the city. Two years later, he found his perfect match with Pierre Duvair.

"I can't believe it," Hugues sobbed. "You're not going to die regardless what those charlatans in white coats told you."

"Look here, *mon amie*. I'm afraid you are wrong. They conducted so many tests that I felt like a mannequin hanging in an anatomy lab. My arms have been penetrated so many times I squirt blood whenever I cough. They abused this delicate body of mine at will. I lost track. I don't care. I give up."

"No, no, Pierre, the cancer can be cured. I'm sure of that."

"Wrong, Hugues. My melanoma is rare. I don't want to overwhelm you with technical terms, but this is what they told me. It can grow in many areas other than exposed skin surfaces. In my case, it damaged the mucous membranes that line my rectum. They assured me it wasn't caused by our...you know, making love. I still have my doubts."

"Are you sure nothing can be done? Why don't you go to America and get a second opinion."

"No, it's too late for that. I want to die in my beloved country."

"How long did they give you?"

"Six months or less."

"Let's leave my studio and go to our private place and commiserate," Hugues whimpered. "We can forget about all the pain and suffering for the time being. What do you think?"

"I think I'm so frustrated wearing these ridiculous diapers all the time. On top of that, I'm depressed knowing I'll be dead soon. But I have to move on, and your idea is timely. I'll call my driver right away."

Pierre directed the limo driver to drop them off a mile from their special place. "Don't you dare tell Andre where you took me," Pierre scolded the driver. "He'll fret and worry about my well-being. When you get back, tell him to take a day off. I won't need him. Same goes for you. Be sure he feeds Louie before he leaves. I'll be in touch."

The special place was located in the Cour des Miracles, an undesirable area traditionally inhabited by unemployed migrants. He didn't want his driver to know the exact location, so he always had him drop them off away from the site. They either walked the remaining distance or hailed a taxi.

Pierre seized the property from a delinquent account when he was at the bank. The small open space was conveniently located above a loading dock accessed by a private entrance. There were no windows, but a skylight allowed outside light not blocked by the building abutting the dock. Using his artistic talents, Hugues converted the upstairs unit to a *studio des asphyxia*. The walls were painted in sky blue and strobe lights were mounted on each ceiling corner.

Hugues taught him the fundamentals of erotic asphyxiation early in their relationship. Initially, Pierre despised the "self-abuse" as he called it but later enjoyed the thrilling sensations it gave him. He designed an armless wooden chair that could be suspended from the ceiling either upside down or sideways. Hugues preferred the chair elevated on a platform three feet high where his shoes were grounded on something firm.

"Get the collars ready, Hugues. I need to transcend immediately."

"Hold on a minute, Pierre. I have some prepping to do."

Hugues had purchased a supply of one-inch adjustable wide collars lined with a firm cotton-like material. The collars had adjustable plastic screw settings depending on the size of the participant's neck. His size was a twelve. Pierre measured a sixteen and paid extra for a collar with a silk lining. Hugues didn't care what material choked him to near death. It was the ride that counted. He was a giggler and enjoyed cross-dressing. Pierre leaned more toward masochism. The restriction of oxygen to the brain gave both of them a cocaine-like high with insurmountable pleasure.

They always started their sessions draining a half carafe of cognac. If Hugues was up first, he always used a half-inch cloth rope first before he transferred to the collar. It gave him a quick high but brought him to the dark edges of asphyxiation.

"I want to spend my last days in Verdun at my place on the Meuse River." Pierre sobbed before he drifted into the final point of near-asphyxiation much too soon. "My older sister lived there and deeded the property to me before she died."

"How did she pass away?" Hugues asked, never having been brought into a discussion about his lover's family.

"Melanoma. She spent every summer in the intense sun at our family retreat on the Cote d'Azur. It was always hot and steamy at times on the Riviera. Thank Jesus, our father was killed in battle, or he'd of died of the same affliction. Seems to run in the family, huh? We were informed that our father was buried at the Douaumont Ossuary after falling in the Battle of Verdun. I guess that's why she spent her last days there instead of Saint-Tropez."

"Don't be so dour," Hugues whispered softly. "We have much more to accomplish before you…ah…cross over."

Pierre didn't hear him. He had passed out.

That night, they slept on the floor curled up in woven quilts Hugues borrowed from another artist friend. The next morning, Pierre arranged for his driver to pick them up. They secured a taxi to return to the same corner where they had been dropped off.

Hugues exited the limo in front of his apartment. Pierre joined him on the street for several long minutes. The driver curled up his fists and slammed the dashboard in frustration.

"Good-bye, my dear friend." He placed both hands on Hughes's shoulders, kissed him gently on the right cheek, and then the left. He followed up by clamping Hughes's left cheek in his jaws and gave him a gentle, full-mouth squeeze with his teeth. Hugues never liked this act because it would take hours before the bite marks would disappear from his left cheek.

Andre was at the Champs apartment, reading the paper when Pierre arrived home. He never took a day off because his life revolved around his master. He had a comfortable bedroom in the back room immediately behind the kitchen. He didn't have anywhere else to live so the arrangement was acceptable.

"You were gone a long time with your friend, Pierre. I would be more concerned about my medical condition, if I were you. You pass out periodically, and that concerns me. Are you trying to speed up your death?"

"Your concern about my health is overwhelming, but my demise will come soon enough regardless of what I do and where I do it."

Andre was suspicious. He didn't believe Pierre had cancer, especially the deadly melanoma. He went on the Internet to check it out. Melanoma was a skin cancer and presented itself as an ugly brown spot somewhere on the skin. He'd seen Pierre naked in the bathroom as recently as last week. He didn't see any spots. He was sure that his master had AIDS. He knew all about Hugues Chaban. The limo driver was his grandson.

Chicago—Valentine's day, 2012

LEAH MALAKA WAS ENTERTAINING a visiting mayor from the east coast when she got the frantic call from Slade. It was midnight. She'd just climbed out of the champagne-filled king-sized bathtub in a private suite in the Hancock Tower. Her date for the evening was a single gay man who had no intention of showering her with anything but gifts. He wanted the type of exposure commensurate with being seen in public by a beautiful woman. He was running for reelection, and the pundits were out in force at the charity ball they attended earlier that evening.

"What's going on, Slade? You knew I was working tonight?"

"I couldn't sleep. None of the pills they gave me worked. I'm in pain every waking minute. Do you have any suggestions?"

"Open the bedside cabinet top drawer and lift out the loaded .357 magnum. Place it to your temple and pull the trigger. You're dying anyway to get it done with in short order. What the hell do you expect me to say? I've told you ever since they diagnosed you there's nothing I could do that would alter the outcome. Go back to bed, and I'll be there soon as this bimbo I'm with falls asleep. I dropped two sleeping pills in his glass of champagne an hour ago. I shouldn't be too late."

Slade was still pissed at her for accepting the assignment from her facilitator. He wanted her to be with him all day and night as this would be his last Valentine's day on earth. His melanoma had metastasized to his lungs, and they gave him fewer than six months to live. She knew he bought the magnum on his return to the condo after digesting the death warrant from his oncologist. Leah was there at the time; otherwise, he would have used the pistol the minute he walked in.

"Fine, just make it snappy, Leah."

"I will, don't do anything stupid, and I'll be there before you know it."

Slade ambled to his desk and sat down at the computer. Every cellular structure in his body was on fire and ached so badly he was shaking. He pulled up the Internet to continue his research on melanoma, hoping to find new data on a potential cure. There wasn't any. Stage IV popped up repeatedly, but he'd already memorized the prognosis that came with the morbid classification. He kicked himself repeatedly for not seeking medical help before it was too late. He vividly recalled the discussions he had with the oncologist several weeks ago.

"Your years of sailing in the Florida sun without using sun screen protection had caught up with you, Slade. I know you don't believe in modern-day medicine, so I'm not going to go into the what ifs with you. It's too late anyway."

"It's not that I don't believe nor don't care, Doctor. I'm more stubborn than stupid."

"I've prescribed pain pills for you to take when the pain gets unbearable. You told me that you have placed your affairs in order, so I have one last thing to suggest. When you reach that period of time where you can't fully tend to yourself, arrange for hospice care. They are angels of mercy in disguise and will provide the comfort you need at the terminal stage of your life."

When Leah came in, he was still at his desk shaking in pain. She started to tell him about the gay guy she was with, but he was rude and interrupted her. "It's about time you got here. Get my pain pills from the bathroom."

"My, my, are you in a good mood or what, Mr. Glick? I came right away. The buffoon I was with apparently developed a resistance to sleeping pills throughout the years. I guess the demands placed on a modern-day mayor cannot be taken lightly."

On her way to the bathroom to fetch his pills, she screamed so loud Slade flipped backward off the desk chair. She had stumbled and fell across his African rock python slithering down the hallway from the guest bedroom. The snake crawled to her and started nestling around her lower legs. She froze, staring blindly at its eyes and at the triangular dark brown spear-head outlined in yellow. When the python opened its mouth, she noticed the many sharp and backwardly curved teeth and screamed.

"What's going on in there?" Slade asked. Silence prevailed.

Leah struggled to free herself as the reptile began to tighten its grip around her ankles. Unsuccessful, she poked a long sharp fingernail into its eye, and the reptile loosened the grip. She raced to the bathroom and slammed the door shut.

"Are you sure you're okay, Leah?" Slade shouted as he retrieved Rocky and returned him to the serpentarium. She came out of the bathroom when she knew the snake was caged.

"Of course I'm not, you buffoon! Why was the slimy devil free to roam the house? I told you before that if I ever encounter him again out of the snake cage, you'd be history. For Christ's sake, Slade, has that cancer completely bleached your mind?"

"I'm so sorry. I forgot that I'd let Rocky out. Having him living with me is comforting as my life is slipping away. I don't know what I'd do without him. Of course you wouldn't understand. Women believe that snakes are God's fallen angels."

She regained some semblance of sanity after being scared half to death. Leah rationalized that her friend was dying and needed her comfort and support, not unmitigated harassment about a stupid pet serpent. He took the pills she gave him, and they settled back down in the living room.

Slade began to feel more human after the effects of the analgesics kicked in. He could still be amorous at times, and this was one of them. He missed her today and was jealous of her arrangement for the evening even though she pulled in a thousand bucks. Money and the prestige that came with it no longer meant anything to him. He'd be gone in a few months.

"Let's go to bed now, Leah. I hope you're still in for a real Valentine's day treat. The Slademan's got the whole package ready, willing and eager to deliver."

They undressed each other, slowly and methodically and crawled in between the silk sheets. They embraced each other while speaking in soft murmurs until Leah got up and went to the bathroom. When she returned, she found him snoring. She opted not to wake him knowing that a deep sleep was exactly what he needed. The sun began to creep across the outline of Lake Michigan. She wondered what the new light of day would bring them.

CHAPTER 6

SAN ANTONIO

BOBBY BIEL WAS A NEW MAN, genetically, physically, and emotionally. He and Jamie celebrated his revitalized status for an entire week before Jamie moved out. He was anxious to pick up Vic from a friend and was greeted with language even he hadn't heard before. It was more enjoyable than being quoted chapter and verse from the Bible. He was tired of hearing about the escapades of Matthew, Mark, Luke, and John. Jamie leased a home in Alamo Heights near the high school football stadium. He and Bobby decided to go their separate ways for the time being. Jamie enrolled in an MBA program at a local university. Bobby had greater intentions. He planned on becoming extremely wealthy with his newly found discovery. It was time to go for a walk. He went to his favorite haunt.

"Is that you, Bobby? You seem different." his bartender acquaintance at Teddy's Tavern asked with a half smile creeping across his face. "I hardly recognized you."

"Yes, indeed, I had some cosmetic surgery done. Do you like my new looks?"

"You're a stud, man, must have cost you a mint. You discover a gold mine or what?"

"Let's leave it at *or what.*"

"Sure, want a pint of Samuel Adams?"

"Yep."

Bobby picked up his beer and walked to a nearby table. The only other customer in the tavern was at the end bar stool and slumped over. Bobby figured the guy lifted one too many glasses of Lone Star beer. He wanted to be alone, needed to think. He learned two valuable lessons when he lived in West Texas as a youngster: how to get high and how to experiment with animals. His brilliant father developed a popular product from mescaline, one of the psychoactive properties of the local acacia trees and peyote cacti.

He recalled a conversation he had with his father when he was an adolescent. *"Why do those people want to pay so much money for your stuff? Son, it instills a powerful belief in them, and that is opening the door to the spiritual world. They gain the benefits of heaven while still living on earth. You can't beat that with a stick."*

Customers paid a steep price to use the mind-altering effects from the compounds his dad synthesized and sold. Mexicans found their way across the border in search of Señor Biel's Elixir. Many years later, through his research on the farm, Bobby learned that he could make methamphetamine much easier than messing around with acacia trees and the peyote cacti on the farm property.

"Ready for another Samuel?" the bartender interrupted his chain of thought.

"Hit me one more time."

"You got it."

Few people knew that Bobby owned the small farm in a secluded patch of rugged land between San Antonio and Laredo where he raised goats, chimps, and produced meth. He called it a farm instead of a ranch because it consisted of only one hundred twenty acres. In Texas, a ranch encompasses massive acreage. Even Jamie Richards was unaware of its existence. Bobby inherited it from his father twenty years ago. He was the only remaining next of kin. It was the ideal place to flee from the rat race in the city where he had labored twelve hours a day. After work, he usually hung out in the bars along the River Walk before heading back to his apartment. On weekends and days off, he'd motor to the farm where he'd constructed a modern laboratory inside of the big barn. It cost him a ton of money, but Bobby rationalized it was worth every cent.

Two tourists barged in, and Bobby relocated upstairs in a corner, which overlooked the long bar below. The sleeper at the end of the bar woke up and soon engaged in an animated conversation with the newcomers. Bobby drifted back again in deep thought.

I need to modify my research laboratory out on the farm. Developing a melanoma cancer cure takes precedence beyond the other businesses. Cha-ching, cha-ching. I love the sound of money hitting the till. I'll put the anti-aging research on hold and give the goats some time off. Their horns will grow longer, which is even better when I grind them into powder for my end product.

At the same time, I'll cut back on the meth operation and notify my distributor that I won't be able to meet his demands for at least the next six months. He's from Matamoros and can find another source of supply to feed his Mexican addicts.

Bobby finished his beer and dropped some money on the bar as he was leaving.

"Cutting out so soon, Bobby? I thought you'd hang around and meet some chicks that frequent this establishment. With that new Hollywood face and chiseled body, they'd be standing in line to take a crack at you."

"Got to run. Places to go. Things to do."

When he returned to his apartment, he booked a roundtrip ticket to the Mascarene Islands in the Indian Ocean. He planned to smuggle out at least two dozen of those miracle sea snails, which he was convinced, had cured him. He would make a fortune developing a serum that would cure the horrible cancer that afflicted him and so many others. He planned to pose as a marine biologist on a research mission for the Conus, the large genus of the marine gastropod family. Biel didn't anticipate a problem bringing the cones back to the US. He had all the requisite credentials and was even known internationally for his work at the San Antonio biochemical research laboratory.

The following morning, he called Roberto Gomez, the trustworthy caretaker he was lucky to retain when he was gifted the farm. The eighty-year-old grizzled Mexican waded across the Rio Grande when he was a teenager and found lasting employment with Bobby's father. He lived alone in one of the outbuildings and didn't speak much English. He was short, powerful, and missing all of his front teeth. He had no neck, and his head sat squarely on his shoulders like a pumpkin plopped on the kitchen table.

"Roberto, I'll be gone for a few weeks. Make sure you tend to the goats and don't lose any through the fence line. You know I paid a deep price for them. Keep the barn locked at all times and don't let any strangers wander around the property. And be sure to clean out the chimp cages. They get messy when they throw food at each other."

"*Si, si,* Señor Biel. No worry here from me." Bobby hung up and smiled. He was like a son to Roberto. The caretaker never left the farm, and he hated outsiders. Roberto always had a long-barreled pistol strapped to his thick waist and took great comfort in shooting rattlesnakes or other varmints stalking the property. He was near death on two occasions from the venom of their bites but survived to hunt them again and again.

At noon, Bobby got a surprise call from his former assistant at the biochemical firm that axed him. He was shocked at the news she relayed to him. "The corporate big shots decided to award you for getting a US patent for the acne vulgaris salve you developed. Teenagers across mainstream America will love you forever. Merck just bought the rights to further develop and market the product."

"I can't believe that. Are you sure?"

"Of course, Bobby. You know I wouldn't be pulling your leg."

"How much?"

"Twenty-five grand, and it will be deposited in your bank account. Personnel told me they still have your account information on file. I'm sure you didn't read the write-up in The *San Antonio-Express News.*"

"Nope."

"How are you doing, Bobby? Your voice sounds different, much deeper. Do you have a cold?"

"No cold here. It's my cedar allergy," he lied. "I feel great and am pursuing a new adventure."

"Like what?"

"Like, it's a big secret, sweetheart."

"You're kidding me. Let me in on it."

"Sorry, cannot do. Anyway, thanks for the call. I hope they're treating you better than the way they hassled me all the time. By the way, is that bastard boss of ours still on board?"

"Bobby, how can you say that? We're engaged to be married. He's a really a nice man."

He hung up in disgust.

Who'd have believed those two would walk down the aisle together. "Birds of a feather," they say. I am beyond shocked that the company decided to share some of that windfall they got from Merck. It came at an opportune time and will finance my trip and some of the research costs. I know that I'll have to buy some more sophisticated equipment to keep those sea snails living. No problem now.

He was surprised when the phone rang again. It was Jamie.

"I haven't heard from you in ages. What's going on? By the way, I like that sexy new voice of yours."

"Screw you, Richards," He laughed.

"No, seriously, is everything all right?"

"Yes, things are great on this end. My former employer received a chunk of money from one of my patents and is sharing a portion of the proceeds with me."

"Fantastic. Great news on top of your miraculous recovery. I'm happy for you."

Bobby decided to keep him in the dark about his upcoming trip to procure the sea snails. He would bring him aboard at the appropriate time.

"How's school coming along, Jamie?"

"It's on hold right now. You wouldn't believe what just happened to me. Do you remember me telling you about that Navy SEAL?"

"Yes, the Cyclops guy."

Jamie responded. "If you ever call him that in person, he'd rip your head off and shove it down your neck. He called me last night and wants me to work an assignment for him."

"What's that all about? I thought you were getting your MBA."

"School can wait. Denis Sweeny works for the US Secret Service. He told me when we were in Somalia, he was going to end up with an exciting job after he retired from the navy."

"And?" Bobby said with trepidation.

"The President of Venezuela is coming to Dallas next month to make a formal visit to the John F. Kennedy memorial site at the Book Depository at Dealey Plaza. Scuttlebutt has it that he's trying to improve his relationship with our government. He purports to be a big fan of the Kennedy clan. I have been asked to be a *secret* bodyguard while he's in Dallas."

"Really? I bet he's there to honor that asshole Lee Harvey Oswald. Doesn't he travel with his own security detail?" Bobby was curious. This didn't make any sense.

"Certainly but our powers-to-be aren't taking any chances on another assassination attempt in Dallas. Sweeny knew that I lived in Dallas before I joined the army. He wants me to work independent of the president's personal bodyguards. I'll be near the main man at all times but not up close. He won't know I'm around, but his security staff will be briefed about my mission."

"Are you going to accept the assignment?" Bobby asked with a sly grin knowing Richards couldn't flush the thrill of dangerous liaisons from his system.

"Sure, why not? There's good money in it, and I miss all the excitement thrown my way from Delta Force. It's high time to get my gear in order and crank up the reliable Bul M-5. I love the 9-mm. handgun even though the Caspian frame was made in the US as well as other internal parts. A fair amount of fitting and machining was involved. You didn't know that, right?"

"Not all of the details you're flaunting at me. Is that the one you told me about where the barrel, barrel bushing, recoil mechanism, and slide were initially produced in Israel?" He also loved fire arms and not only envied the weaponry Jamie possessed but his skill in using the tools of death.

"You got that right, Bobby. I got the longer barrel version and had it threaded to accept a suppressor. My baby has a nineteen-round capacity, not counting the one that's chambered. One of the Mossad intelligence agents I worked with on a mission in Lebanon obtained approval to reward it to me for my service with them. I saved the guy's life."

"You got a permit to carry a concealed weapon, or are you going to wing it?"

"Bobby, I'm a law-abiding citizen now."

"You danced around my question. Don't do anything stupid, Richards. I know you like to take chances."

"Maybe we can get together after I complete the mission, knock down a few cold ones. I haven't been downtown since we got back from our foray on that French island. What was it called again?"

"Reunion," Bobby responded, wanting to change the subject. He wasn't about to tell Jamie about his travel plans, at least not at this point.

"Are you planning on hooking up with that Fort Hood lady, whatever her name is?"

"Always probing, aren't you, Biel? You're like a creeping dentist. No, we're no longer seeing each other. Maria was getting too serious, told me she could put in for a job transfer to San Antonio. She was quick to add that there are numerous civil service positions available in town that she is qualified for."

"And what did you say?"

"I told her to forget it. She bombarded me with a ton of Spanish curse words I dare not repeat."

Bobby had heard enough. "Don't ask me to babysit that stupid bird for you. Be sure to call me when you finish your assignment in Dallas." He hung up and plunked down in a chair rubbing his chin.

I might need Jamie later on during the final experimentation phase of my new endeavor. There are bound to be controversial issues surfacing that could result in personal danger to my research team. My good friend would fit in perfectly. He's got the requisite equipment, skills and bravado to make things happen.

CHAPTER 7

NEW YORK

E N ROUTE TO THE INDIAN OCEAN, Bobby Biel decided to visit
an undergraduate college classmate living in New York. He
needed to consult with him on his Conus sea snail mission.
His friend was a leading malacologist renowned for his study of invertebrate zoology dealing with mollusks. When Bobby had contacted
him to set up the visit, Gar Underwood was elated. He told Bobby to
ask one of the airport staff for directions to his Manhattan apartment
when he arrived.

Underwood had set out to become a physician but left halfway through medical school to pursue his interest in biology. In the
past, he had chaired the zoology department of a local university. It
didn't take him long to despise the dreaded paper mill production
demanded of all senior university department heads. In more recent
years, he spent most of his time in the research laboratories preferring
a low-key working environment.

Bobby knew that malacologists were known for their dedicated
and relentless work in invertebrate labs, not as traffic cops in the
bowels of academia. They spent numerous hours in natural history
museums or on the beaches of the world. Gar was unemployed and
excited to learn all the nitty-gritty details about Bobby's new venture.

"What's the best way to get over to Sixty-Ninth Street on the west side of Manhattan?" Bobby asked the lady occupying the information desk at LaGuardia Airport. I'm visiting a college friend who lives in one of those brownstones."

"I'd take a taxi," she said. "Should run you around thirty-five bucks."

"Why can't I hop on a train? I'm told they are the most efficient means of transportation around these parts."

"Well, son, these parts don't have a train running out of our terminals." She chuckled to herself at the cowboy hat Bobby had propped on his head. She broke out in a laugh when she saw the rattlesnake belt anchored with the silver buckle symbol of the State of Texas.

"How about a bus?"

"Sure, partner, if you don't mind the inconvenience and company of my fellow New Yorkers. Go outside and grab the M-60 but first buy a MetraCard ticket. See that machine by the wall." She pointed to the unit location. "Feed it and it'll spit out your token."

"After I board the bus, where do I get off?"

"Would you like me to hold your hand and go with you?" She was enjoying herself at Bobby's expense. It had been a slow day, and she was bored to death.

"No, thanks. I left my grandmother at home."

"Better write this down, cowboy. Get off the bus at 125th and Lenox Avenue in Harlem. You'll find a subway stop downstairs. Take the 2 or 3 train downtown. Get off at the Seventy-Second Street station. You're close enough to walk to your friend's apartment. Have a super stay in our city, Wyatt Earp."

He found Underwood's apartment an hour later. "Wow, Bobby, you've really changed since we last saw each other. I barely recognized you," Gar said when he led him through the front door of his Manhattan apartment.

"Yes, sir, Dr. Underwood, I have changed considerably. You remember our days back in college when I couldn't lasso any chicks. They weren't looking for any nerdy types to escort them around the campus. You were the leading hen-snatcher in our fraternity."

Gar laughed. "You mean you've come all the way from Texas for me to fix you up with a leading New York model? Forget it, man. I've lost my touch. I'm getting too crotchety for that stuff."

"Well, that's not why I'm here."

"I know that. You didn't give me many morsels to chew on when you called me. What's up?"

"My fortunes have changed."

"Yes, I can readily see that. It appears that you fell under the spell of a plastic surgeon, and now you're looking for a pretty young lady to entertain you. My gracious, buddy, what's next?"

Bobby smiled at the remark from his still good-looking short and slightly overweight friend. "Let's sit down and talk. I want to tap your expertise on the project that I'm undertaking. You can relax. It doesn't involve the opposite sex."

"First, let me fix a pot of coffee and then we'll chat," Gar said, scratching his forehead. "It's too early in the day to hoist a few beers."

"Go for it. This will take some time."

They adjourned to a seating area outside the building and renewed past times. The friends bantered back and forth about women, the ridiculous times they got drunk on homemade wines, and their successful pursuit of doctoral degrees. Bobby was amazed that his friend was forced into retirement. Underwood failed the ultimate academic goal—tenured professorship. He was unceremoniously ejected just like the smoking round he took from the research lab higher-ups in San Antonio. They were two peas in a pod, scientifically driven, research-oriented junkies.

"I'm amazed at your miraculous recovery from cancer," Gar commented after the detailed briefing that led to his friend's visit.

"A true miracle," Bobby proclaimed.

"I have a difficult time believing that the neurotoxin from a Conus sea snail cured your melanoma. Having said that, I know that extensive studies were underway in my own scientific field to learn how various categories of mollusks can alleviate pain in humans. I just caught up on reading my literature last week."

"Gar, it had to be the snail. There is absolutely no other explanation."

"I'm not an expert in human genetics with the genome and DNA implications. But I'm convinced you went through some significant genetic mutations after having been struck by that snail harpoon. Your face and hair are different, the cleft palate is gone, your speech is more pronounced, and you are a walking stud."

"Again, I fully agree. Everybody I know is quick to compliment me."

"Why don't I accompany you to the island and help you harvest the snails? I am extremely interested in your situation, especially since I am considered an expert in the field of mollusks."

"No, that would be too obvious."

"What do you mean? Too obvious to whom and for what reason?"

"You'll blow my cover. We're both internationally known research scientists in our respective fields. I don't want the world to know what I'm up to. The mission must be classified as top secret. Otherwise, the entire pharmaceutical industry will assemble their troops and pull no punches going after my prize."

"So where do I fit in?" Gar asked intently, wanting to squirm his way in on a piece of the action.

"I want you to come to San Antonio and help me develop the product that will revolutionize cancer treatment for all ages. It will be the biggest discovery ever witnessed by the civilized world and we'll be filthy rich."

"Go on," Gar said, sitting attentively on the edge of his chair.

"I already have a limited research laboratory out in the county so isolated that nobody knows of its existence, not even my best friends. You can stay there on the farm and work with me. I'll continue to live a so-called normal life in town, so I don't alert anyone of the secret study we're undertaking. What do you think?"

"I'm in."

"Just like that?"

"Yes."

Bobby hesitated and asked, "What kind of financial remuneration would you be looking for if we hit pay dirt?"

"Seventy-five percent yours, twenty-five mine, pure and simple."

"Contract?" Bobby pushed further.

"Handshake. We'll have a formal agreement drawn up when we develop the final product. It will protect both of our interests."

"Deal," Bobby exhorted and shook Gar's hand firmly. "When can you start?"

"In two weeks, I'll wrap up my portion of a protocol on the commercial use of octopus and squid waste. One of my former students applied for and won a grant from the US Department of the Interior and begged me to help her. How could I refuse the young maiden? She's not only gorgeous but brainy. After I'm finished, I'll join you in Texas."

"Hold on," Bobby asserted. "Octopus waste? Squid waste? What the hell does the government care about shit like that?"

"Excrement from these sea creatures can benefit humanity in many ways."

"Good Christ! Are you pulling my leg, Gar, or am I missing something here?"

"Too complicated to get into at this time. The coffee is long gone from my system. Let's switch to beer and talk about old times."

The sun found a nearby high rise to hide behind. A police car went racing down the street with the siren announcing an emergency event. He regretted not bringing some warmer clothing having forgotten how moody the NYC weather got at times. Gar had retreated to the kitchen to fix some snacks. Bobby agreed to overnight with his friend and catch his flight out of JFK in the morning.

Indian Ocean—Madagascar/Reunion

THE PLANE WAS CIRCLING the runway at Ivato International Airport in Madagascar, and Bobby couldn't wait until it landed. He'd never used a "barf bag" before on an airplane but got sick on the leg out of Paris-Charles de Gaulle. Underwood must have drugged him or something because he wasn't feeling well. Maybe the reason was they stayed up all night drinking and talking. He barely made the flight out of JFK.

"Where to, sir?" the cabbie at the airport asked politely.

"Take me to Jacques-Moreau Marina Supplies. I think it's a long haul from here, but I'm sure you'll find it."

"No problem, sir. I'm a French expatriate and live not too far from Jacques's operation. Might I ask if you're going deep sea fishing? I captained one of his fishing boats but, man, was he ever demanding. No time off and poor pay."

Bobby was surprised at how well the man spoke English. "No fishing expedition today. I need to get some supplies here, for a job I have in Reunion."

"What's that all about? People like you go there to bask in the sun, lie on the beaches, and play games trying to pluck our enchanting native women."

Bobby laughed. "None of the above. I'm on a scientific expedition and will only be there a few days. Need to pick up one of his transportable marine aquariums, which aren't available on Reunion."

I need to change the subject. This cabbie was probing too much. Thank goodness, I made all these arrangements in advance. I'm in a big hurry to get there, secure my miracle sea snails, and hustle back to the USA.

He told the cabbie to wait for him at Jacques. The transaction went smoothly but took two hours. Bobby put the portable aquarium, aerator, and other supplies in the opened trunk and climbed back in the cab. The taxi sped off to the airport, rear tires squealing and loud music playing on the radio. Bobby preferred the earsplitting music to a conversation with the cabbie who asked too many questions.

Bobby relaxed in the back seat, oblivious to the speedy and circuitous route the driver took back to the airport. *This guy's in some kind of trance getting his rocks off on that stupid Bob Marley reggae music blasting on quad speakers. He needs to spend a week in Jamaica, and he'll forget he ever liked any form of music, period. Probably hung up on some cheap hash he got waiting for me while I was in Jacques.*

Upon his arrival in Reunion, he rented a car and drove to the same resort hotel that he and Jamie visited several months ago. Bobby planned to stay three nights. It didn't work out that way. He hooked up with the tall blond from Dallas that entertained Jamie on their last visit. They accidently bumped into each other at the hotel lounge, and Bobby sent her drink sailing across the floor.

"Whoops, excuse me, pretty Texas lady. I'm so sorry. I'm still in a daze about the beauty of your island. Let me get you another one."

"Um, that would work for me, good-looking," she responded in a deep sexy voice.

After initial acquaintances were made and the usual small talk that followed, she remembered Jamie but not him. She shared a story that he found hard to believe.

"Jamie cold-cocked a local thug when *yawl* were here on your last visit."

He gasped. "What the…"

"The idiot tried to put the make on me while I was huddled up with Jamie at the bar. Two of the goon's bearded friends jumped to his defense, but Jamie put all three losers on the floor. I had to constrain him because he went to the bar and got a huge knife from the bewildered bartender."

"You got to be kidding me."

"No, sir, he was going to cut their ears off about the time the local police came and hauled the thugs off. Jamie was spaced out, babbling incoherently about radicals and the misfits planted on our universe. I think the automatic reflexes kicked in, reacting like he was still on that mission to Somalia."

"What mission?"

"I guess he never told you about the band of wayward pirates he was sent to slaughter."

"Slaughter! I have a hard time believing you," he said to the blond. "My friend is not that type."

"Sorry, but I don't think you know much about him."

"Let's talk about us," Bobby suggested and moved in closer, her scent having penetrated his nostrils.

"Sure, what do you want to talk about?"

"Let's go up to my room for a nightcap, and we'll really talk."

The evening became complicated for Bobby. Miss Dallas called a girlfriend, and she joined them in his opulent suite. He was totally out of practice for the action they proposed. Somehow he survived and performed to their satisfaction. Whatever magical potion they slipped in his drink worked. When he woke up in the morning, his head felt like a gigantic vise was squeezing his brain into submission. His body ached. There were multiple bruises on his arms and legs. He figured they tied him up before they took turns sexually assaulting him.

"Where are you taking the jeep?" the concierge asked. He had arranged the rental for Bobby.

"Why do you need to know?"

"Just curious. Were you in a bar brawl last night? You look like shit."

"No, got drunk and fell down the stairs," Bobby snickered. "I'm going to tour the islands, take some pictures of the wildlife, and then do some snorkeling."

"Have fun, sir."

Bobby completed his mission even though entertaining two gorgeous women for one night almost killed him. He captured thirty-five Conus sea snails of varying sizes. He used several empty milk cartons strapped to his waist and was careful to wear specially designed gloves to prevent bites from the dangerous creatures. The previous day he had found help from a local who knew how to prepare the portable aquarium with salt water, live sand, and porous rock. The old seaman sold him a small hydrometer to ensure that the salinity remained at a relatively constant level.

He decided to leave the island earlier than planned. Rearranging his travel schedule at the last minute wasn't a problem. The flights back to New York went without complications, that is, until he arrived at the US Customs desk at JFK.

"I've told you five times about my research journey," he told the officer. "You've already reviewed the official paperwork prepared by my university. What more proof do you need from me?"

"We're going to quarantine the marine life you have in that aquarium you're carrying with you."

"You can't do that."

"Oh yes, we can, Dr. Biel."

Bobby called Gar Underwood and asked him to rush to the airport and bail him out of the mess. He figured his friend had some pull at the airport being an internationally known scientist.

"What's the officer's name who's giving you a hard time?" When Bobby told him, he heard a sigh of relief on the other end of the line.

"Hand him your cell phone and let me talk to him."

"Why, do you know him?"

"You are in luck, my man. He's my first cousin."

Ten minutes later, Bobby and his sea snails boarded a cab and headed to Gar's apartment complex in Manhattan, his booty safely stowed in the trunk of the taxi. He didn't take the time to inquire about other means of transportation. Been there...done that. He briefed his friend on what happened during his stay on the island. Some details were left unsaid. Gar sat back in his lounger and focused intently on the colorful bruises on Bobby's exposed arms.

Biel noticed, smiled, and said, "A pleasant encounter of the feminine kind."

"Good job, buddy, wish I'd gone with you. I've always enjoyed being physically abused by sexy women. Anyway, sounds like you had one hell of a time. Care to share the gory details?"

Bobby laughed. "It would only make you jealous with rage. Knowing you like I do, you'd bad mouth me forever for not taking you along. Now let's make some definitive plans."

"Go for it."

"How soon can you join me in San Antonio?"

CHAPTER 8

TEXAS

Dallas

JAMIE RICHARDS was presented with a unique set of circumstances. He was not accustomed to operating independently from the main body on any operation. The only person he was allowed to contact was Denis Sweeny, his handler on this covert mission. Dennis remained in Washington at Secret Service headquarters but was available 24-7 by phone. Under no circumstance was he to make contact with the bodyguards of the Venezuelan president or even members of the Dallas PD. They were initially briefed about his undercover role but only in general terms. If either entity needed to contact him, they were instructed to go through Denis Sweeny. Jamie thought this was unusual but accepted the instructions like a seasoned trooper.

It was slightly overcast in downtown Dallas with limited visibility. Jamie preferred to work in bright sunlight where he could easily zero in on people and objects. Crowds began to form around the Book Depository, the seven-floor building facing Dealey Plaza. The local newspapers covered the visit as though our president elected to accompany the dignitary from South America. The Kennedy buzz had never left the streets of Dallas.

"Stop!" Jamie shouted at two men in the middle of the crowd signaling to a third person on the fifth floor of a building across the street from them. He rushed over to them as they were slipping away from the small assemblage near the infamous building. The president's motorcade hadn't reached the area yet, but sirens could be heard in the background announcing his pending arrival.

"I said stop. Freeze or I'll shoot!"

"What's going on?" the tall bearded man asked Jamie when he caught up to them.

Jamie flipped out a bogus sheriff's badge made by a metal shop in San Antonio. He figured it would come in handy, more so than the two pages of documentation Sweeny sent him to validate his official status. The tall man looked at the papers and snickered in his face.

"Who were you signaling to up there?" Jamie boldly asked him while still gripping the Bul M-5 inside his coat pocket. The tall man shifted in to a defensive stance.

"Er... Um... We are part of a group filming the president's activities while visiting your great country. It will be shown live back in Venezuela."

"I wasn't told anything about a filming crew from your country working the visit."

"Who are you? You are not in uniform, not Dallas PD."

"Answer my questions!" Jamie snapped. He was agitated, breaking out in a cold sweat.

"The short bald accomplice mumbled incoherently and shoved a laminated card in Jamie's face. It was a picture of both men in military uniform. In one swift motion, Jamie slapped it aside and grabbed the man by the collar.

"What the—" Jamie didn't finish his sentence when he saw a quick movement out of the corner of his left eye. The tall bearded man had pulled a side-handle baton from his jacket and swung it viciously at Jamie's head. He ducked under the weapon's arc, rose up, and karate-chopped the man in the throat. He followed instantaneously with a kick to the dazed man's balls and watched him flop to his knees and then fall to the ground groaning in pain.

"You pig! I kill you," the short bald man stammered as he stood up closer to Jamie's face.

"On your knees!" Jamie ordered him. "Right now!"

The man stood defiantly and, in a flash, pulled a concealed weapon.

Jamie decked him with a powerful thrust of his pointed elbow to the man's exposed jaw. The gun spun out of his hand and landed near his bearded partner still rolling on the ground holding his crotch. The bystanders who opted to remain in the area gave them ample room to spread out and fight. One lady screamed and soon fainted. Two young boys cheered the action shouting, "Go, man. Go."

In a lightning move, Jamie pulled out his Yarborough knife and glared like a zombie at both foreigners. He kicked the gun away from the fallen man and lunged down to the ground grabbing at the shorter man's cauliflower left ear, now oozing bright red blood. He sliced it off in one quick thrust of the sharp knife, spun the ruffian's head around, and loped off the other ear. Out of habit, he licked the dull side of the blade.

Ugh, tastes too sweet! Aha, you prick. See no evil... Speak no evil... And sure as hell, now hear no evil.

"What the hell's going on here?" a Dallas PD uniform snarled. He was on horseback, providing crowd control measures when he heard the commotion and closed in on them.

Jamie released his hold on the man's shoulder and sprung to his feet, sheathing his Yarborough out of the cop's line of sight. His pistol was still tucked away in his jacket.

"I'm an agent here on official business. Call your supervisor immediately," Jamie said defiantly while keeping an eye on the two men still hugging the ground. Neither attempted to take advantage of the confusion and scramble away from the shocked crowd.

"Oh yeah," the cop exhorted. "And I'm the Lone Ranger."

"These guys have an accomplice up there on the fifth floor," Jamie said with conviction while pointing across the street. "I think they are setting up to kill the Venezuelan president when his limo stops at the Book Depository."

The cop dismounted, partially believing Jamie's story not chancing a screw-up and pulled his service pistol. He ordered the terrorists to roll over on their stomachs, grabbed his lapel mike, and then yelled in a code. Within minutes, two other cops appeared.

"What's going on here?" one of the uniforms asked the cop wielding the pistol. He listened to a brief summary of events without saying a word.

After validating Jamie's status, one of the other policemen raced across the street to check out the building. He was instantly rewarded by colliding with the shooter suspect fleeing through the back door of the complex. The remaining cops cuffed the two foreigners and led them to a waiting police van. Not understanding a word of Spanish, they turned a deaf ear to the pleas of the wounded man clamping closed fists against both sides of his head. They'd seen plenty of blood before, and this didn't qualify as an immediate concern, as long as he didn't bleed out.

The police detail supervisor showed up at the scene at the same time the lead vehicle of the caravan entered the crowded plaza.

"Thanks pal," he said. "I think you prevented another murder here through your courageous actions. We don't need that type of adverse publicity to resurface. Believe it or not, we're still smarting from the JFK assassination after all these years."

"My honor, sir," Jamie said meekly and walked away, taking up another vantage point closer to the targeted building.

Damn it, I lost it. I shouldn't have pulled my knife. I'm not in Somalia anymore punishing pirates. The shrinks at Hood told me when I got out of the army, my mind-set might slip back to some of the dangerous assignments I had with the Delta Force. Got to get it together.

Thank goodness the uniforms arrived when they did. Otherwise, I might have killed both of them. Probably should have, but it would be me in the police van straddling the cold bench seat cuffed to the side wall.

The remainder of his Dallas mission transpired without another glitch. The mutilated head of the bald terrorist was purposely overlooked and never surfaced as an issue. Sweeny was thrilled with Jamie and told him that he'd keep him in mind for another opportunity to show off his *manliness,* as only the present-day Cyclops could put it. On his way out of Dallas the next morning at a restaurant, he shot a glimpse of the morning paper and laughed out loud as he read, "An unknown bystander thwarted an assassination attempt on the Venezuelan President during his visit and…"

San Antonio

SWIRLING RAIN BATTERED BOBBY as he climbed out of his car at the farm. The entire state had been under a three-year severe drought. Area lakes were drying up, water sources were becoming scarce, and partial rationing of water supplies had begun in the larger cities. The storm was a welcomed occurrence by all of the farmers and ranchers in South Texas.

Roberto met him at the front door.

"Come in, Señor Bobby, and shed those wet clothes before you catch a cold."

"Thanks. How's everything going with the animals?"

"The storm has spooked all of them except the chimps."

Bobby laughed. "Those guys are aged but tough. You remember when I bought them from the circus caravan trouping back to Mexico. I was told they were too feeble and lacked the energy to perform anymore, a lot like you, Roberto. You all seem to be doing quite well."

Roberto shrugged, flipping his hands to his heart in a "what the hell" gesture.

"I sorry to tell you that one of your prized Austrian goats escaped through an opened gate that I forgot to lock back up. I ran after him but could not catch up. Him too fast, Señor."

"Is that right? I bet you enjoyed the charcoaled *cabrito* instead of those tasteless bean and cheese tacos you live on."

They both laughed. "Not to worry, Roberto. We have plenty of his mates left here. You did a great job keeping up the farm while I was gone. I'm back now, and we have tons of work ahead of us. I'm expecting some company in a few days, so prepare the guest rooms."

"Si, Señor Biel."

After unpacking his suitcase, Bobby drove to the barn and unloaded the aquarium and other equipment. The rain had subsided. Roberto hauled everything into the lab, not having the slightest clue what was happening. Bobby preferred it that way. The less Roberto knew what was about to take place, the better for all of them. Utmost secrecy was the name of this game.

Several days had passed when early one morning, Bobby's cell phone rang. It startled him because he wasn't expecting any calls.

"Gar here, Bobby. Come and pick me up."

"Huh, what? You're not due in until next week."

"I couldn't wait any longer. I'm anxious to get going with the experiment."

"Where are you now?"

"I'm at San Antonio International. How soon can you get here?" Gar was too eager as far as Bobby was concerned, curious about what ulterior motives he had in mind that pushed up his arrival date. He was normally late for everything.

"Six hours at the earliest. Cool your heels and find a soft bar stool in the lounge. I'll get there as fast as I can."

Gar sighed. "I guess I don't have an alternative."

"No, you don't unless you want to hire a commercial helicopter and drop in on me sooner."

An unhappy Gar Underwood smirked. "I'll wait you out." He hated to wait for anything or anyone now that he was retired and called his own shots.

UNDERWOOD WAS A CITY SLICKER and hated the isolated farm and the wild creatures roaming the plains in South Texas. He missed the intrusive car-honking and shrilling police sirens wailing at three in the morning. He seldom ventured outside but was willing to work twelve-hour days in the laboratory without hanging back for relaxation time. He chided Bobby for not having any windows to the outside light.

Bobby was concerned about the increasing costs to conduct their research. The first day in the lab, Gar stated he was not happy with some of the outdated equipment.

"We need to upgrade your centrifuges, the autoclave and microscopes. You don't have all of the chemical reagents we need. Blood pressure cuffs should be available to monitor our patients. What if one of them has convulsions, a stroke or even a heart attack? Do you have a backup medical team available? We're out here in the middle of nowhere for Christ's sake."

"Damn you, Gar. I've already gone through the additional twenty-five grand I budgeted for our experimentation. You're driving me to the poor house. And yes, I have arranged for an ambulance with

EMTs to be on standby when we begin. They'll be stationed at the volunteer fire department we passed at the crossroads two miles from the property."

"Sounds reasonable to me," Gar uttered, still not totally convinced but figured it might be less costly than having them on site.

"You were in medical school," Bobby countered. "I would think you should be able to handle any medical emergency that might arise on the farm."

"Probably, but if we're to succeed, you need to do the upgrades I suggested."

"What the hell. It's only money," Bobby snapped.

After the fourth week of non-stop experimentation, Underwood was getting itchy and started to complain about minor inconveniences.

"When are you going to take me to Mexico?"

"I don't remember you asking me about crossing the border."

"I didn't, but it's time to get out of this place. Cabin fever has set in. We're almost done with our experiment and long overdue for a break in routine. I want to go to a cat house."

"What the hell?" Bobby was floored with the strange request.

"Before you passed out at my place in Manhattan, you told me about Papa Julio's in Nuevo Laredo. You bragged that a dozen beautiful senoritas provided a fantastic service for the Gringos flooding Mexico for cheap sex."

"That was years ago. The border towns are too dangerous now with the feared banditos kidnapping and murdering on a daily basis. Next week, I'll take you back to San Antonio, and we'll have fun. I owe it to you."

"Fine, it won't come soon enough."

Bobby agreed they needed to distance themselves from the farm. He was becoming an expert on the Conus sea snail. He learned more about the hypodermic-like radula tooth and venom gland used to attack and paralyze their prey before engulfing it. He experienced the assault in the warm waters of Reunion but not the *engulfing* part. Observing the snails stalking their prey, he was enthralled by the barbed harpoons extending out of their mouths at the end of the proboscis.

"We'll shoot for next weekend if I'm satisfied with our progress."

"Great!" Gar shouted and slapped his thighs. Now appeased with the notion of time off, he worked more diligently the next few days.

Through many measured manipulations of the aqueous fluids, Gar was able to separate the curative agent from the neurotoxin of the poisonous snails. The end result proved disappointing in that only a miniscule amount of the magic potion was harvested.

"Shit," Bobby lamented. "I don't think any big pharmaceutical company would be interested in the time and expense to pay us for our discovery."

"I'm not sure. The snails worked a miracle for you."

"Right on, but we need to determine if it would result in the same outcome for other stage IV melanoma patients."

Gar was perplexed. "And how will we do that? On second thought, I suppose we could round up some of those Mexicans buying your meth and pay them to find human specimens. Melanoma is not unique to us Gringos. With the lack of specialized treatment facilities across the border, I'm sure they'd locate a couple of willing patients."

"Only as a last recourse. I have a better idea."

"And that is?" Gar had become disenchanted with their progress.

"I'm going to suspend the anti-aging study."

"Why? You're on the verge of proving that the special breed of goat horns ground into a powder can be helpful. Look how long the chimps have lived after you've injected them. One day, I saw that big male humping the female you call Dolly. Hope I still have the means and where with all to perform like that when I'm up in years."

"Were you jealous?" Bobby asked with a huge grin.

"Shut the fuck up!"

Gar continued his analysis. "I've reviewed the preliminary results of your clinical trials that got published in several periodicals. Some of your chimps are beyond sixty-years old and still active and foolish. You've prolonged their life for…we don't know how many additional years."

"Here's what we'll do," Bobby declared. "We'll embed a micro-capsule slow-releasing agent in the chimps containing a mixture of the goat horn powder and the potent snail fluid that we've extracted."

"Why do that?"

"I want to see if they survive the genetic onslaught that will take place almost immediately."

"You're not a geneticist, Dr. Biel. I know enough about the subject to be dangerous. We didn't have that much exposure to the gene thing while I was wasting my time in medical school before I decided to bail out."

Bobby was not to be denied. "I happen to be a renowned bio-chemist with exceptional creativity and unprecedented insight, Dr. Underwood. The chimps have a DNA structure almost 98 percent identical to humans. Both are members of the Hominidae family. So are gorillas and orangutans. I've got to stop Roberto from calling them monkeys, not politically correct."

Gar laughed. He digested Bobby's comments for a few seconds and then added, "The human aspect is interesting because I've read where chimps have adopted other animals in need and raised them as their own. Whales and elephants must also have some of our genes that show human-like capability for empathy and grief."

"I hadn't thought about that," Bobby said. "Enough talk about genus and species. Anyway, watch me run with this. If they survive that potentially dangerous combination that we've developed, we're on our way. Let the testing begin!"

TWO MONTHS HAD PASSED before they took a well-deserved break in San Antonio. Underwood was enthralled with the Alamo and its historical significance. They got drunk in Teddy's Tavern and enjoyed a two-night orgy with some locals that Bobby's bartender friend arranged. One night after a colossal drinking bout, Gar tried to swim in the San Antonio River but was restrained by the Park Police. The New Yorker found time to go home for a week and returned eager to learn the results of Bobby Biel's grandiose tests.

"I hope you have great news for me. Did it work?"

"You bet it worked. After a one-day sleep-like coma, they came out of it full of vim, vigor, and tons of vitality. Dolly has been pestering half the male population to copulate, and most of them obliged. The testicles of our male chimps have ballooned to softball size. I was surprised that the hair of the male chimps turned from black to a light brown. All the chimp faces became lighter, and their noses are no longer flat. I have it all charted."

"Absolutely outstanding," Gar roared.

"One other major change relates to their hands and feet. Anatomically, they resemble human beings so they have limited range in swinging on the cage bars."

"Do they ambulate like humans?" Gar quizzed further, not knowing where this was going.

"Yes, no more walking on their knuckles and back feet. They stand up straight when they walk."

"So have you made contact with Merck, Pfizer, or any of their subsidiary biopharmaceutical organizations?"

"Yes. In fact, I zipped a summary protocol to my contacts at the two giant drug companies asking for immediate or what we call *fast track* analysis of a miracle drug that would alter history and make them billions of dollars."

"What did they say?"

"They were aware of my reputation in the industry and decided to take immediate action. They had been working on parallel studies and knew plenty about toxins and their potential benefits. Unfortunately, they tore my protocol apart deciding the expense to isolate the Conus sea snail curative agent from the other fluids would be cost-prohibitive. Aside from that fact they experienced numerous barriers while separating the curative serum from the poisonous elements. They suggested I continue the research and get back with them when I have overwhelming evidence of our success that it will work. I didn't dare mention in writing my use of the anti-aging powders. It would've raised red flags."

"Shit, I thought we were off and running with this skyrocketing discovery."

"You know how the FDA approaches new initiatives," Bobby emphasized.

"Yep, in phases, and that sometimes takes years. Do we have time for that?"

"No."

"So what's the next step?"

"I have uploaded a fifteen-minute video on YouTube with a testimonial of my cancer cure. There is a studio in Laredo that I have worked with in the past. They had prepared several of my presentations for distribution at professional conferences. Of course we didn't go into detail about the use of sea snails not wanting to spook anybody. They assured me it would circulate around the globe. Maybe we'll get a hit—one million dollars for anybody wanting the cure for a stage IV melanoma."

"You've got to be kidding me. Using YouTube is definitely not the scientific way of doing things, notwithstanding the moral and legal implications involved. Furthermore, how many idiots watch the garbage cranked out on that program?"

"You'd be surprised. Too late for second-guessing. I've already put it in motion. I trust we'll get a response before the sun blankets Gotham City and batman rallies his troops to find someone in dire need of our product."

CHAPTER 9

DATELINE

San Antonio—July 4, 2012

"WHAT'S GOING ON, BOBBY?" Jamie screamed into the telephone. "I was scanning YouTube last night, and I nearly had apoplexy. I damn near fell out of my chair. You got to be out of your warped mind. Who the hell put you up to this?"

"I'm a scientist first, and now I'm going to be an entrepreneur."

"Stop this nonsense immediately, or they'll put you in a strait-jacket and haul your fat ass off for a frontal lobotomy."

"No way, it's totally legit. I hired a lawyer to review my plan. After scratching the rest of the hair off his balding head, he gave me the green light. The whiz created a Texas Limited Liability Company in my name. Told me that an LLC would protect me from personal liability suits."

"Well, you were always crazy. The miraculous cure from your melanoma discombobulated your brain. You need to see a shrink and right away."

"Cool it, Jamie. Have you and that Fort Hood hot potato hooked back up?"

"I told you before that we broke it off. She cut me off, demand-ing that we legitimize our relationship. She wants a kid, and I don't. Simple as that. I'm not ready for a trip to the altar. It's over."

"Hey, friend of mine, why don't you saddle up and come to the apartment? Gar Underwood and I are spending a few days in town. I'll brief you on the entire initiative. Then you'll understand why we went the YouTube route."

"Who in the hell is this Underwood character?"

"Get your skinny behind over here and find out for yourself."

"Roger that, I need a break from my classes. Macroeconomics sucks! Why does anybody need to know the difference between the gross domestic product and the gross national product? By the way, speaking of YouTube, have you had any hits?"

"Thirty-five and counting," Bobby bragged.

Jamie frowned, waiting to hear a detailed explanation. None was forthcoming, so he continued to press on. "I suppose you are fac-ing a bad-news-good-news situation. The bad scenario is that there are many fools roaming this man's earth. The good news is that you might snag one of them willing to pop for a mil."

"Hey, something positive is happening, you nonbeliever. I recorded three responses that look promising. We're in the process of evaluating their worthiness. The other thirty-two can be classified as trash-talk, which I expected."

"Okay, I bite. See ya tonight, Bobby. I want you to mix a batch of Bombay Sapphire martinis, and we'll catch up. I survived a short consultancy in Dallas since we last chatted, and I'll fill you in on the details. You'll be proud of me."

After they hung up, Bobby went into great detail briefing Gar about his long-time friend, Jamie Richards, the ex-Army Special Forces soldier of renown. Underwood was intrigued with a man who sacrificed himself in so many ways for the good of his country. He had planned to cross into Canada if the US government reinstituted the draft and came running after him.

This guy Richards must be a real stud. Can't wait to meet him!

San Francisco—July 4, 2012

KAT KURBELL WAS SO PAIN-STRICKEN she had a difficult time hoisting herself out of bed and getting dressed. Her law firm put her on an indefinite leave status drawing half pay while she awaited the Grim Reaper. She was receiving daily support from a home health care agency that neutralized some of her spasms and discomfort. She was worried that her insurance company would soon pull the plug on that benefit. Barry Gregg was history. Even though he sent her flowers every week with an encouraging note, she couldn't stand the thought of him and refused to answer his repeated calls. She was shocked watching a story unfold on YouTube while wallowing in bed scanning the channels for some kind of humor.

"Mom!" Kat roared in a frantic phone call to her mother in Iowa with the good news. "I need you to come here and accompany me on Amtrak for a trip to Texas. I'm going to get cured."

"What in the world are you jabbering about daughter? Are you overdosing on that despicable weed?"

After a brief discussion about the miracle offering on YouTube, her mother advised Kat to forget it. Some quack was looking for a quick million bucks, and she wasn't about to lead her dying daughter down that path of bankruptcy. Her husband had unexpectedly passed away, and she wasn't thrilled about mortgaging the farm for some hare-brained idea.

Kat cried and told her mom that she had invested wisely since becoming a sought-after lawyer and could pay for the treatment without any outside help. She needed a strong shoulder to guide her through the travel process. Having no legitimate excuse to deny her daughter a last dying wish, she consented to the plea.

"How soon do you want me?"

"Please come right away. Mom, I am so, so glad you'll help me out. The cancer has ravaged my entire body, and I don't think I can last another month. The pain medication has turned me into an addict. I'm no better than the junkies I represented in court. This is my last chance to continue to live a productive life, and I thank God that someone found a cure for melanoma. Believe it or not, the scientist who developed the cure was also on death's doorstep with the devil's disease when he found the key to unlock this malady."

Her mom began to weep, but Kat cut her off.

"I can't fly. I'm too debilitated. When we hang up, I'll get reservations for the train ride to San Antonio. I don't think I'll die en route to my cure if we leave soon."

Kat stumbled into the back room and let Stryker out of his cage. Every day since she was diagnosed as a terminal, as she called it, she would free the big bird. They had bonded in such a unique way she was sure that no other falcon in the world meshed with a master like her.

One time, she let Stryker perch on the end of her steel headboard while she slipped under the depressant effects of Vicodin. She was burning with a fever she couldn't control. The drug brought on nausea and irritability, but the euphoria and drowsiness it caused was a welcomed escape from reality. She thought she felt a poking at her forehead during the night while slowing progressing toward coma status. She never knew that Stryker fanned her throughout the night with his widely spread, powerful wings. He had pecked at her several times, trying to wake her up from incessant moaning and groaning. His dedication and fervor for her prevented the raging fever from burning her up. Stryker was still perched there the next morning when she awoke.

"Big boy, it's time for you to return to your cage."

He let out a disapproving sound and flew to the back room.

When she went to the bathroom, she noticed three minor puncture wounds on her forehead with congealed blood. She cleansed the site with hydrogen peroxide and dismissed the cuts as incidental clawing of her sharp fingernails during the painful and trouble-filled night. Today was dedicated to rest and recuperation from the perils of the previous evening.

The following day, Kat cashed in most of her stock with Fidelity and arranged for the agent to wire-transfer the million dollars. One half of that amount would be deposited into Dr. Bobby Biel's checking account in a San Antonio bank, the remainder in an escrow account accessible to Bobby only on written proof of her cure. She arranged for the lady downstairs to take care of Stryker. The neighbor had softened up and became helpful during Kat's illness, even bonding with her pet. The woman experimented with different things to feed the bird but learned that Stryker preferred young rats. Now all she had to do was hold on long enough for her mother to arrive for the planned trek to Texas.

Paris—Bastille Day, July 14, 2012

THE DARK DANK HALLS of the Hotel-Dieu de Paris where Pierre Duvair was incarcerated only heightened his despair. Being admitted to the oldest hospital in Paris on the left bank of the Seine River next to Notre-Dame didn't dispel his mood. He carried on so much about his sore ass, pain in every bone of his emaciated body, and constant diarrhea that he disturbed every sick patient around him. The beleaguered staff was ready to toss him into the Seine River. After consultation with his attending physicians, they decided to move him to a unit that was distant from the mainstream busy wards and minimally staffed. There was nothing more they could offer him to ward off his impending death from melanoma. He had contributed large amounts of money to the institution in past years, so the administration felt obligated to *warehouse* him.

"I brought you some of your favorite chocolates," Hugues Chaban said, smiling affectionately at his friend as he walked into the stuffy room.

"I can't eat sweets. Toss them in the garbage container by the door," Pierre howled. "You know me better than that. Next time bring me some pork hocks. The food here isn't fit for inmates awaiting their turn at the gallows."

"But...but..." Hugues moaned. He hated to be admonished.

"You forgot to bring Louie his dog food, you idiot."

"I thought they told you he couldn't stay with you any longer."

"Well, as you have witnessed, he's still here, and he's staying put. I need him to cuddle up on my behind and sleep with me. It helps to alleviate my constant pain and loneliness. To a limited degree, Louie makes me forget my utmost dissatisfaction in being imprisoned here."

They ceased being lovers when Hugues almost hung him to death in their secret sex parlor. Strangulation was the quickest way to terminate life, but Pierre was holding out for that one-in-a-million chance to survive. Duvair succumbed to his pledge never to see the artist again. He allowed him to visit the hospital but only one day a week. The nursing aides hated their over-bearing and inconsiderate patient. They wore masks whenever they entered his room, not because he had a communicable disease but because of the stench caused by the incurable cancer.

"Were you able to access our joint account at the bank, Hugues?"

"Yes, but I was questioned why we were sending such a large amount of money to America."

"What did you tell them?"

Hugues hesitated and began a confusing litany of whys, what-ifs, and buts until Pierre threw a pillow at him to shut him up.

"I had a difficult time explaining your medical condition, let alone some odd-ball YouTube pronouncement of the miracle cure. Anyway, I got it done, just as you asked. A half million was wired to Dr. Biel's checking account in a Laredo bank and another half to an escrow account to be released when the doctor certifies your cure."

"I'm so sorry to jump on you, Hugues, for what you've done for me these last few weeks. You tried to help in every way possible while I continue to wither away postponing death. I don't know how to repay you."

"Pierre, I still love you!"

"If you weren't staying up all night watching those imbecile programs like YouTube, I'd never have found out about it. You might be my living savior here on earth. They've given me two more weeks. How generous of them. You might take comfort in the fact that the hospital chaplain administered the last rites to me yesterday."

"Absolutely, but I hope it was an exercise in futility. When are you going to Texas?"

Pierre was quick to answer. "The day the miracle doctor calls me to come after he's notified of the bank deposit. I've already hired a private jet, and the crew is on standby, so it should happen any day now. By the way, I don't want you to come with me."

"All right, have it your way. You may die before we ever get you out of the hospital. What's the big delay?"

"I just told you. You want it in writing? I'll not be found dead in this broken-down excuse of a hospital. Do you hear me? I'm going for the cure even if you have to haul my skin and bones out of here in a coma. Got that?"

"Oh, Pierre, I'm sorry about all of your suffering. You have been very brave. I'll do anything for you, but I must leave now. Andre is ill again and asked me to stop by the Pharmacia and pick up some of those awesome drugs your friend always prescribed for you. Your house butler has been hallucinating for some time now. I think he has dementia."

"How would you know?"

"I moved in with him."

"What! I'm not in the ground yet, and you found another... lover."

"Your disease has taken possession of what was once a brilliant mind, Pierre. How could you insinuate such a distasteful thing? Andre is our friend. I wouldn't think of such a thing. Anyway, he's beyond the age I prefer to snuggle with."

"Get out of here, you imbecile!"

When Hugues left the room, Pierre signaled to his dog. Louie was sleeping on a chair by the window, half-covered with his master's bath robe. His pet never cared to be up and alert whenever that bad person was with his master.

"Louie, come to Daddy."

The dog snapped to alert and, with a slight hesitation, sprung up on the bed next to Pierre. It was a difficult jump for those short legs, but he managed. That same night after nursing rounds, Pierre elapsed into a coma. Man's best friend kept him alive by constantly licking and pawing at him until the near-death experience ended. Louie's wet tongue kept him cool and comfortable throughout the night, staving off the dreaded elevated temperature he was experiencing each night.

When Pierre opened his eyes in the morning, Louie was in a deep sleep, worn out from his mission of mercy the previous evening. Pierre playfully slapped him across the jowls to wake him up. Louie didn't move, and Pierre became enraged.

"Get off my bed, you lazy mutt!" he shouted and then shoved Louie toward the edge of the mattress. Louie awakened and, in an unprecedented act of defiance, snapped hard at Pierre, gripping the Frenchman's fat hand in his tightened mouth. When Pierre pulled back, blood spurted from the top of his hand.

"Bitch dog," he said. "Look what you've done."

Louie hopped off the bed and struggled to get up on the bedside chair. Pierre licked off the several streams of blood, wrapped a linen cloth around the wound, and continued to scold his dog. "That's the first time you ever bit me, and it had better be the last, or you'll get butchered up and made into hot dogs."

His beleaguered pet ignored the threats and fell back to sleep, totally exhausted from his night's work.

The long anticipated call the next day from Dr. Biel couldn't have come soon enough.

Chicago—July 15, 2012

LEAH MALAKA WAS AT WIT'S END. Slade Glick told her he was traveling to Texas and having his melanoma cured by a miracle drug he saw on YouTube. He insisted that it was authentic, especially after checking out Dr. Bobby Biel on Google and LinkedIn. He was impressed with the researcher after reading several of the journals he had authored. The financial windfall Biel's biochemical company received for the acne cream motivated Glick to jump for joy while digesting the article. He had acne as a kid and forced his rich father to spend thousands to make it disappear. The concluding assurance was that Biel himself was cured from stage IV melanoma. Slade was convinced the miracle drug would also cure him.

"Slade, we have the finest medical care available in the city. Have you contacted Northwestern University? I've read where they have superb research programs in place pertaining to cancer and, more specifically, to melanoma. You might qualify for one of their experimental protocols."

"I don't care to be one of those clueless subjects in never-never land hoping that an experiment will save them."

"But to place your life in the hands of some quack advertising a magical cure on YouTube is beyond ridiculous. It's a scam, pure and simple." He was shocked by her biting comments.

"I've checked him out thoroughly, and I'm satisfied. Prop me up on the pillow, Leah, and hand me my cell. I need to make the phone call."

He was delirious with pain and wanted her to stuff a handful of codeine pills down his throat. She read his mind and gave him six of the marvelous pills and a glass of water. The pus pockets on his head continued to ooze. He was fatigued by the constant blotting at the foul smelling liquid with towels. Leah excused herself several times to go puke in the bathroom.

"Hello, sir," Slade talked into the telephone. "I watched your spiel on YouTube. and I've already wire-transferred a million dollars to be deposited in your bank account in Dallas. You switched financial institutions on me, but that's no problem. Can I come to Texas right away?"

Bobby was stunned. *This is the third rich person wanting to undergo the remarkable cure. Physically, I can only accommodate three patients at any given time. Roberto and the construction team have just completed the modification of the research barn. Gar has supervised the workers and is satisfied that we're ready to start the process. Thank the Lord, I have bank accounts in three different cities. The feds will poke their noises into my business, but my lawyer has me fully shielded from probing officials.*

"I'm ready for you any time you can get here, Mr. Glick. Give me a twenty-four-hour advance notice, and I'll have one of my associates meet you on arrival. I presume you're flying."

"Yes, I chartered a private plane out of O'Hare."

After he ended the call with the cancer healer, Leah told him as unobtrusively as possible that she wouldn't be seeing him again in the future. She wanted to let him down lightly. In reality, he was too much baggage for her, and she never loved him. She simply used him just like that east coast mayor used her. Being seen in public with a good-looking male companion enhanced her image. It was good for business. She was dumbfounded with his reaction.

"Go get Rocky out of the serpentarium and put him in my bed."

"Are you crazy or what?"

"He's the only living creature that loves me, and I love him. If I pass away after you've so unceremoniously dumped me for good, I'll die a happy man knowing Rocky was always there for me."

"You are one sick man, in more ways than one. Get up and retrieve your own fucking snake!"

She let herself out of his condo, not knowing if she'd ever see him again. *What if he gets cured? Will he be a different person? Will he ever want me again? Shit, I don't care. I've got to move on. I'll be reeling in fifteen hundred tonight with a Hall of Fame wide receiver. Good riddance, Glick, you prick.*

Slade staggered to the guest room and maneuvered the slithering snake to bed with him. He fortified himself with an additional codeine hit. The aching that had been racking his body subsided. With the loss of constant pain, a sudden chill came on and shook his body. He began to convulse. He started to slip off the bed.

"Help me, Rocky. I can't stand this any longer. I want to die. Kill me right now, please. Don't let me go on living like this."

Rocky grabbed his upper leg and maneuvered him back to the center of the bed. Even though the reptile "mouthed" the leg, sharp teeth punctures caused blood to seep trickle Slade's thigh. Rocky gripped the other leg and coiled around it. The snake began tightening and increasing the coiling process every time Slade breathed out but not enough to restrict the blood flow to his leg. Slade soon fell asleep. After an hour of tightening and releasing, Rocky moved between his master's legs generating excessive body heat. The pet remained in that position the rest of the evening. He wanted his master to stay warm and comfortable throughout the long, stressful night.

CHAPTER 10

FLORIDA

"**D**ENIS SWEENY, YOU GOT THE WRONG PERSON. I'm not a hit man, you fool." The call had come shortly after midnight while Jamie was cramming for a test in the morning. He was tired and cranky and pissed that someone would have the gall to call him at this late hour.

"Hold on there, Jamie. Think about it for a minute. This radical in Florida needs to be taken out for the good of our country. He's been rallying that far out group called Glorious Reformation to take arms against the government and remove our commander-in-chief from the White House. Intelligence tells us that he is planning to make a move next month."

"So why don't you have someone from Secret Service do the job? Isn't that what they're getting paid for?"

"Yes and no. Their primary job is to protect the president at all times, and they have even sworn to lay down their own lives if necessary to ensure no harm comes to POTUS."

"I got the yes part. What's the no part?"

Sweeny hesitated, trying to find the right words to convince him to jump at the opportunity. He needed Jamie, had the utmost of confidence in him, and was out of options. Jamie was the last person on his list, having been denied the assignment by the rest of the operatives he'd used in the past. *"Not enough dough for the risk," they all told him.* This particular scenario was potentially explosive and required the skills of an experienced and well-trained killer. Jamie fit that job description.

"We can't do it in-house because of the adverse publicity that might come from the kill. This zealot has been in the news for the last several months, and the pundits would jump on this. As you might have read, the president's popularity has been sinking in all of the latest polls. Taking this guy out cannot be traced back to us under any circumstances. Please say you'll do it, Jamie."

"How much?"

"Half a million, all up front. Believe me, such an arrangement is a major exception to our standard policy. We really didn't pay you enough for that stint in Dallas. By the way, did you keep the ears?"

Jamie elected not to comment on the reference to the ears, wondering how the hell Cyclops found out. "I'm in. When and where?"

"Tonight, before the sun comes up. Dade County, west of Miami."

"What? Why so quick?" Jamie protested. "I have a major exam in school first thing in the morning. The dean is ready to terminate my MBA program. He claims I don't attend enough classes. He's ready to notify the appropriate authorities to cut off my GI bill. Can't it wait until tomorrow?"

"No, this loon they call The Redeemer is on the move. I'll have a plane pick you up at Kelly Air Base there in San Antonio in four hours. Give me your banking information, and I'll have the deposit wired in the morning."

"When the hell do you plan on briefing me?" Jamie was cranky, tired, and concerned. Sweeny didn't elaborate, preferring a short break in the conversation for Jamie to cool down.

This whole thing was moving too fast for him. It normally took him two or three days to get emotionally wired and super-charged to kill people. There was something about this job that made him feel uncomfortable. *Sweeny must have several other candidates who could murder this freak. Why me? Oh well, the money is good, and I have the credentials to take some rotten maniac out of existence. Yes, sir, especially if he's a threat to my country. My education will have to wait.*

"Don't sweat the small stuff, Jamie. I'll have an agent on board the plane. She will give you the dossier on your subject and answer any questions on your mind. As a bonus, she'll give you a loving pat on your sweet ass when she drops you off. Call me on my cell after it's done. Good luck."

"Denis, when I—" Too late, Sweeny had terminated the conversation.

Jamie texted his friend next door. He was a retired sergeant and loved birds. The neighbor owned several cockatoos in the past but outlived all of them. He'd agree to watch Victoria any time Jamie had to travel. He possessed the combination to Jamie's realtor lock box on the back door knob. He bought Jamie's explanation of being on call 24-7 for an Internet security company.

He sent a text to his economics professor about the need to miss the exam. He hated economics. It has way too much theory for a *hands-on* guy. The professor was a combat veteran of the Vietnam War and enjoyed commiserating with Jamie about the military. He'd understand. He'd been a warrior.

"Now what, Bebe?" a shrill voice came from the back room. Victoria could not pronounce the word Jamie but did the best she could after overhearing urgency in his conversation with Sweeny. He went to her cage and tossed on a cover. She had a habit of yakking all night when she thought he was going to leave her. His gear was stored in the guest bedroom, and he didn't want the bird to see him hauling out his Bul M-5 and Yarborough knife from the security closet.

The executive jet picked him up at Kelly. The pilot introduced him to Sweeny's female cohort. "He really thinks the world of you, Jamie. He doesn't normally use outside resources for sensitive missions like his one."

"What can I say?" he shrugged meekly.

She was a looker. How this heavenly creature ever got mixed up with Cyclops is a mystery yet to be solved. He'd love to be the one doing the solving but that could wait. He was charged up now and didn't want to be thrown off-cycle by the breathtaking person of the opposite sex standing in front of him.

The aircraft put down at Homestead Air Force Reserve Base south of Miami as scheduled. The Redeemer was scheduled to talk at a rally in a convention hotel on the edge of Miami. Jamie learned that management was hesitant to book any far right organization because of possible adverse publicity. However, occupancy had dropped considerably when two modern hotels opened within a mile from his lodging facility. He needed the revenue so agreed. He would beef up his security team as added insurance to monitor the event.

"Hold on a second, Sweeny. Please say again what you just told me," the female agent gasped as she stared in confusion at Jamie. They had started to deplane when she got the call. She stood frozen on the exit platform that had been rolled up to the door of the aircraft.

"Roger that, boss. I'll tell him what you told me."

She motioned Jamie to get back on the plane, and they sat down on the comfortable chairs at a table behind the pilot's cabin.

"What's up?" Jamie asked excitedly.

"We're aborting your mission. The wacko leader of the Glorious Reformation got blown to pieces about an hour ago."

"No shit! How? Who? What?"

"All Sweeny told me was that the pontifical one was found in bed with the teenaged daughter of one of his admired followers. They were discovered in a cabin at the edge of the Everglades. Apparently, they were humping away like rabbits in heat."

"And what the hell happened?"

"When the anointed one left the cabin this morning, someone detonated an explosive molded underneath the rear bumper of his SUV, more than likely Semtex. Pieces of him are now alligator food in the nearby swamp."

"So fly me home right now," Jamie ordered her.

"Not so fast, young man. This plane is going to be refueled, and I'm heading to Los Angeles on another high-priority adventure."

"But...but what about me?"

"Sweeny said to haul your butt to another terminal and ske-daddle back home on a commercial flight." She handed him official government documentation authorizing him to carry the weapons he brought with him.

"Call him when you get back to Texas, and he'll discuss reim-bursement for your time and travel. Apparently, you didn't give him the banking information he had asked you for. It doesn't matter. He'll get it. By the way, Denis pays well, trust me," she added with a soft smile and firm handshake. He would have preferred a tight hug from that gorgeous body and not a gentlemanly "so long stranger" verbal *adios*.

SAN ANTONIO INTERNATIONAL AIRPORT couldn't arrive soon enough for a tired and worn out Jamie Richards. He had to stay overnight in Miami. He was psyched up to kill another human being for the good of the country and pissed that it was called off. He remembered Father Lawrence telling him he would experience emotional highs and lows for the remainder of his life. He wondered how far down the psychological sanity ladder a person could fall for missing the opportunity to murder another human. After a quick cup of coffee at the Starbuck kiosk, he decided to call his best friend. If any person could boost his morale, it would be the *reborn* Bobby Biel.

"Well, I'll be damned if it's not Jamie Richards. Where the hell have you been these last few weeks? I wandered by your house yesterday, but your neighbor told me you had to leave town in a hurry. He said Vic was driving him nuts. What's up?"

"Not anything I can share with you on the phone. Can I come over now?"

"Absolutely, Gar Underwood is with me, and we were trying to contact you to join us."

"Why, what's going on?"

"I need you to support a big project I'm knee-deep in. Just get your sorry ass up here, and I'll explain. By the way, where are you now?"

"At the airport, but I flagged a taxi, and I'll be there in fifteen minutes."

Bobby and Gar Underwood proceeded to brief him on the new endeavor. Jamie was shocked. He never thought that Bobby would turn his good fortunes into a commercial enterprise. He was willing to listen to all the details because he had deep feelings for his high school classmate. Bobby mixed a picture of Bombay Sapphire martinis, and the three of them sat outside on the balcony and talked.

"So why do you two entrepreneurs want to hire me?" Jamie was beyond curious.

"Can you put graduate school on the back burner for a few months?" Bobby inquired.

"Depends on what you have in mind."

"Tomorrow, we have several sick patients coming to town to benefit from our new cure. They are suffering from the fatal illness termed stage IV melanoma. Two of them will have a person accompanying them. One lady is coming from San Francisco via Amtrak with her mother. The other, a man with a female aide, will arrive from Chicago on a private jet. The third person is a Frenchman flying alone from Paris, France. Gar and I will bring the three sick persons to our laboratories in South Texas and begin their cure from the dreaded disease."

"I say again, Bobby, what do you have planned for me?"

"I need you to provide overall support and security to our operation. Initially, I want you to keep an eye on the two people traveling with them. We don't want them underfoot when we begin the transformation. They will be staying at the Menger Hotel downtown. You will be our liaison to them, keeping them busy and out of our hair until their treatment is finalized."

"You got the wrong man, asshole," Jamie shot back. "I'm not a glorified babysitter."

"We know that, but this entire operation could be explosive. We need a strong hand to run interference for us just like I did for you in high school on the gridiron years ago. The performance theatre is much bigger now to the tune of multimillion dollars. We don't want any outsiders checking in on us, wondering what we're doing and how they might be helpful…or even harmful."

"Where in South Texas is this highfalutin experiment taking place?"

"At a location between here and Laredo. I never shared with you that I own an isolated farm property. The big barn has been converted into a high-tech laboratory. I inherited the real estate from my father years ago and spend my spare time there doing what research scientists do."

"What's in it for me?" Jamie asked, scratching the itchy scar on the side of his head. "Bottom line, please. No bullshit."

"You'll get eight percent of our proceeds on this mission of mercy."

"So what am I looking at in terms of dollars that would convince me to put my MBA on hold?"

Bobby hesitated and then said, "Eight percent of three million. You're a graduate student. Do the math. And, Jamie, that's just the beginning."

Gar Underwood spoke up after measuring Jamie's body language. "There may be some trouble ahead for all of us, Jamie. We're not sure that our cure will work but believe strongly in our preliminary findings. We may have three dangerous and unpredictable persons reaching for our throats. When the public gets word of our success or failure, all hell could break loose."

"How's that?" Jamie asked. "I thought you ran clinical trials on other sick people."

"We used chimps," Gar responded with a shrug. "Genetically, they resemble the human genome and have contributed to many successful medical advances throughout the years. Granted, we're taking a gigantic chance to duplicate what happened to Bobby in Reunion when he got nailed by the poisonous sea snail."

"You guys may be certifiably crazy, but I'm in."

"Fantastic!" Bobby shouted. "I knew I could count on you. All the information you need for your assignment is on the table in the back room—full names and pictures of all the people including ETAs and attendants. We've been in touch with air traffic control, and they have cleared the arrival of the private jets. We had a more difficult time with US Customs on the man coming from France but got the green light."

"You're really connected, Bobby."

"No, Underwood has all the pull. The pickup will be made at the private jet park in back of the main terminals. I have a medically equipped van, a medic, and a trusted driver on call to bring you and the three sick people to the farm after you drop the attendants off at their hotel. Gar and I will leave early in the morning to begin the technical setup and prepare for your arrival. Trust me, Jamie," Bobby stuttered, the alcohol slurring his speech. "Gar and I are on the forefront of an international phenomenon that will alter the course of cancer treatment for all ages. There are multiple risks facing us but look at all the great scientists in history that reached the pinnacle of success. They were deemed radical by their peers but continued to function outside the box. We are willing to gamble on the same platform that advanced the good of humanity throughout the ages. You'll be closely tied to this unbelievable achievement."

Jamie nodded, not sure where all of this creativity and activity was headed. Both of them were nationally known scientists. They have been blessed with the confidence and energy to make this happen. He was a warrior, a stalker, a killer. He was confused about his role in this off-the-wall episode but would support Bobby. They've walked the same challenging path together many times. This endeavor was no exception. The threesome drained their martinis and stumbled off to bed.

CHAPTER 11

TEXAS

AMTRAK WAS LATE AS USUAL, but Jamie planned accordingly by first picking up the gentleman from Paris. His flight came in as scheduled. Jamie was shocked at the emaciated body that was helped off the sleek jet. His eyes were hollow. There was no trace of hair evident on his shriveled head. The poor soul was bent over in pain. To add to the unpleasantness, he reeked like a rotten piece of discarded meat. He had been drugged, but the vanishing narcotic high needed reinforcement.

Jamie led Monsieur Pierre Duvair to the waiting van where the medic took charge, much to Jamie's relief. There were no introductions and nobody talked. A jaundiced worn out bull was being led to slaughter. The medical staff attending Duvair signaled the pilot that their delivery task was completed and to head back to France immediately. Jamie thought it was strange that the sick man from Paris didn't have an aide or family member traveling with him.

Good news for me. One less person to keep an eye on.

"Where to now?" the van driver asked. Jamie was seated next to him in utter amazement, anticipating what the next sick body would look like. "The train is an hour late, so let's swing around and meet the other jet coming in from Chicago."

He had made prior arrangements with Homeland Security to proceed directly to the private jet park and pick up Slade Glick and his female associate. They were on schedule. The hefty female aide acknowledged Jamie with a smug smile on her chops. She wheeled around, grabbed the sickly-looking gentleman by both arms, and muscled him to a waiting wheelchair. She avoided his feeble attempt to kick her in the stomach.

"He's all yours now," she told Jamie. "Good riddance. I'm on the next commercial flight to Chicago. Have someone drive me to the United Airline terminal."

He had planned for that eventuality and had a taxi on standby to transport her away. She didn't take the time to wish her patient well. In fact, she couldn't get out of there fast enough. Jamie wheeled the sick man to the medic who immediately took out a loaded syringe and shoved it into the patient's upper arm. Slade jerked his head back and in a few minutes was out like a light. They loaded him like a slab of beef into the rear of the van next to a mumbling Pierre Duvair.

"I sure hope they don't all stink like this," the medic said. "I've been around enough patients leaning toward the heavenly gates, but this last guy tops them all. Road kill has a better scent."

"Louie, Louie," Pierre whimpered. "Where are you?" The air-conditioner in the back of the van was roaring like a twin engine jet. The medic slapped on a surgical mask and went about his chores of making the two sick people comfortable as possible. Their timing was perfect. The Amtrak arrived as they pulled up to the station. Jamie didn't anticipate a problem with the third pickup but was mistaken.

"No, no, I won't let my daughter be led off by a bunch of Texas hillbillies," Kat Kurbell's weeping mother cried out. "I want her to die peaceably in the comfort of a hospital and not on some Texas ranch with all you cowboys."

Jamie was persistent and, with minimal force, led both of the malcontents to the waiting van. Kat tried to object, but she could barely raise her hand in deference to her mother. She was clutching vigorously at her stomach, trying to squeeze out every ounce of racking pain. Her body no longer absorbed the soothing affect of the potent pain medications she'd been on. The scene reminded Jamie of a Mexican standoff.

"I'm sorry, ma'am. My orders are to take your daughter immediately to the site where she will be cured. You won't be able to go with us. The research team issued the instructions. I arranged a hotel downtown for you to rest up and wait until your daughter's treatment is completed."

The lady lunged toward Jamie with a closed fist. "Over my dead body, sir! I won't leave my daughter." He sidestepped her and motioned for the medic to calm her down.

"Get this big gorilla off me, or I'll call the police!" Kat's mother screamed at Jamie and kicked at the medic. She was beyond hysterical and breathing in quick, choking gasps clutching her throat.

Kat stared at her mother, confused by her actions and started to faint. Jamie caught her before she fell. They managed to settle everybody down and took off in the crowded van. Jamie decided to skip the hotel accommodations and lug Kat's mother with them to the research farm. Checking her into a hotel as planned would be a disaster. He'd prefer the distraught lady be within reach. He knew Bobby wouldn't be happy about his decision, but he didn't care. His friend was not in charge of this phase of the operation. After Jamie checked all the documentation Bobby asked them to bring, the van swung on I-35 and took off south.

THREATENING BLACK CLOUDS had formed above the barn while the research team prepped the three sick persons for their procedures. They had to be sedated. Kat continually screamed for Stryker. She cared less about her mother. As far as she was concerned, the mother never existed. Slade wanted them to find Rocky and bring him to the farm. His legs were convulsing in spastic movements. Pierre stopped howling for Louie, resigned to the fact his pet was dead in a Paris sewer. He knew that trusting the old fart Andre with such a huge responsibility was a mistake. He was sure that Hugues blew him off the day he left France for treatment.

Meanwhile, Jamie and Roberto Gomez took a quick tour around the property in a dune buggy with specially equipped rifle mounts and high beam flashlights for hunting feral hogs at night. Local farmers and ranchers used suppressed rifles and panoramic night vision goggles to reduce the damaging herd of hogs that only foraged at night. Jamie was satisfied with the security afforded by the isolated location. Bobby had the foresight years ago to construct high fencing around the property. He recently installed motion detectors at critical junctures monitored by TV screens inside the barn.

"We'd better get back right away. I'm afraid those rain-swelled clouds are about to rip open and drench us. You know Texas storms can be unpredictable and destructive, Roberto."

"*Si*, Señor, but we are in a drought and need the God above to bless us with the rain."

"Fine, but let's hustle back to the barn and check out the next phase of the experiment." In addition, he wanted to test the television monitors to ensure they were working properly.

"No, no!" Roberto declared. "There are demons in there. I don't want anything to do with Señor Biel and his madness. Please take me back to the house, and I'll make sure Señorita Kat's mother is comfortable. I'm happy she settled down. She is a real mountain lion."

"Do that. She seems to like you. She sees you as the only one in this crowd that's not involved with killing her daughter. Make sure the plastic zip ties on her wrists are not cutting off any circulation."

When Jamie entered the research section of the barn, Bobby and Gar were getting ready to complete the process of inserting the microcapsules into the chests of the three sick patients. They wore open cotton smocks and pajama bottoms and were strapped to gurneys. They seemed to be breathing normally. Their eyes were closed and mouths shut. They had stopped conversing with each other.

There was a major problem earlier when the patients began comparing notes. Jamie thought they were probably hallucinating from some of the drugs Bobby had administered. Kat demanded to back out of the experiment on moral grounds but was reassured by the smooth-talking Gar Underwood to hang with them.

Kat opened her eyes when she heard Jamie come in and said, "Jamie, hold my hand before they begin. Please stand by me throughout the procedure. I lost faith in both of those devious scientists. I think they want to turn me into a wild killing animal. I'm scared. I don't want to die. What's going to happen to me?"

"I'm here for you, Kat. I'd be happy hold your hand, but you are way off base on that last comment."

"Why?"

"Because they are internationally known and trusted scientists by their peer groups. I've known Biel since high school and can vouch for him. As far as the Underwood person, I trust my friend's professional judgment of character and purpose."

"Oh, Jamie, you make me feel so much safer in their hands. Thank you."

He squeezed her other shaking hand with a firm grip. He noticed her body relaxing to his touch. She closed her eyes. He wasn't sure nor did he care what medications were being used to drug the three. Such knowledge was beyond his pay grade.

Slade turned and gave them both a look of disdain. He had no use for the lawyer. *She's simply another trick to be had, nothing special in my mind.* They were about to lapse into a coma. The older Pierre Duvair took the lead, Kat succumbed, but Slade took longer. His eyes bulged as he glanced in horror at his cohorts figuring they were in the initial stages of dying. He screamed at the top of his lungs, "Murderers! Murderers!" before he passed out.

The insertion of the microcapsules took twenty minutes for each patient. Underwood monitored them, closely noting the rapid escalation of respiratory functions. There were several jerky movements, but that was expected as the curative agent gobbled up the cancer cells like an out of control Pacman. Slowly, their breathing returned to normal.

"What the hell was that?" Bobby shouted. A gigantic boom slammed the research lab roof shaking the three gurneys so severely that he thought the force would catapult the patients to the floor. The lights went out, and the humming of machinery stopped. It took the backup generator five minutes to kick in.

"It's the storm outside," Jamie said softly.

"What are you talking about?" Gar asked.

"Roberto and I saw the makings of a big one heading this way from the Gulf of Mexico when we were out checking the perimeter. Buckle up folks. I think we're in for a big surprise."

Jamie glanced at the three patients on the gurney. They reminded him of corpses he's seen in the medical examiner's morgue ready to be violated by the impersonal autopsy process. They all looked dead, way dead if there was an estimation of how dead is dead.

What scale is used to measure deadness? He was still holding Kat's left hand and felt nothing. No pulse, no skin sensations, no moisture, and no warmth. He felt sure she was gone.

All of a sudden, a streak of blinding light accompanied by a deafening super-sonic boom exploded from the roof top. Separating in two distinct channels, one leg of flaming electrical energy struck the three gurneys while the other ball of fire shot to the corner of the laboratory. The force threw the researchers to the ground and upended the gurneys. Jamie was the least dazed by nature's assault, but Bobby and Gar went berserk, but they recovered quickly.

"Didn't you install lightning rods on the barn roof?" Gar questioned Bobby curtly.

"Roberto was supposed to do it last summer, but I never checked."

"Guess it's too late now," Gar added with a shrug of his shoulders.

A flash fire started immediately in the corner of the treatment room. Jamie grabbed the commercial fire extinguisher and put out the flames. Bobby searched the rest of the facility to ensure there were no more fires starting. Gar attended to the three patients and needed help to upright the gurneys. The patients were still secured with the strapped belts firmly around their ankles and upper arms. They were in a deep coma, oblivious to the confusion ramping up around them.

"Jamie, check the house for damage," Bobby urged.

"I'm on my way."

He ran into Roberto who was racing out of the house toward the barn. "Señor Richards, I came as quickly as possible to see if everyone in the barn was safe. I heard the big noise and saw lightning strike the top of the barn. I thank *Jesus* for not letting it hit the house."

"What a big relief. We had a bolt that caused a small fire, but we extinguished it. How's the old woman doing in there?" He elected not to press Roberto on the lightning rod issue.

Roberto hesitated, worried that Bobby was going to fire him on the spot. "After you cut the plastic restraints, she quieted down. She even talked to me in broken Spanish, and I spoke to her in some of her own language. The lady asked about her daughter. I told her she could see her daughter real soon and that she was resting comfortably now."

"Good job. Please tend to the chimps and the goats. Make sure they are safe. Stay with them for a time and talk to them. Bobby told me the chimps like the sound of human voices, settles them down when they get excited. I'll check on the mother."

"Si, Señor Richards."

Jamie went into the house and double-checked on Kat's mother. She was placated now as Roberto mentioned, calm and actually considerate. Perhaps Bobby gave her a shot of some mood-altering drug.

He apologized for the use of the wrist restraints. She concurred their use was necessary at the time. She asked about Kat, and he reassured her that her daughter was doing well and that the treatment would be completed soon. He didn't mention the chaos that took place in the barn. Jamie excused himself and walked to the living room to make a few phone calls. He had not expected to receive any incoming calls and was startled when the phone went off in his hand.

"It's about time, Richards! I thought you went AWOL or some ridiculous episode of independent operation," Denis Sweeny roared. "Don't you ever answer your damn cell phone?"

"Sorry about that, Denis, but I've been very busy. What's up with you?"

"I called to thank you for the Florida bit last week. I know you well, Richards, and I'm sure you were disappointed you didn't get the kill. Perhaps another time. I wired ten thousand bucks to your bank account. Talk to you soon."

"Thanks a lot, Denis, I will—"

The phone went dead, and Jamie shrugged.

I really miss that goggle-eyed government, son-of a-nobody, and savior of mankind. One of these days. I need to drive to DC and knock down a few beers with the big man again. I wonder if he and that cute aide are romantically involved. I never asked him if he was a married man nor did he ever volunteer personal information.

CHAPTER 12

SOUTH TEXAS

T HREE DAYS LATER, PIERRE DUVAIR was the first to ease out of a coma. He sat up and looked around at the entire research area. His facial features displayed a difficult time computing images, shapes, and people, but that changed. He focused again on the three people standing next to him.

"Where am I, and what the hell am I doing here?"

Gar Underwood, standing closest to him, was amazed at how fresh and youthful-looking he appeared. Pierre was able to release himself from the loosened restraints. He slipped off the gurney and grabbed the scientist in a strangle hold, trying to kill him.

Underwood hollered for Jamie who was watching the TV monitor screens. There was activity outside at the south end of the property he had to check out right away. Images of either animals or humans were moving around in the dim background.

"Get him off me! He's gone wild!"

Pierre released his hold on Underwood's chubby neck after Jamie gave him a karate chop on the back of the neck. The Frenchman rubbed the aching area several times before apologizing to both of them. "I'm so sorry. I lost track of time and purpose. How do I look? Am I cured? I feel great."

133

"You smell a lot better," Jamie told him as he left the room. He didn't care for the Frenchman.

"Slip off those pajamas and the smock. I'm going to check your body," Gar ordered. "I want to see if all the lesions disappeared from your buttock."

"I don't feel anything back there!" Pierre exclaimed. "All the pain has disappeared!"

Gar examined him and was bewildered. At first, he thought Duvair's facial features resembled one of the male chimps. The face was flatter than before the treatment. His head appeared larger and square. Pierre's nose was shorter with broader nostrils. His ass looked as smooth and clear as a newborn baby's buttocks. He noticed that Pierre's upper legs were much thicker now and heavily muscled compared to his lower legs, which appeared to have atrophied. His chest was much larger, more rotund. Underwood finished all the measurements and charted the results.

Bobby entered the lab area after completing an inspection of the entire barn area to include the upstairs storage rooms and outbuildings. He wanted to make sure the meth storage bins were unharmed. Fire damage could be costly to both of his operations. He validated Gar's findings after a quick visual assessment of Pierre's body.

"You are ready to return to Paris, Mr. Duvair, a new man!" Bobby exclaimed, visibly shaken with his patient's new physical appearance. Pierre was too excited to notice the scientist's concern.

"Thank you, my dear friend."

"Contact my bank and release the other half million," Bobby said. "Jamie will arrange your return flight to France on United Air Lines. Your treatment fee covers the entire transportation costs to include any overnight accommodations should they become necessary."

"Consider it done, Dr. Biel."

"Why don't you take a walk around the property?" Underwood suggested. "Smell the clean air brought to us by the heavy rains."

"Good idea, I need the exercise. By the way, where is my dog, Louie?"

"He didn't come with you," Bobby said.

"What? I insisted! It was part of the deal."

"No, sir. Your earlier e-mail told me that a *Monsieur* Andre would be taking care of him in your absence. I believe that worked out well. Now go outside and take your walk."

Thirty minutes later, both Kat Kurbell and Slade Glick came out of their comas at the same time. They each stared at the strange surroundings, not remembering having been led into the research lab. Kat looked up at the charred hole in the damaged roof. Slade's eyes were riveted to her bare feet. They were absolutely beautiful, he thought. Well-proportioned heels, tiny and appropriately aligned toes, and curved insteps. *This lady is nothing like that gigolo I bedded in Chicago with overgrown bunions and toe nails painted in a color that resemblespuke. Yuck! I want to leap off this gurney and caress them. She'd appreciate the attention. Wait. What did she say?*

Kate spoke out forcibly again. "Where's my mother? Did she go back to Iowa?"

Nobody answered her. The research team members were still in an assessment mode completing their findings. Slade continued staring at her feet, a swell beginning to rise in the front of his pajama bottoms. Without thinking, he covered the erection with both hands. *Good gracious, man, nothing to be embarrassed about here,* he thought with gushes of unbridled pleasure. *The old joystick is poised for action. Thank goodness. I wondered if I would lose any parts of my manhood undergoing this procedure. After all, I just paid these scientists a million bucks to assault my gorgeous body!*

Jamie came in after checking the fence line.

"Everything okay out there?" Bobby asked.

"I confronted some illegal immigrants drinking the bottled water."

Bobby looked relieved. "No problem. Local ranchers are of the opinion that making the water available will keep the transients from breaking into their property for food and drink. I've been practicing that belief for years, and it has worked to my advantage."

"Real smart, cowboy," Slade commented as he joined the conversation. "Were they on their way to attack us?"

"No, of course not," Jamie said. "They ran away when they saw me approaching in the dune buggy. I checked on your mother while I was outside, Kat. She asked to come to the lab and check on you but decided she'd wait in the farm house. She's doing fine. Roberto has been taking good care of her for you."

Kat demanded to see her right away. All three members of the team were shocked at how great she looked, stunning and vibrant. It appeared to all of them that she grew another three to four inches in height. The remaining growth of hair on her head had changed to a frizzy brunette. Her peachy face glowed like the rising sun. She was pretty.

"Draw the curtain and step out of there, Jamie, so we can examine her more thoroughly," Underwood said. Bobby nodded in agreement. Kat didn't object.

"Hey, wait a minute," Slade butted in. "Frenchie told me before he went out strolling that we should be able to witness the miraculous changes that took place in our friend. I'm sure she wouldn't mind."

"Not going to happen," Bobby said sternly. "It would serve you best to mind your own goddamn business." He threatened to put him back into a coma, and Slade settled down. Pierre came in, and Slade briefed him on his proposal. He told them he didn't care either way.

The researchers examined her in the makeshift privacy platform. Her upper arms were more muscular, and her shoulders seemed broader. The dermal papillary ridges forming at the base of the hair follicles of her upper arms could not be explained. She was pain-free, excited, and more than ready to begin her new life.

"Thank you, doctors! I feel marvelous."

When they threw the curtain back open, Slade checked her out in deep admiration, planning an assault on her cute body if they were ever left alone. She reminded him of the feisty Leah Malaka.

Bobby walked in front of Slade, cutting off his view and said, "Kat, when you get back to the farm house, be sure to notify the bank to release my escrowed money. I know you'd feel remiss in your utter happiness if you forgot to perform that simple task when you returned to San Francisco."

Jamie led her out of the barn and to the house to reunite with her mother. She held his hand again, reassuring him that she appreciated his polite behavior throughout the long grueling process.

"Hey, how about checking me out," Slade interrupted Underwood who was busy making notes in their charts. It didn't take him long to forget about Kat's feet, now wanting answers on his own condition. *I think the other two look different. The lady's facial appearance improved considerably. but the French guy looks more like an animal. I'm curious to find out if I changed in any way. They need to install full length mirrors around here.*

Bobby and Gar studied the man intensely, alarmed at his new emergence. His nose seemed more elongated but, at the same time, more…*aristocratic*. His eyes grew larger, a brighter green set off by thick black eyebrows. Their first thought was that Slade, like Pierre, had developed large muscular thighs. Gar palpated Slade's lower back just above the anus and sensed that a digit or bony structure was beginning to grow out of the skin. He didn't say anything to the cured man, hoping it was his own imagination gone wild.

"Well, Doctors Biel and Underwood, how do I look?'

"We are happy with the results, Slade." Bobby scrambled to find a mirror and gave it to him.

"Wow! Neat. I feel like a million dollars, excuse the pun, and twenty years younger. All of the excruciating pain left my body. The young maidens had better watch out now. The Slademan cometh with his full bag of tricks."

Both of the scientists smiled in relief. Jamie came in but didn't say a word. He was having a difficult time sorting all of this out. He was a warrior, not a magician reconfiguring a human body. He was worried about the potential fallout but didn't say anything.

"When can I return to Chicago?" Slade asked impatiently. "My pet sitter advised me he could only take care of Rocky for two weeks."

"Jamie will take all of you back to San Antonio tomorrow morning. Please arrange with my bank to release the balance of the money before you leave."

"I'll do it right away. Let's get back to the ranch house, so I can get my cell phone."

"Jamie, please bring Pierre and Slade back to the farm house. Help Roberto fix some food for them. They must be starving. Gar and I will remain here and finish up some paperwork."

When the group left the barn, Bobby assessed the damage caused by the storm. There wasn't any internal fire damage, but he'd call a company from Laredo to fix the roof. The electrical storm was a rare event. He wasn't going to crucify Roberto for not taking care of the roof. The storm wasn't predicted by the weather team on local television nor on the internet. He joined Gar at the desk where he was entering data into his computer.

"Well, Dr. Underwood, are you pleased with the results of our hard work?"

"Yes, to a degree."

"Please explain what you mean," Bobby asked with a concerned look.

Gar began. "First and foremost, I'm convinced we wiped out the cancer. For example, as a starter, one glance at Slade Glick's forehead supports that fact. No brown ugly splotch. To be 100 percent certain, they should be fully evaluated by their own oncologists. We lack the sophistication here to validate that finding on our own."

"So far, I agree with you. What's the other degree you're referring to?"

"All three have evidenced drastic changes in their external appearances. We didn't program that to happen, did we, Bobby?"

"No, but look at me, I experienced the same thing. You knew how ugly I was when we were together in school. Age didn't factor into my changed appearance. It was the miracle on Reunion Island that did it. Hail to the Conus sea snail!"

"Well, something more dynamic, maybe even catastrophic happened here," Gar proclaimed. "I'm convinced that severe genetic mutations took place while the three of them were strapped to the gurneys. I don't want to attempt a DNA analysis for fear of what we might find. Anyway, we don't have the proper equipment available. Maybe our formula was flawed. Should we have mixed that goat horn powder with the snail curative agent?"

"Why ask that question?"

"I theorize that electrical currents from the lightning storm ionized their entire cell structure when it hit them."

"Ionization?" Bobby asked with a puzzled look.

"Yes. As you know from physics, the process of ionization works slightly differently depending on whether an ion with a positive or a negative electric charge is being produced. I suspect it's a combination of both the ionization and the goat horn powder fusing upon ionization."

"Pretty heavy duty *stuff* you're throwing at me, Professor Underwood. You may be right. Kat looks like she's starting to grow feathers on her upper arms. Pierre is built like a bulldog, and that Slade character is growing a tail."

Gar was in deep thought about the genetic mutation hypothesis. "We need to delve deeper into our presumptive findings. Maybe there is an outlier here we haven't uncovered."

"I'm listening."

Gar was beaming. He loved to theorize, even prophesize if given the opening. "Perhaps this can be explained by the unlocking of previously blocked developmental pathways encoded in our genomes. A small percentage of the human genome is dedicated to encoding proteins using the triplet genetic code. Molecular biologists used to call the other stuff *junk DNA*. One of the roles of the so-called junk is now known to encode developmental instructions to guide us from the fertilized egg-to birth-to adulthood and on to an advanced age. It is apparent that ancient developmental programs still linger in our genes."

"That may well be," Bobby said. "I went to grade school with a girl whose hand resembled a pig's foot, a sweet thing bearing an awkward appendage."

Gar was starting to feel more comfortable with his scientific analysis. "There is a well-studied mutation in fruit flies called antennapedia in that legs appear where the fly's antennae should be. Thank God, they signed the documents your legal counsel prepared."

"Amen," Bobby said.

"The lawyer wisely attached the three doctors' statements you asked each of them to bring with them," Underwood continued. "Certifying they were terminal and that no further treatment would alter their impending demise gave us the green light to begin our process."

"Sometimes, attending physicians are hesitant to make such statements," Bobby said. "It's reassuring to know we can't be held personally liable for any adverse situations that might arise. By the way, what made you think of having their doctors prepare the documentation?"

"Jamie Richards. He's done his share of killing and recommended that legal safeguards be put in place for all of us, including him."

"I'm glad we decided to snap before and after pictures of the three patients. I'm stretching this observation a bit, but upon further study of the pictures, I think we improved their looks. I don't think we'd be sued for that. At the same time, we can't take pictures of their genetic makeup. They may be vicious animals for all we know. Hey, that's a joke!"

"I think we're overtired and exaggerating our perceptions here, Bobby. Let's finish the treatment records and retire to the farm house. We need to relax and see how our charges are getting along with each other. I need a strong drink."

In the evening, the treatment team assembled in the kitchen with their newly created charges. Everybody enjoyed the ample servings of margaritas that Roberto prepared. For many years, he experimented on his own to make the potent tequila. It was no problem harvesting the blue agave plants strewn on the property. A meal of fajitas, meat enchiladas, and homemade corn tortillas accompanied the margaritas. The conversation was flowing.

"Mom, stop telling stories about my childhood challenges on the farm in Iowa. You're blowing them all out of proportion."

"The truth hurts, dear."

Kat's voice had slipped into a shrilly, bird-like chirping sound. Everybody was under the influence of Roberto's own liquid cure and acting too foolish for anyone to notice except Jamie. He'd heard that sound before but couldn't place it.

"I want you three to make an appointment with your oncologists as soon as you return home," Bobby directed.

"Not me," Kat said.

"No need for that nonsense," Pierre added. "Waste of time."

"Why?" Slade countered.

"They need to clinically validate the absence of your melanoma. We're not set up to conduct that comprehensive level of testing in our lab here. We know you're cured, and you know you're cured. They will document it in medical-legal terminology for you."

"Oh, why not," Slade said with a grin. "Could help us in the long run."

Kat, Pierre, and Slade looked at each other and nodded in agreement.

Gar had the feeling that Bobby was whistling Dixie. These three were not going to take the time or make the effort to see their doctors. They would be totally satisfied with the results, running around like proud peacocks in their own backyards.

After dinner, Kat was flapping her arms at everything Slade was telling her. Jamie observed that Pierre's eye teeth seemed much longer now as he smiled at Bobby's comments. Slade had his right leg twisted around the table leg where he was sitting across from Kat. Periodically, the table would wiggle.

Jamie watched Kat, Slade, and Pierre intently all evening. They didn't seem normal to him; something was way out of kilter. Maybe it was the tequila. Their mannerisms and darting eye movements alarmed him. He recalled the images and locked stares of several bad hombres just before he killed them.

Has the treatment turned these people into some kind of animals? I've witnessed soldiers in their final stages of violent death, eyes piercing mine, asking me to help them. I think I witnessed the same thing tonight but not as clear-cut as on the battlefield. I'll be happy to get them to San Antonio and be discharged from my responsibility. It's time for me to resume my studies and get back to hitting the books if I'm still enrolled.

CHAPTER 13

SAN ANTONIO

J AMIE RICHARDS WAS NOT A HAPPY CAMPER when he tried to round everybody up and load the van for the trip back to the Alamo City. Pierre couldn't be located after breakfast, deciding he wanted to take a quick spin around the farm fence line and bird watch. Roberto mentioned to him before he raced off in the dune buggy that he'd be disappointed. "Ain't any good-looking birds around here," he'd told the Frenchman.

Slade decided to take another look inside the barn and convinced Kat to accompany him. Jamie and the driver had loaded the gear into the van while the two research scientists were holding a lengthy conversation with Kat's mother. She had the insight to ask them what she should expect in the future with Kat.

"She'll be fine," Bobby suggested. "The successful treatment of her deadly melanoma has opened up a whole new chapter for her."

"Yes, of course," Kat's mother said. "But she seems to be a totally different person now. I think she's prettier than before. I hope that's not a problem."

Gar laughed and then offered a comment. "In my eyes, being pretty has never been a problem for a woman. On the other hand, we scientists are well aware that sometimes the cure is worse than the disease itself. In this case, I think you'll agree that Kat will now have a long life of total fulfillment. By the way, you don't look well. Do you have a medical problem we're not aware of?"

"Not really," she sighed. "I'm just eager to get back to my own farm in Iowa."

When they entered the research barn, Slade took Kat's hand and placed it on his chest. She didn't appreciate the heartfelt initiative and yanked it away. He'd never forget her glare.

"What do you think you're trying to do, Mr. Glick?"

"Um, I have to tell you how much I adore you, Kat. I'd like you to come back to Chicago with me. I have a luxury condo overlooking a beautiful park with the astonishing Lake Michigan off in the distance. The city is vibrant, and you could even practice lawyering there. I have a close friend planning to expand his law practice."

"No, thanks, I would never leave San Francisco. I'm engaged to a super fellow who lives there, and we plan to get married when I return," she lied.

Slade grabbed her by the shoulders and forced her to a corner of the research lab. He shoved her hard against the wall and tried to lift her blouse up over her head.

"Stop it!" she yelled and swung viciously at his face with a balled fist and went for his eyes with the long fingernails of her other hand. He ducked the thrust to his eyes. She kicked him in the groin and raced out of the barn as he sunk to the floor groaning in pain. She ran head first into Jamie when she rounded the driveway corner to the ranch house.

"Hey, what's wrong, Kat? Why the big rush?"

She threw her arms around him and said, "Hold me, please. That animal Slade Glick tried to rape me in the barn."

"What?"

"You heard me correctly, Jamie. I need you to protect me. He's gone wild."

"Get in the house. I'll go in the barn and have a chat with that deranged man."

When Jamie reached the barn, he couldn't find Slade. He searched the entire area but could not locate him. On his way out, a long arm reached out and grabbed him, jerking him forcibly back into the barn. It was Slade, holding a giant pitchfork and bleeding profusely from his aristocratic nose.

"See what that bitch did to me," he shrieked as he pointed to his nose.

"Drop that weapon, Glick, or I'll bury it in your gut."

He obeyed and flipped it on the ground next to Jamie. Pent up with rage and screaming vulgarities at him, Jamie grabbed Slade's bare upper arm, punched him on the chin, and then tossed him to the ground.

Good God, this guy's flesh feels different, like coated with fish scales or something!

"What the hell!" Glick shouted. "You're crazy."

"You got that right, you no-good Chicago gangster." Jamie reached around to his belt and pulled out the trusty Yarborough he always carried. He grabbed Slade's right ear and screamed, "You low-life prick! I'm going to cut your fucking ears off and feed them to the goats behind the barn. If they like the taste of them, your balls are up next. We don't tolerate rape in these parts."

"Stop, please!" Slade begged. "I didn't do anything. She led me into the barn with an unbelievable promise to spread her legs for me."

"What are you talking about?"

"She claimed she hadn't been with a man since she was diagnosed with cancer. She had that certain look in her eyes that told the whole story. I politely told her that now is neither the time nor the place for sexual exploits. I invited her to come to Chicago with me, but she refused. Go ask her yourself, but I'm sure she won't admit it. They never do."

He sheathed the big knife and glared at Slade still prone on the ground. "Shut up. Let me think for a minute."

Who the hell should I believe? They both have convincing stories. Whatever, I need to keep them apart until we get back to San Antonio.

"Get up and let's go. The van is loaded, and everybody is eager to leave the farm."

Nothing more was said by either accusing party when the van was back on I-35 heading to San Antonio. Jamie was smart enough to seat Kat in front and Slade in the rear. Kat's mother continued her discussion with the two scientists. Pierre was reading a summary of the entire treatment episode they furnished each patient. They wanted to determine if he had any questions before returning to Paris. He was still convinced his former lover Hugues Chaban had infected him with the melanoma. Pierre wouldn't believe his doctor when he said it wasn't a sexually transmitted disease.

The van parked in front of the Menger Hotel, and everybody off-loaded except Jamie, Glick, and Duvair. They left immediately for the airport to catch their respective return flights. Bobby checked Kat and her mother in at the front desk while Gar headed to the famous bar he'd heard so much about.

"Pierre, I trust you'll have a safe trip back to Paris," Jamie said when they arrived at the airport and got out of the van. "I have plans to visit your great city next year." He had warmed up to Duvair, probably because he had no use for Slade Glick.

"Ah, that sounds great, Mr. Richards. Please let me know in advance when you're coming, and I'll arrange everything for you." He kissed Jamie on both cheeks, ignoring Slade as he disappeared through the entrance doors almost knocking askew one of the uniformed baggage personnel in his haste to leave America.

"I'll bet you're happy to get rid of the *Frog*, huh, Richards? He's weird, even spooky now that he's cured. You know he's gay, don't you? Those French people live a different lifestyle than we do in the US."

"Look here, Glick. I care less about that sexual orientation garbage. How about hauling your ass to the United Airlines counters and get out of Dodge City. I've had enough of you and your outlandish behavior. Any other good Texan would have crippled you for life if you tried to rape someone."

Slade scowled and took off, never looking back at him. Jamie returned the van to the rental agency and picked up his own car. He was ready to revert back to normal everyday life in the city. On the way back to the Menger Hotel, he reflected back on the tight squeeze Kat gave him back at the farm. The olfactory sensations of the beautiful woman never left him. He pondered whether to pursue her.

I'm not sure about Maria anymore. When she visits me in San Antonio, she nags at me all the time. The woman is convinced I actively seek excitement and adventure in remote and dangerous places. She wants me to stay at home, watch television, and revert to a Johnny-be-good kind of guy. I'm not built for that, and I won't take that from any woman. On the contrary, I'm curious what it would be like to jump into a relationship with the stunning and exciting lawyer from San Francisco. She wants me. I can feel it. Slade Glick might be right on this one. She needs a man. Why not me?

"Any problems at the airport?" Bobby asked when he entered the lobby of the Menger.

"Not really, two down and two more to go." He wasn't looking forward to Kat and her mother's departure the next evening. He learned that they had cancelled their return on Amtrak in exchange for an American Airline flight. He was now determined to arrange some one-on-one with Kat.

"Where's Gar?" Jamie asked.

"He's in the bar with Kat. She came down from her room when her mother decided to take a nap. Said she wasn't feeling well. Kat

147

said she was ready for a stiff drink and learn more about the history of San Antonio."

"I better check on them," Jamie said. "I don't want your associate to get too friendly with Kat. I've noticed him eyeing her more and more since he first examined her after the cure. Must like what he saw. I've heard too many stories about New Yorkers and their quest for free love."

"Stop worrying about him. He's only interested in what he sees under the microscope, not under the sheets."

"I'll believe it when I see it. In any event, I hope our classmate isn't tending bar. I never cared for the loudmouth braggart, but you always got along with him."

When he entered the bar, he looked twice at the pretty female bartender. *I think I've seen her somewhere else. Oh well, doesn't matter. I have more pressing needs to attend to.* He saw Gar lift off his stool and walk out the side door to Alamo Plaza. Kat lifted her glass signaling for another margarita when Jamie drew beside her. She looked at him and smiled, almost as if expecting him to arrive in time to bail her out.

"Teddy Roosevelt must have been a real stallion to ride in here on his big horse and round up a bunch of cowboys to help him fight that war in Cuba," she said with a slight grin.

"I see you had ample time to look at all the pictures on the wall in between downing margaritas and listening to the exploits of Gar Underwood."

"He's harmless. What about you?"

"What do you mean by that remark?"

"I'd like to find out if you are the man I think you are."

"How do you propose to do that?"

"First, let's get out of here. Call your friend Dr. Biel and tell him we're going on a tour of the city and will check back in later tonight. Ask him to alert my mom, so she doesn't worry about me."

"And what's for seconds?" Jamie asked seductively.

"Follow me."

They walked hand-in-hand to a hotel on the other side of Alamo Plaza. She first noticed the hotel's unusual architecture when they rode by the historical plaza to check in at the Menger Hotel. They had a drink at the bar before checking in to a suite. Five hours later, physically exhausted, they barely found their way back to the Menger in the dark.

The following morning, everyone met for breakfast. Bobby had arranged to take Gar and Kat's mother to the airport for their flights home. Kat decided to stay in San Antonio for a few more days, arguing that she needed more rest and recuperation before returning to busy San Francisco. She didn't fool her mom who knew the reason why she was staying behind. His name was Jamie Richards. Multiple tears enveloped in sheer relief were shed by the two women when the van left for the airport.

"Want to see where I live, Kat?" Jamie asked.

"Can't wait."

Broadway Street was congested at that time of the day, so they relaxed and bantered back and forth between signal light changes. They drove around the high school stadium and went inside his house. After a brief tour of his home, they collapsed on the couch. A knock on the door startled them. He checked through the peephole and opened the door greeting his next door neighbor carrying a jabbering Victoria in her cage.

"She heard your car pull in and wouldn't shut up."

"Thanks so much for taking care of Vic. Want to come in?"

"No, thanks, I got errands to run."

Jamie introduced Vic to Kat. She immediately fell in love with the bird and began to talk to her. He had a hard time understanding all the muted words she whispered in a sing-song manner of speech. Vic immediately picked up on it, twisting and turning her head in some form of acknowledgement. Shrieking out a few unintelligible words and ignoring Kat, the bird jumped to the back swing of her cage. Jamie carried the cage to the back room and partially closed the door, knowing Vic didn't like to be totally shut in.

"I like your home, but your pet wasn't very friendly with me. At least, my Stryker is polite and cheerful, not nagging at me all the time. If I were you, I'd enroll Victoria in one of those avian discipline classes I read about."

"Why do that? She always communicates with me in a special way. I think she was tuning you out. I'm used to it. At least, she didn't dump her entire vocabulary of curse words on you."

"How do you know what she was telling me?"

"I haven't the slightest clue, Kat."

"You need to have more conversations with Vic. You'd have a better idea of what she's all about. She's a female and can't be closeted for too long without showing some emotion."

He didn't want to talk any more about pets, not the reason he brought her home. "It might be early, but how about some wine?"

"Only if it's a California blend."

They sat on the couch, sharing a bottle of Napa Valley's finest merlot. Vic was squawking and banging against the side of her cage. Jamie got up and slammed the back room door shut and then opened it a slight crack. It quieted the bird.

"So what do you have planned for the next three days, Mr. Richards?"

"Some touring of this fine city and getting to know you a lot better."

"Socially or carnally?" she whispered in his ear.

He laughed. "A smidgeon of the first, a ton of the second."

A screech was heard through the back room door followed by some muttered words. "Don't, don't, don't… Sinful… Go to hell. Father…bless soldier boy… Bless them all."

Jamie jumped off the couch, walked to the back room, and covered the bird cage. He went to the kitchen and grabbed the bottle of wine. Holding Kat's hand, he led her to his bedroom. They made love until the sun came up the following morning. He was concerned about her upper body strength and bumpy skin that became more prevalent later in the evening. Maybe it was his imagination, but he thought he felt small, soft feathers when he caressed her arms and back but blew it off in the height of the sex act.

In the morning. they managed to maneuver themselves out of bed and to the kitchen looking for something to eat. They were both spent and still naked. He checked her out in the light of the morning but saw nothing but beautiful gleaming skin on the arms and upper back.

"Why don't you come back to San Francisco with me?"

"As much as I'd love to, Kat, I need to finish my schooling."

"I take that as a…you don't love me enough."

"No, you're wrong there."

"Soldier boy needs to move slower?" she taunted him.

"How did you know about my military background?"

"Vic made reference to it. I always take the time to check out my new lover's home. I enjoy looking at pictures and reading award citations tacked to the walls in offices and hallways."

"Oh, let's just take this one step at a time. You go back home and put your life back together now that you're cured. I will come out there at the end of the semester. If our relationship is still strong and meaningful, I'll look for a job pending receipt of my MBA. What do you think?"

"I think that's a mountain of outright bullshit, Richards. That's what I think. All you want to do is use me to fulfill your sexual fantasies and then toss me to the wolves. That's what soldiers do all the time. You're hedging here and I don't buy a word of what you're telling me."

"But, Kat—"

"I smell the odor of another woman who has been hanging around here. That's why your bird doesn't care for me. She's attracted to the other female. You never told me you had a live-in."

"There's no way I'm having another woman in this house. What a ridiculous comment to make after what we've done."

"Take me to the airport tomorrow. I want to go home."

"Nope, won't do that. You're staying here with me until we get this impasse resolved. I can't let you fly home feeling like this. I've never been in love, so I don't really know how to interpret my own feelings for you. We need our relationship to develop, mature, and grow stronger before we make a major mistake and live to regret it."

She didn't hear a word he said to her. Her hands were tied to her face as she wept. He waited her out. They got through a bowl of cold cereal without talking. She stared at the ceiling most of the time. He tried to rationalize his thoughts but couldn't make things jell in his mind.

"Jamie, I love you so much!" she shouted, causing him to spill his cup of coffee. "Please forgive me for everything I told you. I was mean, self-centered, and not my normal self."

"But, Kat—"

"Quiet, my dear Jamie, let me talk. You were correct. Why did I question you? You mean the world to me. We need to spend some time and space apart from each other to see where we're heading. We'll know what we have together if we're patient."

They leaped off the kitchen chairs and flew into each other's arms. They hugged, kissed, caressed, and assaulted opposite ears with sweet whispered words. Jamie sighed, looked into her eyes, and then disengaged. He went into the back room to remove the cover from Victoria's cage and let her out. He encouraged the bird to talk to Kat. Victoria snubbed both of them as she ended up perched on top of a light shade in the living room. "Out...out of here," she jabbered over and over until he shooed her into the back room and closed the door.

"Let's go touring now," Kat suggested. "You promised to show me the highlights of your San Antonio and its glorious past."

"Agreed, let's get going."

They walked the famous San Antonio River Walk and stopped in the nearby mall. Kat wanted to take in a movie at the IMAX theater and convinced Jamie to sit through the *Alamo: The Price of Freedom* on the big screen. After the movie, they went to the Thai Princess Book Store, and she bought a copy of *Three and Out: The Saga of a San Francisco Apartment Manager* to read on the plane. She stayed two more days before returning to San Francisco.

CHAPTER 14

DATELINE

San Francisco—Halloween, 2012

THE *SAN FRANCISCO CHRONICLE* REPORTED another killing in the Presidio Heights neighborhood. It read as follows: "This was the second murder that occurred in the vicinity in the past month. Some animal has been ravaging young men after the local bars along Union Street closed for the evening. The SFPD inspectors were amazed at the autopsy findings. The victims were bludgeoned to death, but in each case, the medical examiner was unable to identify the instrument of death. Both of the deceased had their eyes plucked out by the killer."

Kat Kurbell decided not to return to work. She had enough money saved up even after the exorbitant cost of getting cured. Her mother was killed in a car accident shortly after returning from San Antonio. It was reported that she had suffered a stroke while entering the on-ramp of an expressway. Kat inherited the farm and immediately sold it. She was financially set for life.

Periodically, in the early evening hours, Kat took Stryker to the Presidio, a nearby national park where he could hunt over open water. Before darkness overtook them, Kat loved to watch Stryker barrel into his victim. He used a clenched foot that usually stunned or killed the prey upon impact. He would swivel to retrieve it as it fell from the sky. When the prey was too heavy to haul away, Stryker dropped it to the ground. He plucked away the feathers or outer coating and began to feast on the remains.

It was a typical cold and windy day in the city. Kat was taking a nap when her cell phone startled her. "Hey, Kat, Barry here."

"Hello," she said coldly. "What do you want?"

"I heard through the grapevine that you're back in town. You were gone a long time. Where in the hell have you been, and what were you up to?"

She sidestepped the question. She hated him and was about to hang up when she heard the magic words.

"The tanning company our group sued on your behalf offered to settle out of court. I couldn't reach you, so as your attorney in the lawsuit, I agreed to their terms. Five hundred thousand spread out for five years was put on the table and I accepted. What do you think of that?"

She hung up on him without responding. She didn't need the money but was happy with the outcome. Barry was a complete ass and a total bore. The man never shut up about his courtroom conquests. She had no use for him anymore. In fact, she wanted him dead. He called back on the land line, but she let it ring until he gave up. She stopped using her answering machine. Stryker was sitting on her upper arm and pecked lightly on her cheek, informing her it was time for another outdoor stroll. It was dark. He was hungry.

"Be patient, loved one. We'll go after I watch the late news."

Tonight, she decided to change course and head to the Marina Green. This time, she would kill, and Stryker would watch. To ease his hunger, she fed him one of the short-tailed shrews she kept caged in the far corner of the garage before they left. At midnight, the weather turned stormy. Feathers in her arms grew out twelve inches, her arms extended out several feet, and her fingers reformed into sharp claws. She was ready to go hunting. This phenomenon happened every night after twelve o'clock when the slightest sign of lightning appeared in the skies.

At first, she was alarmed at the changes in her body. She vacillated back and forth, trying to digest the fact that she and Stryker belonged to the same genetic family. She learned to adjust with the slight discomfort her condition wrought. Kat salivated at the power and strength possessed by her bird-like body. She was now driven. Driven to forage and kill with Stryker, her new animal family member. On the average of twice a month, they would take turns seeking their prey. Sometimes they scored, and other times, they flew off without engaging.

"Let's go, Stryker. My turn to kill."

It was an hour past midnight when she backed the car out of the driveway. Her huge bird-like body made it difficult to maneuver her car. She decided to drive to the Golden Gate Bridge and park. A Volkswagen bus was rocking back and forth in the parking lot with two teenagers sprawled in the back making out. With Stryker perched on her arm, she walked to a familiar location on the bridge. It was the exact spot where Barry Gregg stopped her from committing suicide.

"Are you ready, my love?" she asked Stryker.

He fluttered his wings in acknowledgement, and they both soared off the bridge heading for Crissy Field on the Presidio. They flew over an incoming freighter. Not finding anyone in the marshes or pathways that lined the former airfield, they continued their flight toward Fort Mason. She slowed when she spotted an elderly man walking at a slow gait up the pathway. As she sped in for the kill, Stryker circled in front, steering her away from the intended victim.

"What are you trying to do, bird friend?"

He continued to nudge her away, pecking at the back of her head.

She realized the kill was aborted for the night. They flew up and away, far above the gigantic trees lining the rear property of Fort Mason and settled on one of the long piers facing Ghirardelli Square. She told Stryker that he was selfish for not letting them both feed on the carcass of a human. Together in a tight formation they flew back to the bridge, got in her car and drove back to her apartment. She was sad, unfulfilled and upset with her pet.

"Go to sleep in your own cage, bad boy," she admonished him. "No way are you sleeping with me tonight!"

She became alarmed when she woke at dawn and found globs of dried blood on her pillow. She felt the back of her head and massaged the series of welts she located. While she knew changes took place in her body when she morphed after midnight, it still surprised her that her bald head would regain a full growth of new hair in the morning.

Paris—Halloween, 2012

HUGUES CHABAN GREETED HIM at the door with a whisper. "Sh, quiet, Pierre. He's resting now. Poor Andre is sick and not expected to live much longer. He took ill while you were in America. His doctors have not been very encouraging about a recovery."

"What's going on here, Hugues? Have you moved in while I was away?"

"Didn't I tell you that when I notified you of Andre's turn for the worse?"

"My memory got all tangled up with the aches and pains of my recent illness."

"Well, let's face it, I had to. Andre called me from his doctor's office and asked me to come live in the apartment and care for him. He suffered a severe heart attack and has not recovered. On top of that, the doctors found an incurable liver cancer that had been eating away at him for a long time. He must have been suffering right up to the moment you left. Louie is in there sleeping with him now and keeping him warm and comfortable."

"I suspected Andre was sick, but the cripple never confided in me. I guess I forget all about that having been under major duress myself. By the way, how do I look?"

"Um, different but I can't put a finger on all of the changes. You appear hardy and well with lots of good cheer. You have a full head of curly black hair, which is new. I thought it was one of those high-priced wigs. The treatment must have worked. I've missed you."

Pierre's mood changed drastically, and he threw himself on Hugues. "Get your things together and get out of my house. Now! I don't want you around me anymore. You're the one who caused me to suffer from that terrible cancer. I can't stand to look at you or be in the same room with you."

Hugues was stunned. "But I can't leave. What about Andre? He needs me now more than ever."

"I'll babysit the old goat and tend to his needs until he dies." Pierre was fuming with rage. "You've done your good deed for humanity. Now get out of here."

Louie heard the commotion in the front of the apartment and came bounding in to greet his master. He jumped up on Pierre's leg and began to sniff him. He slobbered until Pierre pushed him down. "Easy, boy, Daddy is home now and will take good care of you."

The dog sat quietly at his feet. Hugues raced by both of them with his suitcase strapped to his back and didn't say a word as he sped through the front door. Pierre knew he had a bicycle and would bike back to the Montmartre. He was in good shape and could easily negotiate the hilly ride up to his apartment.

"Oh, ah, good to have you back," Andre moaned when Pierre walked into the bedroom. "Where's Hugues?"

"He decided that he wasn't needed here anymore."

"Come closer to me. You look different."

Pierre didn't respond to him and left the room. He was not going to explain everything to nosey people prying where they were unwanted. He didn't expect bad things to happen so soon. He was enjoying his newfound lease on life until ten days later. Andre fell into a deep coma and never recovered.

He buried him with full military honors. Only five people attended the sober ceremony. Needing change, Pierre gave up his beautiful apartment in Paris. He decided to move to his isolated estate on the Meuse River in Verdun, 220 kilometers east of Paris.

AS HE DROVE THROUGH THE HISTORICAL CHATEL GATE, the only remaining part of the medieval city walls he was reminded of the infamous Battle of Verdun during the First World War. Almost a million French and German soldiers were killed in the one-year siege, but Germany failed to bleed the courageous French nation to death. He made a note to visit the interment site of his father who fell during the battle.

The home on the thirty-acre estate required major repairs. The loft had been damaged by a leak in the tiled rooftop. Masonry was peeling off the wall on the sides of the structure. Clusters of moss were hanging from tree branches near the river's edge, resembling gray or greenish hair. He remembered his sister referred to the lichen as an "old man's beard." The plants circling the front porch were in need of major resuscitation. Inside the house, small bits of animal feces were strewn throughout the dank basement. He was ready to torch the entire premise.

Remembering the last time he and Hugues stayed there, Hugues threatened to leave him. They had argued continually about the need to sell the deteriorating estate because it was draining Pierre financially without ever being used. Hugues wanted him to sell, but he refused. Pierre told his former lover that it was none of his business. Hugues pouted for two days before he abandoned the miserable place during the night.

Duvair lived alone, having no friends except his trusty and beloved Louie. The dog curled up and slept with him every night. Some midnights, Pierre would wake up, creep outside, and search the sky for major star groups. If the full moon was out he became hypnotized by its shape and the blinking messages at its circumference. Most of the communiqués were interpreted by Pierre as a call to action. Within minutes, his head grew square and larger. His eyes widened, set down low in his skull. His nose shortened, but the nostrils broadened, and the lower jaw protruded outward, and his fleshy cheeks hung over the underlip in front.

At night, a sudden storm-produced lightning with beautiful colors bouncing off the muddy Meuse River. "Come, my dear Louie, it's time to seek out our next malcontent." The dog barked in acknowledgment that it was time to get moving.

Louie had become more nervous and hesitant on each midnight run. His master would command him to attack female drunks or lowly prostitutes, knocking them down with a thrust of his powerful hind legs. He would keep the prone women in place until his master arrived for the kill. This dark night was no different.

The two hopped in Pierre's Peugeot and motored to Etain, a village twenty kilometers northeast and parked on the main road near the Laffite Tavern and waited. Pierre always carried a double-loop garrote choke wire he had from his days in the French Foreign Legion. They spotted her a block away, weaving and tripping as she walked.

"No… No!" she cried out when Louie pounced on her.

"Time to die, you slovenly woman," Pierre barked at her.

Louie released her, and while stunned, she began to sit up on the sidewalk. Pierre darted over and grabbed her. It was over in less than a minute. Blood poured out of the huge gash in her throat. She bit her tongue so hard, she lopped off the front tip. It bounced off Louie's head. Pierre picked it up, sucked on it, and then tossed it into the street. He bent down and chewed off her left cheek and spat it out at

Louie. The dog refused the invitation to eat human flesh and waddled back to the car. Ten minutes later, they were out of town.

The local newspaper, *Le Messager Verdun*, had a running commentary from the *Gendarmerie*, concerning the vicious murders perpetuated in and around Etain. All were female victims found choked to death, some with a bite-sized chunk of flesh missing from their left cheek—always the left cheek. They couldn't determine if the attacks were planned or spontaneous. They were confused about the shape of the bite where the flesh was ripped off. Was it human or animal? Both possessed the same general characteristics.

After the third murder, Louie resisted his master's midnight command to go for a ride. Instead, he would run outside and hide in a thicket near the lower river tributary. Pierre would crawl after him on all fours but could not pick up his scent. Frustrated, the master would abort his killing mission for that night and wait for the next full moon or thunderstorm to resume his hunt. When morning came, Pierre was excited to let Louie back in the house and showered him with dog treats.

Chicago—Halloween, 2012

SEVERE THUNDERSTORMS PROMPTED a halt in the downtown Halloween activities. The annual children's parade was canceled at the last minute because of pelting rain. Fall was easing its way toward winter as temperatures hovered in the midthirties. Several of the colorful floats were damaged waiting for the parade to begin.

Slade Glick was in a quandary. He wanted to contact Leah Malaka and renew their friendship. He was only interested in the physical component of any relationship. He had never found a more responsive and aggressive lover even though she was paid royally for focusing those talents on well-healed customers. He would take her back if she gave up her lucrative profession and dedicated her entire life to pleasing him. He knew that wouldn't happen. She was too independent and didn't need his wealth to keep her happy.

"Come in here and snuggle up with me," he called to Rocky.

Upon his return from the cure in Texas, he had allowed Rocky to roam freely throughout the condo. His magnificent male snake almost died while he was gone. The alleged herpetologist he hired from a notice in Craigslist failed to visit Rocky daily and feed him the new supply of monitor lizards he'd purchased before the trip.

"Good boy," he said as the snake made its way into the living room. "You are looking quite well this late afternoon. I'm going to kill that pet sitter the next time I see him, Rocky. In fact, maybe I'll let you do it for me."

It was dusk, and the parlor was unlit. Slade was enthralled with the side-to-side undulations of the moving reptile in the near dark. Six feet of smooth, twisting and turning of the thick chestnut colored body excited Slade, sending a shiver up and down his spine. The triangular head marked on top with a dark brown "spear-head" outlined in buffy yellow exuded supreme confidence. Slade never witnessed any living creature as indescribable as his pet.

"I love you," Slade whispered.

Rocky slithered up his body and wiggled around his neck. Slade loved to stroke his smooth scaled body and massage the visible pelvic spurs he believed anatomically meant to be legs. Periodically, he'd reach around behind him and feel the bumpy area on his lower back.

"Tonight, we'll go for a hunt. You'll get better real soon. Trust me."

Rocky hissed back at him in agreement and looked in the direction of his carriage. He started toward his beloved transporter.

"Whoa, big boy, not yet."

The python was displeased and hissed back at Slade.

"Shame on you, Rocky. Daddy knows what's best for you."

Slade had purchased a baby buggy from an Outlet store and modified it to use as a carriage to wheel Rocky around outside. They both loved fresh air and wouldn't be denied the opportunity to take advantage of it. He got tired of the other strollers asking to see his baby when they neared him. He'd head off in the other direction. Slade decided to remedy the slight embarrassment it caused him. To preclude gawkers from eyeing the snake, he affixed a sliding mount that extended from the foot of the buggy to the upper hood. There was no need to alarm people and upset his pet. He would just say that the baby was sleeping, and he didn't want to wake him.

The following Sunday's edition of the *Chicago Tribune* reported a bizarre murder in Millennium Park, a popular section of Grant Park. A young female was found murdered at the edge of Lurie Garden. Her throat was slashed from ear to ear, and a toy snake was stuffed into her esophagus with only the tail portion protruding out. The medical examiner estimated the time of death at two in the morning. The newspaper article quoted the medical examiner as saying that "the cause of death was cardiac arrest and not from the mutilation of the throat that occurred sometime after the victim died. We cannot explain the significance of multiple contusions we found around the victim's abdomen. We join in the police department's cautioning singles from walking the park at that late hour."

Criminologists were at a loss to determine the significance of the toy snake. They couldn't find a parallel case anywhere in their exhaustive search of recorded crime histories. The investigating authorities did establish she was a prostitute known to solicit in Grant Park. They concluded the murder was an isolated incident and didn't see a need to increase security in the park. Nobody came forward to claim the deceased's body.

Eight days later, a second murder in Lincoln Park with the same modus operandi marshaled the investigative police to action on the far north side of Chicago.

CHAPTER 15

SAN FRANCISCO

T HE GOLDEN GATE BRIDGE BELOW BECKONED them to the City by the Bay with dense fog concealing the upper structures of the behemoth. Alcatraz rose up through an opening in the gray cover and an oil tanker was seen creeping toward Angel Island in no hurry to leave the upper sanctuary of the bay. Jamie Richards and Bobby Biel were conversing in first class as the United Airlines flight began its descent to SFO. The pilot announced that incoming flights don't normally circle the Golden Gate, but heavy air traffic in the area necessitated the alternate approach. The flight attendant scrambled to pick up the tray of roasted pine nut hummus, wheat thins, and half-empty glasses of a Napa Chardonnay.

"Why don't they just call it a garbanzo salad?" Bobby asked.

"In reality, it consists of chickpeas," Jamie clarified with a serious stare at his friend.

"Ugh, enough with names. The pasty creation was really good."

"Why did you insist on coming to San Francisco with me, Bobby?"

"I hate to spend Veteran's Day alone in a military city like San Antonio."

"What? You're not a veteran, if I recall correctly."

Bobby smiled. "Nope, they didn't want a geek like me carrying a rifle and anyway, I couldn't pass the optometry hurdle. They didn't call me four-eyes in high school for nothing."

"But look at you now," Jamie said.

"Why?"

"You're a Charles Atlas look-alike of the first degree."

"Is that right? Convince Kat to fix me up with a Charlene Atlas when we get there. I'm ready to share some of that West Coast legalized pot with some hottie in Haight-Ashbury."

"You're too much, Biel. You need a prescription for the medical marijuana. Seriously, why did you come with me anyway?"

"I'm troubled."

"About what?"

"You may not remember, Dolly, one of our experimental chimps we used to develop the cancer cure."

"No, why should I?"

Bobby took a deep breath as the airplane touched down on the runway. "Well, Dolly used to be gentle, caring, and even amorous with the male chimps. She's turned into a she-devil, attacking any male that approaches her. Roberto tells me she bites and claws even the larger ones, like she's going for a kill. I'm afraid the special formula we embedded in her has made her vicious."

"So why come to San Francisco?" Jamie asked with a frown.

"I want to examine Kat to see if there are any adverse complications from her successful cure of the melanoma. The last thing in the world I need is for her to become a violent woman with the intent to harm any male she comes in contact with."

They secured their backpack carry-ons, deplaned, and headed to the BART ramp to grab a train into the city. It was crowded and noisy, which contributed to Bobby's migraine. He had recognized the slight aura and motor disturbance coming on after they flew over the Rockies. The ibuprofen he carried with him failed to relieve the aching in the back of his head and the accompanying nausea.

"Are you in pain?" a concerned Jamie asked, not experiencing his friend's problem in the past.

"I'll live." He knew from research that fluctuating hormone levels and genetics were thought to be contributing factors. He started to experience the migraines after he was cured of his cancer but thought nothing of it until now. He remembered his father had complained of the severe pains in the back of his head and upper neck, which he blamed on the hard farm work he experienced as an adolescent. Bobby concluded it was a genetic phenomenon, a negative fact because he didn't inherit his mother's good looks.

"Where are you staying, Bobby?"

"At the Hyatt Regency on Market Street near the Ferry Building."

"Great, it's not too far from the financial district where I plan to make some calls for possible future employment."

"But you haven't finished your MBA yet."

"I'm working on it."

"Why aren't you back home in school? You seem to attend class whenever your heart desires. Don't they have an attendance requirement?"

"Of course, they do, but they consider me as one of the exceptional students in the program."

"Bullshit, I been there, done that, Richards. You are only exceptional in the eyes of the beholder, and in this case, you are the esteemed beholder."

"Screw you."

"I'm not finished with you yet. Tell the truth, did the power structure at school let you back into the program after your last arrangement with that government agent? I thought you received a pink good-bye slip. I for one know the significance of that crappy piece of paper. Isn't it premature to set up interviews?"

"Military-trained folks plan ahead, buddy. As long as I complete the homework assignments and take the scheduled exams, I'll make it. You know how brilliant I am, never studied much in high school either."

They got off the BART at the Embarcadero Station. The crowd dissipated like a disturbed anthill belching the brown critters in every direction. They found a nearby Starbucks and huddled at a small table near the front window cuddling their expensive lattes and lemon pound cake squares. It was drizzling outside but the sidewalk traffic didn't seem to notice or care. Liquid moisture was part of the landscape for these city dwellers.

"What's the plan, Jamie?"

"Kat knows I'm coming today. I'll call her and get directions to her place. We'll catch up with you tonight. She knows you're with me but not the reason for the visit. I told her this is your first visit to SF, and you'll be the proverbial tourist. Make reservations for dinner somewhere near here and leave a message on my cell. I expect we'll be pretty busy."

Jamie's cell phone rang. He expected Kat was checking in on him.

"Denis Sweeny here, don't you have anything better to do with your time than people-watch in San Francisco, you washed-out soldier?" He laughed into the phone.

"What the f—" Jamie was caught off-guard, as if he had been leveled by a blitzing linebacker.

"I'm looking at you as we speak. Glance back at the table near the restrooms. I was perusing the newspaper with some associates when I saw you and your pal walk in here."

Jamie turned back to look but didn't see the former SEAL. Two guys and a pretty lady were seated at the table. The bigger guy waved a newspaper back and forth signaling Jamie to join them. He told Bobby that he needed to pee and headed toward the rear table.

"You big ape, Sweeny. I didn't recognize you in that ridiculous bearded disguise you're wearing. I didn't know POTUS was going to be in San Francisco. What the hell are you doing in town?"

Sweeny got up and bear-hugged Jamie and introduced him to the other two at the table.

"I had an opportunity to transfer to the CIA, Richards. No more babysitting the president. A former SEAL that headed up the training program when I first joined the navy took a familial liking to me. You know, like you did when you first met me. The big man now heads up the Maritime Branch of the Special Activities Division that focuses on amphibious operations for the CIA."

"And who are your friends, Denis?"

"That ugly dude sitting there and the beautiful young lady are an integral part of my special team on assignment."

"You didn't answer my earlier question. What are you doing here?"

"Patience...patience was never one of your virtues, Richards."

"Right on, my benevolent Denis Sweeny. Please take your time and tell me why I'm talking to you at a Starbucks in downtown San Francisco with two other spies."

"Of course, I will. Sit down. Confidentially, we'd been asked by the local law enforcement folks to help them solve a couple of mysterious murders that took place on or near the waters surrounding the city. They think that some foreign radical group is in town and setting up shop. As you know, there are tons of harbor locations that could be mined with underwater explosives and create havoc for all concerned."

"But why would they take down one or two victims and not blow up a major building and wipe out tons of people? That's what they do."

The young lady spoke up. Jamie was sure he recognized her from some event in the past. "We finished up yesterday after two weeks of undercover work and found nothing." Pointing to the small man next to her, she said, "Bubba here stumbled on a possible lead the other night while knocking down a few at Lefty O'Doul's watering hole. He overheard two bearded customers sporting colorful turbans whispering something about Alcatraz. Not having his trusty five-thousand-dollar listening device with him, he thought he overheard something about bomb devices or boom-booms or even big-bang machines."

"So what actions did you take?" Jamie asked.

"Cyclops here took us on a hazardous dive inspecting the underwater approaches to Alcatraz Island. You wouldn't believe the trash tourists dump overboard on their pricey sightseeing excursions to The Rock, as it's affectionately called. We found some interesting contraband presumably left behind by a band of Aboriginal peoples from the San Francisco area. They took control of the island for eighteen months in late 1969. Bottom line, a waste of our time."

"Sounds like it."

Denis Sweeny was having a problem with his false eye, scratching and tugging at it simultaneously. In desperation, he maneuvered it out of the socket and flipped it in his half-empty glass of ice water. The clunk startled several coffee drinkers at the next table staring in bewilderment at Sweeny. The operatives sitting with Jamie gasped in concert with each other. He expected such an event to happen at some point in time during his relationship with the former SEAL.

"Sorry, folks!" Denis shouted at the top of his lungs. "Mr. Eyeball needs to be cooled off. He's acting up again and giving me a terrible headache."

Three teenage girls at the table near the restrooms witnessed the act and screamed when they looked at the bearded one-eyed monster. Two other tables emptied immediately. Bobby came running to see what was happening.

"Hey, guys and girl, meet my best friend, Bobby Biel from San Antonio. Bobby, this is Denis Sweeny and his two team members from spy city, USA."

"Pleasure to meet you all," Bobby said with a slight laugh, paying special attention to Sweeny. "I hope this doesn't insult you, sir, but Jamie tells me you are a character. He thinks your militaristic attitude leans several degrees to the left of Attila the Hun."

Denis laughed so loud, tears formed in his good eye. He slapped his chest in triumph, retrieved the prosthesis and scurried off to the bathroom.

"How long are you guys going to be in town?" Jamie asked the young lady.

"We're leaving tomorrow."

Jamie remembered where he'd seen her before.

How come my stodgy brain didn't pick this up right away? She was the agent on the plane that Sweeny sent to Miami in pursuit of the Redeemer and his Glorious Reformation movement. He must have recruited her to join him when he transferred to the CIA.

Maybe Sweeny has something going on with her. She's pretty and exudes sensuousness in every gesture and expression. Cyclops can be engaging and attract people in a moment's notice. Good for him, a man's got to do what he got to do! He surrounds himself with great people.

Starbucks had returned to normal when Denis returned with the glass eye secured in his head and without his beard. Jamie and Bobby bid farewell and continued their stroll down Market Street toward the Hyatt Regency. Neither of them said a word until they reached the hotel.

"Give me a few days to mess around, Jamie. Call me when I can see Kat."

"I guess you don't want to go out to dinner with us tonight."

"No."

"That's fine with me. Meanwhile, don't get into trouble with any of the locals. I might not be available to bail you out."

"Trouble? Who, me? Maybe I can attract a California cutie and make mad passionate love for a few days before I rejoin you on my scientific assessment of one Kat Kurbell."

AT SIX O'CLOCK IN THE AFTERNOON, Jamie and Kat were sipping drinks at a wine bar on Union Street. He'd been encouraged by her warmth and attentiveness. She seemed excited again to be in his presence. In the middle of a pleasant conversation, Jamie felt a series of vibrations from the phone nestled in his back pocket. He retrieved it and clicked on the cell.

"Jamie, it's me. I need help. How soon can you get to Haight-Asbury?"

CHAPTER 16

THE BAY AREA

"WHERE THE HELL ARE YOU?" he screamed into his cell phone while hailing a taxi and leaving a frustrated Kat stranded at the bar. Three hours ago, he told his friend not to get into any trouble. It was obvious to Jamie that his words of caution were useless rhetoric.

"I'm at the corner of Divisadero and Page Streets, not too far from Buena Vista Park. Please hurry, they're going to kill me. I hope that—" Bobby's phone suddenly went dead.

Jamie gave the cabbie his destination and told him to "fly this machine as fast as you can!"

As the taxi rounded the corner at Van Ness, he spotted a medical equipment store and ordered the driver to stop. The cab screeched to a halt and Jamie ran into the store, reappearing ten minutes later. He was carrying a wooden cane and gray wig designed for patients after chemotherapy had robbed them of their hair.

"What's that all about, mister?"

"An emergency, now haul ass!"

On the way to the Haight, he slipped the long rubber cup off the bottom of the cane and took out a small knife. He always carried a sharp jackknife in situations where he couldn't bring along his deadly Yarborough. He carved the end of the cane to a fine point resembling the end of a pencil and slid the cup back on. He wiggled the tight wig on his head for a better fit, checked the mirror on the passenger's side, and was satisfied with the image staring back at him.

"Going to some kind of masquerade party?"

"Shut the fuck up and stop dragging your butt on the road. Hurry up!"

Beads of perspiration broke out on Jamie's hairline. The wig was hot and uncomfortable but not the cause for the sweating. He started to tremor and mutter words to himself. The driver began to squirm in his seat afraid that his passenger was going into cardiac arrest. Jamie's adrenaline rush was off the charts, resembling the immediate effect of an EpiPen plunged into a major artery. Years ago, he remembered his Special Forces instructor termed the scenario the "fight, flight, or freeze response." It was further defined by the shrinks as a physiological reaction that occurs in response to a perceived harmful event, attack or threat to one's survival. He was going into battle!

"We're here. Get out," the driver ordered. Jamie flipped him a hundred-dollar bill and told him to stay parked. He shot out of the cab and headed for the small mob assembled in the park near the tennis courts. *Well, I'll be damned. Some of the girls do have flowers in their hair. Great lyrics.*

"Make way for an old man. Clear the way!" he shouted as he wobbled through them with an unsteady gait, supporting himself with the cane. As he neared the south end of the tennis courts, he saw a young lady repeatedly slapping Bobby's face. Three men were wedging his arms behind his back. Scratch marks were drawing blood on both checks.

"Leave my son alone. Release him right now!"

"Go to hell, Gramps. Can't you see we're busy," the lady screamed.

"He has a bad heart," Bobby cried out. "I don't want him to die in the park."

"Stay away or you'll get hurt," she warned. Turning to Bobby, she snarled, "Fuck his heart and fuck you too!"

The tall guy holding one of Bobby's arms released his grip and strolled to Jamie's side. He resembled one of those clowns panhandling for money on Fisherman's Wharf. He still had the silver cream smeared on his face and a top hat to match his silvery shirt and pants. Jamie thought he was pushing seven feet tall.

"Look, Pops, we don't want you harmed. Just go home, fix a cup of hot, tea and take a nap."

"Say what, asshole?" Jamie roared as he slipped the curved loop of the cane around the guy's neck, pulled him down hard to waist level and then kneed him viciously in the head. The loud *pop* could be heard by the mob. The goon grabbed his broken jaw. Jamie stepped back and hammered his head three times with the gooseneck portion of the cane. Not finished with him yet, he kicked the moaning man in the crotch as he slumped to the ground.

"Holy shit," the fat guy holding Bobby exclaimed while relaxing his grip on the arm. "Did you see that?"

Nobody responded.

Jamie turned to the woman and shoved the bottom end of the cane in her face and told her to hit the road. She laughed at his feeble order and slapped Bobby again. The fat guy pulled a pistol from his belt and told Jamie to hug the ground next to the tall guy. As Jamie duck-walked by the fallen comrade he slipped the rubber cup off the end of the cane and speared the fat dude's left arm above the hand grasping the weapon.

"Jesus Christ!" the man yelled in pain. "He's trying to kill me!"

Jamie grabbed the weapon out of his hand, pointed it at the third guy, and said, "You're next."

"I'm outta here," the third man whimpered and took off running up the hill.

Bobby whipped around and slugged the lady on the chin. She fell unconscious to the grass next to the big guy. The fat guy kneeling on the ground was trying to stem the gush of bright red blood squirting from his lower arm. Jamie ripped off half of his right sleeve, scrambled to the man's side, fashioned a makeshift tourniquet, and then love-tapped him several times on the face.

"Who's next?" Jamie shouted at the group of hippies behind him. Some were clapping their hands and hooting while others simply walked away. One young girl wearing an orange headband and smoking a thick black cigar hollered out, "Way to go, Grandpa!"

"Are you ready to get out of here, Dr. Bobby Biel?"

"Hell, yes. Let's go. Nice outfit."

Jamie took off the wig and tossed it to the young hippie with the orange headband. He tossed the cane to the fat guy with the arm wound and said, "A keepsake for you as a reminder not to pick on stupid out-a-town fools."

"You have a lot of explaining to do," Jamie scolded him as they walked back to the waiting taxi.

"You won't believe what happened."

"Try me."

"I will, but I'm too embarrassed. Can it wait?"

"Wait for what?"

"Until I get these cobwebs out of my head."

The cabbie dropped them off at Bobby's hotel.

Jamie called Kat and apologized about his sudden departure from their wine-tasting session on Union Street. She didn't question why he rushed off, figuring he'd fill her in later.

"Take the number ten bus to Pacific Heights. I'll be waiting for you."

She lived a block off the bus route. She enjoyed riding the city buses, rubbing elbows with every walk of life. The city did not offer convenient or inexpensive parking so commuters used the bus system to the maximum. Many residents didn't even own an automobile, renting one periodically when duties or chores dictated their leaving town. Kat didn't own a car any longer even though she could afford to operate one.

"Welcome to my city, Jamie," she said after she closed the door. They hugged, kissed, and then sat on a worn leather couch. He was shocked that the living quarters were so Spartan. Only one large oil painting of two pirate ships engaged in battle adorned the entire living room. He had his fill of pirates and their merciless quest to obtain ransom. A bronze three-foot statue of a falcon with bulging eyes stood guard to the entrance of the hallway. A multi-colored, bound scrapbook sat on a small glass coffee table next to the couch. A copy of the *Yale Law Journal* was on top of it. Faded wallpaper clung to all four walls. The room was dank and dim.

He heard a commotion in the back room that reminded him of Victoria squawking every time he had returned from a trip. He knew Kat owned a pet falcon, figured the bird was exercising its lungs to let the visitor know of its official presence in the home.

"So how have you been since I shot off in the cab? You look absolutely stunning."

"Thanks, I haven't done anything since I walked home." She put an arm around his shoulder.

"You only called twice since you returned from San Antonio," Jamie said. "Have we drifted that far apart?"

"Speak for Jamie Richards," she said without passion. "Your infrequent e-mails led me to believe our relationship had cooled off. Was it too difficult for you to pick up a phone and call me once in a while?" She removed her arm from his shoulders and crossed them in her lap.

"Hey, hold on a minute," he blurted out. "Let's not get tangled up in trivial talk. I'm so excited to be here and spend a few days with you. I've missed you immensely, but I guess I have a difficult time expressing my inner feelings."

"Yes, I agree. It's a man thing."

The late afternoon sun sunk in the Pacific Ocean, taking with it the moisture that had accumulated during the afternoon. Street traffic below announced the return of the working class to the neighborhood for their evening reprieve until another day beckoned them back to their livelihoods. Kat turned on the only lamp in the living room and went to the kitchen to pour a glass of red wine for them. He preferred a martini, but she drank only California's finest export from the Sonoma Valley.

"Where's Dr. Biel?"

"I thought I told you he was staying in a hotel downtown. He is recovering from an unusual episode that occurred his afternoon about, which I am sworn to secrecy." Jamie was confused. *Was she more interested in seeing the doctor?*

"I don't remember you telling me he was going to stay in a hotel," she lied. "Let's drink our wine and plan the two days that you and Bobby will be in town."

He didn't like the direction this conversation was heading. He planned to spend all his time with her, night and day. Apparently, she thought differently.

Did she and Bobby have something going on between them? Did he inject her with some kind of love serum at the farm? But we made unsurpassed love in San Antonio. Was she visualizing it was Bobby on top of her during the grunting and groaning sessions?

"What do you have in mind to pass the time?" He was past being curious.

177

"Tonight, we'll have dinner at my favorite restaurant on Union Street, and after eating, you can grab a taxi and scoot back to your hotel."

"Wait a minute, Kat. I don't have a hotel room booked. Are you telling me that I'm not going to stay here with you tonight?"

"Yes, you heard it right."

CHAPTER 17

THE BAY AREA

J AMIE PITCHED A COMPLETE SHUTOUT the previous night. Looking back with a sour taste in his mouth, they'd rushed through dinner at the crowded Betelnut on Union without sharing much conversation. She told him that she hadn't been feeling well, and on top of that, it was the time of the month that most women of child-bearing age hated. She insisted he wouldn't enjoy making love under those extenuating circumstances. He didn't agree. Having come all the way from San Antonio and drawing a total blank in the lovemaking department was not an option. She'd won out, and he retreated to the Hyatt Regency, hoping that Bobby had reserved a suite. He did. Bobby was shocked when Jamie called him from the lobby at midnight.

"What's going on with her? Is she frigid or just not interested in you anymore?"

"I think both," Jamie said. "What's your room number?"

Bobby opened the suite door, and they settled in the parlor area. He was in a white bathrobe and black slippers. There was an opened bottle of Bombay Sapphire hugging the corner of the end table. He had been drinking and appeared a wee tipsy to Jamie.

"About this afternoon, talk to me, Bobby."

"Sure, you have a right to know. I wanted some weed, so I went to the Haight and asked this lady standing on a street corner where I could get some medical marijuana."

"Was she the one slapping your pretty face in the park?"

"Yes."

"Please continue."

"She said that wouldn't be a problem and told me she had a prescription she'd lend me for a hundred dollars. Told me the drugstore across the street from us supplied most of her friends."

"Don't tell me that the intelligent scholar and internationally known cancer healer that you are could not borrow the marijuana script with a firm handshake and a soft smile."

"I tried and she laughed in my face."

"Smart kid."

"She told me a friend borrowed the script and was going to return it today, but she had to meet him in Buena Vista Park. She suggested I come along with her and she'd cut the so-called user fee to fifty bucks."

"And you agreed?"

"Not initially. She began to soften up and suggested I get the pot and we'd go to her apartment and get high. She said she never did this kind of thing before but I seemed special."

"Special? You idiot!"

"Hold your horses. You saw how good-looking she was, and frankly, I was horny."

"Why were the goons slamming you against the tennis court fence in the park?"

"When she introduced me to her three friends, I knew I was in trouble. The big one told me he had the script and it would cost me five hundred bills to borrow it. I told him I didn't have that much cash with me."

"So?"

"They started to push me around, jabbing at my back and stomach, and threatened to kill me. They accused me of propositioning their female friend. I was scared. Some of their hippie friends started to gather around, shouting names at me, encouraging the three men to beat the shit out of me. They were in the process of roping me to the fence, ready to crucify me."

"What did you do?"

"I told them I could call a rich friend who'd rush here with the dough."

"You bastard, Biel."

"There's more."

"Enough... Enough." Jamie had had it. "I don't want to hear anymore. Let's get drunk."

Morning arrived, and Jamie struggled to wake up. He wasn't in the practice of getting drunk, but last night was an exception. His cell phone was propped on his pillow. While he was collecting his thoughts, wondering if he'd been on the phone during the night, it suddenly beckoned him to action. It was Kat.

"Sorry about last night, but I feel much better today. Can you come see me now?"

"Sure, after I shower, but don't discard me like a slice of last week's leftover pizza."

"Course not. You mean too much to me, Jamie." She hung up.

"Who the hell was that?" Bobby asked as he came in the bedroom with the newspaper.

"Kat."

"What'd she want?"

"Me and as soon as possible. I think she's hot to trot."

"I'm going with you."

"No way, Jose. Get off your ass and go find your own girl."

"You mean like yesterday?"

"Hell, no, and if you ever try that trick again, call somebody else to bail you out. Am I perfectly clear on this point?"

"It won't happen again."

"All right. Why do you really want to see Kat?"

"I need to check her out. I continue to worry about possible adverse effects from my treatment."

"Look here, cowboy. I had this gut feeling about you and Kat. Did something above and beyond the curative treatment go on between you two?"

"Like what?"

"Like are you sexually attracted to each other?"

"Hell, no, strictly professional."

"I'll sit on that explanation for the time being. While I shave and shower, how about calling room service for breakfast. Make mine pancakes with three sausage links and loads of syrup. The syrup flushes whatever alcoholic residuals are haunting this man's body."

"Yassah, Master, right way."

Bobby made the call and retreated to the sitting room with the *Chronicle*. He usually skipped the front page in favor of the Sports Section. The 49ers were his team. He liked their uniforms with the big SF affixed to the helmet. He picked up the front page and zeroed in on the article about the vicious murder that took place at Crissy field last night. The eighteen-acre tidal marsh linked to the San Francisco Bay with the dune habitat, shrubs, and wildflowers was a popular picnic and jogging area for area residents and tourists alike.

The headline read, "The Eye-Plucking Murderer Strikes Again" in bold print.

"Oh, God no, not again!" Bobby shouted out loud and began to fidget. He tossed the paper aside when the loud knock on his door signaled the arrival of their breakfast. Jamie was already out of the shower and dressed.

"I'll make you a deal, Jamie. You can have Kat all to your lonely until midafternoon. Get whatever has to be done between you two, and then she'll be mine."

"Let's say she's *ours* because I want to be there when you conduct your assessment. I think she'd want it that way."

"Fine with me, but I don't want you to interrupt the process. I know how you are, Richards. Quick to pull the trigger and then beg forgiveness."

Jamie decided to take a taxi this time. The bus was overcrowded yesterday, and he jostled with passengers most of the way to Kat's apartment. He was saving every ounce of energy for the big event.

She'd better be ready for me this time, no apologies and no holds barred. I didn't come all this way to be sidetracked by excuses. I can't believe she forgot the special time we had together in San Antonio. Maybe her cancer got to her brain and wiped out all recall capability. I don't care. She's healthy now even if her brain might be skewed off-center.

He was pleasantly surprised but alarmed when she opened the door to let him in. She was standing naked with the big falcon propped on her shoulders. The bird looked as though it was ready to strike at him. She held him back with a restraining strap from her wrist to his powerful clenched foot. Her breasts appeared much smaller than he remembered, almost like shrunken plums. Yet her shoulders were muscled like a weight lifter. Her face was alive with adventure.

"About time you got here," she scolded him. "Stryker couldn't wait for your arrival. I told him repeatedly that my new lover was coming to visit us. He's a little agitated for some reason. Maybe I should go back there and put him in his cage."

"Please do so and lock the cage door and cover him up. I don't want any interruptions when I devour you, my fair lady."

"I may have mentioned that Stryker likes to be present when I make love to a stranger."

"What!"

"Just kidding, but I think it would be a neat experience if he sat in on us when we fuck."

Jamie could not believe what he was hearing. *Maybe I should get done with it right away and call Bobby to come for the much-needed assessment. Something is amuck. Has she been groveling with other men? I should have been more persistent in calling her.*

What Jamie didn't know and had no reason to know, Dr. Bobby Biel had come to California twice after Kat returned home. And he didn't come to pan gold at Sutter Creek.

After a brief pause and with a less serious look on his face, he chuckled. "From what I saw of his claws and beak, you can forget that whacky notion."

"But—"

"It's either Jamie Richards without the bird, or I go home. Take your pick."

Her eyes began to tear up, but he put a hand softly to her face, and she smiled. He had a decision to make, and either way, he didn't think she'd be happy.

"Instead of the *vulture* watching the ceremonial act, why don't we get Bobby here right now? If you need another set of eyes to witness the copulation, I trust my friend more that that raptor caged in the other room."

"Forget it, Richards. Let's go for a walk."

"If that's the therapy you need at this juncture, I suggest you get dressed first." She went to the bedroom and came out sporting a pair of frayed pink shorts. She wore a purple tank top with the words "Smoke Pot-Get Hot" embroidered across the midriff. He hoped she'd change it before Bobby arrived. Cannabis in any shape or written form was *verboten* in his mind after yesterday's crisis with the hippies in Buena Vista Park. She opted for flip-flops, which failed to hide a gnarled set of long toenails.

He started down the stairs, but she ran back to the house claiming she forgot to do something. They walked down to the Marina Green and curled up on the lawn. Shuttles to Alcatraz looked like ants making their way to a new hill. Several young boys were attempting to windsurf but were thrashing in the water more often than balancing on their surfboards.

"This is my favorite place in the whole city," she said, pointing both long arms skyward. "People come here to exercise, relax, roller blade, and jettison their cumbersome worries. Hang-ups disappear here, Jamie. Look out there at the view of the bay. Birds of every variety exercise their unrestrained freedom. I wish human beings could do that, don't you?"

"I care less about birds. What's going on with you? You've changed so much I hardly recognize you. Where did that Midwestern upbringing go? You act as though you don't give a shit about yourself or anybody near you. What do we have to do to resolve our differences?"

"I don't think we were meant for each other, Jamie. I've changed. You've changed. The cancer had obliterated my life—that is, until Bobby reversed my fortunes. I feel totally different now, free and easy. I don't think a long-term relationship is in the makings. I just want to be alone, like a hermit. Live alone with my Stryker."

He was at a loss for words, unable to calculate in his brain what was going on with her and that fucking bird. Perhaps he should accept his losses and head back to San Antonio and resume a *normal* life.

Who the hell wants to come to San Francisco and live with these unusual, spaced-out zombies? Not me, that's for sure. Bobby could well be a candidate the way he's been acting. On second thought, maybe he can put his educated finger on this mess and decipher it for me.

"Let's go back to your place. Bobby should be there by now," Jamie suggested.

She got up bouncing three feet in the air and did a one-eighty spin in front of him. Her arms extended out laterally. Her chin thrust out with feet kicking back and forth as though she was attempting a takeoff. He reached up and grabbed her arm pulling her to his chest with great force.

"Leave me alone!" she shouted at him. "I'm only trying to burn off some of this excess energy I have bundled up inside of me." She walked ahead of him to Marina Boulevard toward the Safeway grocery store. "I'm famished, and I need to get some food in me. I'll pick up sour dough baguettes and some lunch meat, and we'll eat at home. I'll call Bobby and have him join us if he's not already there."

Jamie wanted to ask how she happened to have Bobby's number so handy but shrugged it off. He reasoned that the sooner his friend got here, the better. He had a knack for sorting things out and would clarify what the hell was going on with this woman.

"Bobby said he was already at my place. Let's finish up shopping and get out of here. Grab a couple bottles of red wine, and I'll meet you at the checkout counter. We'd better hustle up there. I left the front door unlocked and Stryker out of his cage before we left on our walk."

The front door was closed when they got to her apartment. When they opened it and walked in, Bobby was sitting on the couch with Stryker perched on his shoulders. Jamie couldn't believe it, lifting up his arms in dismay, and turned to Kat for an explanation. She smiled at his hand and arm gestures and rushed to the bird and returned it to the cage. Bobby got up and followed her to the back room. Jamie sat down and waited for the two to return to the living room.

"Glad you did your best to get here, Biel. I noticed that you and the raptor have become good friends. Care to explain how that has happened seeing you've never been here before?"

"My, my Jamie, you are a suspicious one. I know about these beautiful creatures. I am a scientist, you might remember…minored in zoology in my undergraduate years before earning my doctorate in biochemistry. The door was unlocked when I got here, so I opened it and went in. Stryker was caught in that frayed curtain by the bay window. He apparently was trying to look out the window, but got those big feet snagged in the woven scarf draped on the curtain rod. I hesitated trying to unhook him for fear that he'd attack me."

"Claws, Mr. Zoologist…not feet. So what action did you take?" Jamie had a difficult time buying the story.

"I looked around for something…anything that would distract him enough so I could help him. He was exhausted from trying to disengage from the loosely woven trap he'd gotten into. Stryker enjoys a special treat that Kat gives him when he's been a good boy, so I searched the house and couldn't find one. I went outside and into the garage, and there they were, in a cage in the far back corner clamoring around like street urchins. I reached in and grabbed one of the shrews and raced back in and offered it to Stryker. One claw had worked its way loose, and he pinned the shrew against the curtain rod. While he was pecking the life out of the rascal, I unhooked the other claw from the drape, and he flew into the back room with his prize."

"Bravo, my hero," Jamie said without emotion and not believing a word of it.

"Thank goodness you were here," Kat said. "He could have died if it weren't for you. Why don't we sit down and have our lunch now. Stryker enjoyed his?"

They fixed sandwiches and drank wine. Jamie remained quiet throughout while the other two bantered back and forth. He felt like the odd man out.

Something suspicious is going on between these two people, but I'll give Bobby the benefit of the doubt. Maybe he has this special way of evaluating patients, a technique that even I can't understand. He is well-trained in the dynamics of biochemical therapies. I should trust him. It's Kat who bothers me. Perhaps I should give up and run back to Texas. Maybe it's just not time to go the amorous route with this one. Women sure can be a pain in the rump!

CHAPTER 18

THE BAY AREA

THE CABLE CAR RIDE UP CALIFORNIA STREET was the last venue Jamie had on his checklist for the visit to San Francisco. Yesterday had been a complete washout for him. Kat was so spaced out, he couldn't handle it. Bobby aggravated him. He moved his gear out of the Hyatt and found a small hotel on Sutter Street near Union Square. Their long-term friendship was in jeopardy. He didn't trust Biel anymore. In his mind, Bobby was a fucking lizard, changing colors more times than a chameleon. He was convinced that his miraculous cure from melanoma in the Indian Ocean was responsible for his bizarre behavior. The ring of his cell phone jump-started him back to reality.

"Where the hell are you, Richards?" Bobby was shouting at the top of his lungs.

"Shut up!"

"Look, there is absolutely nothing going on between Kat and yours truly. My interest in her is strictly clinical. Understood?"

"No."

"Do you want me to elaborate?"

"No."

"Jesus Christ, Jamie, what do I have to do to convince you?"

"Go to hell, Biel. You've been jaunting out here behind my back, romancing *my* woman. I repeat, *my* woman."

"Hold on, soldier friend. What if I told you she may be involved in several vicious murders here in the city?"

"What the—"

"Again I ask, where are you now?"

"I just got off the cable car at Van Ness."

"Grab a taxi and meet me at the Ferry Building. I'll be sitting on a bench out behind watching the seagulls swoop for food. We need to talk and now."

Jamie showed up fifteen minutes later, out of breath and out of patience. He was willing to give Bobby one last chance to redeem himself; otherwise, their friendship would be history.

"Thanks for coming. Let's go inside and talk. The wine merchants offer some good red as well as tasty munchies."

"Sounds like a plan though I'm not hungry."

The Ferry Building Marketplace was teeming with activity. Two bay transit shuttles belched out a mob of eager commuters. Several of them peeled off to purchase coffee, cheese, chocolates, or other food items from the friendly vendors lining the first floor of the historical building.

"What evidence do you have to suggest that Kat is a killer?"

"Plenty. Have you read the *Chronicle* since we've been here?"

"No, I hate politically deranged newspapers."

"Get real. They don't manufacture murders on the city streets. They report the facts and circumstances surrounding the tragic events."

"True, but I do like their *Sporting Green*."

They drained the first carafe of a new wine label the merchants were pushing. It was now late morning, but they needed to kill four more hours until boarding their return flight to San Antonio. Both of them had already checked out of their hotels and had their backpacks with them. A second carafe came with a plate of cheese and crackers.

"So what was reported in the paper?"

"A few days ago the SFPD found a body floating behind Fort Point. The head was mutilated, the eyes gouged out of the poor soul's head."

"Good God, who the hell would do anything that gross?"

"It's the fourth case in the past month…same MO and no tangible leads to pursue. Some crazy or crazies are getting off on shit like this, Jamie."

"So why implicate Kat?"

"What I'm about to share with you is confidential and must not be repeated. Swear to me, Jamie."

"Of course."

"I have examined Kat on three separate occasions. Each time, she exhibited different signs and symptoms. While eliminating the melanoma, I think our curative therapy is turning our friend into another creature—half human, half animal."

"How did you come to that conclusion?"

"Conclusion is not the appropriate word at this point of our discussion."

"But you just said—"

"I know what I said. It's theoretical and at the same time potentially explosive."

"What else have you found?"

"I think Stryker is a party to the killings."

"What say you? A bird that seeks out humans and kills them?"

191

"Here are two alarming facts. The investigators found bird feathers embedded in the chest of the remains of all four victims. They have yet to identify the exact species. An expert from the world famous San Diego Zoo is working with them."

"And what's the second fact?"

"You recall me explaining how I retrieved Stryker from the drapes at Kat's house, right? When I ventured into the back corner of her garage to get a shrew mouse, I discovered a strange five-gallon glass container. It shocked the living hell out of me."

"So what was in the bottle?"

"It contained eyeballs floating in some kind of liquid preservative. There must have been a dozen or more slimy eyes staring me in the face."

Jamie was stunned. He couldn't believe what he'd just heard from the quivering lips of his good friend. He slammed his half-drained glass of wine down and shattered the stem. Wine spilled on his trousers, blood oozed from the hand that held the glass.

"Are you saying that Kat is responsible?"

"I don't know for sure. Her upper body strength is phenomenal. Her back is severely pock-marked. Something is happening back there. She may have severely infected sebaceous glands involving the papilla of the hair follicles. Maybe feathers are growing underneath her skin. Did you see her bare feet when you were at the Marina Green? Are her feet are gnarled? Scientifically, it's called *Anisodactyly* where three toes are forward and one turned back. This is common in hunting birds like eagles, hawks, and in our case, falcons. They attack the eyes of their prey."

"Don't confuse me with scientific facts, Bobby. Is Kat a fucking bird?"

"The jury is still out. When I visited Kat, she always insisted that I leave before midnight. We'd go out for dinner and come back to her place for coffee and Danish. No explanation, just get out by midnight, she always insisted. I didn't argue with her but suspected that some bodily transformations took place after midnight."

"Does she fully comprehend what happens to her after midnight?"

"That, I am not sure of. At times, I think she's cognizant of the changes. But whenever I tried to discuss it with her, she denied it ever happening."

Jamie was in deep thought while he clasped a napkin to the cut on his hand. The blood congealed within minutes.

Did that lightning strike that crashed through the roof of the research barn in Texas have anything to do with Kat's problem? If I recall, it happened shortly after midnight. Is that the magic hour when she transforms into a bird, a killing bird like her winged pet?

Bobby interrupted his thoughts. "We'll resolve this later. I had to get this off my chest. We'd better grab our gear and get to SFO, our plane leaves in two hours."

They ambled down to the Embarcadero Bart station and jumped on the next rain to the airport. Halfway to the airport, Bobby's cell screamed out. He answered it, and after listening for some time, he grimaced in disgust. He tossed *The Wall Street Journal* he was reading across the aisle, bouncing it off the train door. Jamie spun around, reached over, and shook him.

"What the hell was that all about?"

"Robert called and—"

"Who?"

"Sorry, it was Roberto Gomez, my caretaker at the farm in Texas. Surely, you remember him. He could hardly speak. Half Spanish and half English words came out of his mouth. He started to whimper, apologized, and then blurted it out."

"Come on, Bobby. Get hold of yourself. What did he blurt out?"

"Gar Underwood stole the remaining Conus sea snails that I was hoarding for another experiment. That bastard! I should have known better. The prick cheated his way through college. I even authored some papers for him and actually took one of his final exams."

"What? He flew from New York to San Antonio, got a rental car, drove down to your place, broke into the research barn, and casually swiped the specimens. Simple as that?"

"Not quite. Roberto said there were two state troopers that accompanied him. He had no choice but to turn the snails over to them."

"State troopers? Maybe aliens from the planet Pluto dressed as cops."

"Get serious, Richards. That's exactly what he said. Roberto started to tell me about the other major problem that happened, but I couldn't understand him. He was wailing like a sick baby."

It was a long flight back. Neither of them spoke much. They consumed their maximum allowable share of alcohol while seated in first class accommodations. The flight attendant elected not to talk to them when they stumbled off the plane in San Antonio. The last words Jamie heard from his friend as they went their separate ways was, "I'm going to kill that fucking Underwood!"

CHAPTER 19

FRANCE

Pierre Duvair and Louie were hunkered down on a cold morning in November. Both were exhausted from the previous evening's hunt in Etain near the former Sidi Brahim Barrack area several blocks from downtown. Pierre preferred to hunt in the small village and not around Verdun. His beat-up Peugeot was known to most mechanics in town, so he operated far enough away from his river estate not to draw unnecessary attention from the nosey ones.

They could not find a suitable malcontent to kill last night. He figured most of the potential female victims were coupled up, hand in hand talking about the upcoming Thanksgiving party the local mayor was hosting. He didn't want to kill males, especially older men who were to be dignified. In his mind, all French women were sluts except his mother and sister. They transmitted terrible diseases.

"Come here, Louie, and sit. Today, we are going to visit my father's grave. You haven't been there yet. You need to see the hallowed grounds of our French soldiers where they were slaughtered by the greedy Hun."

The dog silently obeyed.

Pierre looked at him in pity. He knew this breed had limitations. His former lover Hugues Chaban ranted constantly about hiring

Louie out as a stud dog. Pierre knew that many French bulldogs are incapable of naturally breeding because they have slim hips, making the male unable to mount the female to reproduce naturally. They had to be helped. Ugh! He didn't want to force undue embarrassment on his pet.

"I'm going to put you outside for a short time. Hustle out there and do your duty and come in and sit on your comfy dog bench. It won't be too long, Louie, but I have to attend to my chores inside before we leave for Verdun. You get in my way too often when I work."

The dog barked an objection. He didn't like being left outside for long periods trying to escape the hot sun. The master had a habit of forgetting about him being left outside. The constant barking for relief was a waste of time.

"Hush up, dog of mine."

Louie did as told and flopped to the cold wooden floor, mulling over several issues. *Today is acceptable, but on hot days, he fails to remember that I have a difficult time breathing and regulating my body temperature. And while I'm complaining, he throws sticks in the Meuse River and expects me to retrieve them. Fun? Maybe for him but not for me. He doesn't seem to get it. I am top heavy and have difficulty swimming. But I am an obedient guy and always try to please him, except I hate his new game. I love humans. They are always so kind to me. Why does he want to kill them?*

Pierre washed and dried the breakfast dishes and swept the floor. He hated to cook even though his family was known as the crème ala crème of French cooking. He decided to take a short break before the next task of hauling the vacuum out of the closet to suck up the balls of fuzz on the thick rugs. He missed the old fart Andre who took care of all the inconveniences of life. Reclining on the couch, he shifted his thoughts to Hugues Chaban.

I hate the man but miss the times when he coiled the rope around my throat and sent me on an enlightened mission of fantasy and ecstasy.

Oh…oh, I'm getting hard. Rush to my side, sweet Hugues, and do me, please. I can't hold off any longer. Ah…ah.

"Come on in now, Louie. Hop in the car. We mustn't waste any more time." His pet didn't move. "Okay, okay, I'll get you a treat."

The dog responded. His tongue was wagging back and forth like windshield wipers in a heavy rain storm. Pierre slammed the car door shut. They headed to the Douaumont ossuary, a memorial containing the remains of soldiers who died on the battlefield during the Battle of Verdun.

"Quite a sight," a deep voice directly behind him said loud enough for Pierre to hear.

"That it is," he replied, turning to face the man.

"I cry every time I visit the hallowed ground and the tomb of the brave soldiers who fought here. Several of my ancestors bravely gave their precious lives for our country."

"As I do," Pierre said with a shallow grin. He checked the young man out, and a sudden sensation raced through his body, causing him to shiver several times. He hoped it wasn't too obvious. Pierre was attracted to men in uniform.

"I see you are in the service of our great nation, young man. Where are you assigned?"

"At the Étain—Rouvres Air Base. I belong to the 3ᵉ Régiment d'Hélicoptères de Combat."

Pierre knew of the well-maintained, front line French military base. In fact, he tried to gain access several times to meet military men, but the reputation of his past service in the French Foreign Legion failed to unlock the big gates out front.

"Are you alone?" Pierre blurted out almost too quickly.

"Oh, yes sir, they prefer to assign single men to the base. We're on call all day and night. I'm afraid that having a wife would result in undue hardship."

"Sure, I understand," Pierre said, linking the word *wife* to *hardship*.

"Look there on the right at those small thick outside windows," the airman pointed ahead of them. "The skeletal remains of almost two hundred thousand unidentified soldiers of both nations are piled up in the alcoves at the lower edge of the building."

"What a pity, war and the ravages of humanity it entails," Pierre said, lacking expression. He was trying hard to control his attraction to the young man standing beside him, perhaps not hard enough though. The airman was quick to pick up the vibes.

"That's why I serve—to discourage countries from attacking us. And if that fails, we have the means to counter their thrusts in order to protect our own interests."

"My father is buried there," Pierre offered, trying to gain a quick dose of sympathy.

"Wow! You must be proud of his service."

"Yes. Would you like to go somewhere and have a glass of wine or hot cup of coffee? It's cold this morning. I know of a comfortable establishment in downtown Verdun."

"Yes, sir, that's a nifty idea. I've had enough of this monument for a day… Been here since sun-up. Bus from the base dropped me off."

"By the way, what's your name?" Pierre asked.

"Rene. Rene Gibeau," he replied. "And yours?"

"Pierre Duvair."

"Where are you from, Rene?"

"I was born in Longuyon."

"If I'm correct, that's not too far away from Etain. I remember reading about the Royal Canadian Air Force staff and family members living there back in the 1960s. I think they operated an airbase in the vicinity."

"Yes," Rene confirmed. "Actually, it was located at Marville. My grandfather worked there when the base was active. I read a lot about the history of the base in school, and that's what prompted me to join our own military force."

They shook hands. Pierre felt an immediate charge running through his stubby body. Rene was tall, lanky, and wore a thin moustache across a broad freckled face. His ears were two sizes too large for his head, but the blue beret he wore held them in check. After releasing their grips, they strolled to Pierre's Peugeot. He let Louie out and encouraged him to exercise and do his duty. Always the stubborn one, the dog neglected the exercise order but managed to drop a hot load near Rene's feet.

"Oops, that was close. Fine-looking dog you got there. Does he bite?"

"No."

After pumping the gas pedal too many times, he flooded the motor. Rene told him to relax and wait several minutes before trying again. A spark ignited the engine on his third attempt. They drove to Verdun proper, crossing the Meuse River at the Châtel Gate leading to La Roche Square. Pierre drove across to Café Dumond and parked in front. Louie remained in the back seat, hoping they would return with some leftovers for him. It was late morning, and he longed for a snack. They found a table outside under a colorful umbrella facing the river. Pierre ordered a carafe of *vin de pays*, a country wine slightly better than ordinary table wine.

"Would you like something to eat, Rene?"

"No, thanks."

"Um, do you have a girlfriend?" Pierre was probing, his interest in the young man gaining momentum.

"No, sir. I always stayed away from them. They're nothing but trouble. My mom ran out on dad when I was five."

"I'd like to think there are dozens of fine women around these parts," Pierre assured him. *A good-looking specimen like this airman should have them swooning all over him. He's more attractive than that deadbeat Hugues Chaban. I always preferred tall men, and this young lad is much taller than Chaban. Does he like men, or am I simply mis-reading the body language?*

They finished their wine and several miniature baguettes with a plate of cheese, compliments of the café. Their conversation stalled, and Rene suggested they take a walk along the Meuse River and check out some of the beautiful structures that lined the riverfront. Pierre didn't like to go for meaningless strolls. He had his own property on the water but caved, hoping to develop a more *meaningful* relation-ship with the energetic young man.

"I have a home on the Meuse, Rene. It's comfortable with the picturesque wooded surroundings. You'd like it. Perhaps someday you could come to my chalet, and we'd hunt small game or even do some fishing." He emphasized the word *chalet*. "Would you like that?"

"Yes, I sure would, but think I'd better head back to the base. It's getting late. Would you give me a ride to the bus stop?"

"I'll do one better. I'll take you back to Etain. I have nothing else programmed for today."

"You are a kind man, Pierre." He bent down and kissed the older man on both cheeks. The gesture startled Pierre sending mixed sig-nals to his mind. The French were always polite but…

The short trip to the base was delayed by an overturned furniture truck halfway to Etain. Sofas, kitchen chairs, mattresses, and tables of varying sizes were strewn along the oil-slicked highway. A sudden rain had surprised the commuters who failed to adjust driving speeds and take other safety precautions. Pierre bypassed the scattered debris and arrived at the main gate.

"I don't know how to thank you, Pierre. You remind me so much of my father, the kind of dedicated man that raised me alone. How can I thank you?"

A thousand thoughts went racing through the older man's head. "Why don't you spend next weekend with me? We'll have fun, at least go fishing, and I'll cook you one of the finest meals you'd ever taste in these parts. What do you say?"

"Book it. You've got a date."

The weekend came and went. Pierre tried repeatedly to contact Rene at the number he'd left him. It was the gate guard pavilion at the base, and they wouldn't forward the call to Rene's unit. Pierre was frustrated and angry. He felt like he got stood up by a puppy dog kid who didn't have the courtesy to follow-up his gracious offer.

Screw him, I'll find another young man, one more willing to spend time with me and enjoy my company.

Late that Sunday evening after midnight, he gathered up a disgruntled Louie and drove to Longuyon. He had no intention to connect with René or any of Rene's family still living in the city. He drove all around the town, which was minimally lit up at the wee hours of Monday morning. He was searching for prey, any French slut that might be roaming the streets. His chest had inflated to such a degree he had difficulty breathing. His hands had turned into paw-like mittens, and he had a difficult time gripping the steering wheel of the Peugeot.

When he crossed the Crusnes River, he spotted her. She was alone and walking at an unsteady gait. He pulled one block ahead of her, parked, and turned off the ignition and lights. Louie began to bark in defiance, sensing what was about to happen, and he wanted no part of the action. Pierre quieted him with a slap across his head. When she approached, he opened the door and slid off the seat. She hesitated briefly and smiled at him.

"*Monsieur*, how kind of you to stop and offer me a ride home."

In the dim light, Pierre surmised that she was in her late thirties, pretty but drunk or on dope, half-staggering toward him. He smiled, nodded, and reached into his back pocket and pulled out his double-loop garrote choke wire and shoved it in her face. He started to talk, but the throaty voice came out of his mouth with a growl. He had a difficult time mouthing each word.

"You filthy street walker…disease-carrying French whore…you deserve to die."

"No, please don't. I have two children at home who need me!"

"Woof, woof…I don't care."

Her death was immediate. With great force, the tightened loop almost took her head off at the neck. The wire sliced through the cartilage past the cervical vertebrae. He released his hold allowing the dead woman to slump to the ground. She was naked under her long trench coat. A stream of urine and fecal matter pooled at his feet. Pierre knelt down and took a two-inch chunk of flesh off her left cheek and swallowed it without chewing. It made him gag, but esophageal reflexes managed to shove the tasty morsel down his throat. He left the victim in a curled heap at the curb, climbed over her limp body to his car, and sped away. Louie vomited in the backseat.

Rene called him three days later. "I've been trying to contact you but apparently scribbled down an incorrect number. Operator assistance in Verdun was able to locate you through your former Paris telephone number. Is your offer still good?"

Pierre hesitated answering the young airman, questioning the validity of his story. He was still reliving his thrilling encounter with the French tart in Longuyon. Raping her had crossed his mind but was ruled out. He wouldn't screw them if they were alive, so how could he even consider doing it if they were dead? Murder rejuvenated him, made him feel strong, all-conquering, and not vulnerable or accountable to anyone. He recalled his earlier invitation to Rene to hunt game or even go fishing in the Meuse River.

"Of course, Rene. When can I pick you up?"

"I'll hitch a ride with a friend who is planning to visit the Verdun battlefields tomorrow. I can have him drop me off at the cafe where we had the food and wine. Would that be all right?"

"You remember how to get there?"

"I'm a military man, you recall. I drew a strip map after you dropped me off at the base. I have an unbelievable memory. My peers call it a photographic phenomenon."

"Mighty big words, young man. How long can you stay with me?"

"I have a three-day pass."

The next day could not arrive soon enough for Duvair. He tidied up the house, went to the nearest food store, and picked up enough provisions to last a week. He already had enough cognac and wine to serve a troop of airmen. He dusted off some pornographic DVDs that he and Hugues Chaban viewed to increase their sexual appetites before they engaged in near suffocation with the rope. It was never that necessary for him, but Hugues took much longer to get aroused. The high was unbelievably erotic and orgasmic. It surpassed the combination of drugs he took when he was in the Foreign Legion to achieve such an unworldly lucid, semi-hallucinogenic state. He hoped it wouldn't be difficult to lead Rene to the rope.

"Please jump in, and we'll be at my home before you know it," Pierre said when he picked him up at the cafe.

"Thanks. How soon can we go fishing? I haven't dipped a worm since I was thirteen." They had pulled into the stone-cobbled driveway. Rene was all eyes when he spotted the river through the thick stand of trees.

"I set aside time to fish tomorrow. Today, we'll simply relax and get better acquainted."

Pierre could see the disappointment in the airman's eyes. He ushered him to the guest bedroom and helped him stow his meager belongings. They reconvened on the porch outside the main quarters.

Pierre offered a glass of wine, and Rene seemed more relaxed talking about old times. He allowed the airman to go on for an hour before interrupting.

"Do you miss your home town, Longuyon, I believe you told me?"

"No, I was glad to leave for bigger and better things. By the way, did you hear about the brutal murder that happened there a week ago?"

"Um, no, it wasn't in the Verdun paper. Tell me about it."

"My uncle called me at the base and told me about it. A young mother with a couple of kids was ambushed on her way home from tending to a seriously ill aunt. It was late at night. The killer almost cut her head off and took a slice of meat off her face. Nothing as repulsive has happened in Longuyon for decades. Sick bastard who done it to the poor woman. They ought to cut his balls off and stuff them down his throat when they find him!"

Pierre was silent for a few minutes. He had a bad dream the other night about a person being chewed to death by a mad dog. He awoke, drenched in sweat, and screamed at the top of his lungs. He continued wailing until Louie jumped in his bed and quieted him.

"Agree, human beings at their worse. They need to be brought to justice. What you suggest is way too kind for a deranged animal. The killer should be tortured and skinned alive, layer after layer after layer. More wine, Rene, or would you like to shift to something smoother, say cognac?"

"One more piece of information about the murder, and I'll get off the subject."

"I think I've heard enough." Something was bothering Pierre, but he couldn't put a finger on it.

Rene continued anyway. "A witness to the killing told the gen-darmeries that he saw the animal that perpetrated the act. While it was dark at the time, he made out the figure of a large ape or even a muscular dog. The animal was standing on two legs as it assaulted her. He heard repeated, deep grunts, maybe even the growling of a dog. Before he could run down the street and stop the attack, the animal got on all fours and jumped into a car and sped away."

"Did they get the make and model of the car?" Pierre asked with sudden interest.

"The witness thought it was a new Citroen but couldn't remember the color though."

"They'll get the bastard soon enough," Pierre assured him. He was aroused watching the kid's gestures and emotions describing the unfortunate demise of the young mother. Rene had grabbed his own scrotum and simulated cutting the killer's nuts off. Duvair almost had an orgasm. Recovering from the slight embarrassment, he made a mental note to activate the security monitors he installed when he moved back. It wasn't that long ago that he'd read about the series of prostitutes murdered in Etain. A savage killer is on the loose. For all he knew, the exterminator could even be living next door.

"Are you ready for that cognac now, Rene? You've worked yourself up about the murder. Do they show x-rated movies at the base? In the Legion, we saw them on weekends. Never mind, you need to relax and enjoy your stay with me. We'll have fun." Without waiting for a response, he went back inside the house and retrieved the cognac.

By midnight, they were both drunk. Louie was bored with their rambling conversation and went to his bed. They watched two DVDs portraying three uniformed soldiers sodomizing each other. Initially, Rene was repulsed, but the alcoholic stupor urged him to get bolder. He asked Pierre if he knew any of them or were they just actors. Pierre answered positively by mentioning Hugues Chaban as the tall soldier. Pierre figured it was time to introduce the rope to his house guest. Shocked by his positive response, he led him to a room already rigged for the event.

"Tighter, Pierre, pull tighter. I'm almost to the top of the Swiss Alps," the nude airman shouted.

"Hang in there. Drop the pick ax. You don't need it anymore to scale higher. You're past all the overhanging ledges. Start now, you shouldn't wait any longer, or you'll miss the peak.

"Oh…oh…ah," Rene moaned. He was giddy, lightheaded, and slipping into a lucid, semi-hallucinogenic state. Pierre was amazed at the manhood staring him in the face. The organ resembled a swollen finger shaking at him and pointing like a school teacher disciplining a wayward student.

"A bit longer, and we'll switch places," Pierre coaxed the nearly dead airman clinging close to death. Twenty minutes later, the hanging body went limp.

Why did I let this happen? I could have prevented the young man's death. Yet I have this inner feeling…this great impulse to snuff out life. Why a promising, patriotic male? Did it have anything to do with my being drummed out of the Foreign Legion years ago? Probably a rebellion against authority.

Louie is not going to be happy when he learns of this. He was comfortable with Rene and even let the young man wrestle around with him on the rug. Of course, the tasty goodies he brought for Louie went a long way toward developing a special relationship. I'm jealous. Louie has been indifferent to me lately no matter what treats I tossed at him.

On a cold, dreary evening in an isolated estate, a French airman from Etain-Rouvres Air base met his creator. Pierre went to the bedroom and woke Louie from a deep sleep.

"Come with me, Louie. It's time to take our young friend home."

Louie let out a mumbled growl. He knew what had happened and wanted no part of it.

Pierre tried to persuade Louie by tossing a few of Rene's treats in front of the snub-nosed dog. He didn't budge. Pierre defiantly let loose with curse words that Louie understood but stood his ground.

Frustrated, he dragged the dead man outside by the feet and threw him in the trunk like a shriveled bale of rotten hay. The next morning, Rene Gibeau was discovered in Longuyon draped over a bridge on the Crusnes River, two blocks from the neighborhood where he grew up. The entire left side of his face was missing.

CHAPTER 20

CHICAGO

LAKE SHORE DRIVE WAS BUMPER TO BUMPER as usual on a chilly Monday morning commute. A fender-bender at the Randolph Street exit delayed the traffic flow. Mid-November weather was unusually cold in the city. Downtown residents were hoping for a light snowfall by Thanksgiving, but the weatherman would not sign off on it. The beloved Chicago Bears were contending for the Central Division lead having already beaten the Packers, Lions, and Vikings. Slade Glick had an early appointment at Jon Jon's to have his fingernails and toenails manicured. He was elated when Jon Jon added three Vietnamese women to his staff for the delicate procedures. He would skip the coiffure. He didn't want anybody to mess with it. In his mind, his hair was even more perfect since his melanoma cancer cure.

"Good morning, Jon. Thanks for taking me so early."

"Your schedule must be tight today," the hairdresser suggested with a quick wink of his right eye.

"I should slow down, but I have so much energy to burn off."

"Your body is even more beautiful than before, Mr. Slade. Maybe I should take a trip to Texas and undergo whatever you did."

"I was dying, but miracles do happen, especially if you can afford to foot the bill."

"Are you still dating that Hawaiian queen?"

"She is not a queen, my friend. You are…that is, if I have to remind you again."

Jon laughed. "Oh, stop it. Stop teasing me."

"No, I'm not seeing her anymore."

"Why not, if I can so boldly ask you?"

"If I told you, I'd have to kill you." He laughed so loudly that the Vietnamese woman tending to him shrieked and jabbed his big toe with her sharp instrument.

"Back off, woman," he snarled in pain.

Jon interceded on her behalf, and they settled down, her with a big smile, he with a tight grin, and Jon with a "who cares?" attitude streaked across his heavily made-up face.

He returned to his condo and was greeted by Rocky at the front door. Slade forgot to hustle up giant rats, and his pet reminded him by twisting around his lower legs and pulling him to the floor. Slade unwound the reptile and told him he'd go out and bring home a special treat for him. He drove across town to a pet store and bought a rabbit. When he got back to his condo, he reached into the box, grabbed the rabbit by the ears, and tossed it in the opened door. He then closed it. Slade went downstairs and disposed of the cardboard cage. It was time to go outside and relax in the fresh air. He was in no hurry to go back upstairs and interrupt Rocky's banquet.

An hour later, he returned. Rocky was in the back of the house, and Slade felt the vibes that he didn't want to be disturbed. He made a note on his to-do list to buy more food for his pet. He always seemed to run out at the most inopportune times. He needed him to stay healthy and well-nourished for their nocturnal activities. For some unknown reason, he enjoyed maneuvering around a quiet city in the very late evening. The telephone rang. It was Gar Underwood.

"Hello, Dr. Underwood. What a surprise to hear from you. Are you in town?"

"No, Slade, I'm just checking up on you. How are you feeling?"

"Super good."

"Have you followed up and visited your oncologist like we suggested?"

"Um, not yet. Why should I bother the wacko who didn't have the skills to cure me like you and Dr. Biel?"

"I have a favor to ask you. I hope you can help me."

"Of course, I owe you my life."

"Do you still own that big luxurious schooner down in Miami you told me about?"

"Yes, I plan to go down there next week and take it out of dry dock. Can't wait to get out on the open water again. Why do you ask?"

"I have a proposal, one that could make big money for both of us. Are you interested?"

"Sure, the Slademan never turns down an opportunity to rake in more dough. What do you have in mind?"

"I want to convert the vessel into a floating research laboratory."

"What the hell are you talking about?"

"I need a facility, preferably one on or near the water to cultivate my Conus sea snails. I am going to expand the research that Dr. Biel began, but I'm sorry to say it was suspended."

"Are you working with Biel again? You two made an excellent team. Why did he discontinue developing an astounding discovery for a market willing to pay millions for the cure?"

"He committed suicide a month after you left Texas."

"Oh my god, why?"

"Nobody knows the reason, but he had a severe history of mental illness. I guess he couldn't get the *monkey* off his back. He tried to kill himself when we were back in college, but this time, he was successful. Dr. Biel put a pistol to his head and blew his brains out on the farm in South Texas."

There was a pause in the conversation. Slade didn't hang up but placed the phone down on his desk. He had to think, needed time to run the numbers on this. *Poor Dr. Biel, the terrible stress accumulated throughout the years of dealing with people and their problems. Maybe I can help continue his dedicated work with Dr. Underwood and be a facilitator, an agent for change, a boost for my fellow mankind. On top of my generous gift to society, I can make millions doing it. What the hell, Slade, go for it.*

"I'm in, Dr. Underwood. Are you still on the line?"

"Yes. I thought you'd hung up on me."

"What's the plan?" Slade asked, now breathing in quick gasps. He was excited and couldn't wait to get things rolling.

"Drive down to Miami and get your schooner out of dry dock."

"I already decided to do that."

"Yes, you told me. Do you know where Islamorada is located?"

"Sure, in the Keys. I've sailed by that location many times."

"Good. We need to locate a secure, yet isolated marina. Check out the area near Caloosa Cove. I have a marine biologist friend who lives near the Tavernier Creek Bridge. The guy went to college with Biel and me. He was a football player and an intercollegiate boxer and won several titles in his weight class. Who knows, he might be of assistance to us when we start our project."

"Can I bring my pet snake with me? Rocky loves to sail and shimmies with the undulations of the sea. He won't be a problem, honest."

"Sure, don't see any harm in that. Call me when you get established down there but make it happen soon. I'm having some difficulties keeping my sea snails healthy."

Several days had passed. Slade decided to celebrate his good fortunes. He needed a woman, not just any woman but his Hawaiian princess. He remembered those perfectly tanned, long brown legs wrapped tightly around him screaming for help, a Polynesian strangle hold she'd perfected. The legs ended at perfectly turned ankles and feet to die for. He called Leah Malaka to see if she was available to party with him tonight.

"Why contact me now, Slade? You cast me off like yesterday's leftovers. Now you want me to come crawling back and take care of you. I thought you'd be long dead by now. I've been checking the obits every day in the *Trib*, but I guess I didn't miss anything."

"I have great news to share with you, Leah."

"Tell me something I want to hear."

"I'm cured of my cancer. I can't remember if I told you about my trip to Texas. I underwent an experimental procedure using a one of a kind drug that cures melanoma. It did. I'm a new man."

There was a delay on the line. She didn't know what to tell him. *I really liked him, but that was before he got sick and became the city's number one asshole. He sounds great, energetic, and sweet at the same time. Maybe I should check it out. He's never lied to me before, and of course, the sex was terrific.*

She arrived late He had a carafe of expensive Bordeaux at the ready. He expected her at eight, but it was after midnight when she knocked on the door. She was dressed in white slacks, a green tank top, flip-flops and a plumeria lei decorating her long neck. He became intoxicated with the aroma of the plumeria flower whenever she donned the fragrant plant. She took one long look at him and screeched, shocked at the new appearance.

"Slade, you are actually beautiful. Your skin is so milky, I could drink it. Your nose looks like Charles de Gaulle's but much more Roman. And your eyes, they're brighter and greener, if that's at all possible."

"Thanks for the compliments. Can we go to bed now?"

"No, we need to talk."

"About what?"

"Commitment. It's a word that you may or may not remember the meaning of."

"Refresh my memory, Leah dear."

"Before we hop in the sack, I want and demand a firm guarantee from you. I changed my life around. I'm no longer a high-paid call girl. I'm not the Virgin Mary anymore, that's for sure, but a brand-new person. I mothballed my psychology practice after being recruited by the *Chicago Tribune* as a fashion reporter. You, for one, know how I'm so into high-priced clothing trends. I feel refreshed and enthused."

"Bravo for you. I thought I was the only fashion maven in my circle of friends."

"I demand a change in your selfish life style, if we're to take the next step, Slade."

"Like what do you want me to become?"

"A respectable gentleman no longer imbued with greed and gigantic self-esteem. I know you're rich beyond all means, but that doesn't impress me anymore. Lastly, I want you to become a one-woman man. Can you see yourself moving in that direction?"

"Of course," he lied. "As long as you are the one woman."

"Let's take it in smaller steps and see where it all ends. The first step is not to bed me tonight."

"What? Isn't that a bit drastic? I haven't seen you in ages and missed you so much."

"No, Mr. Glick, not if you want me to be your main squeeze. Denial…denial of excessive animal desires whenever the whim strikes us, that's our defining moment."

Slade sat back and took a long swig of red wine and stared at her. *Good lord, she must be freebasing cocaine. I can't believe what's coming out of those sensuous lips. She's trying to corner my market, and I'm not about to fall into that trap. I enjoy the company of many women, even several at the same time. No living person on earth is going to dictate my behavior now that I am healthy and an obvious gift to the weaker sex.*

"I've heard enough of your nonsense. I'm leaving for Florida in two days, and I need my batteries fully recharged for the trip. Either put out or get out!"

She slapped him hard in the face. Shocked and in disbelief, he whirled around and raced to the back room to let Rocky out. He hadn't fed the pet in days and knew that Rocky would be hungry. The long reptile slithered and wiggled to the living room, but it was too late. She was halfway down the outside hallway to the elevator doors.

CHAPTER 21

EN ROUTE TO FLORIDA

THE TRIP TO FLORIDA WAS UNEVENTFUL until they hit Miami. Slade found few places to let Rocky outside in the rest areas along the route when he got restless and needed to stretch out. He decided not to bring the buggy. It would take too much room in the back of the vehicle. Instead. he brought the large collapsible metal grocery cart he used when shopping at the supermarket to haul his bags of grocery items back home. Using an old bed spread, he improvised a non-descript cover for the conveyance.

It was hard to find an isolated area where his pet could roam freely and forage for food. Rocky loved the outdoors and always fought him when it was time to get back and motor on. He tried to explain the nature of the trip to him and that he would love sailing again. He reminded the pet about the excursions they enjoyed in the past. His words of comfort and reassurance seemed to quiet Rocky and at least placate him for the time being.

"Thanks for calling ahead, mate," the boat storage manager said to Slade upon his arrival at the storage site. "*The Glickster* is cleaned up and ready to go."

"Appreciate that. It's time to set sail again. I've missed her."

"What kept you away so long?"

Slade was in a hurry to get his boat out of storage. He didn't need to discuss his past history with the man. The manager was bored and welcomed any visitor to his storage kingdom. Not many boat owners came in late November to secure their floating treasures.

"Too complicated, my friend. Just take the final steps for me to set sail."

"Where ya headed?"

"The Keys. Why do you ask?"

"There's some bad weather out that way. I keep these weath-er-beaten ears to the nautical channel on my shortwave radio. New Town in Key West just got hammered. How far down the Keys are you sailing?"

"I haven't decided yet." He refrained from sharing specific details about his plan with anyone. Dr. Underwood told him that this entire arrangement was a secret mission—something about advanced research for the government. If successful, they would become famous, with an outside chance for a Nobel Peace Prize nomination. The possibility suited him well. He didn't need any more money, but world-wide recognition would satisfy his inflated ego.

"Where's your crew?" the manager asked.

"I don't have one."

"Did you forget how challenging it is to sail alone, especially with adverse weather conditions staring you in the face?"

"You're right. You have an educated fix on the landscape around these parts better than most folks. Do you know of any experienced hands that might be available to hire on with me?"

"Well, maybe. Pointing to the corner, he said, "See that old man sleeping on the cot. His name is Tiny. He served in the US Merchant Marines and allegedly knows the ropes on the open waters. He helps me do chores around here when he's sober. Offer him a hundred bucks and a bottle of Jack Daniel's, and he'll jump at the opportunity."

"Are there facilities near here where I can park my car for several months?"

"Of course, you forgot that your boat storage contract provides for six months of free parking whenever you take your boat out of dry dock. I'll give you an extra month and charge the going rate of a hundred a month thereafter. Park it in one of the empty slots in our long-term parking lot out front."

"Much obliged. I'll leave my car keys with you if it has to be moved for any reason."

Slade and his new crew member set sail out of Black Point Marina. Getting Rocky aboard *The Glickster* was another problem, but he had foreseen the challenge. Prior to securing his schooner, he went to a hardware store and purchased a trunk large enough to haul his pet wherever he wanted to go. Small air holes were drilled on both ends and layers of straw provided a makeshift bed for his pet. He picked up a small rabbit at a pet shop and tossed it in the trunk. Dinner would be waiting for Rocky when they sailed out of Black Point.

"That fucking snake kill?" the old salt asked when he was introduced to Rocky.

"Only if it dislikes you, Tiny, so be good to him."

"Never been good to any slithering reptile before and don't intend to change my ways this late in life. Just keep him locked up, and we'll get along fine."

"No problem." Slade smiled. *Maybe I'll feed the prick to Rocky when we complete the trip.*

An hour out of port, he called Underwood. "Hello, Doc, Slade calling. Can you hear me?" The answering machine kicked in. "This is Slade Glick, your new research partner, Dr. Underwood. I'm at sea on the way to Islamorada. Just want to keep you informed. I'll call again when I find a marina."

The storm that hit the lower Keys swept south into the Gulf of Mexico. Islamorada was spared. It was an all-night trip struggling with the challenging winds. The hired hand did surprising well, at times offering Slade several suggestions that worked. They arrived in midmorning, docked at Caloosa Cove, and found a restaurant. He needed food and permanent docking information. Tiny needed another bottle of Jack and disappeared with his hundred-dollar bill. It was the last time Slade saw him.

"What'll you have?" the heavyset waitress asked with a wink of her withered right eye.

"Two eggs, over easy, and a half of slab of bacon, burned."

"You mean crisp?"

"No, are you deaf? Burn the hell out of the pig slices."

This time, she winked the other eye and turned in the order. He overheard her telling the cook to "burn the shit out of the bacon." After bantering back and forth with her, he thought the bitch was trying to hit on him. It wouldn't be the first time or the last. He was sure of that. He'd take a rain check on this one strictly for emergency purposes.

"By the way, lady, what do folks around these parts call you?" He figured at least he should get her name.

"Constance. My good friends call me Connie. You can too." She leaned over, put her elbow on the counter, and rested her chin in her right palm. One chubby breast couldn't contain itself in the open-neck blouse and peeked out at him.

"Where can I get info on docking my boat?"

She hesitated answering. She watched the words coming from the most sensuous pair of lips she'd ever seen. An older gent sitting across from the counter sipping a huge mug of coffee did hear Slade and chimed in.

"I might be able to help you out. Tell me about your boat and how long you plan to stay in our beautiful area."

"Who are you?" Slade asked, peeved but loosened up. He hated people with elephant ears always wanting to join in on somebody else's private conversation. "Why do you ask? Do you own a marina?"

"Yes, I do, but it is fairly isolated, so most folks don't know much about it."

"Tell me where," Slade asked, now interested in hearing what the old man had to say. The word *isolated* came through in capital letters.

"Have you heard of Teatable Key?"

"No, where the hell is it?"

"It's northeast of Lower Matecumbe Key, not too far from here. There is a small public beach on the island. I own a marina near a private road that leads to a gated residence. I have my speedboat slot there and one other slip. Potable water and electricity is available. If your boat is not a large ocean-going vessel, it should fit nicely in the slot. Boaters around these waters think the place is on far-away Mars. The slot stays vacant for long periods of time. Are you interested?"

"Yes, take me there after I eat."

"I will. By the way, my name is Hap." After the short introductions, they left the restaurant and walked by *The Glickster* toward his speed boat. He stopped for a few seconds to look back at Slade's boat.

"Wow, you didn't tell me you had a luxurious schooner. I thought we were talking about a tiny sailboat. How long is she?"

"Sixty-five feet and sleeps anywhere from six to eight."

"Tell me more about your prized possession."

Slade beamed. "It's a two-masted, gaff-rigged ball of energy with square top sails. It has a shallow draft with a steel hull, computer-controlled electric winches controlling the sails, and a dedicated power-generation system. It can almost sail itself anywhere she elects to explore."

"I'm impressed," Hap said and whistled in a high pitch.

"Most of my friends are also."

"It should fit in the slip I'm going to show you. The US Coast Guard asked me to construct a dock large enough to accommodate their biggest cutters in case they needed a site for an emergency mission. Being the devout patriot that I am, I agreed. Of course, some of Uncle Sam's cash didn't hurt matters."

They skipped off in Hap's motorboat, weaving in and out of the wakes of a dozen other boats and arrived at Hap's Landing. He said it was named after his grandfather, a seafaring bard who fought in the Spanish American War. Slade was amazed.

This guy had to be pushing eighty and richer than Warren Buffet. He owns half the island.

Hap showed him the complete setup. Slade stepped it off and measured the distance between piers. It would fit in there with ease. Hap offered him a one-year lease provided his schooner wasn't going to be a party boat or a commercial tourist shuttle around the Keys.

"This works for me, Hap. I'll be joined by a friend who is an author and needs the serenity and privacy this place offers to write his books."

"What's his name? I'm an avid reader?"

"I'm sure you never heard of him. He writes scientific journals."

"Forget it, way out of my genre. I prefer those scary paranormal books. I'd better get you back to *The Glickster.* I have several errands to run, and I want to get them done before dark. As you might have noticed, there aren't any floodlights at the marina. I like it that way as I never leave or return here in the dark. I hope that's not a problem."

"No, sir, the darker, the better." Slade laughed and shook hands with Hap, sealing the deal. Dr. Underwood would be right proud of him.

They returned by the most direct route to Caloosa Cove. Hap questioned whether Slade needed another hand to help him maneuver the schooner back to the landing. He was assured that it wasn't necessary. He waved his farewell. Slade liked the man and knew he had an ally living in the area. It was reassuring to know he could call upon the chap if he needed help for anything.

He came aboard to check on Rocky and call Underwood. Rocky was sleeping in the tomb-like box he traveled in. Slade planned to sleep on the schooner tonight and head out to Hap's Landing in the morning. He had to stock up on provisions for both of them. Hap told him there were limited resources available near his marina so better to shop here.

After repeated attempts, he got through to Underwood. "Absolutely perfect, Slade. I couldn't be happier with the setup you described. I plan to drive my Land Rover down there. At least, we'll have one vehicle to get around in if need be. By the way, I found the telephone number of my marine biologist friend. His name is Zack Seltry. Write down his telephone number and call him after we hang up. Give him a heads-up about my planned arrival but don't go into details about our project. I'll brief him after I arrive. I'll see you in three or four days. Thanks so much for all of you efforts. You won't regret it."

He decided to wait until evening to call Gar Underwood's friend. The phone was answered on the first ring.

"Sheriff's Office, Zack speaking. How can I help you?"

CHAPTER 22

TEXAS

J AMIE RICHARDS WAS UPSET AND VISIBLY SHAKEN. His dear Victoria was gone forever. When he returned from San Francisco, his neighbor was waiting for him on the steps of his porch with the terrible news. "I am so sorry, Jamie. I let her out of the cage to partake of much-needed exercise. You had often suggested this whenever I tend to her. I'm sad to say that I left the front door of your house ajar when I came by two days ago. I didn't want to call you. I feel so down and sad about the misfortune."

"Accidents happen, my friend. Don't take it so hard." He had a difficult time containing his own emotions. Grief swelled in his mind. He loved the little jabberer more than he'd ever thought. The neighbor was an outstanding and considerate person.

"But I—"

"Maybe she'll return," Jamie suggested. "She's one tough bird, and I wouldn't doubt for a minute that she'd survive out there on her own."

"I'll buy you another one," his neighbor offered.

"Not necessary. We'll wait and hope. If she doesn't come home, I won't replace her. I travel too much to take care of a pet in the manner they deserve."

It was a long night for him, knowing that he'd never see Victoria again. He decided to call Bobby and share the bad news with him. After explaining about the accident, Bobby was in no mood to offer consolation. In fact, he was cold and brisk.

"You don't need a pet to tie you down the way you rush off at a moment's notice. Shit happens, Jamie. You'll forget about her in time. Anyway, they're a dime a dozen."

"What kind of shit-face response is that?"

Bobby expected the comment but let it slide. "I'm glad you called. I was about to pick up the phone and dial you up."

"What's going on now? You in some kind of trouble again?" Jamie asked sarcastically, not satisfied with the burning remarks about his loss.

"I had a message from Roberto Gomez when I got home. He's been thrown in jail down in Laredo."

"What the—"

"You heard me correctly. You remember me telling you on the airplane about Roberto's frantic telephone call, right? Just to refresh your dormant memory, that asshole Gar Underwood and two state troopers raided my farm and stole my sea snails from the research lab. In the process, they discovered something else."

"Oh no, they found your meth lab in the outbuilding."

"Correct. I was so excited about the new project, I never shut it down. Apparently, Roberto couldn't stop them from searching the entire premise for contraband or whatever the hell those officials were looking for. My guess is that Underwood sent them off on some kind of a scavenger hunt. It gave him time to gobble up my precious sea snails and stow them in his rental car before they returned."

"Did Underwood know about the meth lab?"

"He accidentally stumbled on the meth storage site during one of his walks around the farm. The guy is cunning, street smart, and no doubt was looking for something to hang me."

"So now what?" Jamie asked, forgetting his own misfortunes.

"I called the Laredo jail and spoke with the sheriff. He told me to get down there right away or he'd have the Bexar County Sheriff corral me and haul my ass down there. He said they had to clear the books on the meth operation. The state troopers even snapped some pictures. When I get to Laredo, they will release Roberto on bail."

"Get legal counsel, Bobby."

"Don't need it."

"Why?"

"Think, Jamie, think hard on it. I am a scientist. The government is paying me to do research on the adverse effects of methamphetamine on obese adults of Mexican American descent. I got papers to prove it."

"And who did you bribe to spring with the false documents?"

"Believe it or not, the crook Underwood prepared them for me. He has the skill of a Harry Houdini. Can get out of anything. I had no other recourse but to tell him everything about my side business…even brag about its success. He was eager to know more but told him I had planned to mothball the business."

"Let's hope he leaves it at that," Jamie said.

Bobby nodded in agreement. "We had some downtime when we cured the three cancer patients, and he took out his trusty computer and went to work. He pulled out a copy of another government protocol that he'd worked on and simply swapped out verbiage."

"Will it hold up in court?"

"Probably not, but I know how to do business with our law enforcement friends on the border. My daddy taught me how years ago, a lesson I'll never forget."

"Oh yeah, and how's that?"

"*Mucho dinero*, my friend."

"But wouldn't the official government documentation be enough?"

"Perhaps a conscientious person would have a nearby federal agency validate it."

"I would if I were the sheriff," Jamie asserted.

"You're overlooking the outlier here."

"Outlier?"

"Yep, in this case, Jamie, it's the *mucho dinero* in the same folder as the fake protocol."

"Do you want me to motor down to Laredo with you?"

"No. I'm leaving as soon as we hang up. Roberto is a basket case, and I need to get him out of there before he spills the real beans. I just wanted to keep you in the loop."

Ten minutes after hanging up, Jamie got a call from Maria Serrano. He had to hesitate for a few seconds before responding, curious what she had in mind.

"Hello, Jamie, I am so glad I caught you at home. I was afraid that you'd be gallivanting around in some dark dangerous part of this crazy world of ours."

"Not anymore, Maria. I'm done with that nonsense. I need to shift into high gear on my schooling before they toss me out of the program. Anyway, I'm down in the dumps right now."

"Why, someone I know passed away?"

"Actually, yes… It's Victoria. Remember the Myna bird Father Lawrence gifted me? My neighbor accidently let her fly the coop when he was petsitting for me. He let her out of the cage not remembering that he hadn't shut the front door of the house. I'm hoping she has homing pigeon genes and flies back here."

"I'm so sorry. I know how much you loved that bird...almost as much as me, right?"

"Um, it sure is nice that you called. I thought for sure I was history."

"No, silly man, I tried to forget about you many times, but you constantly resurfaced in my head. Do you miss me?"

He hesitated, wanting to be sure he said the right things without backing himself into a corner. "Of course, Maria, but I thought you broke it off with me after the last time we chatted. You were mad as hell, even tossed the 'conquering hero' crap in my face. I thought I'd never hear your sweet voice again."

"Somehow, I knew we'd get together. When can I drop by?"

"Hold on a minute. Where are you now?"

"I'm at my new home as we speak. I moved to San Antonio and bought a house in Stone Oak. The neighborhood is located north of Loop 1604."

"Don't tell me you accepted that job transfer with Civil Service."

"I did. Yours truly is the new billeting officer at Fort Sam Houston."

"Congratulations! That's a big jump from a simple clerk to head honcho, I might add."

"You should know me by now, Jamie. I interview well, blew 'em out of their chairs. The main man with the approval authority served with Daddy in the same tank unit at Hood. Networking always pays off. It didn't hurt that we conducted a portion of the interview in Spanish."

Listening to that honey-crusted voice, punctuated by an occasional sigh turned him into putty...putty in the hands of a seasoned sculptress. She could do that to him, anytime, anywhere. Maria Serrano always got what she wanted.

Maybe I was too quick to dump her. She's glad Vic is out of my life now, so she can have me full time. I'm getting older. I need to settle down, have some kids. That's what she wants. Perhaps I should accommodate her. Making a baby would be fun. Never had a lady with that thought in mind.

"Why don't you come over, or are you still at work?"

"I'll be there in thirty minutes. I took the afternoon off, had some comp time coming. We'd been working day and night on a big base housing project that we completed yesterday."

"Let me give you directions to my house."

"Not necessary, sweetie. I've driven by your place a dozen times. Your address is in the phone directory, and my GPS is a crown jewel. I hesitated to stop and knock on the door. I don't fare well with rejections, especially from those I have a fuzzy feeling for. I'll be there before you know it."

When she walked in, he glanced at her with a stare that could penetrate steel.

What a specimen of femininity, not a blemish, scar, or tattoo on that magnificent body. I forgot she was tall but slimmer than I remembered. I'm thankful she doesn't wear all those gadgets and trinkets women feel necessary to attract the opposite sex. She doesn't look a day past forty. Not an ounce of extra fat on her light brown body. Ah, God help me!

The sex was unworldly, and astronauts would be proud of them. Maria was the aggressor—no foreplay, no distractions, no bird squawking in the background, no traffic outside, only tons of built-up sexual anxiety being turned loose in his humble abode. He gave in and didn't use any protection. She appreciated his unconditional surrender, knowing that she could get pregnant. They did it from every angle. She tossed in a new one that he'd never imagined possible. She called it the sky-hook-swoop. They kissed, caressed, and uttered words during the act that neither heard nor cared. Four hours later, Jamie suggested they shower and go out to eat. He was famished. She didn't object. She had her fill of him, and that was enough.

"Suit yourself, woman, but this man lives on three squares a day. I need sustenance to continue operating this body at such a high octane level. You should know that by now."

"Bullshit, Jamie. You're no different from any other man in that regard. I mean, the eating requirement. By the way, I like your house, at least the part of it I saw until you coaxed me into the bedroom."

"Turn on the boob tube and relax. I'll be back in twenty minutes with some fried chicken from Church's."

On his way to the fast-food joint, he received a call from Bobby. It didn't sound good.

"What? Oh shit, I don't believe it! Say that again. A helicopter picked you up on the rooftop of your apartment and whisked you off to Laredo. You had to get down there that soon?"

"Yes, of course. My Roberto Gomez has been beaten up and is in a holding cell in a jail across the border in Nuevo Laredo."

"You mean he's in a rotten Mexican jail now?"

"As we speak. The state troopers had released him to the local sheriff in Laredo. When the higher-ups learned he was an illegal immigrant, they lugged him across the border. He was tossed in the steel can, awaiting further action."

"What further action do they anticipate?"

"The Mexican officials think he's part of the Los Zetas organization."

"Because of the tie-in with the meth lab?"

"Don't know for sure."

"Well, what in the hell do you know?"

"They did buy my explanation and paperwork documenting my bogus study of obesity in Mexican American adults. The Laredo magistrate is in the process of releasing the hold on the outbuilding where the meth lab is located."

"So they declared that you were not a part of the Zeta organization, but Roberto was a card-carrying member because he was here illegally? Come on, Bobby, lay it out for me. I'm getting confused."

"I think everybody on our side of the border decided to wash their hands of the whole mess. It was an easy decision to free me because I am a legal citizen. On top of that, I'm authorized to do the important research. It was a different story for Roberto. In their eyes, he belonged back in Mexico."

"What now? I suggest you leave Roberto alone and come home."

"I can't let him rot in a Mexican lockup. He'll die before their court system gets around to him. We need to go to Mexico and break him out of jail."

"What do you mean by *we*? Have you been snorting your home-made crystal, for Christ's sake? The Zetas are the most dangerous cartel in Mexico. They spring criminals out of prison like it was kid's play. You need a small army for that to happen."

"Jamie, you know how to handle adversity. You've maimed and killed the worse kind of animals on earth. We have one element going for us, and it's major. He's not in a maximum-security prison where the Zetas strike when they want to break out groups of their gang members. After feeling sorry for me, the Laredo sheriff told me the exact location of the holding jail. It's on the outskirts of Nuevo Laredo and minimally staffed by municipal police."

"Look, Bobby, I'm tied up right now. Let me think on it, and I'll call you in the morning."

"Absolutely not. We've got to move on it right now. If you don't leave San Antonio in the next few minutes, I'll do it myself, you chicken shit!"

"Hold your horses, you damn idiot. I'm on my way."

Jamie went back home, packed his Bul M-5, Yarborough knife, and a small supply of C-4 explosives with assorted detonators. Maria was stunned and disappointed with his one-minute explanation.

"So here you are again, soldier man. Off to war and not giving a loved one any consideration. You haven't changed a bit, Jamie. The consummation of our lasting love for each other that took place between the sheets meant nothing to you. Don't expect me to be here when you get back home...in the flesh or in a goddamn wooden box!"

CHAPTER 23

LAREDO

THE STRIP MAP TO THE JAIL HOUSE was accurate. Earlier, Bobby had visited his banker friend where the balance of his million-dollar deposit still remained. On his way to meet Jamie, he remembered the conversation and stern warning he had received from the banker after divulging his secret arrangement to free Roberto.

Don't do anything stupid, Bobby. The Los Zetas have everybody in their back pockets including city and law enforcement officials. I'm originally from Nuevo Laredo and was raised in the El Remolino neighborhood. My home is a few blocks from the jail you intend to visit. I scribbled a map for you and remember, trust no one, and get the hell out of there as fast as you can!

He met Jamie at the designated truck stop on I-35 near the outskirts of Laredo. Jamie parked in the back of the gas station and unloaded two backpacks into the trunk of Bobby's car. At the last minute before leaving, he threw in a pair of night vision goggles and a sawed-off shotgun his dad passed on to him. His sister was also fond of guns and pissed when the father bypassed her. He climbed in with his carryout of Church's fried chicken. They snacked on the cold chicken tenders and flushed them down with swigs of whisky Bobby brought from home.

"I'm glad you're here, Jamie."

"Thanks. What's the program?"

"Roberto is still in a holding cell. He's awaiting further transfer to a federal maximum security prison on the far southern edge of the city. According to my banker friend, our target jail is located in a remote area of Nuevo Laredo and lightly guarded. He told me the building is old and constructed of adobe and brick. The last time he visited his mother, he had occasion to drive by the site. He informed me that the structure was falling apart at the seams."

"How do you intend to cross the border? Swim the Rio Grande?"

"Not quite. We're going over on the Texas Mexican Railway International Bridge and, in some cases, underneath it." He was surprised at Bobby's detailed planning effort.

"Why not hop a train?"

"Too well-guarded."

"I can't believe there are many people trying to sneak into Mexico." Jamie laughed.

"It's been known to happen. How do you think Roberto got to see his parents before they died?"

Jamie hesitated to respond, still hung up on their proposed point-of-entry excursion.

"He wasn't a US citizen, stupid. Have another swig of rot gut."

They bantered back and forth, waiting for dusk. The plan was to drive into Laredo proper and park several blocks away from the railroad terminal. When darkness set in, they would skirt the manned barriers and maneuver to the tracks from below. Crossing to the other side, they would hike to the Calle Victoria road and head west toward the El Remolino area. The brush and undergrowth was abundant, and if they needed more cover, they could traverse the unimproved terrain most of the way to their target.

"Let's do it, Bobby. It's dark enough now."

Jamie could feel the tremors coming on again, followed by excessive sweating and rapid heartbeat. He remembered Father Lawrence back at Fort Hood and the way he framed his words when granting him absolution for his sins.

"I'm glad you're getting out of the Army, Jamie. You have a whole new world ahead of you to thrive in—a life devoid of killing and maiming other human beings. I've given you absolution for your sins, so you should leave here with a clean soul and healthy conscience. Good-bye and go forth and serve the Lord to your fullest."

Would the good priest forgive me again for what I'm going to do tonight? Does the absolution have a short or long shelf life? I probably have to kill again, the human trait indelibly etched in my DNA. I'm going to hell anyway for the sins I've committed in the past even though sanctioned by my government. It doesn't matter that Father Lawrence's intervened on my behalf.

"Jamie, Jamie, snap out of it! You're mumbling incoherently and shaking like a hula dancer gone wild. What the hell is wrong with you?"

"Nothing. Forget it. Move out."

They strapped on their backpacks and executed the plan. The railroad landing on the US side was temporarily shut down for repairs. This was an unexpected bonus for them as busy repair crews were busily laying a section of new track. There were no security guards or border control personnel at the site. Halfway across the railroad bridge, a spotlight shone twenty yards ahead of them.

"Down, Bobby. We need to crawl under the bridge for cover."

"Right, something is happening on the Mexico side."

They scurried underneath the bridge in time to witness a self-propelled railgrinder maintenance car roll overhead. Two railroad workers were aboard the conveyance, laughing and talking in loud Spanish.

"What the hell was that all about?" Bobby asked, unable to interpret the conversation because of the loud racket above them.

"They're vehicles used to restore the profile of worn rail track by removing irregularities from the track. We used a prototype when I was in Special Forces training. They make deadly combat vehicles when mounted with .50 caliber machine guns with night vision capability."

"Did you ever use one in combat?"

"Hell no, they had no flexibility and were moving targets."

"You probably used camels. I heard they were spitting-good combat vehicles."

"Shut the fuck up, Bobby. Get your mind back to the operation at hand."

After waiting an hour, they made their way to the other side of the bridge to the border without further incident. There were no uniformed police in sight. They only saw maintenance workers tending to the specialized equipment. One crew was mounting new floodlights on a cargo receiving platform. They easily bypassed the workers and stopped to rest.

Bobby took out the strip map for a quick review and surveyed the area. "There's the Calle Victoria." He pointed ahead of them. "We'll turn west there and walk several miles to the jailhouse. There's plenty of cover off to the right if we encounter heavier traffic. These folks must hit the sack early around here."

"Don't count on it."

"I won't."

Jamie took out his night vision goggles and scanned the area immediately ahead. He saw some flashlight activity a hundred yards down the road. He pulled Bobby aside, and they knelt down.

"Something's going on ahead of us near the target area. We need to take cover in the bushes and wait till it's clear. Maybe the Federales suspect a jail break, or maybe it's a group of youngsters on a night bike ride. Either way, we don't want to be seen here."

They waited thirty minutes until the activity ahead ceased before they struck off again. Ten minutes later, they saw the jail in front of them and huddled behind a parked car. He gave Bobby the double-barrel shotgun, twenty rounds of ammunition, and two flash bangs or stun grenades as the military preferred to label them. Jamie opted for a better vantage point to complete his surveillance of the property and surroundings. He located a monument across the street from the jail that had thick bushes on each corner of the small plat.

"Stay here behind the car while I go to the monument and reconnoiter the entire area."

"But what—"

"Stop talking so loud and whisper," Jamie said. "I need to get a closer look to see what we're facing."

"Be extra careful. Roberto and I are depending on you."

Jamie crossed the street, and tiptoed to the monument. The jail house was lit up with dim external floodlights, half of them flickering on their way to full burnout status. The two-story adobe structure was literally coming apart at every corner of the edifice. Pock marks in the old building showed where bricks were once embedded. The jailhouse was smaller than his fifteen-hundred-square-foot home in San Antonio. Four tiny windows were located on each floor, the openings secured with iron bars. The wooden door entrance to the jail had no security bars. A peephole was in the top right hand corner of the door. Jamie had seen enough. He had a plan and walked back to Bobby still sitting on the curb by the parked car.

"We're going to sit here and wait another hour."

"Why not spring into action now? We don't have all night."

"I want to be sure of two things—first the traffic density. There can't be any cars or trucks operating in the area when we strike. And then, I want to see if there's a shift change at midnight."

"Anything else, Commander Richards?" Bobby was getting impatient.

"Yes. Judging by the size of the building, there can't be more than four holding cells in the entire complex. I'm sure the prisoners are incarcerated upstairs. From my training experience in a SWAT drill, downstairs should house the office, a kitchen, and a sleeping room for the staff. My guess is that there are two policemen in there."

"How did you come to that conclusion?"

"Intelligence gathering. That's what I'm getting paid big bucks for, right?"

"Yeah, of course, but I don't pay as well as your Cyclops tosses government money around. You better not be wrong here because I'm rushing upstairs to free Roberto when we barge in."

"Hold your horses, Tonto. You'll do what I tell you."

They waited another hour and no shift change occurred. There wasn't any traffic. The last vehicle observed was a beaten-up truck barking down the street without a muffler. It passed by an hour ago. Jamie reviewed the plan. They moved to the monument, waited another fifteen minutes, and walked to the jailhouse door. Bobby took a position immediately behind Jamie, partially concealed by a twin wooden pillar. Jamie rapped loudly, three times, and repeated the sequence of knocks three more times. There was no response.

"Anybody home?" Bobby whispered but knew better.

"Count on it."

They held tight for five minutes, and still nobody inside acknowledged the staccato raps on the jail door. Jamie turned back to Bobby and shrugged his shoulders as if to suggest something funny was going on inside. His partner was at ready with the shotgun loaded and cocked.

"Lower that damn cannon and get your stun grenade ready. I'm going to kick the door open," Jamie ordered while double-checking his Bul M-5 to ensure that a round was chambered with the safety off.

"Aye, aye, Captain Jamie."

Jamie took one step closer to inspect the wooden door for the best location to stomp it in. The dim overhead light showed an iron-plate housing the handle that was reinforced with thick metal—not an option. He noticed a foot long crack in the left center of the door adjacent to the middle hinge which looked vulnerable. Inspecting more closely, he peered through the wide crack and saw a uniformed guard prone with his face plastered to the cement floor. He turned and whispered his finding to Bobby.

"I see one on the floor—sleeping, drunk, or pretending to be passed out."

"Who would've guessed that?"

It was time to strike. The door shattered on impact. Bobby lunged forward and tossed the flash bang into the anteroom. The guard on the floor came alive when it bounced past him. He took a kneeling position and tossed aside the empty bottle of tequila he had been hugging. The last thing they witnessed before the explosion was the guard reaching for his service revolver.

Bobby and Jamie closed their eyes and covered their ears while a blinding flash of light, and loud noise erupted. The concussive blast of the detonation was intensive enough to disorient anybody down-stairs. The guard was sent sprawling backward to the floor; his pistol fell from his hand skipping out of reach. They waited a few more seconds and rushed in.

Jamie shouted to no one in particular. "Drop your weapons, or I'll kill you."

He didn't see the blur coming at him from his left. Five steps inside the jail, Jamie was hammered across the chest with a lead pipe.

He fell hard to the floor on top of the stunned guard. His Bul M-5 slipped aimlessly from his hand bouncing along the damp floor.

Bobby hesitated long enough to witness the big brute winding up for another swing, this time aimed at his own exposed head. He ducked under a vicious whiff and blew the attacker in half with the first blast of the sawed-off shotgun.

"Go to hell, you scum bastard!" he yelled as bits and pieces of bloody flesh and slimy intestines spewed out of the dead man's belly blanketing his partner still dazed on the floor. Jamie had escaped the rain of body parts by rolling off the screaming Mexican and secured his Bul M-5. He looked toward the stairway and saw a third guard running up to the next level for cover. He tapped out three shots to the back of the half-dressed guard's head.

"Watch out, Jamie!" Bobby hollered at the top of his voice. "The bubba on the floor found his gun." He started to reload the double barrel shotgun, forgetting that he had a second round still chambered.

Jamie spun around, Yarborough knife clutched in his right hand, and skewered the guard in the throat twisting the big knife upward and outward until it peeked out of his opened mouth. He jerked the dagger out of the wound, wiped the blood off on his trousers, and grabbed the man by his right ear. Bobby knew what was on his agenda.

"Christ Almighty, don't cut his ears off, you blood-sucking idiot."

"Shut up and mind your own business!"

"Listen up, I hear shouts from upstairs. We need to get Roberto out of here right now before reinforcements arrive. Let that dead bastard die with his ears still glued to that fat head."

Jamie hesitated briefly and then released the dead guard while trying to discern the meaning of the garbled words wafting down from the stairwell. Bobby took the stairs two at a time, veered around the dead guard at the top of the landing, and noticed four cell blocks—two on the left and two to his right. Three of the units with opened steel gates stared blankly back at him. There wasn't a prisoner inside any of the trio of cells. Jamie followed a close step behind his friend. They arrived at the only gated cell where the unintelligible shouting was coming from.

Bobby peered into the darkened corner of the cell at the frightened old man holding his arms over his head. He wasn't sure the withered, beaten man was Roberto. There was not enough light.

He shouted in perfect Spanish, "Who the hell are you?" He was shocked at the weak response.

"*Yo soy Alejandro Espinoza.*"

CHAPTER 24

TEXAS

A FTER THEIR FAILED ATTEMPT to extract Roberto Gomez from the Nuevo Laredo holding jail, they made their way back across the border without incident. Bobby was depressed and kept blaming himself for coming up empty. The remaining prisoner in the jail told them Roberto had been moved earlier in the day to the maximum-security prison on the other side of town. They decided it was too risky to attempt springing him from the fortress-like facility.

"Let's head back to San Antonio," Bobby said reluctantly. "I can't do anything more about him. He'll rot in that miserable place or even be executed on trumped-up charges. It's a first-class snake pit."

"Maybe you can find a lawyer who knows the Mexican penal system and free him through some appeals process."

"Good point. I'll look into it when we get home. Meanwhile, let's blow this place. You drive."

There wasn't much conversation during the ride home. Bobby was curled up sleeping in the backseat. They were hungry and frustrated. Jamie knew his friend would find a way to get Roberto out of that hell hole. He was resourceful, had the right connections and the money to make it happen. But he would put it on the back burner.

All he talked about before conking out was getting even with that prick Gar Underwood for stealing his sea snails and causing this entire rotten mess. They hit the outskirts of San Antonio when he woke up.

"Take me to Earl Abel's, and we'll get some breakfast," Bobby ordered.

"Sounds good to me, that fried chicken we gobbled down is long gone."

"So what's the plan?" Jamie asked him after the waitress picked up the dirty dishes, slipped the check under the napkin container, and began to wipe off the table.

"You know me better than to ask such a stupid question, Richards. I'm going to New York and settle up with that dirty thief. I still have a hard time coping with his traitorous act."

"And what are you going to do when you catch up with him?"

"Nothing."

"Huh?" Jamie shrugged his shoulders.

"I am not going to do a thing. You are."

"Oh no, Mr. Biel, it's your conflict, not mine."

"I'll pay you to kill him. Lots of money, Jamie. You'd know the best way to pull it off. Let's face it. You are a mercenary at heart, trained in the nuances of stalking the enemy and eliminating him at all costs. I can't do that. You know I'm a scientist."

"Bullshit, Biel, you did just fine down there in Mexico. Clean up your own damn mess."

"Are you telling me you won't do it for your best friend?"

"Yes, I mean no."

"Screw it, I don't need your help. Take me home now."

Jamie dropped him off at his apartment on Houston Street and drove down Broadway to Alamo Heights. Rush hour was underway, and he encountered an accident at the intersection with Hildebrand.

While waiting for the traffic cop to untangle the mess, he figured she'd be there waiting for him. He remembered how the situation played out after he returned from Somalia. The same scenario happened again. She wasn't there when he walked in. There was a note propped up on the desk next to his computer.

Jamie dear, call me when you get home. I'm sorry I said what I did when you rushed out of here to help your best friend. I'll make it up to you. With much love, Maria.

He called her immediately but soon hung up, knowing that she was at work and didn't want to leave a message. He'd catch up with her tonight and maybe surprise her with a dozen roses. He felt guilty. She deserved better. He fixed a pot of coffee, sat down on his favorite soft chair, and reflected back to Bobby's drastic plea to kill Gar Underwood. *Perhaps I should do some preliminary legwork for him and gather the latest intelligence on the wayward scientist. Surely, Underwood has gone underground with his prized snails. Where would he go? How can I find out?*

The obvious answer hit him squarely between his eyes—his Navy SEAL buddy, Denis Sweeny.

"Is national security involved in this personal vendetta, Richards?"

"Well, maybe indirectly."

"Be more specific."

"This mad scientist might be developing some kind of biological warfare agent for all we know." Jamie filled him in on the background, embellishing the story where appropriate. He wouldn't outright lie to Sweeny but needed an element of urgency to solicit his help. "In the devious hands of conniving radicals, those snails could contaminate a municipal potable water supply."

"The agency doesn't subscribe to witch hunts." Sweeny was curt but polite.

"What's with you? Having a bad day?"

"I've had a rough few weeks solving the dilemma in San Francisco and need space, lots of space, and comp time to return to normal"

"What happened in my favorite city?"

"My team recovered twelve high-explosive charges wired to one of the underwater towers supporting the Golden Gate Bridge. The hardware they used was sophisticated, Richards. We hadn't encountered the wiring schematic before. On an anonymous tip, three radical Islamists were found with remote detonators on a boat anchored in a Sausalito harbor."

"I bet it was that sweetheart agent of yours who uncovered the plot."

"How'd you guess? She figured the person who wired the explosives was a left-handed dyslexic. In any event, their hairy asses are sitting in Guantanamo while the government is sorting out which federal agency will prosecute them...the usual jurisdictional bullshit we have to live with."

"Congratulations for a job well done."

"Thank you, soldier boy."

"Now one last time, will you help me out?"

There was a long pause on the line. Jamie didn't know if he got cut off or whether Sweeny was considering his request. After what seemed like a five-minute pause, he came back on the line.

"Help you out with what?"

Jamie knew immediately that his SEAL friend had been under tremendous stress. He sensed that Cyclops's life of jumping in and out of life-threatening scenarios was catching up to him. He repeated his need for assistance.

Sweeny balked, then said, "I guess I comprehend the importance of the distorted facts you presented me. I'll take a chance and move on it. Send me all the information you have on this mysterious Dr. Gar Underwood."

Jamie went to bed, exhausted and completely frustrated with his truncated life. Wrestling with a thousand what ifs, he succumbed to sleep minutes before noon.

On the other side of town, Bobby was too charged up to sleep. He decided to test the waters at the Menger and knock down a few Sam Adams in Teddy's Tavern. He always met interesting people when his high school acquaintance was not behind the bar and bending his ears. Six people were enjoying the historical rendition of the saloon conducted by a female bartender he had not seen before. He got bored and left.

His head was throbbing and signaled a need to catch some shuteye right away. On his walk home, he zigzagged through a large group of international geologists congregating in Alamo Plaza. They were rehashing their controversial last session of the day. Ten minutes later, he was in his apartment, consumed with the idea that he had to find Underwood as soon as possible. Before he went to bed, he called him. When he dialed him up in New York, he got a weird message on Underwood's answering machine. He played it back three times and still couldn't make sense out of it. The message was brief. "Hello sports fans. I'm out to sea, gone fishing for fun, and will return your call when I get my catch. Ta ta."

At six in the evening, Jamie was startled by his cell phone jumping up and down on his bedside stand yelling crazy things at him. He swore he'd find a different setting for announcing an incoming call. He grabbed it before it reverted to the message mode. It was Sweeny.

"I found your guy, Richards. He's in Florida."

"What in the hell is he doing there?"

"Don't know. Not my job to find out. You asked me to locate him, and I did."

"Where in Florida?"

"In the Keys on a small island, not far from Islamorada."

"Is he alone?"

"No, he's living aboard a boat with some dude named Slick or Glick. My agent said his conversation with an informer got muddled up. Be my guest and draw your own conclusions on the name."

Jamie was dumbfounded. *What in the hell are those two jokers up to? I bet they are developing another cancer cure with Biel's snails. Bobby will have apoplexy and never recover if he finds out what they're up to.*

"Thank you so much, Denis. I really appreciate it."

"You owe me one, Richards."

"Name it."

"There's some preliminary talk about another mission to Somalia. This time, it's a hostage situation. You're at the top of my list to lead it."

"Shit, Denis. I'm no longer a part of Delta Force. I put all that behind me long ago. You're well aware of that. Stop pulling my leg."

"Bullshit. People like you never change."

"I have. I'm seeing a shrink now," he lied. "He thinks I suffer from a chronic case of post-traumatic stress related to my combat days. He told me if I didn't want to go out the way of suicide, I had to give up running around and killing people."

"I always knew you were crazy. Why change course now?"

There was a pause in the discussion until Jamie said, "Thanks for the info, buddy. Got to run. Take good care."

He picked up the phone to call Bobby and report his findings from Sweeny. Instead, he hesitated for a brief moment and decided to call Maria first. She had just walked in the front door of her house and caught the call on the final ring.

"I'm glad you're home safe and sound. You got my message, right?"

"Yes, and I appreciate the thoughtfulness," he said sincerely. She felt his emotions vibrate through the telephone line.

"Don't start dinner, Maria. How about going to the Barn Door for a steak?"

"Sounds great. Do you want to meet there?"

"No, I'll bring a bottle of champagne to your house. We'll have a cozy chat before we chow down."

When he walked in, she put a choke-hold on him and kissed him hungrily on his lips, cheeks, and neck. He set the bottle of bubbly in the ice bucket on the kitchen table and led her to the bedroom. They undressed each other, slowly and passionately. They switched roles, and he became the aggressor. Their lovemaking was rough, quick, and wordless—animalistic in nature and without emotion. They showered together but washed separately, a ritual she always preferred because he was one…two…three and done.

"Let's eat. I'm famished." She always skipped lunch, a habit she developed years ago trying to keep off extra poundage. It didn't work. She made up for it at the evening meal. She wasn't overweight, but he knew if she ever became pregnant most of the gestational gains would hang around forever.

"Not yet. We have to polish off the bottle of Moet."

"But, Jamie, it's been a long day. I need to eat, not drink."

"I understand. We'll get a drink at the Barn Door."

Bobby called him as the car swung into the restaurant parking lot. She gave him a mean glare, hoping he'd let it click to the answering mode. She hated cell phones; they controlled everyone's lives, not the other way around, the way it was meant to be. Surprising her, Jamie didn't answer. He climbed out of the car, came around to her side, and opened the door. He leaned over and kissed her on the cheek as she exited the vehicle.

"I love you, Mr. Richards," she whispered when they approached the entrance. The restaurant wasn't crowded, which pleased both of them. They needed the relaxed atmosphere to continue their serious talk. She ordered an appetizer to quell the hunger pains while he was satisfied with a glass of ice water. They didn't say a word to each other while they ate. All they talked about after dinner was how super their steaks tasted.

He wanted to go back to her house and open a second bottle of chilled Moet. She told him she was worn out and had a big day ahead starting at sunrise. Fort Sam Houston was undergoing a manpower survey geared for personnel cuts. The billeting office was reputed to be the second most overstaffed support activity on post. She was prepared to plead her case but had to be well-rested to fight the bureaucrats. He dropped her off in front of her house and went straight home to return Bobby's call. He knew Biel would be sitting on his phone waiting for him to respond.

"What's up, Biel?"

"Something strange is going on with Underwood. He's not home, and he's not in New York."

"Where is he?" Jamie was leading him on. He knew the situation down to the exact dirty detail. He waited for Bobby to elaborate.

"Fucking gone fishing somewhere."

"So what's your next move?"

"I made airplane reservations. I'm flying to the Big Apple tomorrow morning. I'll track him down. No thanks to you, my so-called friend who never comes through for me."

"Are you home alone?"

"No, I got two of Hooter's finest twin peaks sitting on my lap drinking mimosas, you idiot. Of course I am!"

"I'm on my way to your apartment. Sit tight."

"Why? It's getting late."

"I have some breaking news about your mischievous friend."

"You mean Gar Underwood?"

"No, Albert Einstein, you former hare-lipped nerd."

"Stop your idiotic oration. What breaking news?"

"I got Underwood in my crosshairs."

"Get your sorry ass up here right away, Richards. We can't afford to lose any more time."

CHAPTER 25

FLORIDA

GAR UNDERWOOD HATED FLORIDA with a passion. He was bugged by the high humidity, overcrowded freeways and gobs of senior citizens elbowing their way to the early evening discount at overpriced restaurants. His parents retired in Orlando with a host of other seniors from New York. They were dead now, remained ensconced in an isolated graveyard bordering a pest-infested swampland far south of the city. It was raining and getting dark outside. He hated to drive with opposing headlights and windshield wipers distracting him. Outside of Miami, he called Slade Glick for specific directions to the pickup point they discussed last week. The phone rang. Nobody answered, so he left a message. He repeated the call an hour later and got the same disappointing results. He found a motel at the next interstate exit.

AROUND MIDNIGHT slade woke up from a brief nap. He had a headache, sore muscles, and a dry mouth. His body had morphed again, his head and upper body resembling a larger African rock python. He thought he'd heard the phone ring earlier but wasn't about to be bothered by some obnoxious caller at night. Rocky was curled up next to him in a deep sleep. He was allowed to roam freely on board and preferred to stretch out on the open deck absorbing the late afternoon sun. Slade would scoot him down to the lower deck if any activity took place near the marina.

"Are you ready to take your nightly stroll?" Slade asked his pet. "We'll go across the water and find a good place to exercise." The thunder and lightning had subsided. Rocky didn't respond to him. He was getting tired of his master's late-night stalking and killing other humans. He was satisfied to capture and devour the four-legged morsels caged in the next compartment and didn't need any more excitement.

"I said let's go, Rocky. It's time." The snake understood the urgency in Slade's voice and started to flex his muscular body.

The scheme for the evening had to be aborted. He had a major problem lowering the Zodiac from the hoist. The cable jackknifed and locked in place. He couldn't untangle the jammed links because his arms had begun to morph back into his body. In a fit of anger, he kicked the snake and decided to wait until morning to rectify the situation. The Zodiac was left at half mast for the remainder of the night.

The pair only had one successful hunt since docking at Hap's Landing, and it was not a good experience. They almost got caught by a sheriff's deputy on a stormy morning before daybreak. Slade had maneuvered his Zodiac water craft to a small marina at Islamorada several nights after arriving and located a small park within walking distance. He had a special carrying case for Rocky and was never questioned about its contents. The black carrying case for a large tuba musical instrument served the purpose. A bronze-plated *R* was affixed to the left side. The container had a four-inch roller mounted at the base for ease of movement. When loaded, the case was heavy, so he didn't like to venture too far wheeling his pet on foot.

Slade relived that night several times in his dreams. It was the first non-Chicago lady he did. In his mind, she tasted better than his other victims, a little sweeter than the bitter taste he'd experienced before.

"Who are you?" she asked in a shaky and frightened quiver as he came up beside her. She gasped when she saw the outline of the triangular-shaped head.

"A musician on my way home from band practice. What kind of dog is that you're walking?"

She didn't answer and increased her pace. Five yards ahead of the stalker, the black Labrador broke free from his tether and circled back to Slade. Anticipating an attack from the growling animal, he opened the case and Rocky lurched out. The dog stopped in his tracks, showing sharp fangs with intermittent barking. The girl screamed. Rocky knocked the dog to the ground on the first lunge and wrapped his body around the Labrador's chest, pinning him to the wet grass. The lady watched in shock as the snake started to squeeze the life out of her charge.

"Interesting how the forces of nature entertain us," he said with a wide grin.

He didn't see her withdraw a police whistle from her purse. She blew it as hard as she could several times. It startled Rocky, and he temporarily relaxed the coiling action constricting the dog's chest. Slade jerked back and covered his ears. The dog got up and began snapping at Slade. It didn't see Rocky slither toward him. The serpent mounted the bewildered dog again with twisting, turning propulsions.

"You are going to die, woman," Glick said with a high-pitched voice and mounting excitement.

"Please! No... No... I'm—"

He threw her to the ground and held her down until Rocky maneuvered his muscular trunk around her chest. Rocky quashed every breath of air out of her lungs. The vicious process took less than fifteen minutes. He got up and positioned the limp body next to her dead dog, both without heartbeats and each with crushed chests. He knelt down and fondled her—licking, licking, licking her pretty face, her sinewy arms, and her long legs. He reached into his pocket and pulled out a rubber snake. He tried to shove it in her mouth but couldn't force it past her clenched teeth.

He poked a hole in her esophagus with his box cutter knife and wiggled the snake through the bleeding orifice.

"Hurry, Rocky, get back in your case. I see headlights approaching."

On closer inspection, Slade saw a vehicle with opened windows pulling up to the curb across the street from the park. A tall man slid out of the driver's side, panning the western edge of the park with a high beam flashlight.

"He's looking for us, Rocky."

Slade changed directions and jogged to the opposite end of the wooded area to the pathway where he initially entered the park. He was lightheaded and breathing under great duress pulling the pet case with his stubby arms.

"That lousy excuse for a woman must have alerted another passerby with that stupid whistle. Somebody around here called the cops." Rocky whacked the inside of the carrying case with his tail acknowledging Slade's frustration.

As he rolled the case aboard the moored schooner, he saw the sheriff's patrol car racing down an adjacent street with red lights whirling and a loud siren announcing to the whole world that an emergency situation struck the small island.

The sun poked its head through a flat mushroom cloud as he got up to pee. He was exhausted and couldn't figure out why his body ached so much. Peeling off his sweaty pajama bottoms, he noticed the red light blinking on the antiquated but dependable answering machine. He listened intently forgetting that he was supposed to tell Gar Underwood where he'd meet him in Islamorada.

The hell with it! He can wait. I need sleep, and I need it right away. He's sacked out in a luxury hotel on Miami Beach. At noon, I'll call the number he left for the return call. I sure as hell wish he'd get here soon.

"Where in the world have you been, Glick? We were supposed to hook up last night. Why did you stiff me?"

"Sorry about that, Dr. Underwood. I didn't have my cell phone when the EMS rushed me to the emergency clinic," he lied.

"Huh? What happened?"

He exaggerated the false statement. "They thought it was an appendicitis attack and kept me five hours for testing and observation. The physician concluded that my severe pain was a case of indigestion, more likely from the partially cooked seafood I ate for lunch. When I got back to schooner I went to bed immediately."

"Thank goodness it was nothing more serious than a common bellyache."

"Yeah, dodged the bullet. Where have you been?"

"I stayed overnight in Miami. I called Zack Seltry to get the directions to his place, by odd coincidence where I'm presently chatting with you. He's that college friend I told you about, a former marine biologist and now the county sheriff of all things. He left to investigate a horrible homicide last night in a local park. I plan to leave my Range Rover next to an outbuilding on his property. I'll come back tomorrow to unload my precious contents. His wife is home and agreed to drive me to our pickup site later in the afternoon. By the way, where are we going to meet?"

Slade gave him specific directions to the restaurant where he first met Hap. He figured he'd do some shopping before Underwood showed up. He wended the Zodiac through the choppy waves and moored at the usual dock. Two hours later, he ventured to the restaurant.

"Well, my gracious, look who the west winds blew ashore," Connie said with a quick smile. She was disappointed he hadn't called her since his arrival.

"Hello there."

"Where ya been? Haven't seen that handsome face around here for some time? Saving that luscious body for somebody else?"

"I'm storing everything up for you, Connie. Maybe next week I'll give you the privilege of draining my pipes. I hope you make time for me."

"Oh… Ah… Sounds nice and juicy."

She led him to a booth near the restroom entrance, poured a cup of coffee for both of them and slid in next to him. "All bullshit aside, give me a call some day. I'll show you the sights and sounds around here. Must be lonely living on that miserable atoll my friend Hap calls home."

"Not really, I like it."

"Heard you got a big snake."

"What? Who the hell told you that?"

"Hap saw it one day sunning on the deck of your boat. Said it was a whopper."

"Um, er…I don't have it anymore."

"What happened?"

"Best I can tell, it crawled overboard and drowned. Snakes can't swim."

"I know. Sorry to hear you lost the pet."

"Thanks. Don't you have some work to do?"

In a snit, she lurched out of the booth and returned to the kitchen without saying another word to him.

Prick thinks he's God's gift to womanhood!

An hour later, they came in laughing and slapping each other on the shoulders. Zach's wife was a stunner. Her long blond hair gathered in a bun the size of a softball and no doubt tainted by the magical bottle. She was wearing cut-off shorts revealing the finest set of legs Slade had ever seen. As they approached the booth, he shot a glance at her open-toed beach shoes. He muttered his silenced disapproval when he saw both big toes adorned with miniature pendants swinging from quarter-inch silver toe rings. The toenails on each foot appeared to be an inch long and painted in gaudy Halloween orange. The polish was chipped like a shattered mirror. His mood went from excitement to disgust and vowed he'd never have a thing to do with her.

"Hi, Slade," Gar said when he spotted him. Six or seven plastic cream dispensers were strewn by the sugar bowl still leaking their white contents.

"It's about time you got here, Underwood. You're more than an hour late."

"Sorry about that. Mrs. Seltry took forever to get ready. She wanted to make a good impression on you. I told her you were a walking advertisement for *Esquire* magazine. Slade, you know what makes these island ladies tick."

"I'm aware of that fact. My girlfriend, Leah Malaka, is from Hawaii." He didn't tell them she had shared her awesome body with different men every evening on a pay-as-you-go carousel. They didn't need to know that spicy bit of information. He presumed the good doctor had something going on with this hussy behind her marine biologist-sheriff's back. It was in his nature to make judgmental calls on women. He was always correct in his assessments.

"Nice to meet you, Mrs. Seltry," he fibbed.

"Please, call me Uriel. I don't jive on formality." He let the comment drop and drained his fourth cup of coffee, which was now cold and lost its biting taste.

"We'd better get going now," Slade said. "I heard on the radio that a storm was brewing off the Gulf and my Zodiac doesn't like counter-punching the elements."

The three of them walked to Slade's Zodiac, and Underwood tossed in several duffel bags and a suitcase. He hugged Uriel, bade her a warm farewell, and climbed into the shuttle boat.

"Take good care of him for me!" she hollered back as Slade revved up the motor, and the Zodiac took off like a spooked stallion.

Gar Underwood was pleased with the location, perfect for what he had in mind. After a tour of *The Glickster*, he encountered Rocky sunning himself on the bow.

"Jesus H. Christ, Glick, you never told me about this giant man-eating serpent. I was expecting something more…conventional as your pet even though you mentioned a snake."

"He's harmless as a baby. You'll see. All I have to do is keep him fed."

"What do you feed him? On second thought, I don't want to know. I didn't look closely at those small cages hidden in the storage area behind the galley. I'm sure they're his rations for the week."

"Good observation. What do you think of my floating bundle of joy?"

"Other than the zoo component, I think the lower middeck area beyond the galley would be the best location to set up my lab."

"You got it. In the morning, we'll go back to Hap's Landing and pick up the rest of the gear at your girlfriend's house. I believe you told me you had to get those snails here as soon as possible. Will she be home tomorrow?"

"Yes. She told me to dial her up before I come. The snail shelf-life, as you non-scientific types would define it, is short when not living in their native habitat."

Underwood was eager to get started, and glad at this point, he hadn't briefed Zack about his purpose for being on the island. No doubt the sheriff would introduce numerous barriers to his entrepreneurial venture citing zoning laws, marina restrictions, trademark violations, and other binding legal technicalities. He knew Zack had been active in all professional matters pertaining to marine biology before he opted out of his chosen scientific field for an unexplained run at law enforcement.

At midnight, Glick became restless. Minor physical changes were taking place in his head and lower body. The storm from the Gulf that was promised by the weatherman to invade their location never happened. Rocky was sleeping comfortably beside him. Underwood had retreated much earlier to his quarters after punishing the best part of the bottle of Jack inadvertently left behind by Tiny.

At two in the morning, his lower legs started to tingle, his head hurt, and his tongue had narrowed, flicking in and out of his mouth. He thought he heard muted conversation and laughter coming from Underwood's quarters. Past experience taught him that too much alcohol tends to interfere with sleep patterns and generate horrific dreams so his guest might be hallucinating.

Thirty minutes later, he jumped out of bed, grabbed his .38 caliber snub-nosed police revolver, high-beam flashlight, and then tiptoed to the ladder leading up to the main deck. He glanced around, looked up, and saw the outline of a person moving across the opening. The ambient skylight wasn't bright enough to identify the person. Frustrated, he shot his high beam upward but the moving image had already disappeared.

"Who goes there?" he shouted loud enough to disturb Rocky who he heard thumping against his cage door. There was no reply. He climbed up to the top deck and saw the figure rotate around the back of the launch, which secured the Zodiac.

"Stop right there, or I'll shoot!"

The spotlight caught the darting figure.

"What the—" He was stunned.

A naked Uriel Seltry raced to the outer rail and dove into the cold tumultuous waters below.

CHAPTER 26

MIAMI

T HEY DECIDED TO DRIVE TO FLORIDA. Jamie wanted to stop in New Orleans on their way cross-country. He'd spent several steamy days and long nights in the French Quarter with two of his Army buddies on leave from Fort Benning. He never forgot the good times they had there. He relished the thought of wolfing down those hot, powdery beignets chased by intermittent swigs of the chicory coffee. Bobby vetoed the idea with pleas of urgency to get to the Keys. Outside of Baton Rouge, Jamie got a call from Sweeny.

"Sorry to disrupt your session on the padded leather couch with your sexy young therapist, Richards, but I got an update on Underwood."

"And a jolly good afternoon to you, Cyclops. What's going on?"

"Underwood is in the intensive care unit at a hospital in Miami."

"What the hell happened to him?"

"There's a sheriff down there named Zack Seltry who put two .225 caliber slugs in him. Some domestic family dispute best we can tell. According to our contact down there, he has a violent temper, gets away with a lot of crap, and has the undying support of the municipal big wigs. I wouldn't tangle with him if I were you."

"What hospital?"

"Dade County Memorial in South Miami."

"Whoa, a long drive from where he was shot."

"Yah, there was a good reason for moving him to that hospital. Another agent covering Dade County found out Underwood had been in touch with an old medical school classmate. The surgeon heads up Dade County Memorial's emergency services teaching program. The doctor made arrangements for the wounded patient to be moved there. He was satisfied the patient had been stabilized enough for the trip."

"You've been a great source of info. Appreciate it, Denis."

"Keep your powder dry, crazy man."

They were taking a break at a rest area when Sweeny had called. Jamie sucked in a big breath of muggy air. The mission to Somalia didn't come up. He briefed Bobby on the conversation.

"Pray that they keep Underwood alive long enough for us to find the hospital," Bobby said.

"Why? You want him dead, don't you?"

"No. I plan to castrate him with your Yarborough knife like a farmer slicing off a young shoat's masculinity. Forget the ears, which you would never do, family jewels have a higher priority in this case."

The first night on the road, they stayed in Pensacola on the Florida panhandle. Jamie hit the sack right away, but Bobby got on the Internet. Out of curiosity, he scanned YouTube to see if there were any further developments on their miracle drug. He bolted out of the chair when he viewed an episode filmed in France with English subheadings. He woke Jamie out of a horrendous snoring marathon.

"That's got to be Pierre Duvair they're talking about."

Jamie was still half asleep and couldn't concentrate, hearing the French words while reading the English version. "What does all that mean, Bobby?"

"It means we might be in deep *kimchee*. The gendarmes are searching for a serial killer in the Verdun area. The assailant seeks out women and garrotes them to death nearly decapitating them."

"So what? Shit like that happens everywhere."

"Before or immediately after the kill, he chews off half their left face. They think the teeth marks are of a certain breed of French bulldog."

"Ugh, sounds like a creature from outer space. Maybe even a deranged zombie?"

"Get serious, Richards. The killer doesn't leave any human foot-prints, but the officials have found two sets of prints resembling that of a dog. One set was larger than the other."

"Where are you going with this?"

"Underwood and I gave our three patients a complete physical before and after their miracle cure. Duvair's body seemed different. His legs and barrel chest were more muscular, and he had an under bite and flabby cheeks drooping down his jowls. His face looked like a bulldog, if you really concentrated on the comparison."

Jamie jogged his memory and recalled Pierre talking about his dog and wishing he were with him while undergoing the cure. He knew the man served in the French Foreign Legion and was well-versed in killing by choking a victim with a wire or rope.

"Bobby, this may be far-fetched, but do you think your therapy turned these three into killing animals? We harbored this thought about Kat and the newspaper accounts of a serial killer operating in the Bay area."

"I don't know. Maybe."

"Think hard. You were transformed by the Conus sea snail when you were struck by one in the Indian Ocean. Remember?"

"True, Jamie, but I didn't turn into a killing animal. At least, not yet although I've wanted to slaughter you on more than one occasion."

"Did you alter the curative agent in any way?"

"Of course not! Wait a minute. We did inject a measured amount of a creamy compound we harvested from goat horns that had been proven to slow the aging process. We tested it on the chimps and got good results. They were more active than before the procedures but didn't try to kill each other."

"So what other variables could have caused such a severe genetic mutation?"

"We know that about half of our genes have been scientifically determined to be non-essential genes serving as so-called floaters that guard against mutations having severe life-changing consequences."

"Pretty heavy-duty stuff, Mr. Genetics," Jamie proclaimed sarcastically, biting hard on his lower lip.

Bobby continued. "I'm convinced it was nothing organic, chemical or synthetic."

"Could it be traced to an environmental cause?"

"Holy Jesus, Jamie, remember that big electrical storm we had when our treatment was in process? All three were in a coma when their gurneys were upended by that tremendous bolt of lightning that came through the roof and torched our lab."

"Would that have exacerbated the curative process?" Jamie was probing at every conceivable angle, a byproduct of a short stint as an intelligence analyst.

"Maybe, just maybe that happened. I don't have any scientific reason to reject your assumption. Hey, it worked for Dr. Frankenstein didn't it?" Bobby chuckled.

"Let me throw a curve ball in here while we're at it. Wasn't Pierre Duvair from Paris? Your video clip said the murders took place in

Verdun. If I remember correctly from my military history, the battle of Verdun was fought during WWI. Verdun is a hundred miles east of Paris. Are we fingering the wrong man here, Bobby?"

He shut down his computer with the YouTube findings pounding his brains and sat back in deep thought.

Maybe Richards is correct. Maybe the serial killer is another deranged person. Duvair was an aristocrat of sort, a true Parisian if I ever met one. And how about the other two? Is our beautiful San Francisco former lawyer a killer? We've been there, seen her, and lived with her. Or did we? Have we missed something? And look at Slade Glick. Why did Gar Underwood hook up with him of all people? What's the connection?

We need to get down there right away and see if he orchestrated Underwood's dalliance with Zach's wife that resulted in the attempted murder. I wouldn't put it past him. He was always a womanizer.

They worked their way down to Miami the following day. On the road, Jamie got a call from Maria, wanting to know if he was coming over to see her that night. She planned to take in a movie at Santikos but didn't want to go alone to a scary flick, one of those far out Stephen King productions. He told her he had another commitment he couldn't get out of. It was true. No way he could dream up the mess they were in. She pressed him for details. Now he had to fabricate a story. He hated to deceive her but had no alternative.

"Maria, do you remember the Navy SEAL friend I talked about?"

"Yes, of course. Is he undergoing major surgery to have that weird eye fixed and need you bedside to hold his hand?"

"Don't be silly, Maria. Nothing of that sort."

"Well, why bring up his name here?"

"He needs my expertise in a top-secret security operation. Because of the sensitivity of the mission, I'm not at liberty to discuss it with you. I tried to beg off but he threatened to have me called back to active duty if I didn't help."

"Can he really do that?"

"Yes."

Her voice began to shake. "Where are you now?"

"I'm in Miami on my way overseas. Sorry, all I can tell you for now."

"Please be careful, Jamie. I don't want to live without you."

"Aren't you being dramatic here?"

"I'm a woman, Jamie. I have feelings…feelings for only you. I'm sorry if you can't understand what I'm saying."

He felt guilty, a different kind of guilt, not a killing guilt for which he was supposedly absolved from by someone on high. This one tugged at his heart. He began to perspire and tears formed at the edges of his eyes. She loved him, and he loved her.

"Got to run now. I love you," he said in a hushed tone and hung up.

"That bad?" Bobby blurted out.

"Yeah."

CHAPTER 27

MIAMI

IT WAS PAST MIDNIGHT when they pulled into the hospital parking lot. They had decided not to spend any time at Cape Canaveral other than driving by the perimeter of the John F. Kennedy Space Center. It was a minor detour and didn't kill much time. Bobby hoped Jamie wouldn't complain after denying him the visit to Bourbon Street. The heavy rain that belted the car traversing I-95 subsided. After a heated discussion that almost came to blows, Jamie refused to give him the Yarborough knife. He argued that there was a time and a place for killing and cutting someone to pieces, and this was neither. They entered the hospital through the busy emergency room and were directed to the main information desk.

"What room is Dr. Gar Underwood in?" Bobby asked the clerk.

"Are you his brother?"

"Um, yes, came all the way down from New York. Why'd you ask?"

"My info card here says that only family members are allowed visiting privileges."

"Why's that? Is he still in ICU?"

"Heavens, no, he's in room 625."

"Does that info card list his home address?"

"I'm sorry but that's privileged information." She blushed as she looked directly into Bobby's striking eyes. Her legs weakened and she began to melt.

"Mother asked me to get it for her. She's flying in tomorrow but won't come here to visit him. She almost died in a hospital last year and pledged never to cross the threshold of one again. She plans to go directly from the Miami airport to his home, wants to get it ready for his recuperation when he's discharged."

"On second thought,"—she flashed a smile—"he's your brother."

"Thank you." Bobby scribbled the address on the back of his hand and whistled, "I never heard of Teatable Key. Where's it located?"

"I have no clue, but there is a note underlined in red to call a certain Sheriff Zach Seltry if anyone inquires about the patient."

"Got a number?"

"Yes."

"Please give it to me. I may need to contact local law enforcement when I get down there. Who knows, I could be the next shooting victim," he joked. She relented and with a long sigh gave it to him. This time, he wrote the number down on the back of his other hand.

As they headed to the elevator banks, she rose up, whirled around the info desk, and grabbed Jamie's shirt. "Sir, you have to stay down here in the lobby area. Apparently, you didn't hear me say that only family members were allowed."

"I did, my dear young lady. I'm Father Lawrence."

"I'm so sorry." She blushed. "I didn't see your white collar. Please forgive me. Of course you may go up with his brother."

Bobby laughed as they got on the elevator. "Quick thinking, Father." The night nurse on the sixth floor surgical ward caught up with them as they walked down the wing of patient rooms toward

625. "Where are you gentlemen going? You need to sign in at the nurse's station before you visit any of our patients. Who'd you come to see?"

"Dr. Underwood but don't tell him we're here to visit him. We want to surprise him."

She laughed. "That won't happen, gentlemen. He signed out against medical advice about four hours ago."

South Miami, six hours earlier

THEY WERE SITTING IN THE BACK SEAT of a speeding taxi. Traffic out of Miami proper was heavy for that time of the evening. Because of the adverse publicity and sensitivity surrounding the murder attempt on his boat mate, Slade Glick thought it best to hire a cab for the trip to the hospital. Even though he had a spare set of keys to Underwood's Land Rover, it was too dangerous to venture over to the Seltry's where it was parked.

"Thanks for coming up to the hospital to pick me up," Underwood uttered to Slade as they exited the hospital. I wasn't sure whether you'd respond to my urgent call. I had to get out of there, had my fill of questioning by the detectives and probing by the news media. You'd have thought I was the perpetrator instead of that fucking Seltry."

Slade laughed and then said, "Frankly, I was surprised, thought you'd be stretched out on a cold slab in the county morgue by now. From what I heard on the radio, the sheriff used you for target practice. What's up with you and that cheating wife of his?"

"I'll fill you in later, Underwood said. "We need to get back to the schooner and get the hell out of here?"

"Why the rush?"

"Because I'll never forget the last thing Zach Seltry shouted at me when the ambulance carted me off from the scene of his attempted murder."

"What did he say?"

"He said if I was lucky enough to survive round one he'd send in a hit team to the hospital and finish the job."

Slade ordered the driver to drop them off a few blocks from the mooring at Caloosa Cove. Even though it was after midnight, he wanted to make sure they weren't seen by a soul. He was satisfied that Underwood could ambulate without too much of a problem. His stitched wounds seemed to be healing properly. He still had pain walking with the cane he swiped from the hospital. When they passed the wooded park, Slade broke out in a cold sweat.

Have I ever been here before? It looks familiar.

He couldn't put his finger on the reason for his jitters. He wouldn't walk by the front entrance so they detoured back to the docks another way.

"What was all that about, Slade? You look like you saw a ghost back there."

"I hate dark, dense parks. Gives me a chill."

Underwood had read in an old newspaper Slade had on board about the murder of a school teacher in the park. It was grizzly reading Sheriff Zack Seltry's quotes of "viciousness…never seen before… sick, sick killer." He was alarmed when he read on further about a rubber snake stuffed in her neck. He remembered seeing some of those toys in a plastic bag on a shelf behind the refrigerator. He never thought any further about the weird coincidence. For all he knew, Rocky may enjoy playing with them.

"Need any help getting into the Zodiac?"

"Just brace my shoulders when I step in. I'm tossing this cane when we get to the landing."

Slade happened to glance down to the bottom of the boat and thought he saw a piece of paper. A ray of light from the street lamp near the mooring revealed a sealed envelope. He picked it up and ripped it open. He was able to make out the scribbled note. He reeled back in horror. Underwood saw the shocked stare on his friend's face as he read and reread the note. He reached over and grabbed the note out of Slade's hand, read it, and shoved it in his back pocket. Slade didn't object. A blank stare and puckered mouth temporarily paralyzed him.

We know it was you who killed that lady and we're coming after you!

Underwood was fatigued and fell asleep on the way across. The soothing ripple of the waves and the singing winds conquered his restlessness. The trip to Hap's Landing gave Slade a few minutes to interpret the meaning of the suspicious note and to replay the events of the last several days.

What in the world is going on here? Who's playing a joke on me? Do they think I was the killer? How could they come to that conclusion? Did I do it? I've had dreams of a mutant taking the lives of innocent ladies. Sure, I've had a few restless nights since docking in this spooky village, sleepwalking for the most part. But murder!

And what about Underwood? Are they coming after him too? Has that wild-assed sheriff organized a posse to hunt us down? His messing around with that no-good Uriel is going to get us both killed. I think we'll pull anchor tomorrow and get the hell out of this haunted piece of real estate.

When they returned to the schooner, he told his mate they were packing up and sailing out in the morning. They got into an argument. Underwood was upset because he was on the cusp of starting his project with the Conus sea snails and demanded to stay, even offering Slade a thousand dollars to take a day and rethink his decision. Slade began to piece things together in his mind that maybe he was involved some way or another with the murder of the lady in the park. He was at a loss for the reason he saved the damning newspaper article.

Was there a connection? Did I assist the killer some way?

"Holy shit!" Underwood cried out when he walked into his sleeping quarters. "Come here, Slade! Run! Hurry up!"

"What's up?" He asked as he climbed down the ladder to the lower deck.

Out of breath and tired of Underwood's shenanigans, he couldn't believe what he saw on the floor stretched out before him. Rocky was gnawing on the head of a uniformed deputy sheriff lying next to him in a pool of dried blood. It looked like the python was ready to start swallowing the dead man. He had to be deceased for at least a day based on rigor mortis setting in. His left arm extended vertically resembling the mast of a flagpole. In his clenched fist was a rubber toy snake.

"My god, what do you think happened, Slade?"

"Your guess is as good as mine. More than likely, he thought the trunk with the suspicious air holes down below contained some illegal contraband. He decided to open it and Rocky sprung out at him."

"To begin with, why would a cop be out here on the boat?" Underwood asked, certain he knew the answer.

"A better question is why did Rocky kill him? He's a pet, not a wild animal in some far away African jungle. We have to disappear from this island post haste. No way can I round up another hand in the midst of this chaos. I trust you've recovered enough to help sailor *The Glickster* out on the open sea."

"I'm pretty resilient. Either Seltry is a lousy shot, or he didn't want to kill me. The slugs missed my bones and vital organs. I think everybody overreacted and were simply trying to cover their collective asses. I've sailed before, and I'm strong enough to help."

"We developed a plan, so let's get on with it," Slade said.

"What are we going to do with the dead cop?" Underwood was shaking. He anticipated a major problem with the law.

"Slice him up in pieces and toss the body parts overboard when we get out on the ocean. There are sharks out there waiting for something delicious to feast on."

"You can't be serious, Slade."

"What's your take?"

"That's…that's so inhumane."

"Well, don't expect Rocky to eat him even though it looked like that would happen. He doesn't like the taste of human flesh or you'd have been dead by now!"

"Help me carry him up to the deck, and we'll toss him in the ice bin. It's convenient. We stored big game fish there to keep them out of the hot sun until we got back to shore. Grab some buckets and get some ice from the freezer down in the kitchen. We'll cool him down for the time being and chop him up later."

"I'll have no part of that," Underwood protested but then relented. He couldn't drum up a better alternative.

"We'll check in on your feelings later. Now get going."

They hauled him to the top deck after Underwood's minor rebellion. He filled several buckets as ordered. They plunked the cop in the cooler and tossed ice over his body. They were exhausted. The dead man was at least fifty pounds overweight. Slade suggested they sit underneath the canopy and catch their breaths.

"I'm not sure if they are coming after both of us. More than likely, the target is you," Slade commented as he began preparing the schooner for its departure. He cranked up the powerful engine and let it idle. He pushed the lever that sprung into action lifting the anchor from twenty feet of water.

"Well, I'm shocked. Are you certain you don't have any blood on your hands, Slade?"

"Zack Seltry is on a vendetta to get you for tapping into his wife. I haven't done anything to warrant pursuit by the law. By the way, you never shared any details about your liaisons with Uriel Seltry that nearly got your scientific ass blown off. Was she a good enough fuck to risk your life?"

"I guess I owe you an explanation but remind me when we're hours away from this nightmare. I'll fill you in if you tell me about that bag of rubber toy snakes. Why did that lawman have one clutched in his hand?"

Slade walked down the gangplank to the pier and untied the ropes anchoring the schooner to the dock. He unhooked the water and electrical umbilical lifelines, returned to the boat, then manually turned the crank to pull in the aluminum walkway. He noticed that Hap's speedboat was not docked and wondered where he was off to this late at night.

Maybe he's boinking Connie, the old fart! They seemed joined at the waist every time I went there to eat. She doesn't really want a piece of me. She wants to screw the old fucker to death and inherit the valuable property he owns on Teatable Key.

"Where are we heading, Slade? I need to get these stitches out pretty soon. The doctor wanted me to return in ten days."

"North, by the Outer Banks of North Carolina."

"Why there?"

"I have an uncle from Chicago who owns a marina not far from the Cape Hatteras National Seashore. He's stored my schooner in the past, so I don't see a problem. It's a thriving tourist haven. We'd be able to blend in with the rich New Yorker crowd until this stink goes away."

"Maybe you can dock somewhere before we get there. I can locate a doctor to check my wounds and take the stitches out."

"No, sir, red flags would go up. They'd want to know how you got shot. We can't afford that. I don't plan to stop until we arrive at our destination. You'll have to rip out the stitches. You're a doctor, so you should be able to take care of the minor issue without a problem. I store hydrogen peroxide in my medicine cabinet. I heard it's a good disinfectant."

"I guess I can do that, not having a choice in the matter. How convenient to have a rich uncle we can depend on. When Seltry learns that *The Glickster* is no longer anchored at Hap's Landing, he'll put out an APB. On second thought, with his deputy missing, I bet there's one already transiting the air waves. What about your car at the boat storage facility in Miami?"

"I have plenty of time to run back there to retrieve it whenever I need it. Our first order of business is to get as far away from Haps Landing as possible."

"Yeah, and quickly," Underwood stressed.

"Speaking of cars, are you going to donate your Land Rover to Zack Seltry's motor pool?" *I would prefer that vehicle over my own but realize that's not an option. Maybe Uriel will find the keys and run away in it.*

Underwood thought for a minute and responded, "Before he tried to kill me with that dinky pistol, he screamed repeatedly about impounding my car. As I was drifting off to never-never land, I think he said it would be held as physical evidence in the slaying of that lady in the park."

"What in the hell are you talking about?"

"You got me. I think he's trying to pin the murder rap on me. That's another reason to leave these parts immediately." *I'm beginning to think more and more that you and that slimy snake killed her. I need to watch my step around here. I could be next on the drawing board.*

South of Miami Slade decided to deviate from the route. In hopes of picking up another helper, he piloted his boat to the familiar storage facility. He knew it was a slight risk in the event Seltry was able to trace where he kept the boat in dry dock. Underwood didn't measure up, moaning and complaining every nautical mile they distanced themselves from the Keys. He needed a reliable seaman for the reminder of the voyage. He figured that a two and a half crew composition could negotiate the tasks ahead. It was early morning when he tied up at the dry dock. The manager was outside readying another boat for release from storage.

"Ya back again?"

"Just passing through and wanted to say hello."

"Well, hello. What do ya want?"

"Is that withered whiskey-sipper still hanging around here? I could use his help again if he's not drunk."

"You mean Tiny?"

"Yep."

"He's out back. Never completely sober…always in between. Ya know what I'm saying?"

"I get the main drift."

"Wait here and I'll round him up."

The conversation was short. Tiny wanted to know if the giant snake was still living on the boat, claimed he became friends with the serpent. This time, Slade had to throw in the cost of transportation back to Miami in addition to the two hundred bucks Tiny negotiated. The sot had to hitchhike back home from the last stint with him. He deplored the fact that motorists don't stop for hitchhikers like they did after the war.

"Let's get the show on the road, friends." Slade was anxious to disappear before the storage manager started to ask questions about the change of plans. If the law was in hot pursuit, he didn't have time to stand there and create misinformation.

Six hours out on the Atlantic, Slade cornered Underwood on the bridge. "Time to dispose of our big game fish. Take Tiny below and pour enough Jack Daniel's down his gullet, so he won't have a clue what's about to happen."

"Aye, aye, skipper. That shouldn't take too long." Tiny was elated when he learned he was going to have a liquid meal all to himself. As a precaution, Underwood tied his ankles with a rope and anchored it around an exposed metal pipe. He told the old salt it was for his own protection. Tiny shrugged. *Protection from what? If that's what it takes to get boozed up, so be it.*

They pulled the dead cop out of the bin and dropped him unceremoniously on a thick plastic sheet and proceeded to hack him in pieces with a machete Slade kept on board. Underwood had time to rethink his position on the disposal plan. He joined in on the savagery. Rocky was on the top deck at the time and witnessed the scene. In disgust, he slithered down the main stairwell and crawled back to his trunk passing and ignoring Tiny in the narrow hallway.

They were both spent after heaving the body parts overboard. Slade watched intently for the dorsal fins of the sharks to appear. Five minutes later, he was not disappointed and cheered in delight. He was mesmerized by the swirling choppy waves generated by the sharks' voracious assault on the clumps of flesh.

"Get that empty fat container in the kitchen with the sealed lid," Slade ordered the retching and vomiting Gar Underwood."

"What for?"

"I want to stuff it with that bloody plastic drop sheet and small pieces of chipped bone strewn on the deck. We'll also put his uniform and shoes in with enough fishing line weights to send it straight to the bottom. Evidence is convicting, and we don't want that to come back and haunt us."

They finished their chores and relaxed in the two captain chairs underneath the control panel canopy. Underwood's color returned to his face, and he seemed to accept his responsibility for the despicable act. He thought that some meaningless conversation might improve his disposition.

"I suppose you want me to tell you the story about my tit-for-tat with Uriel Seltry."

"I'm all ears," Slade said with a lecherous grin. "Can't wait for the juicy details."

"You knew that Seltry and I were college classmates. Uriel was a freshman cheerleader at the same school. I always made it a point to sit in the stands as near to the playing field as possible. The ploy was not to watch the stupid game but be closer to her. She was the best looker on the cheerleading squad. We began dating after the first game. My friend Zach was a defensive halfback and was jealous that I held sway on Uriel."

"As a star player, couldn't he attract any of the split tails on his own?"

"We all thought Zach was gay, but he began dating some real hags with big tits. One evening in the dorm, he approached me and warned me that he was going to take a crack at Uriel and would I mind. Of course, I was at a loss for words but told him to go ahead. I was sure she'd tell him to take a hike because we really were on a romantic tear with each other. She had shared with me after our third date that I was the first virgin she corrupted."

"I get it now. He had a bigger pair of balls, and she dropped you like a hot potato."

"Sort of. We did sneak away one night at an alumni affair five years after graduation. It was a masquerade party. I was in graduate school getting my PhD. They were also attending the celebration, married and had no kids. Zach got drunk and spent the night passed out at in a hotel room with two of his football pals."

"Yuck, I know what's coming next." Slade loved the narrative, reliving the script as though he were the leading man in the Broadway play *Sex on the Run.*

"She told me he was sterile, couldn't father a kid, asked me if I'd be a substitute, and do the job for my good friend Zach."

"And you reasoned that duty called you to…ah…bail him out."

"Not quite, Slade. I resisted at first, but I think she put a Mickey in my drink, and the next thing I knew, we were in a cheap downtown hotel."

"So the Lolita Palido look-alike dropped her panties, and you mounted her. The masked Zorro gave her a kid?"

"No. Apparently, I shot blanks that night."

"Well, kiss my ass! The sheriff sure as hell didn't shoot any blanks last week when he caught up with you and the witch temptress."

They both laughed and went below to join Tiny, drunk but coherent enough to have snapped the anchoring pipe freeing the captive ropes. Water was dripping from the break. He was perched on a bench next to the marine aquarium housing the precious sea snails. Shaking from delirium tremors, he took the whiskey bottle in both hands and drained it in one last slug.

He whispered in a shallow voice, "Professor, them snails are all dead."

Underwood bellowed out in anguish. "No, no, no! It can't be!"

CHAPTER 28

DATELINE

San Francisco—Thanksgiving, 2012

SERIAL KILLER STRIKES AGAIN was the main headline in the *Chronicle* on Turkey Day. Kat was shocked when she read the paper and hoped they'd catch the heinous bastard soon. She figured this was the fifth victim yet the case-cracking wizards in the SFPD were still stumped. They brought in another expert on bird feathers from an avian sanctuary in Europe. Kat thought she read a ridiculous statement in the paper that some kind of human birdman might be the killer. The telephone rang. She hesitated before answering, not caring to be disturbed. It was Barry Gregg.

"Did you read today's paper?"

"Yes, I'm reading it as we speak. Now we have birdmen maniacs cavorting around our city. What's this world coming to anyway?"

"Are you civil now, Kat? Can we meet for lunch? I need to talk to you about a new case that I'm involved with."

"I don't do lawyering anymore. I've told you that before, but you discarded that fact. Every time we meet face-to-face, something negative erupts. Haven't you found another female to add zest to your boring life?"

"That's a low blow, Kat. I have to beat them off with a stick. I can't get you out of my mind. If lunch is out of the question, please have dinner with me tonight."

"I already have a date."

"Can I come to your place right now?"

"No."

"Why not?"

"I don't know how to put this in gentler terms, Barry Gregg, but I think you're despicable. I can't stand you. I hate everything you represent. The money-raping of clients using vague, but defensible legal arguments should be outlawed. It would be if we had decent citizens in Congress instead of you, fucking purse-snatching lawyers!"

He hung up in disgust. This time, he got the message loud and clear. She gave him credit for one thing—persistence. Stryker had been sitting on her shoulder listening to the conversation. He'd been content until last night when she insisted on yet another search for satisfaction—her satisfaction.

When will it all end? I prefer to hunt alone, to seek out vulnerable wildlife for food and not human animals for pleasure. Why does she take their eyes out and bring them back here? I am all through helping her fulfill her quench for snuffing out another poor defenseless person, no more!

Kat missed Jamie Richards and wished he'd come alone the next time. His scientist friend was a sex maniac, and all he wanted to do was fondle her body, feel her arms, and palpate her breasts. At the same time, she was thankful for the cure. She was never able to figure out why some mornings she was so tired and unable to get out of bed. She felt punch-drunk, like going five rounds with Muhammad Ali. The article in the newspaper about a serial killer began to bother her. She couldn't put her arms around it. She decided to call Jamie and invite him for Christmas.

"Hello, Jamie. Thought I'd give you a call and see how you're doing. It's Kat. What's up?"

"Oh, hi, I sure wasn't expecting a call from you."

"You mean you have another admirer competing with me?"

"Certainly not, you are my one and only."

He wondered why she was calling. He and Bobby left San Francisco not sure if they'd ever hear from her again. She castigated Bobby Biel for his episode in the park with the zonked out locals in search of weed. *Apparently, my unsuccessful pursuit of her luscious body didn't put a damper on her amorous instincts.*

"Where are you?" Kat inquired. "I hear car horns blaring."

"Bobby and I are on an interstate in Florida, trying to catch up with a former acquaintance."

"If you find him, are you going to kill him and cut his ears off?"

"What the hell kind of question is that?"

"I know you're a hired killer, and that really turns me on, Richards. Has any other woman confessed that to you? I'm shivering with goose pimples as we speak. Would you like to slash my throat from ear to ear?"

"I will if you don't shut the fuck up?"

"Just kidding. When you get to a big city where you can hop on a plane, forget your silly manhunt and fly out here. I can't wait much longer to have sex with you again."

"You got to be on smack? Bobby told me he saw needle marks the last time he examined you."

"Don't be ridiculous. He told me they were pox marks and didn't know what caused them so we left that topic alone. Seriously, if you can't travel here now, will you come for Christmas?"

"Can you hold off that carnal desire until you see the whites of my eyes?"

"I guess I'll have to if that means you'll come."

"I give you my word. I got to hang up now. We're pulling into a small village in the Keys."

Kat went to bed that evening with a thousand thoughts racing through her disjointed mind. She couldn't sleep. It was after midnight and she began feeling uncomfortable.

My back hurts again, she thought. *My fingers and feet are so arthritic I could cry all night in pain. What's wrong with me? Sometimes I feel like taking Stryker and fly out of this damn city. The so-called bird murders are scaring me. Am I a bird? Am I the killer?*

Paris—Thanksgiving, 2012

PIERRE DUVAIR PULLED A RIFLE OUT OF THE CLOSET and was planning to kill Louie while the dog slept. It was late evening. The big hand and the small hand on the grandfather clock settled on twelve. He was disappointed with his pet. Louie disobeyed all the time, refused to jump in the car on command, and even snapped back at him one evening.

Enough is enough, he thought. *The dog has got to go.*

Earlier in the day, he baked a fat turkey and stuffed it with his favorite bread dressing. He ate alone, drank alone, and was miserable. He met an older man yesterday while on his daily walk but didn't like his attitude, reminded him too much of Andre. The guy was limping along the road pushing an aluminum walker whistling "La Marseillaise." His skinny chest was puffed out in exaltation as though he had written the verses of their lovely national anthem. He recalled the conversation.

"Live near here?" Pierre asked.

"I do. The beat-up shack a mile up the road is my fiefdom." He *snickered and spit a wad of chewing tobacco at the road, barely missing Duvair's new shoes.*

"*Do you live by yourself?*" Pierre was curious. *The guy was decrepit, unshaven, and dressed like a circus clown.*

"*No, sir. Got a shriveled up woman in there with me. Shoulda died years ago. Dementia, dysentery, and can't hold anything down. Damned if she doesn't crap all over the place.*"

"*How long you been there?*" Pierre probed.

"*Long enough to know your sister. She was a sweetheart, ran errands for me, and helped bring Mom to the doctors in Verdun. It was a sad day in my life when she died unexpectedly. You got the house, huh?*"

"*Yes, she willed it to me.*"

"*Well, sir, be careful in there. The house is haunted.*"

"*What are you talking about?*"

"*I haven't seen it, but it's rumored that a wild animal creeps out at night howling at the moon.*"

"*Where did you hear that?*"

"*A friend who lives across the river said he seen it, heard it one night.*"

"*He consumed too much vin des pas that evening.*"

"*He said it looked like a gigantic dog.*"

"*Is this guy across the river about your age?*"

"*Oh no, he's got me by a number of years.*"

"*Thanks for the warning. Have a good day.*"

Thunder claps shook the area, and it began to rain. The sky heaved down the wet stuff until the fading light of day gave way to the darkness of night. He carried the rifle outside remembering what his neighbor shared with him that afternoon. He surmised the fool on the other side of the Meuse River suffered from the advance stages of Alzheimer's like everyone else around there.

Frustrated and angry, he blasted off fifteen rounds across the river at an outbuilding near the main house. Pierre listened intently to any sound that would report a hit. His Legionnaire buddies razzed him about being a bad shot. He cared less. He wasn't trying to kill the loony-tune living there, maybe scare him for telling ridiculous lies about him.

A big dog howling at the moon…how stupid!

Louie woke up after hearing the ruckus and pushed the door open to go outside. He shook his fat head in awe as he witnessed a naked Duvair pumping rounds out of a loud gun. It hurt his ears. He was puzzled by the antics and thought it was his duty to steer his master back into the house.

"Whoosh, Louie, get back inside, or I'll turn this rifle around and blow your head off." The dog obeyed. At midnight, Duvair decided to go the rope routine alone. He shuffled to his computer and typed in his favorite website. He began to salivate when he read and reread the definition.

"The sexual practice is variously called asphyxiophilia or auto-erotic asphyxia. Colloquially, a person engaging in the activity is sometimes called a *gasper*."

"So I'm a gasper. Aha, nothing else compares to it. Maybe I should string up Louie. He'd love it. Oh no, he's too heavy for me to lift up there. He might fight me, even bite me. Forget it, I'll do it alone. I know how…did it before I met that radical Hugues Chaban. Fuck him! Fuck everybody!"

He emptied a bottle of cognac while watching several pornographic movies. He envisioned himself as the muscular actor on the last show before he turned it off. The liquor caused an exuberant disorientation.

Maybe it really was me. Kinda has my good looks.

Louie found him the next morning on the floor with the rope still engaged around his neck.

Stupid man, the dog thought. *Why do humans carry on like that?*

Lower Matecumbe Key—Thanksgiving, 2012

USING HIS GPS, BOBBY LOCATED THE SHERIFF'S OFFICE and asked to speak with Zach Seltry. He was told the sheriff was on a call but should return soon. They were advised by the deputy to come inside and wait for him in the conference room. Two hours later, Seltry sauntered in and asked how he could assist them. Bobby was surprised how thin the former athlete looked, wondering if he was suffering from some major malady, like melanoma perhaps. He expected to see some form of the renowned Joe Palooka, the muscle-bound comic book boxer. After cordial introductions, Bobby explained that he was a personal friend of Gar Underwood and heard he was in some kind of trouble.

"Had breakfast yet, fellows?" Seltry asked, ignoring the reference to Underwood.

"No, but if you're hungry, we wouldn't object to go somewhere and eat. Jamie was starved. He felt they skipped too many meals on their rush to get to the Keys. They climbed into the sheriff's big Land Rover with Underwood's New York plates and drove several blocks to a restaurant at the pier.

Connie was behind the cash register talking to a customer. A cigarette was dangling from her lips, about to drop a slug of ashes into the opened till. When she saw Seltry with the two handsome men, she let out a sigh. "What did I do to deserve the presence of three beautiful male specimens? Is this an official call or are you gentlemen here to eat?"

"We're starved, Connie. I told these guys your food is the best in the county." Looking around the restaurant, he paused and asked, "Where's Hap?"

"He should be here soon. Said he had some things to clean up around his landing."

"Suppose you want some privacy again, Zach. Why don't you take these boys in the back room, and we'll serve you in there."

When they got settled, a cute young waitress sauntered over to them, introduced herself, and took their orders. "Connie is cooking this morning. This is your lucky day."

"What's that mean?" Jamie inquired, hoping he was in for a big surprise. His stomach was sending SOS signals to his brain. She poured them coffee and flipped open her pad to take the orders. Seltry told her to have Connie fix her world famous ham and cheese omelets.

"They fired the cook yesterday, skimming off food and who knows what else. He was a lecherous old prick, grabbed me on the ass several times. Good riddance. Be back with your food before you know it."

"Interesting gal with the big mouth. Can't be more than sixteen," Bobby deadpanned.

"She's Connie's daughter by her second husband. The poor bastard was killed in a bar brawl last year. He had a criminal record, saved me tons of work down the road."

Bobby needed to clear up an issue that had been bothering him. "Gar told me you were a marine biologist. What gives with the law enforcement uniform?"

"I got tired of the water and everything swimming around in it. Not exciting enough and high-paying projects were few and far between, so I ran for sheriff and won. Enough about me, let's talk about Dr. Gar Underwood. Is he or is he not in trouble, you ask?"

"Yes, that's why we're here," Jamie said.

"I'll make a long story short. Gar called me before he came down here. Told me he was on a government grant to do some research but couldn't be specific because it was classified top secret. We went to college together. I went on a football scholarship. He got his free ride because of the gray matter between his ears. He figured I could be of assistance to both Uncle Sam and his honor personally."

"Did he know you were no longer a marine biologist?" Jamie asked.

"I didn't tell him of my new venture in law enforcement. After we talked, I was eager for him to work down here. He dated my wife when we were all in college. We partied together like there was no tomorrow."

Bobby and Jamie looked at each other with a slight grin. The waitress carried the food in on a large tray. Jamie almost fell off his chair when he saw the size of the servings. Without making a big deal out of it, cutie pie plopped the plates on the table in front of them and then walked off without saying a word.

"Must be pissed at her mom," Bobby laughed. "Let's chow down while it's hot."

After they ate breakfast, Zach continued his story. "We thought Underwood committed a murder in the county park. A young school teacher walking her dog at night was found with her throat slashed. A witness came forth and told us he happened to be near the edge of the park and saw the atrocious act going down. He was almost sure it was the *new* guy in town who cut her up. Underwood was a high-society type, and the gossipmongers around here had a ball talking about him."

"We heard you shot him," Jamie said, pushing hard for a conclusion.

"That's a horse of another color, and I'll get to that. We were all set to bring Underwood in when this strange guy popped in here and confessed to the murder. He said he was on a drug-induced high, and Satan told him to do it. He claimed to be homeless and was napping in the park when he saw her walk by with the dog."

"Why didn't he call 911 and report it?" Bobby asked.

"Said the evil spirits told him to run and hide but after several days he felt guilty, was going to commit suicide. He feels a lot better after getting everything off his chest."

"Where is he now?" Bobby asked.

"The DA ordered him to sit in cold storage awaiting trial. I cancelled the APB on Underwood. We had just released the wire so had to retrieve it before the world wasted time going after him."

The waitress came by to clear the table. She was in a better mood this time and even told the sheriff an off-color joke. It wasn't funny and nobody laughed except her. "You handsome men have to come back tonight for the big Thanksgiving feast Mom is preparing."

"Um, sounds good," Seltry said. "But the wife has made other arrangements without even consulting me, really pisses me off." Bobby told her they also had other plans.

She told him the sheriff that Hap was waiting out front to talk to him. Seltry told her to fetch him and scoot him to the back room right away. She curtsied while blowing a softball-sized bubble from a full pack of Bazooka.

"I want you gentlemen to meet Hap here." Seltry smiled when the waitress playfully shoved him into the back room. "Nobody knows his last name. Claims he doesn't have one. Connie out front is the only person around here who might know but apparently has been sworn to secrecy. What's happening, Mr. Hap?"

Hap pulled up a chair and looked at Bobby, ignoring Jamie. He tried to recall if Slade Glick ever mentioned their names. He knew Gar Underwood who came to town recently but wondered what the connections were with these two men.

"Sheriff, something odd is going on around here," he said.

"Well, I'll be damned, Hap. Spill the beans."

"I saw one of your uniforms motor to my landing the other day, docked next to my boat."

"Yes, that was Shorty. I sent him to your Key to check out some complaints we'd received about the beach. Nothing major but had to respond. Told him to take a few days off after he finished. He'd been working double shift ever since the park murder."

"He must have decided to camp out on the island somewhere," Hap said.

"Why do you say that?" Seltry asked with a puzzled look.

"Because his motorboat is still parked at my dock."

"Where's *The Glickster?*"

"I don't know. You'd have thought that Slade Glick would have been decent enough to inform me if he was leaving for good. Maybe he and that hotshot scientist friend are just cruising around for a few days taking in our breathtaking shoreline views."

Both Bobby and Jamie listened intently to the story the senior citizen was spinning. Bobby thought Hap was out of touch, maybe even imagining things or creating situations to cause more excitement around the small village.

"Thanks for the info, Hap. We'll check it out. Go tell Connie to fix you her specialty. Breakfast's on the department." Hap left the table rendering a smart military salute.

"I don't think we have a problem with your friends," Seltry said, picking his teeth with a thick toothpick. "My guy Shorty is a party animal. He's still sleeping it off somewhere in your friend's neighborhood across the channel."

Bobby was getting restless and pressed the sheriff for an explanation of Underwood's gunshot wounds. He wanted clarification of the "family dispute" comment from Jamie's conversation with his CIA buddy.

"Why did you shoot, Underwood?" Jamie asked pointedly, taking the question out of Bobby's mouth.

"Out of self-defense. I'm embarrassed to tell you this, but he was sleeping with my wife. Uriel has always been a free spirit, but I never suspected she was a hooker-type. I hate to use that word when describing my wife, but it's true. This wasn't the first episode, but I'm damn sure it will be the last."

"Why is that?" Bobby asked with a concerned look on his face.

"I filed for divorce so she's free to do what she wants with that *botoxed* body of hers. When we had arguments about sex, she always reminded me that she was Gar Underwood's first lover and taught him all the tricks of the trade. I suspect she never put him out of her mind."

"You said self-defense," Jamie interrupted.

"Yes, I did. I'd had enough when I found them bopping each other like deranged rabbits in the backseat of his Land Rover conveniently parked in my yard. He jumped out of the car with his pants off and pulled a switchblade on me. I backed off warning him to drop the knife. He had to be high on something because I'd never witnessed that merciless stare in his or anyone else's eyes before."

"And he didn't drop the knife," Jamie blurted out.

"Correct."

Bobby was in awe as the story developed, thought it would make a good soap opera on TV. Maybe Judge Judy would sit in and handle the case.

Zack continued. "I ducked two of his violent thrusts, backed away, and pulled my service weapon. I thought seeing my gun would change his mind about attacking me. It didn't, so I shot him a couple of times just to disarm him. I had every right to kill the bastard."

"What did Uriel do when that happened?" Bobby finally chimed in.

"Screamed and called me all kind of filthy names and ran to the house and called 911. An ambulance pulled in, EMTs gave him immediate first aid, and hauled him off. I haven't seen him since. I heard he ended up in a Miami hospital."

"Why weren't you temporarily suspended from you duties? Isn't that routine in your business when an officer shoots someone?" Jamie knew this was the universal protocol in cop shootings.

"Yes and no. The county judge is a golfing buddy of mine. The mayor is a shirttail cousin. This is a small community. Everyone looks out for each other. Underwood was an outsider, operating far outside the proverbial *box*, and frankly, no one gave a shit about him. Foremost in our citizen's minds was the first murder in the annals of the Lower Matecumbe Key where a school teacher was murdered in the park. And who better to catch the bad guy? Me, of course. End of story."

Bobby and Jamie were ready to hustle out and get on their way. They excused themselves and left the sheriff seated. He could also pick up their tab. They sensed they were out of options to find Underwood. Jamie decided it was time to head back to Texas. If they drove straight through they might get there in time to celebrate Thanksgiving. Maria had never cooked a turkey but promised Jamie he'd be the first human being to experience her culinary breakout. On the way out of town, Bobby got a call on his cell phone.

"Hi, Bobby. Gar Underwood on this end. Can you hear me?"

CHAPTER 29

TEXAS

T HEY ARRIVED HOME IN TIME to get some of the late trappings of Thanksgiving. Jamie surprised Maria who wasn't sure he'd get there in time. Bobby went to the Menger, hoping it wasn't too late to get turkey. It was, but he was pleased when he wandered into the bar where they were serving leftovers, gratis. Management was scuttling the leftovers from the main meal of the day. A new lady was mixing drinks behind the bar. He thought he recognized her, but it was late. His mind was on cruise control.

"What'll it be, handsome?"

"Fix me a margarita and tell me your name."

"I'll do the first but not the latter. You look like you're trolling for a woman."

"Not necessarily but you fit the bill. Are you a local?"

"No."

"Well, where are you from?"

"Nowhere and everywhere. Here's your drink."

Several hours later, Bobby was reaching the point of inebriation. The pretty lady behind the bar had given him the "last call" warning twice. He found his way to a booth and plunked his numb body down. He was wrestling with the telephone call he'd received from Gar Underwood. He wasn't sure what to make of it.

"I imagine you are ready to send your armed killer friend to waste me, Bobby, and I wouldn't blame you. I am so sorry for whatever hardships my actions might have caused you. I will do anything to make it good for you. I can't return your precious snails. That wormwood idiot Slade Glick failed to take care of them for me while I was in the hospital. I had an appendicitis attack requiring emergency surgery."

"You mean—" Gar cut him off midsentence.

"Oh yes, the very same Slade that we cured down at your research facility in South Texas. We hooked up again in Florida… Accidently ran into him at South Beach in Miami when I was vacationing. Something is wrong with this guy, Bobby. I think our curative treatment turned him into a different person, an animal, a creature that comes to life after midnight and goes on a killing spree. I'm flying to San Antonio tomorrow… Stop. Don't say anything that would cause me to change my mind. I'm coming whether you want to see my ugly face ever again. We need to flush things out. It can't wait another day. We may be in big trouble."

"But I—"

Underwood had already hung up.

On the walk back to his apartment, Bobby remembered where he had seen the bartender before. It was in Reunion when he traveled back there to harvest the snails. She was the other sexy woman who joined in the orgy that sent him fifty shades above casual entertainment. He wasn't sure why or how she showed up in his city. Maybe she told him she lived in San Antonio, and it didn't register with him at the time.

"Are you up yet?" Jamie was in a cheerful mood but not reflective enough to jettison his friend's world-class headache."

"Jesus, Richards, it's not even noon yet. Call me back in two hours."

"Sounds like you got a hangover."

"Do birds fly south in the winter, you idiot?"

He clicked his cell phone ringer off and went back to bed after a handful of aspirins trickled down his parched throat. As he crawled back in bed, a second call came in. He elected not to answer it and was snoring before the bed turned warm again.

When he woke up at three in the afternoon, Jamie was standing at the foot of his bed. Through Biel's bloodshot eyes, he looked like a twelve-foot-tall ogre—a hideous, humanoid monster of the worse kind.

"You scared the shit out of me. How'd you get in?"

"I still have the same thumb affixed to my hand and the identical thumbprint your sophisticated code recognized. You ought to redesign it so a person can only use it for a one-time entry. Just think, Bobby, the pizza delivery guy you call to deliver the pies to your upstairs unit has access to your place at will."

"I hadn't thought about that, Papa John's, but you made your point," he muttered as he tried to shake the blazing fireworks display out of his woozy head.

"Get your rear end out of the sack. We got things to do."

"Like what?"

"Pick up Underwood at the airport."

"How'd you know he was coming?"

"Your cell phone was blinking, so I picked up your messages. He left the second message."

"Who left the first one?" Bobby asked as he threw on his robe.

"A chick with a sexy voice who wouldn't reveal her name. She wanted to know how you were feeling. Who's the broad? Are you holding something back on me? It wouldn't be the first time, that's for sure."

"Who calls me is none of your business, Richards. It's my secret." He had a difficult time recalling who this mysterious woman was that his friend was chomping about, and then it smacked him between the ears—the bartender last night. He was curious.

Did I convince her to come home with me last night and seduce her? I know we got cozy and chatted at the door before she locked up. I feel like shit. Maybe I did some strange things with her last night. In fact, I wish I had.

"You shouldn't be snooping around on my cell phone. Who do you think you are, the FBI? Did that Cyclops character grant you unmitigated access or did the president sign an executive order allowing intrusion privileges to a former grunt?"

Jamie laughed at his comments and got serious. "Why is Underwood coming to town? Did you lure him in under some kind of false pretense to finish the job we set out to do last week? Too late, Biel. My Yarborough is home under lock and key."

Yawning and scratching his head with rapid-fire movements, Bobby said, "I'm beyond that now. He wants to kiss and make up. I'll listen to whatever he has to say, and maybe then I'll take him up to the Tower of the Americas and toss him off."

"He's a no good liar and a thief. Why give him a second chance?"

"Don't you remember someone named Father Lawrence? How many second chances did he give you with the Lord God Almighty?" Jamie forgot he had shared that personal relationship with his friend.

"Fuck you, Biel. Get dressed and let's ride off to the airport. When we get there, I'll get you a pot of coffee and a couple of breakfast tacos." Bobby took a cold shower before they left his apartment. Traffic on Highway 281 was backed up all the way to I-410, so they took a detour and went to Jim's Coffee Shop for the much needed sustenance.

"How was your Thanksgiving?" Bobby asked.

"Couldn't have been better if you know what I mean. Maria outdid herself in the kitchen. I'm not sure where she learned how to cook, but she surpassed the fixings of an Army mess hall turkey day bonanza. Of course, you wouldn't know how the mess sergeants of the world go all out on Thanksgiving and Christmas."

Bobby didn't respond. With food in his belly and caffeine romping through his veins, he was ready to pick up Underwood. In the back of his mind, he was concerned about how Jamie would react when the two see each other again. He went ballistic on their return from Florida about not catching up with the "Beelzebub, Prince of Darkness," a new moniker he pinned on him.

"There he is." Bobby pointed to the arrival curb at United Airlines. Underwood was clad in a sharp business suit carrying a huge, boxy briefcase. Coming up from behind and standing next to the scientist was a lady they both knew well. Both were paralyzed, not knowing what to think or say to each other as their vehicle edged to the curb.

"What the hell is she doing here?" Bobby blurted out.

"Damned if I know," he said. "Strange things happen at home-coming events."

Kat Kurbell smiled warmly at both of them when they jumped from the car to greet them. She rushed to Jamie's side and gave him a bear hug, winking at Bobby in the process. The squeeze was so forceful, it knocked the air out of him. Gar Underwood observed her amorous attack without comment. He was not sure how Bobby would react to the unexpected visitor, nor did he care. Bobby would be thrilled when he found out.

"I brought along an old acquaintance of ours, well…as a surprise. She was excited to join me when I called her to discuss my proposed visit to San Antonio."

Kat released the series of vise-like squeezes and Jamie came around. She kissed him hard on the lips, sucking and swirling her tongue in and out of his mouth until he pushed her away. He shot a glare at Underwood.

What the hell are these two planning? What if Maria finds out about her? No way am I going to put those two together for one minute.

"Neither of us have any checked baggage, so let's get on with the show," Kat chirped.

"What show are you referring to?" Bobby asked.

Kat turned to Gar and nodded for the explanation.

"We're here to get Roberto Gomez out of that jail in Mexico."

"What the hell is going on? How did you know he was incarcerated across the border? I don't ever remember mentioning that to you."

"*Mucho dinero.*"

Underwood dropped the bomb. He'd let them try to defuse it.

CHAPTER 30

SOUTH TEXAS

B OBBY TOOK EVERYBODY BACK TO HIS APARTMENT for a pow wow and not a homecoming celebration of best friends. Against his better judgment, Jamie called Maria to join them. He sensed that sooner or later, she was going to inquire about Kat and assess his relationship with her. It was a gamble but one necessary if he wanted to keep Maria in his life. He loved her and vowed to dispense with his lying practice at every convenient turn of events. It wasn't fair to her. She wasn't home but left a message that she was in Killeen visiting her father and other relatives for a few days.

"How did you find out that Roberto was at a federal prison in Mexico?" Bobby asked Gar with suspicion mounting.

Why should I trust him after what he did to me? He couldn't wait any longer after wrestling with different scenarios on the drive from the airport.

"On my expedition to your farm to *borrow* your sea snails, I befriended one of the state troopers who by accident stumbled on your meth stash in the outbuilding."

"Accident? That's pure horse shit, Underwood. You led him to it," Jamie blasted out.

Underwood did not respond to the accusation but continued his explanation. "The state trooper felt bad about hauling Roberto off to Laredo and releasing him to the authorities. After lunch, as we were leaving the border town, he pulled me aside. Told me to call him any time, and he would brief me on what would happen to Roberto. I gave him a hundred-dollar bill and thanked him."

"And that's how you knew my farm hand was transferred to the federal prison?" Bobby said.

"Yes, sir, but that's not all."

"Please, let's terminate this conversation right now," Jamie cried out. "It's going nowhere."

"Hold on a minute. My state trooper friend called me several days later. He reported that Roberto was in a temporary holding cell in Nuevo Laredo pending transfer to a maximum security federal prison. At some point during the transition, and he didn't know exactly knew when, another criminal element down there tried to break him out. You two gentlemen wouldn't know anything about that, would you?"

"Of course not," Jamie said with a smug laugh. "I think it's time we had some liquid refreshments."

"Nice place you have here, Professor Biel," Kat changed the subject after settling in a lounger with a view of downtown and the Alamo. "Do you own the place?"

"He wishes he did," Underwood suggested. "He can afford it."

"I'll go fix us a batch of Margaritas," Jamie said. "We'll have you break out the specific details of your surprise visit after sipping some of my *especialies*."

"Before you start bloviating about Roberto's situation," Bobby said defiantly, "Tell me more about Slade Glick other than you think he's a killer. Specifically, where is he now and what's he up to?"

"The last time I saw him was at The Outer Banks in North Carolina."

"What were you doing there with the alleged killer?"

"Slade wanted out of Florida, kept looking over his shoulders. He thought the law was after him. He pleaded with me to help navigate his boat out of harm's way. We put the boat in dry dock at his uncle's place in North Carolina. He headed back to Chicago. I returned to New York…end of story."

"You liar!" Kat contradicted, "You flew out to San Francisco to visit me."

Jamie picked up pieces of the conversation as he strolled in to serve their drinks. He couldn't believe what he'd just heard. "Why did you visit Kat?" he asked Underwood.

"She called me shortly after you and Bobby had your fun time with her several weeks ago. She said she wanted a second opinion on her post-therapeutic recovery. Said she wasn't sure that Bobby had evaluated her thoroughly enough."

"Is that right, Kat?" Bobby asked defiantly.

"Sort of. He said that you asked him to visit me and take a look at my progress."

Bobby denied it. The conversation got heated and Bobby threatened Underwood but backed off knowing they'd discuss this later. Now he was more interested in learning Gar's plan to spring Roberto from the Los Zetas-controlled Mexican prison. Jamie was completely confused and glad that Maria was not sitting in on the conversation… he'd never be able to explain it to her, at least to her acceptance.

"Tell us how Kat can help down in Mexico," Bobby asked Underwood, now draining his third glass of the greenish white concoction.

"She's part-human, part-bird woman?"

"What the hell do you mean?" Bobby was flabbergasted.

"She asked me to sleep with her and observe what happens to her body after midnight. She knew there were unusual changes that took place but, in the morning, had no idea what happened during the previous night."

"Did you bang her?" Jamie asked as though he still had a vested interest in her human body.

"Shut up, Richards. None of your damn business," she said angrily, looking over at Underwood.

Gar continued. "The first night, nothing happened. She snored like a trooper. Her pet falcon squawked all night, but she was oblivious to the commotion. On the second night, a storm blew in from the Pacific, and that's when it happened."

"You gentlemen are not going to believe this," Kat said. "I didn't. However, the jury is still out."

Underwood went into great detail about what he'd witnessed. "She had risen from a deep sleep during the middle of the storm, and her body transformed into a much larger replica of her pet falcon. Her wingspan was at least…ten or twelve feet, her hands and feet claw-like, and an elongated nose that came to a sharp point. She didn't say a word to me, took her pet outside, and they both flew up and away off the porch. They returned several hours later, arguing with each other. An hour later, she morphed back to a humanoid and crawled back into bed."

"What were they arguing about?" Jamie inquired.

"Oh, that incident. I couldn't interpret the sounds. They were vibrosynching,"

"Huh?" Bobby had a blank look on his face.

"Vibrosynching is how they communicate with each other. He sends out vibes. She interprets them and *vibes* back to him."

Kat had no idea what Underwood was talking about.

"Do you think your other two patients talk to their pets in the same manner?" Jamie asked.

"Slade and his pet snake communicate that way."

"What about the Frenchman and his dog?" Bobby inquired.

"I believe they use another modality called audioblasmic airways."

"I guess this means they can't pick up each other's vibes but have the ability to understand sounds, moans, groans, and also barking and coughing," Jamie chipped in, now consumed with interest. He stood up and shook his head in amazement.

Garwood smiled and said, "Basically true. Dogs are *eared* like humans, so vibes don't work as effectively."

"Somewhere along the line I missed out on these tidbits of scientific information. I guess you researched it thoroughly," Bobby commented.

"Folks, I read and reread scientific journals. Also, one sunny day in the Keys before my *incident* with Zach Seltry, we had an interesting discussion on this same topic. He said dolphins and other sea mammals talk to each other...even give their offspring names. I was so intrigued I had to dig further into animal communications."

"Dr. Underwood, you're crazy." Kat laughed. "You have no idea what you're talking about."

After a brief pause, Bobby was the first to speak. "Let's talk specifically about Kat's situation. Gar, you have validated what I believed to have happened but did not witness."

Jamie had heard enough. His thought processes had suddenly reverted from minor bewilderment to total lack of comprehension. "Bullshit, you...you three hypocrites. I don't buy a thing that was said. I demand Underwood and Kat undergo a drug screen and a lie detector test. I can set it up for tomorrow."

"Don't waste your time, Richards," Gar said sternly. "I have it documented on film and also recorded the conversation between Kat and her falcon when they left the house and the argument that ensued when they returned. I have proof locked up in my safety deposit box in New York."

Jamie backed off on his threats. Kat fell asleep after one glass of the margarita drink. He was relieved, worrying that she might turn into some other kind of diabolical monster.

Bobby pulled Gar aside. "What's in that oversized briefcase you brought with you?"

"Aha! I thought you'd never ask."

Gar retrieved the suitcase-sized bag from a corner near the front entrance and opened it.

"Explain the contents," Bobby said. "All I see is wiring, fuses, bulbs, switches, and a headset. What goes?"

"I never told you I went back to school in my midthirties to become an electrical engineer."

"No, but I wouldn't put it past you. Nothing you say surprises me anymore. Why'd you bring it along with you?"

"I created a machine that will replicate an electrical storm. The headset is for Kat. Here's how it works. I strap it to her head and attach the leads to both sides of her temple. When I activate the switch, electrical currents race through her head and entire body. In fifteen minutes, the overwhelming but non-lethal charge transforms her into a gigantic falcon."

"Have you actually tested it on her?"

"Yes, and it works. She never understood what happened, didn't even demand an explanation."

Jamie was still coping with the concept. It started to make sense. He went over to Kat and examined her head. "Is that why there are some burn singes above each ear?"

"Yes, they are minor, and most folks won't see them when her hair grows longer. Her eyesight is exceptional, but the bird mind can't process the slightly charred skin. She thinks it's a flaw from the makeup she wears, so I leave it at that."

Kat woke up from her snooze and wondered why the three men were all hyped up. She sat on Jamie's lap and asked him if he was having fun. He gently nudged her to the floor and walked back to the kitchen and fixed something to eat. Bobby thought he knew what was coming next but waited for Underwood to spell it out.

"So, Bobby, got it all figured out yet?"

"Partially."

"Ah, Dr. Underwood, tell him and let's get on with it." Kat was laughing and chirping at the same time. "Hold on. I want Jamie to hear your pitch."

"Pitch on what?" he asked while setting the cheese and crackers on the end table.

Gar got up, snatched a slice of cheese, and shoved it into his mouth. He raised his arms in triumph and bellowed out, "Kat is going to fly to the prison in Mexico during their afternoon outdoor exercise break. She'll snatch Roberto from the outer yard and bring him back to our waiting arms on the US side of the border."

THEY STAYED IN BOBBY'S APARTMENT OVERNIGHT. Kat was disappointed because she wanted to slip away with Jamie and shack up in that hotel they stayed in after her cure. He refused, telling her he was married now and gave up messing around with other women. She didn't believe one word of it but stayed psyched up for the rescue mission.

In the early morning, they set off for Bobby's farm in South Texas. Underwood told him he had to perfect one more technicality to insure the prison snatch would work. Bobby wanted to know what was missing, but Underwood told him he'd discuss the particulars after they arrived at the research facility.

They stopped halfway down I-35 and had breakfast at a local Mexican restaurant. Kat refused to eat, arguing that the only thing edible in Texas was smoked brisket with gobs of sweet sauce. She mouthed off to Bobby stating that breakfast tacos were for people like Roberto Gomez. No urbanite from San Francisco would eat *menudo* or any other disposable animal parts.

Bobby signaled to the passengers. "We're almost there."

"I sure don't remember the ride. I was deathly sick," Kat said. "In any event, there's really nothing worth seeing anyway. Why do people live out here isolated from the rest of humanity?"

"You would never understand," Bobby responded.

When they pulled in, Jamie was happy to get on with the mission. He wasn't sure what part he would play in the overall scheme of things but his adrenaline was running on overtime. He broke out in a cold sweat but told himself not to slip out of control and not overanticipate what could backfire.

Bobby had hired a neighbor to take care of the animals in Roberto's absence. He was heartsick when the farm hand told him that Dolly had died. All the other chimps were thriving. The goats were milked on schedule, and the proceeds of the sale were kept by the neighbor. That was part of the arrangement. Bobby noted that the new lightning rods were in place on the roof of the research barn. In addition, all the damage caused by the earlier electrical storm was repaired.

"Gather some twigs and pieces of wood for the firepit," Bobby directed. "It'll be dark soon. We'll knock down a few bottles of Shiner Bock. I've given up on Sam Adams. I'm sure Gar Underwood is eager to amplify his explanation for retrieving Roberto."

"Go ahead and get the fire ready," Gar acknowledged. "I'll be in the research lab. There's one more piece of equipment I have to wire up, and we'll be all set for tomorrow."

"I'll go with you," Kat said.

"No, you won't," Jamie snapped. "Let him be. You'll help us collect the wood."

"All I wanted was to see the inside of the research barn again."

Jamie scowled. "Not going to happen."

Several hours later, the fire was lapping at the sky with kaleidoscopic colors. Sparks were flicking out sideways and sucked upward with the shifting wind. Underwood returned from the barn and told them he had to insure that the heat sensors in the unit were working properly. He had some earlier trouble with the component because of its high sensitivity to rays of bright sunlight. He hoped the weather forecast reported last night would hold true for tomorrow afternoon. They needed the overcast sky and absence of any signs of rain or lightning.

"Okay, Dr. Underwood, clue us in on your plan," Jamie suggested. "Tell us the purpose of the accessories you've been playing around with all day. They look sophisticated."

"First, I'll address the equipment part," he said as he emptied the big briefcase. "This box is my electromagnetic, hyperdigitalization kit. I call it my EMHD kit for short."

"Huh?" Bobby said with a blank look in his eyes.

"Correct. It's designed to trigger nighttime brain function. I've tested it several times and am satisfied with the results."

"Explain how this toy works," Jamie taunted, thinking Underwood may have slipped off the edge of sanity.

"I'll try to simplify so bear with me. Sleep experts theorize that our sleep consists of two components called non-REM and REM sleep. REM means rapid eye movements. We cycle through the two components every hour and a half to two hours. During the non-REM stages, our brain waves and muscle activity slow down, eye movements stop, and our heart rate and brain waves slow down. Finally, our blood pressure falls, our breathing slows. and our body temperature decreases."

"What's in the REM component?" Jamie was now totally confused.

"This is where the EMHD kit is so valuable. All of the functions I mentioned speed up in the REM stage but our limbs become paralyzed. Most of our dreams occur in this component."

"So what?" Jamie still didn't get it. Bobby sat back and smiled.

"Listen up. Tomorrow afternoon, when we stop near the Mexican border, I'll put this headphone-looking device on Kat, connect the unit to my EMHD box, and switch it to the positive mode. She will fall right to sleep, and her brain will notify her system that it's after midnight. At this stage, she cycles into the REM phase. Then I'll switch the lever to the negative mode. This activates the thermo-dynometer charge, which kicks in and simulates an electrical storm."

"I think I get it now." Jamie smiled. "You have to accelerate past the early sleep levels to get to the REM stage, the only position where your EMHD kicks in."

Gar and Bobby nodded in agreement.

"Kat will be physically transformed into a large, eight-foot falcon with a ten- to twelve-foot wingspan. A massive genetic mutation will create a humanoid-animal relationship similar to her precious pet. That's what we made her into when the electrical storm hit the gurneys in our research lab when she and the others submitted to our melanoma cure."

"Hurrah!" Kat exclaimed. "I suspected that happened and played along. Now I know for sure. I get the shivers to think I become a mutant of sorts. I also believe the transformation happened to that bastard Slade Glick and the queer from Paris. I forget his name and the name of their stupid pets. Can we now be called the Tri-mutants or the Triode Mutants?"

"Shut the fuck up," Jamie said. "It's not funny."

"I'm serious whether you believe it or not."

Bobby recollected the big jar of eyeballs he stumbled on in Kat's garage. It all started to make sense to him. Jamie sat back and wrestled with Underwood's wild dissertation. He remembered the time in

San Francisco when he knew something was out of kilter with her. He understood the second part of Underwood's explanation how Kat was going to free Roberto.

"C'mon, Dr. Underwood, tell them what Kat Mutant's going to do." She was antsy to help.

"Tomorrow morning, before we leave, you will spend time in Roberto's bedroom. I want you to smell and store in your nasal passages the scent of his dirty clothing, bedding and everything he may have touched in there."

"Why?" Jamie asked.

"When she flies into the prison yard to snatch Roberto, she will have the smell of him impregnated in her senses. This heightened sensation will help her find him among the many prisoners spread out in the yard. And, as is the case with many birds of prey, falcons have exceptional powers of vision. The visual acuity of one species has been measured at almost three times that of a normal human. Sight and smell will lead her directly to our man."

"How's she going to know where to fly to once we release her in Laredo?" Jamie inquired. "Even though her vision will be enhanced, the topography of the Nuevo Laredo area will be difficult to read. We learned on our earlier attempt that the prison is integrated into the industrial area of the city. There are several small factories and warehouses surrounding it."

"I'm glad you asked, Jamie. I also witnessed Bobby's eyes questioning my explanation. Here's the scoop. My EMHD kit has a built-in and rather sophisticated GPS system. I'll preset the exact coordinates of the prison. She'll be electronically wired with most direct route to the prison yard before she flies off on her mission to Mexico."

Immersed in deep thought, they drank one more round of Shiner Bock before dousing the fire and heading off to bed. Kat wanted to sleep with Jamie again. She was still stymied why he refused her in San Antonio. He was steadfast in his rebuttal, couldn't be coaxed no matter what she tried. She was so upset she decided to sleep in the research barn against his earlier objection to go out there.

Maybe he'll change his mind and search for me. I know deep down he wants to bed me. It'd be so exciting to pull the three gurneys together, climb on up, and copulate till it feels like we died and gone to heaven!

CHAPTER 31

MEXICO

Bobby prepared a hardy breakfast of beans and eggs. The group waited patiently for Kat to return from the barn. When she didn't come in at the preplanned time, they went looking for her. She wasn't in the research barn, but they found her next to the outbuilding where the stash of meth was stored. Somehow, she was able to pop the lock from the door and help herself to some of the contents. She was sprawled on the ground chirping at a squirrel twenty feet away. Bobby found evidence of snorting sufficient enough to reach heightened euphoria. He knew that most addicts ingesting higher doses induce manic behavior with accompanying feelings of high self-esteem and increased libido. He'd been there, done that. They were able to awaken her and lead her back to the farm house. Gar Underwood was sure her wayward behavior would not impede his plan but decided to hydrate her just in case. Their departure was delayed, but the window of opportunity was still open to attempt the jail extraction.

"What time do the prisoners take their afternoon exercise break?" Jamie asked Gar as they sped down the highway.

"Between three and four, according to my state trooper contact."

"Good, we're almost there," Bobby said.

Several miles before the city limits of Laredo, they exited I-35 onto an isolated farm road heading west. Twenty minutes later, they found a small thicket of oak trees and behind them an open field. There weren't any farms or other structures within miles. They had a clear view of the Rio Grande, twisting and turning across the land like a giant serpent. While they saw clusters of buildings across the border, they weren't able to identify the exact location of the federal prison. The GPS was a necessity to complete the pull out. It was one o'clock, hot and humid with overcast skies.

"Everybody, out of the car," Bobby ordered. "It's time."

Underwood took Kat back to the car, sat her down on the back seat, and retrieved his EMHD kit from the trunk. Jamie trained a pair of binoculars across the river but was unable to sight the prison. Bobby went back and retrieved his camera out of the glove compartment.

Underwood hooked up the headset and flipped the lever to the positive mode. Kat fell asleep immediately. Ten minutes later, he flipped the lever to the negative mode. The sound of thunder and lightning prompted Bobby to put his hands to his ears. He was close to Kat observing the transition. The rumblings didn't bother Jamie because he was off conducting a perimeter check.

They waited another few minutes and then yanked Kat from the back seat of the car. Morphogenesis was setting in, and she was growing faster than Gar expected. Her developing wings knocked him to the ground. Jamie returned from his surveillance and whistled at the dramatic changes to her body. Bobby hoped that Underwood was in complete control of the emerging large falcon. All they needed was the gigantic bird to attack them and abort the mission. It was three o'clock when Underwood reached into the kit and switched on the GPS.

"Off you go, sweet bird woman," he sang out. "Find our Roberto and bring him back here as soon as possible."

Her screeching chirp acknowledged the command. It almost broke their eardrums as she blasted off the ground like the launching of an NASA space shuttle heading toward the Rio Grande. The wingspan was so impressive, Jamie ducked as though he was about to climb on an engine-revving helicopter. Bobby was so enthralled, he failed to snap a picture of the huge bird.

Ten minutes later, the giant falcon found the prison and hovered a hundred yards above the clamoring group of prisoners. She descended incrementally and then pulled the picture of Roberto that Underwood planted in her bird memory bank. She confirmed her prey through a sensitive olfactory system.

"Oh my god, look up there," a prisoner yelled at the top of his lungs while finishing up a set of pullups on overhead bars.

"What the fuck is that?" a second prisoner shouted to nobody in particular. He froze in place and stared at the incoming blur.

"It's a rocket falling off course!" screamed a third prisoner.

"Bullshit," said the second prisoner. "It's a goddamn small jet with the engine conked out. Let's get the hell out of here."

The bird-like Kat descended two hundred miles an hour toward the floor of the prison yard. Small bony tubercles on her nostrils guided the powerful airflow away from the nostrils. The function enabled her to breathe more easily by reducing the change in air pressure. To protect her eyes, she used a third set of eyelids to secrete tears and clear any molecules of debris while maintaining vision.

"Son of a bitch!" Roberto screamed out as he saw the bird zero in on him. He ran toward the steel door leading to the interior of the prison. It was too late. She seized him with clenched feet and whisked him upward and away from the prison grounds. A guard stationed in the near tower could not believe what he had witnessed. Gaining control of his senses, he opened fire at the monster bird but was way off target. Roberto had passed out from fright, unaware of his plight.

"Here they come!" Bobby shouted out.

"I don't believe what I'm seeing," Jamie whispered.

Kat dumped the bewildered Roberto to the ground and perched on a nearby live oak tree. She flapped her wings repeatedly as though trying to rid them of a foreign substance that she may have picked up on the return route. Roberto was mumbling streams of Spanish melodies. Bobby interpreted them as bedtime stories told to the young children in Mexican families. Underwood started running back to the car to fetch his EMHD kit.

"Why are you in such a rush, Gar?" Bobby asked. "Enjoy the magnificent sight from the friendly oak tree."

Underwood had no time to engage in conversation. He was hell-bent on getting on with the next step. Bobby remembered his camera and snapped off several pictures of the big bird. It was now picking at different body parts as though flicking off fleas or other air-borne insects.

"I need to reverse the process and restore Kat to her humanoid form," Underwood said.

"How do you do that?" Jamie asked when the scientist rushed past him.

"I reverse the process, turning night back into day."

"Don't you need to put the headset back on the bird?"

"No, the reversal is done by remote control."

"Jamie, go to her but stand clear. When I flip the lever back, she will revert to human form in about five minutes. As this reversal happens, climb up the tree and steady her. She will not have any strength for about an hour. I don't want her to fall off the tree and get hurt."

How in the world did I ever make love to this she-animal? She could have killed me, plucked my eyes out, and tossed me to the dogs. I must have been high on something other than uncontrolled passion. On second thought, I wonder what it'd be like to screw this...this thing. Bestiality is outlawed in most countries, but I witnessed it in Africa when I was deployed there.

Stop it, Richards, for Christ's sake. She's a human being first, manipulated by the forces of nature. I ought to kill that Underwood prick for his violations of every moral code attributable to man. Bobby would never have allowed this to happen if he were in charge!

"Roberto, wake up!" Bobby said, slapping him gently in the face.

"What... Where... Who?" Roberto said out loud as he came to and turned his head. "Oh Señor Biel, praise the Almighty One for guiding you to that hell hole. I had a horrible dream that I was taken out of the prison yard by a bird as big as *su casa.*"

"Not to worry now, Roberto. Forget the entire episode. Someday, we'll share a bottle of the best tequila, and I'll tell you what happened."

"*Si.* But that man with you is bad, bad," Roberto whispered as he pointed to Underwood.

"You'll have to forgive him. He arranged your daring release from captivity. Let's leave it at that."

"Is that Señorita Kat standing by the tree with Jamie?"

"Yes, she is visiting us from San Francisco and came along for the ride."

"She is so nice. We got along so well at your farm house. I also remember her kind mother."

"I know."

"Does Jamie love her?"

"Sh, you're talking way too much, Roberto. Why don't you get in the car and we'll all go home."

Bobby led him to the car. Gar joined Jamie and Kat. They were now underneath the oak tree.

"How do you feel?" he asked her.

"Tired and worn out from the heat and humidity, but I see we got the job done."

"Certainly did. Do you remember anything, Kat?"

"No, let's get the hell out of this forsaken stretch of real estate. I'm hungry."

They all jammed into the car and started back to the interstate, avoiding a group of whirling tumbleweeds enveloping the farm road. A roadrunner raced across the road in front of them. Kat wanted them to stop the car and check the "poetry in motion" as she called the native bird. She got overruled. They found the restaurant where they had breakfast earlier in the day. Kat commented how she loved the chicken enchiladas and refried beans. She said the proprietor should open up another restaurant in San Francisco. She assured them it would be an immediate hit.

It was decided to stay the night at Bobby's farm before returning to San Antonio in the morning. The first thing on Roberto's agenda when they pulled into the driveway was to check on the animals. Bobby overheard him telling the goats and chimps how much he missed them and was glad they were well. He started to cry when he didn't spot Dolly in the cages. Bobby walked over to console him. He told Roberto there was a move afoot nationally to stop using chimpanzees for medical research.

"Do you mean they are going to take away my friends, Señor Bobby?"

"I think we're safe for the time being. Let's go celebrate your release from hell!"

This time, Kat didn't want to go anywhere near the research barn and opted to sleep on the couch in the living room. Jamie was afraid to go to sleep, thinking that she might sneak into his room and crawl in bed with him. He didn't have to worry; she found her way to Gar Underwood's bedroom shortly after midnight. She never forgot his visit to San Francisco and the steamy time they had in her bed.

CHAPTER 32

SAN ANTONIO

"YOU OUGHT TO PATENT THAT GIZMO," Jamie droned as they streaked down the freeway toward the city limits of San Antonio. Underwood gave him a nod and continued to massage Kat's arms. She complained of terrible soreness stating that she had never experienced the problem before. She confided in Underwood earlier that she never remembered what took place when she assumed Stryker's body. He told her she carried a tremendous load traversing several miles and that the arms and shoulders would be sore for several more days. She asked him softly in his ear if they did it last night. He denied intimacy, telling her she simply had a bad dream.

"No, Jamie, the fewer people who know I have the EMHD kit, the better."

"Why is that?"

"If placed in the hands of the criminal element of the world, we'd never be able to control them or their progenies. People have to experience both the non-REM and REM components of sleep."

"We need to use Underwood's system again, Jamie," Bobby said. "We have two other people to check out and determine if they experience the same transformations as our friend Kat."

She laughed and made fun of the other two male characters she spent time receiving the cure on the gurneys in South Texas. "Those boys are bad news. I'm sorry to have to divulge the information to you three gentlemen commiserating with me. I'm convinced that the human male is a dangerous species and can be molded into raping and killing machines. Look at what that bastard Slade Glick tried to do to me on the farm."

"Why do you think that?" Bobby asked.

"You of all people should know. Sitting right next to you is a perfect example of what I'm talking about."

"Me?" Jamie asked, incredulous.

"Yes, you are a professional, blood-thirsty murderer, skillfully molded into a killing machine by our obnoxious government. I know what you did when you played, soldier boy."

"I don't recall telling you about my *black* past."

"Let me think. Was it Bobby or Gar when we were together in San Francisco?"

Nobody responded. The passengers remained silent as Bobby drove into the downtown parking garage near his apartment. He informed his out-of-state passengers that there was no more party time left on his agenda. They had to catch a flight home as early as tonight. Kat booked an eight o'clock to San Francisco, and Gar was lucky to get a red eye back to New York.

Jamie called Maria and was thrilled that she had returned from visiting family in Killeen. She offered to come by and pick him up. He talked her out of it, not willing to take a chance on her mingling with Kat. Bobby asked Gar to join him in the back room. He told Jamie and Kat that they needed to hash out a few scientific issues while they still had a few remaining hours together.

"Fine with me," Kat said. "Jamie and I have to discuss our future together."

"What the hell are you talking about, woman?"

315

"You remember what you told me in bed last night at the farm?"

"No, I don't. I think you are getting me confused with the doctor from New York."

"I am not! You fell asleep in the overstuffed chair by the fireplace. Gar Underwood was uncomfortable sleeping in the guest bedroom. He came creeping to my couch in the living room. He told me this sad story about his inability to fall asleep unless I was in bed next to him. He was too drunk to do anything. After twenty minutes of frustration, I kicked him out, told him to get back to his bedroom. It wasn't ten minutes later when you came crawling on the couch wanting to 'test the waters one more time,' as you put it."

Jamie became stupefied and delved into what might have happened last night. *What the hell did I do late last night? We all got hammered with that cheap tequila Roberto hauled out of his room and essentially poured down everybody's throat in ceremonial fashion. I remember Kat jumping from lap to lap and hugging Roberto like he was some long lost uncle reincarnated. I recall dragging my ass to an easy chair before I blacked out into a deep sleep. Not sure how I got this sore back. Maybe I'd better call Maria and make sure she doesn't come over to pick me up.*

Bobby and Gar stared at each other with a quizzical look on their faces and then walked to the back room. "Gar, I think we have a serious predicament on our hands," Bobby said with a deep frown on his face.

"Yes, I know exactly what you're thinking about Kat."

"No, not the lawyer-bird-mutant but the other two. We simply can't take any chances," Bobby said. "We have to act now. Do you want to go to Chicago or France?"

"I've had enough of that Slade Glick character to last a lifetime. You go check him out and I'll run down Monsieur Duvair. They both have unusual pets. The million-dollar question to be answered here is whether they morph like Kat and take the animal form of their pets. Obviously, the hour of midnight or the presence of lightning or perhaps a combination of both triggers the transformation."

"What are we going to do about the illustrious Kat Kurbell?"

"Maybe we can have Jamie tail her in San Francisco. We need to know more about what she does at night. I'm not totally convinced she is killing people. I didn't witness anything when I was there the last time. At least, the law enforcement folks haven't fingered her."

"I'm not too sure. Deep down, I think that we both know the answer. How do you explain that jar of slimy eyeballs in the garage that I told you about?"

Underwood shrugged.

"How soon can you get to Paris?" Bobby switched gears, not wanting to believe they created a murdering monster.

"I need two days to clean up some things, and then I'll board Air France and see the night lights of Gay Paree."

"Watch out for him. He may be a serial killer."

"Bobby, you always seem to overreact. I got it covered."

When they came back into the living room, Jamie and Kat were still arguing.

"Hey, hold on, sports fans," Gar interrupted. "We are all good friends here. What's the problem, Jamie?"

"I think Kat is hallucinating. Bobby, you got any meth around your apartment so she can snort it and back off the unwarranted attacks on me?"

"She'll be fine. You know how thoroughbreds are, always on their high horses. Kat, sit down and relax."

Before they could sort everything out, Bobby's sophisticated intrusion system announced that Maria was downstairs. Jamie was surprised that she didn't follow his instructions. "I'll go down and meet her in the lobby." He was more than ready to go home.

Kat wanted to know about the mysterious lady downstairs, but Bobby interceded. "It's a female taxicab driver we all know from the past who's coming to pick him up."

"Good-bye, Jamie. I'm counting the days until you come to San Francisco and visit me again." She moved to give him a good-bye hug, but he backed off and slipped out the door.

Later Bobby, Gar, and Kat had a delicious meal at the Houston Street Bistro. The maître d' found them a quiet table in the rear and offered each a complimentary glass of Bordeaux wine. Kat declined, telling him she preferred a Napa wine if available. After dinner, they went to the San Antonio International Airport to get Kat on her flight. Bobby expected a problem from the feisty lady but was pleasantly surprised when she smiled at the agents manning the security checkpoint. She passed through and waltzed out of sight down the long corridor to the planes. She never turned back to wave a good-bye.

"What do you think, Gar?"

"About what?"

"Her."

"Let's put our thoughts about her on ice. We'll get Jamie out there in a few weeks. I would love to reach a final verdict on these three people so we can put our worries to bed for good and move on with the rest of our lives."

"Amen to that."

They hung around the airport bar until Gar's departure flight was announced. Realizing they may have caused more problems than either of them expected, Bobby forgave Underwood for his transgressions involving the Conus sea snail escapade. They both agreed that their continued research in developing a melanoma cure was past history. They were wealthy enough to entertain other exciting ventures. Bobby told him he was going to dismantle the research lab and wind up his methamphetamine business. He and Roberto talked about developing their own brand of tequila from the ample supply of agave plants on the farm.

"I'd better get going, they're about to close the gate."

"Call me before you fly to Paris."

"I'll do that."

They shook hands, gave each other a friendly hug with gentle slaps on the back. Gar waved one last good-bye when he went through the gate. The attendant chewed him out for holding up the flight's scheduled departure and zinging their on-time, top-ranking departure in the industry. When he was seated in his first-class accommodation, his cell phone rang.

"Gar Underwood, it's me."

"Who?" he shouted through the bad connection.

"It's me, Uriel Seltry from Florida."

"Oh hi, can't talk to you now. I'm about to take off on a flight back to New York. They just announced that we have to turn our cells off and kill any other electronic equipment for takeoff."

"Thank goodness you're on your way back home. I just got off a flight at LaGuardia, and I'm hunkered down in a taxicab heading to your apartment. It's raining like hell."

"What?" I can't hear you."

"See you soon, love."

MARIA SERRANO WAS DELIGHTED to see Jamie again. After picking him up at Bobby's apartment, they stopped at a wine bar in the Quarry Mall. It was crowded with the young set that frequented the popular place every night after work. They were seated outside at the last unoccupied table. She told him how much she missed him and hoped he felt the same. He reassured her that he'd been constantly thinking of her, which was true to a point.

"Did you spend any time in your old stomping grounds at Fort Hood when you visited your family in Killeen?"

"Sure, I had a chance to recall all the good times and revisit the place where we first met. It was my first priority. The family came in second. Dad is getting frail. He walks with a cane now. My favorite cousin returned from his tour in Afghanistan. They are two peas in a pod. I wasn't sure if I should've believed the stories they told."

"How's that, Maria?"

"Dad said he enjoyed blowing up buildings when he was a tanker. My cousin did one better. He bragged that he blew up a whole city block housing the Taliban." What she didn't tell Jamie was that her cousin knew him. He'd told her that Jamie Richards had a bad reputation on base. He was known to be temperamental and made it known he loved to kill. Maria loved her cousin but dismissed his comments as some kind of professional jealousy among seasoned troops.

Jamie changed the subject. "Any changes at the base?"

"Yes, dear, we're both gone."

"Yeah, times have changed…for the good."

"I don't know about policy changes, Jamie, but the same people still work there."

"How's your new job at Fort Sam coming along?"

"Great. We survived the manpower survey team visit with flying colors. They only cut three positions."

Jamie took her hand and cuddled closer to her. He had a hard time hearing with all the background noise slapping his ears. A ruckus was happening at the table behind them. Two guys were arguing and pointing their fingers at each other. One of the ladies at their table tried to separate them but was pushed backward. She fell hard against Jamie.

It all started again. He took several deep breaths, but it didn't help. His body shook, his heart beat was racing out of control, and beads of sweat formed at his forehead and under his arms. Maria placed a firm hand on his arm, shook her head, and told him not to get involved. He lifted the lady off of him and sat her back on the chair she'd just vacated. The larger guy broke off his spat with the other man and glared at Jamie for touching his date.

"Come get me, you prick, and I'll slice you up," Jamie said defiantly. He automatically reached around to his back waist area and padded around—it wasn't there.

"Stop! Stop it, Jamie! Let's go, now!"

She pulled him away forcibly and shoved him in the direction of their parked car. He looked back as management intervened, and the altercation at the other table subsided. When they got back in the car, she pulled him to her chest.

"Why don't we go straight home and tend to your aggression in another, more appeasing manner," she cooed.

"Are you thinking what I'm thinking?" he asked.

"Yes, it's the only sure way I know how to settle you down."

An all-nighter with a sexy woman was what he needed, and she delivered in ways he only saw on porno flicks in the barracks. No normal human female could replicate half the moves. In the morning, he woke her gently and offered to fix her breakfast in bed. She nodded her approval with a warm and inviting smile. Soft-boiled eggs and bacon strips fried to a crisp were her favorites. Wheat toast was optional, based on availability of the bread. He joined her in bed to eat the meal. They didn't have any clothing on and fed each other, spoon by spoon, bite by bite. It was one of the most sensuous byproducts of the sex act he'd ever experienced. She witnessed a tenderness that she'd never seen or felt with him before.

"Let's fly to Vegas right this minute and get married," she said seductively.

"Bare ass naked?"

"Of course not, you fool. How about it, Jamie?"

"Let's not rush into it."

"Why not?"

"I want to be sure."

"About what?"

He knew where this was conversation was heading. Every time they had sex, she begged to get married. *Why can't she be happy the way things are with us and stop backing me in the corner about getting hitched? I know she wants a kid and appreciates the fact that I don't use an umbrella hoping it happens. How can I keep putting her off and continue to enjoy the fabulous sex we have together? Kat never harped about going to the altar after we did each other. Then again, we didn't know each other that long. Where am I going wrong here? Oh, I know what to do. I'll buy her an engagement ring. Should put her off for a while. If I knock her up, I'll make a decision to get hitched at that point in time.*

"Jamie, wake up. You started to doze off on me. Am I too much for you or what?" She laughed.

"Or what is the answer to that question."

"Well, Mr. Richards, is it Vegas or not?"

"I made some commitments I can't get out of right now."

"You're kidding me, right?"

"No, Maria, but I have a plan."

"It better be good."

"Let's get dressed and go to James Avery's and get a ring."

"Oh my goodness, a wedding ring?"

"No, an engagement ring."

"Does that mean we engaged now, Jamie?"

"Yes."

They swept the breakfast trays off the bed, smashing the half-empty coffee cups in pieces on the tile floor. She jumped on him and gave him a headlock he couldn't get out of. He wrapped his legs around her waist and began to caress her breasts. She was breathing out of control as she massaged the jagged scar lines on his back and the side of his head. His cell phone rang. He elected not to answer it, letting it slip over to voice mail. As they were about to consummate their official engagement, he couldn't ignore the message being recorded.

"Jamie, Denis Sweeny here. Call me right away."

CHAPTER 33

FRANCE

PIERRE DUVAIR WAS IN TROUBLE. He knew he had to get out of Verdun. Everything was closing in on him. His neighbors had no use for him, his dog despised him, and he was bored to death. He missed the excitement of Paris and the fine dining found on every corner of the enchanting city sporting the historical Seine River. He had changed—a change he deemed for the betterment of society. He was no longer sick and had the capability to commit to volunteer work at the Louvre, the best museum in the entire universe.

But something was gnawing away at him. Some mornings he felt totally spent, muscles ached and terrible headaches pounded away at him. This happened after a thunderstorm swept across the region. He wasn't sure if he was having horrible dreams or simply walking miles and miles in his sleep.

"I see yer packing up. Going on a long trip?" The pest from down the street had seen him loading boxes into the trunk of the Peugeot.

"Oh, hello there, neighbor. Yes, you might call it that. Need to take a sabbatical from my writing. Fiction writers need to seek new stimulation periodically, and I'm no different than the rest of them."

"Didn't know you were an author. Whadya write about?"

"Just some pornography. You wouldn't be interested in any of the stories."

"You're wrong there, Mister. Mom and yours truly love the stuff, especially Mom. She couldn't live without it. Sorry we had to give it up when her brain froze up on her. She used the camera given to her as a birthday present when she was a snotty-nosed kid. It still works to a certain degree. Every Sunday, we'd ride around and take pictures of our beautiful countryside. I preferred pictures of the old cathedrals. She only worked with black and white though. Photo shop downtown told her years ago that the gadget is archaic, whatever that meant."

Is this old man hard of hearing or what? He thinks I said photography. "Where's your aluminum walker?"

"Broke it. Tossed it at Mom one night."

"Why?"

"Peed again on the carpet. Does it several times each day. You'd think her twinkie had radar vision because she always hits the same damn spot."

This ancient mariner is something else. I wonder if he dresses himself in the morning! "Maybe you should place her in one of those old folk's homes."

"Can't afford it. Maybe I'll snuff her out tonight and get it over with. Oh, that reminds me, have you heard they caught that serial killer in Etain?"

Pierre gasped, wasn't sure he heard him correctly, and asked the neighbor to repeat what he'd just told him. More animated, he stammered out the same story. He told Pierre the killer lived directly across the river from him. The Verdun newspaper reported that the man's much younger wife lived a double life. During the day, she was a school teacher. On weekends, she was a "lady of the night." The husband learned about it from a military friend who had purchased her services on successive weekends during the past summer.

A car honked to pass them, and they ambled to the shoulder. Pierre studied the old man and fell silent. *Last night, I had his ugly dream that I was a notorious killer and people called me the second coming of Jack the Ripper. His attacks involved female prostitutes who lived and worked in the slums of London. Their throats were sliced open before he mutilated their bellies. Ugh, how gross!*

"Hey there, snap out of it. Thought for a moment you were turning to stone on me. Got to do the runs now. Oh, excuse me. Slip of the tongue. Got to shuffle along. Have a good trip."

The old man was out of sight when Pierre returned to his house and told Louie they were moving back to Paris. Louie sat on the floor motionless. He was getting used to the inconvenience of moving. He thought his master was crazy anyway, so leaving the riverfront home for another apartment in busy and crazy Paris wasn't about to change him.

A week later, Duvair boarded up the house, loaded his car, coaxed Louie to jump in the back seat, and took off. He couldn't wait to get back to his beloved city and regretted ever leaving it. He was lonely and distraught. He needed another lover, someone who cared for him and appreciated his many fine qualities.

GAR UNDERWOOD LANDED AT CHARLES DE GAULLE AIRPORT in time for a nap. He was overtired, not having slept in his lush Air France first-class seat. The meal service was typical sauce and gravy French. The braised pullet, smothered with a dry wine mushroom concoction was simply world class. The food and wine he consumed wasn't the reason for his dismay and restlessness. He attributed that to the unexpected visit of Uriel Seltry two days before he planned his trip to France. He deplaned half-asleep, then clearing French Customs presented a sticky problem.

"You can't bring that machine into our country. We're going to confiscate it and hold it for the bomb squad to check it out."

"But I have papers certifying that my EMHD kit is a technical device to support my scientific research. I've got the papers here."

"Show the bomb squad when they arrive."

The problem got resolved two hours later. The forged documents prepared by an associate in Manhattan did the trick. He was exhausted, couldn't go on any further. Instead of trudging outside to hail a taxi, he stretched out across three seats near the baggage conveyors. His unshaven face, rumpled clothing and staggering gait alarmed a young lady sitting across from the vacant seats. She mumbled a few words he didn't understand and left in disgust. Just before he dozed off, he recalled the two-day period prior to his trans-Atlantic flight. Uriel Seltry created such an unexpected diversion he almost cancelled his trip.

He had met her on the doorsteps to his apartment. "How did you find my place, Uriel?"

"Gar, honey, did you forget that my Zach Seltry was a cop among other things? One lonely night when he was out of town, I decided to access his work computer. It was easy to hack into his personnel database, and I found your address. I hope my surprise visit didn't alarm you. We need to catch up on a few things."

"I'm very busy, Uriel, I'm scheduled to leave for France in two days. What do you want?"

"I thought you'd like to know that the old crony in the jail who confessed to the park murder committed suicide so Zach formally closed the bizarre case. You're home free, darling."

"Look here, sweet thing. I didn't kill that lady in the park!"

"I didn't say it was your doing, Gar."

"Thanks for the assurance. Um, hear anything about the missing deputy?"

"How'd you know about that?" she asked him pointedly.

"I read about it in the local paper. Heard he had a family."

"He was a disgrace to both his family and the department. Best Zach could figure the jerk wanted to rid himself of his family responsibilities and took off for parts unknown. Zach knew he'd experimented with drugs at one time but thought he was clean. He kept him on the force because of the wife and four kids."

"I got to go in now, Uriel. Can you call me tonight?"

"You don't sound hospitable, Gar. Did you forget the sizzling nights we had in the Keys?"

"Um, no, of course not, you were hot to trot, and the sex was first class."

"I missed my last period."

"Huh, you still have that mess every month at your age?"

"Yes. What if I'm pregnant?"

"You're married, right?"

"We officially separated."

"My congratulations to Zack. Separated or not, he always wanted kids."

"It wouldn't be his kid... He's sterile."

"Look, Uriel, you have been sleeping around with every Tom, Dick, and Harry. Why finger me?"

"Because I want you to marry me!"

"Wake up, sir, you're talking so loud in your sleep you're drawing a crowd," a young Frenchman said as he shook Underwood's shoulders.

"Thanks, I was having a terrible dream."

He collected his belongings and hailed a cab. He booked a hotel two blocks from Pierre Duvair's apartment on the Champs-Elysees and sacked out the rest of the day and night. Refreshed and energized, he set out the next morning to find Duvair. Frustration set in when he learned that his patient didn't live in the swank apartment building anymore. He was mad at himself for assuming the Frenchman lived in the same location listed in the documents they had on file.

"Where did he move to?" he asked the apartment manager.

"I'm afraid that's personal information, and I can't release it to you."

"I'm a doctor. I came all the way from the United States to personally tell Monsieur Duvair he has a life-threatening disease." He opened a briefcase and showed her enough bogus papers that she was convinced and apologized for harassing him. She remembered somebody saying he went to America to seek medical relief for a serious problem.

"On top of that, the disease is contagious. I need to get to him as soon as possible or the whole city might have to be quarantined." He felt the comment was extreme but needed her to react.

"Please come inside and settle down. I'll get us a glass of wine while I check our file of forwarding addresses. It's locked up in a file cabinet in the back. It'll only be a few minutes."

Underwood surveyed the large room and loved the tapestry. The design had to go back to the days of Napoleon. Small area swag lamps were out of place but they were ornate enough to get by. The low-hanging chandelier had stubby candle lights which more than likely came from the same period as the tapestry. The room and everything in it smelled musty, but the red wine was superb.

"Here it is," she said coming through the foyer. "He moved to Verdun."

"Where is Verdun?"

"I'm not sure, somewhere west of here by the Atlantic coast, maybe in Normandy. There was a big battle in Verdun during one of our wars. We beat the stuffing's out of the raping Hun invaders. General Adolph Hitler was sent straight to hell!"

"I'm familiar with the history." *Stupid French lady with the hairy legs has no clue about her country's infamous war involvements. Doesn't seem to know much geography about her beautiful country.* "Give me the exact address, and I'll find it."

"Would you care for some hot croissants?" She was warming up to the visitor. *He's short but is so handsome. I'm old and fat, but maybe he has a weakness for French women of any age and dimension.*

"No, thanks," Underwood said. "I'm in a hurry. Remember what I said about the communicable disease?"

"Of course, I'll show you to the door."

INSTEAD OF MOVING BACK TO THE CHAMPS-ELYSEES, Pierre elected to move to the Montmartre. He found an apartment near the Pigalle station on lines 2 and 12 of the Paris Metro. The station was located under the Boulevard de Clichy and served the famous Pigalle red-light district. The rent was reasonable for a large, two-bedroom unit. The complex didn't allow pets, and the manager was adamant about refusing to rent the property to him. He returned the next day with false documentation and Louie wearing a red woolen service dog vest. An exception to policy was granted.

"I'm sorry to have questioned you," the manager said.

"Not to worry. I couldn't live without my service dog. Got blinded while serving my country."

He didn't bring any furniture with him from Verdun. He was fortunate because the previous occupant had to vacate in a hurry and left all his furnishings behind for the landlord to sell. Pierre got a steal even though he hated the thick, heavily wooded kitchen table and four chairs. The bed was hard, and the oversized chair had lost most of its stuffing. He did like the psychedelic pictures on the wall of naked male nymphs with oversized gonads dancing with Dalmatian dogs.

The neighborhood couldn't compete with his elegant apartment gracing the Champs, but it would work for the time being. He was in no hurry to find a more permanent residence. He relented from his earlier position and made contact with Hugues Chaban. He was lonely and wanted someone to talk to. He wasn't interested in getting together for sex. He didn't want Chaban to infect him again with the deadly melanoma disease.

He was sipping a glass of red wine when the door bell rang. He wasn't expecting company.

"How in the world did you locate me, Dr. Underwood? I'm so happy to see you again."

"When I didn't find you in Verdun I called back to the United States and had Dr. Biel check your records for a number to call in case of an emergency. You listed your good friend Hugues Chaban. I called him, and he gave me your address but only after some serious haggling."

Duvair laughed and said, "He always tried to shield me from the public. You knew that I was a local celebrity, didn't you?"

"Um, no I didn't. What are you famous for?"

"I was a war hero. I saved a general from being captured during the battle for Dien Bien Phu when Ho Chi Minh fought us for control of Indo-China."

He couldn't have fabricated a better story, but Underwood had his doubts. His impression of Duvair was that of a yellow-belly coward and not of a national hero decorated for valorous actions in combat.

"So how did you pry my address out of Chaban?"

"I told you it was difficult. I stressed repeatedly about the need to find you. I told him you were still not cured and needed immediate surgery or you'd be dead in a month. He was still hesitant."

Pierre chuckled. "That's what good friends are for, Dr. Underwood. I wonder what made him change his mind."

"Money. I offered him five hundred Euros, and he buckled."

"Did you pay him?"

"Yes, I had my bank send a wire transfer."

"That no-good bastard!"

Underwood explained the reason for his visit. He assured Duvair that he was permanently cured but was subject to periodic assessment. Pierre invited him to stay in the guest bedroom for the few days of testing after which he would escort him around Paris. Underwood declined. He was set to complete his assessment and head home. He had to rule out whether Duvair was a genetically altered mass murderer.

They went out for dinner that night, celebrating whatever event they cooked up under the influence of several small carafes of cognac. Duvair not only became a national hero, but he was a major donor to the world renowned *Musee du Louvre*. Louie ignored both of them when they came stumbling back to the apartment. Testing began the next day.

"What's that weird-looking contraption you got there?" Pierre asked excitedly when Underwood pulled out the EMHD kit.

"It's too complicated to explain in detail, but suffice it to say, we need it for the testing."

"I'll take your word for it. Is it okay if I keep Louie at my side during the entire process?"

"Yes, if that makes you calm and attentive. Let's begin now."

After two days of testing, Underwood witnessed his patient morphing into a huge dog closely resembling his pet. The simulated electrical storm after midnight was the key again, as it was in the case of Kat Kurbell. He looked powerful with the broad chest, block head, and muscular upper legs. Duvair didn't act out of the ordinary the first night, but the second night was scary, even dangerous.

Gar followed him out of the apartment, Louie at his side. They walked for thirty minutes when Duvair spotted a lady smoking a cigarette at a bus stop. He got down on all fours, growled, and started toward her. Louie trotted around in front of him and shoved his body as hard as possible against his master, knocking him into a fire hydrant. He didn't want any more of this hideous anti-human behavior.

Duvair swatted the dog aside and continued stalking the woman. Louie rolled on his side and began wheezing. Before Underwood could devise a plan to stop the assault, the woman saw the monster approaching. She screamed, took out a police whistle, blew it at the top of her lungs, and then took off running like an Olympic sprinter. Her defensive actions saved her life. Underwood wouldn't be able to prevent the inevitable. Duvair stood back up on two legs, walked over to a whimpering Louie, and headed back to the apartment, oblivious to the fact that Underwood was walking side by side with them.

"Louie needs to go out for his daily walk," Pierre told him the following morning. "I'm exhausted. I didn't sleep well last night and need a good dose of fresh air. By the way, did it storm last night?"

"Not really, enjoy your walk. I've got to pack up for my three o'clock flight back to the States."

"Relax, my good doctor. Finish that pot of coffee, read some magazines, and we'll be home before you know it."

After they'd left the apartment, Underwood paced the floor while downing a second cup of coffee. He spotted a small scrap book on the end table near the front door. The book highlighted Duvair's family exploits. When he reached the middle of the scrapbook, he fell back in shock and slapped his thigh. Several clippings from the Verdun and Paris newspapers were loosely paper-clipped to several pages. Staring at him in the face were articles reporting the heinous murders that took place in Etain.

"Why are you leaving so soon?" Pierre asked him after they returned from the walk.

"I can't afford to miss this flight. It's the first day of December, and I have tons of scientific projects to finish before the end of the year."

"Oh, I understand. When will I know your findings?"

"What findings? Oh, I'm sorry. The results of your tests, you mean."

"You've been holding back on me," Pierre said with a deceiving smile.

"Not really. Let's see now. You are in good shape. There is no evidence of the cancer returning. Consider yourself cured. I'll send you a written report after I get back. By the way, did you ever check back with your oncologist like we suggested?"

"No, of course not. I'm cured."

"Oh, I see the taxi outside. Thanks so much for your hospitality."

When he climbed into the cab, he let out a big sigh of relief.

I have to get home right away and compare notes with Bobby who should be back from Chicago by now. I'm speculating he'll tell me what I already know. We have three mutants on our hands. For our good and the good of humanity, they need to disappear from the face of the earth, and the sooner, the better.

CHAPTER 34

SAN ANTONIO

JAMIE PUT IT OFF LONG ENOUGH. He felt obligated to return Sweeny's telephone call. Maria wasn't home. She left for work several hours after they'd purchased the engagement ring. He waited until after lunch, dreading the conversation because he remembered the words "Somalia" and "you owe me one" in their last conversation. The morning slashing rains had subsided. Looking out the kitchen window, he saw the most magnificent rainbow he'd ever seen. There had to be a pot of gold sitting on one of the ends of the jaw-dropping display. Maybe something positive was in the works.

Cyclops was ecstatic and wanted Jamie to be the first person to know.

"I can't believe you're getting married, Denis."

"Trust me, Jamie. She's the right woman."

"Do I know her?"

"Remember my agent who brought you to Miami on that ghost run to get the Redeemer?"

"Yes."

"She's the lucky one."

"No, Sweeny. I can't believe that gorgeous slice of womanhood is willing to share your bed with you. Was she on dope when you asked her?"

Sweeny laughed. "Your call. Will you be my best man?"

Jamie fell silent for a moment. He had a hard time reconciling the fact that the one-eyed giant considered him as one of his best friends. *I am honored to be associated with the big galoot. It was obvious the pretty lady was enamored with him. Who wouldn't be?*

"Certainly. When is the big event?"

"Five days after everybody's New Year's Eve celebrations."

"Why five days after?"

"I want you and all my good buddies to be completely sober, Richards!"

"It's the second of December already. Isn't that a bit soon for such a humongous undertaking?"

"Nah, we opted for Hawaii in a chapel on the slopes of Diamondhead."

"Dress blues and tennis shoes, big SEAL man?"

"Bathing suits and flip-flops, Army man."

"I'll make a hotel reservation today."

"Done that already. I have an entire floor of suites at the Hilton Hawaiian Village in Honolulu on the widest stretch of Waikiki beach."

"How about airline reservations? Christmas and, of course, New Year's Eve in Hawaii are mob fests."

"Jumping Jesus, Richards. Do I have to do everything for you?"

"I take that as a no."

"You're brilliant, Richards. Swim across the Pacific if you have to. Just get you're ugly face to Hawaii on time, no boondoggles to delay my primetime event or your ass is grass. Thank you so much for agreeing to be my best man. So long, Jamie."

"Out on this end," Jamie said and hung up the phone in relief.

From Somalia to Hawaii, what more could a good Christian ask for? Maybe Maria and I should speed up our nuptials and join Sweeny side by side with his main squeeze. Maria would veto the idea, opting for a large wedding somewhere closer to her extended family in Texas. I agree with that. Getting hitched at the start of next year is too soon for me. We need to slow down and make sure this is the right thing for both of us.

Bobby called shortly after Jamie terminated his call with Cyclops. He flew in from Chicago last night and wanted to brief him about his visit with Slade Glick. It was not good news. He also shared that Gar Underwood was on his way to San Antonio after an overnighter in New York. They planned a strategy session in Bobby's apartment after they picked up Underwood at the airport.

His flight was delayed. When it did pull up to the gate, they were too tired and cranky to hash out any debriefing activity which could go on all night. They opted for a welcome home drink and then hit the sack. Jamie elected to sleep at Bobby's place. Maria had no problem with being the odd person out. She didn't understand the importance of the Three Musketeers' urgent mission as she began to refer to them. She knew Jamie would fill her in when he felt comfortable enough.

"Top of the morning, everyone." Gar Underwood was the last one to get up. He joined them at the breakfast table where Bobby had prepared a meal of oatmeal and burned toast. Jamie fixed the pot of coffee because Bobby never made it strong enough to suit his taste. They seemed refreshed after a good night of sleep. Jamie cleaned up the mess in the kitchen and joined them in the living room to begin their session. Underwood was first up.

"I'm totally convinced the Frenchman is another Henri Landru, the real life Parisian 'Bluebeard' of the late 1800's. More young women would be dead if it weren't for Duvair's pet dog, Louie. I found newspaper articles describing how the killer garroted their throats and chewed off half their faces. I tested him over a period of two days. My EMHD kit worked like a charm. I am convinced beyond a reasonable doubt that we made him into a killing machine."

"I tend to agree," Bobby said. "We both witnessed the same thing with Kat morphing in San Francisco and once again when we rescued Roberto. It wasn't simply an isolated happening. I'd bet that her pet falcon assuredly saved others from an untimely death."

"What about Slade Glick?" Jamie asked.

Gar Underwood went into great detail telling them about his experience with Glick in the Keys and his own tryst with the sheriff's wife. They both already knew about it. They were not entirely aware of all the details pertaining to the murder of the lady in the park. He told them about the pet snake's behavior and what appeared to be a declining relationship with its master.

"Gentlemen," Bobby scowled, "I'm totally convinced our scientific protocol was foolproof until that son of a bitch lightning storm shattered their entire DNA structure while they were in a coma on the gurneys. Severe genetic mutations turned them loose, following in the animalistic footsteps of their pets. Amen, enough said."

"No, I don't buy the *amen* bit," Jamie interjected. "What caused them to morph into giant-like versions of their pets?"

"I'll explain the scientific details," Bobby said. "Gar had signed off on my assessment because we conducted a thorough exam of each patient after they were cured in the research barn. All three had recent bite scars on their bodies. We found it unusual that they hadn't completely healed by the time they had arrived here. Kat had three puncture wounds on her forehead that we believe were inflicted by her pet falcon. She alluded to a recent event were she lapsed into a coma one night and found Stryker perched on her bed headboard in the morning. When she got up, she noticed the puncture wounds in the mirror and treated them."

"That's it?" Jamie commented.

"Hear me out. We believe that there had to be a miniscule amount of the bird's saliva transported into the open wound and assimilated in Kat's body. I don't want to get too complicated here, but the absorbed genome in the saliva is the entirety of the falcon's heredity information that got encoded in Kat's DNA."

"What about Glick and Duvair?" Jamie asked.

"We noted strange bite marks on Glick's thigh, and we asked him what happened. He wasn't sure but told us he thought his pet python bit him one night when he was semi-comatose suffering from pain so severe he thought he was going to die. Underwood Googled info about the African rock python and its teeth structure and concluded the bite was indeed from his pet. We believe a speck of saliva or a virus was absorbed into Glick's body, and the genome was replicated in his system."

Jamie commented that he had noted an ugly bite mark on the top of Duvair's hand that hadn't healed properly either. "When I questioned him, he said that his stupid dog bit him in a snit of displeasure. He said that was the first time his pet turned on him. Based on the saliva and your genome theory on the other two patients, I suspect it also happened with Pierre Duvair."

"You got that right," Bobby said.

"Now that we have created a trio of monsters, what do you propose we do with them?" Gar asked, knowing quite well that the answer sat directly across from him.

"Jamie," Bobby said in a deliberate and serious tone.

"No… No, guys. I'm washing my hands of the entire debacle."

"Are you willing to sit back and witness the violent deaths of more innocent people knowing you can stop the slaughter?" Gar asked, with emphasis on the word *stop*.

"Let somebody else do it."

"No, Jamie. You are in the middle of this predicament with us," Gar said.

They argued back and forth for an hour. Jamie stressed the fact that his goal was to get his MBA as soon as possible and secure a real job in the community. Bobby wondered aloud whether Denis Sweeny could arrange to have them killed. He could justify the action based on a national threat to all of America. Jamie said he wouldn't go there because the CIA only handles international threats. He reminded the two scientists that Cyclops's group has enough on their plates with the surge of radical Islamic threats to the society.

Bobby ushered Gar to the back room for a private conference. When they returned, Jamie had just hung up on a call to Maria. He asked her to get reservations for the week after Christmas to attend Sweeny's wedding in Hawaii.

"Jamie, we hashed out the dilemma and came up with the best and simplest course of action."

"And that is—"

"We'll pay you a million dollars to eliminate the three of them."

"Well, that sounds more like it," Jamie hedged, still not sure if he would do it. "What would you two brainy people suggest I do with the dead bodies?"

There was silence as Bobby looked at Gar, and he in turn looked at Jamie. Bobby broke the stalemate. "Arrange it so that their beloved pets turn on them and kill them."

"Any suggestions on how to convince their pets that they would be better off without their owners?" Jamie shot back. He hated it when somebody else had all the answers but none of the solutions. "Besides, weren't the pets trying to prevent the horrific behavior of their mutant masters?"

"That's the answer, gentlemen, if we can prove it," Underwood quipped. "However, we don't have that kind of time. We're not getting anywhere with all this hassling. We have to act now. Jamie, why don't you sleep on our generous proposal for twenty-four hours? I'm sure that an experienced Special Forces soldier will come up with a doable plan."

"I'm outta here," Jamie said and left the apartment.

"Think he'll do it, Bobby?"

"I have absolutely no doubt in my mind. I've known him since we were kids. He never shied away from a challenge when the risk-reward ratio was in his favor. A million bucks would preempt getting that silly MBA degree. Trading a sharp military uniform for a tailored business suit would ultimately bore him to death in the scheming world of corporate America."

"Want to bet on it?" Gar suggested with a wicked smile on his face.

"Of course, five hundred says he'll jump at it."

"You're on, Bobby."

"How about another two hundred says he call us by nine in the morning." Bobby didn't hesitate to take unfair advantage of the New Yorker.

"Sure, why not. Let's get the celebration drink. I'm beyond thirsty."

They continued to banter back and forth on their way to the Menger. Bobby was disappointed that the young lady he told Gar about was not behind the bar. They didn't stay long and went back to Bobby's apartment and turned in for the night.

The call came in the next morning at exactly eight-thirty.

CHAPTER 35

SAN FRANCISCO

Week before Christmas, 2012

KAT KURBELL WAS IN A CONSTANT STATE OF DENIAL about her alleged morphing history. How could such a metamorphous be humanly possible? Confusion permeated her mind, and she dismissed the thought as a hoax whenever it surfaced. She assumed the curative treatment she received permanently muddled up her brain. The daring escapade in Nuevo Laredo disappeared, reappeared, and then slipped away as though it had never existed.

One day, while cleaning out her garage, she noticed the big glass jar tucked away in an alcove. At first glance, the contents appeared to be large marbles. She secured the jar, opened the lid, and peered into the murky contents. She reached down and grabbed one of the slimy orbits, looked at it, and almost fainted. How these human eyeballs got deposited in her garage was a mystery to her. She never used the garage for her car. Sometimes, she would leave Stryker's yummy meals back in the far corner of the garage, but nowhere near the small alcove where the eyeball jar sat.

She contemplated calling the SFPD and hesitated, wondering if a serial killer lived in her complex or nearby. Maybe bringing in the cops would alert the would-be assassin. She had been a successful defense attorney and wrestled with a dozen scenarios in the past where the killer had been spooked and slipped away. She decided to lock the garage and go indoors to game plan her next moves when her cell phone beckoned her.

"Hey, sweet thing, it's Jamie. What are you up to?"

"If I told you, I'd have to kill you."

"Hard to do that when I'm in San Antonio."

"I'm resourceful. I'd find a way."

"What are you doing for Christmas?"

"Nothing planned, maybe some year-end house cleaning."

"Why don't I come to SF and help you get all that stuff done?"

"Oh, Jamie, that would be wonderful, but what would your wife say?"

"I ain't married."

"Not a problem. Call me when you leave Texas."

He and Maria had not moved in together. They discussed it and decided to wait until after his friend's wedding in Hawaii. She was confused with his explanation for the San Francisco trip. He told her an Army buddy was killed in a car accident and the family asked him to be one of the pall-bearers. He never discussed having a friend in San Francisco. She wondered if he was up to his usual trick of suddenly having to disappear without an adequate explanation. But they were engaged now so she trusted him to do the right thing.

Jamie intended to drive instead of flying because his trade tools wouldn't clear airport security. In addition to his Yarborough and 9mm Bul M-5, he packed a hack saw, surgical gloves, duct tape, a partial roll of heavyduty black vinyl sheeting, and a small portable blowtorch. He was glad Maria was at work and hoped she wouldn't slip back to pick up something she had forgotten. Even though they weren't living together, she maintained several draft projects she was working on at his home. She valued his input. Today, she was scheduled to interview a new assistant manager. He felt it was safe to spread the equipment out on the living room floor and pack.

He drove through the night, and all of the next day, stopping only for food and gas. He wanted to surprise Kat, so he stayed in a cheap motel on Van Ness, not far from her apartment. He sacked out most of the day and called her at six o'clock.

"Oh my goodness, Jamie, you're in town already. Please stay with me and Stryker. I promise you that he'll be a good boy. I'll be a bad girl."

"I'm exhausted. I had to sack out in a cheap motel, catch some needed shuteye, so I'd be pumped and primed for my visit with you."

"Oh, that sounds so sexy. Come over right away."

"I'm on the way."

He almost T-boned a Mercedes failing to stop at the Divisidero Street signal light turning on to Union. The mustached gentleman driving the vehicle gave him the *bird* as he burned rubber spinning away. All he needed was an accident and his trunk searched exposing his assortment of paraphernalia packed away for the kill. He saw an open parking space in front of Kat's apartment and sped to it before a BMW convertible riding his tail nailed it.

"I'm so happy you're here for Christmas, Jamie," she said as she led him inside. "I've been sad and depressed for the past several weeks, even flirting with suicide. I keep having these frightful dreams that wake me in the middle of the night, shaking and in a cold sweat."

"I'm sorry. What are they about?"

"The rescue of some notorious prisoner in Mexico."

"Huh?" Jamie didn't want to go there.

"In reality, maybe I'm hallucinating. I picture myself as a giant bird of prey flying all over the countryside. Some nights, I kill. Other nights, I save someone's life. I tried a brain dump but still couldn't erase that prison scenario from my head."

"Have you been taking sleeping pills?"

"Handfuls of Silenor, washed down with vodka."

"Maybe you need to cut the vodka."

"Doesn't matter. Will you sleep here tonight after we wear ourselves out with naughty sex?"

"Yes and no. Yes, I'll stay with you. I didn't plan on going back to that motel. No, I won't bed you. I'll sack out on the sofa and intermittently keep an eye on you to see what's going on. I'll also check on Stryker to make sure he stays caged. In light of your depression and bad dreams, we can hold off making love until tomorrow morning."

"Not sure I can wait that long, handsome man."

"I'm twenty times better in the morning."

"Well then, I have no choice in the matter. Are you hungry?" she asked.

"Yes."

They had a casual meal at a new Italian Bistro on Scott Street. He really wasn't that hungry but had to kill time before they went to bed. He didn't drink any booze, wanting to keep a clear mind for his mission. She put away four screwdrivers and became woozy when they walked home. She fell asleep in his arms sitting on the sofa. He cradled her and carried her to the bedroom. Stryker was uneasy, not sure what was in store for all three of them.

Jamie wasn't tired and decided to check out her telephone logs and computer messages. He was thrilled to find a persistent trail of communications by a lawyer named Barry Gregg and a string of e-mails from other friends. He couldn't believe how stupid the Gregg guy was, intelligent lawyer or not. He simply couldn't take no for an answer.

At two in the morning, he heard her thrashing and crying in bed. He tiptoed in but didn't wake her. Soon, she slipped back to a normal sleep pattern. In the next room, Stryker was pounding on the cage as though trying to smash his way out. The thick metal enclosure was too strong to allow his escape.

He went outside to the trunk of his car and secured the medical kit, surgical gloves, duct tape, and a special cloth only obtained from the black market. The cloth was used by the criminal element to remove fingerprints. Inside, he donned the gloves and sat down at her computer. He typed a suicide note to Barry Gregg, printed it, and set the note on her desk.

Jamie read and reread her messages to three friends, all female. She had shared with them her problem coping with depression. Only two responded offering her moral support and recommendations to seek professional help. He prepared an e-mail in her name and sent it to all three with wording that suggested the drastic act of taking her life. He wiped clean the telephone, computer, and every hard surface in the house he may have touched.

He knew it was time for action by the accelerated heartbeat, the profuse sweating, and slight tremor all over his body. His mind sluiced back to his conversations with Father Lawrence. Jamie began to cry, moan, and one last outcry was so loud he couldn't contain his grief. Gaining control of his emotions, he feared Stryker would go ballistic when he came out of his cage. He walked into Kat's bedroom to make sure she was still asleep. He filled a syringe from the medical kit with a full load of Benzolanine, a sleep-inducing drug he bought from a Mossad agent. He buried the syringe in her neck and emptied the contents before she could react to the pinprick. Within ten seconds, she went limp.

Jamie decided against duct-taping her mouth and securing her hands and feet with plastic slip ties. A thorough ME would find evidence of the tape marks on her face and skin abrasions around her wrists and ankles from the thin plastic restraints. With that evidence in hand, the ME would repudiate the police report that it pointed to a suicidal act. He'd used the drug on several covert operations with the Israelis because it was not traceable in the victim's blood in a post-mortem exam. The syringe needle was extremely thin and would not be an issue after the deceased floated aimlessly in cold salt water for any discernible amount of time.

He was quick, methodical but loud. Stryker sensed what was happening and struck harder rattling his cage. Jamie picked Kat up, draped her over his shoulders, and headed for the front door. He heard a shrill whistling sound behind him. Before he could turn around, he was knocked off his feet by a powerful thud on his back legs. Kat went flying against the door frame. It was Stryker. He was free. Jamie thought his right leg might be fractured at the knee but the pain subsided a few seconds after the attack.

Eyeing a baseball bat next to the door, he rose to his feet and picked it up. The falcon was circling for another strike, this time zeroing in at his head. He swung the bat as hard as he could and snapped the bird's left wing, almost whacking it clean off the body. Stryker went gyrating backward, simulating an airplane with a missing wing spinning out of control.

Shit, now I'll have to come back here and clean up this mess.

Jamie picked Kat up by the hair, repositioned her on his back, and walked out the front door. He heard the screeching animal lapping at his wound before the door slammed shut. He stopped immediately and checked to see if anybody was walking the streets at this late hour. It was all clear, so he tossed her in the back seat of the car, half sprawled on the backseat with her arms dangling to the floor. He took off for the Golden Gate Bridge.

Jamie pulled up next to the stature of Joseph Strauss. Getting out of the car, he didn't see the man approach. "You sure are up late," an elderly jogger commented as he took a swig of water from a bottle strapped to his waist.

"Yes, it is, but I have a good excuse."

"Son, you don't need one to satisfy my curiosity."

"I'm a shirttail relative of the famous bridge builder," Jamie said coyly. "I just came in from Texas to visit his plaque here in the plaza and walk the bridge in his honor," He pointed to the license plate on his car to validate where he was from. "It was a long tedious drive but sure worth the effort."

"Welcome to San Francisco."

"Thanks."

"It looks to me like your wife is asleep on the back seat. Better wake her up and make sure the two of you walk the entire span of the bridge. It won't disappoint."

"I will and you have a great day."

He watched the jogger take off in the direction of Crissy Field and soon was out of sight. Jamie glanced in every direction and didn't see a person on either side of the bridge. An occasional car passed by, but he expected that. The driver would notice two intoxicated lovers walking with their arms around each other and oblivious to passersby.

He opened the trunk and took out the sack containing the vinyl sheet, hacksaw, and blowtorch. He slid her off the backseat and eased her out of the car. She was mumbling incoherently in her sleep and didn't fight him. The drug circulating throughout her blood stream was effective. She could ambulate and, at the same time, not offer any resistance.

They paused at the first huge superstructure, which had a twelve-square-foot open area shielding them from traffic. He saw the lights of Alcatraz off in the distance and wondered if he would eventually end up in a federal joint like this mothballed behemoth. He broke out in a sweat.

He opened the sack and spread the vinyl sheet out in the concrete foyer area placing the blowtorch and hacksaw in the middle of the sheet. There was a slight rain dampening the road but no evidence of approaching thunder and lightning. It was decision time. He stretched her out on the vinyl sheet and sat next to her. He began rehashing his plans for her demise.

This must look like a suicide. I've waited long enough to see if she was going to morph again into an eight-foot-tall falcon with the twelve-foot wingspan. According to Dr. Underwood, she would have been in the REM status of sleep now, and that's when the transformation normally took place.

I brought the hacksaw along in case I had to saw off those humongous wings if they sprouted out. She would have flown away from me and aborted the mission. The blowtorch would do a great job searing the flesh and bone around the shoulders if needed. Charring would prevent an incriminating trail of blood to spill out on everything including my clothes.

My plan involves wrapping the two bleeding arms in the vinyl sheet and disposing them separately from the body. The problem of course is that if the crabs and sharks don't feast on her and she's later found dead with severed arms it wouldn't look like a suicide. Now it appears that I won't need to use any equipment.

Checking up and down the walkway, he pulled her up and propped her up against the steel column of the bridge. He wrapped up and tied the vinyl sheet with the tools secured inside and tossed the sack in the corner. He may have waited too long to act. She started to come around. The drug should have held her in abeyance much longer, but then, he reasoned she was no longer a normal human. She started to murmur incoherently and thrash at his face. He slapped her hard across the side of her head.

"Shut the fuck up, you bitch. I'm going to toss your cheating ass off the bridge."

"No, no, Jamie. I love you and only you."

Her eyes widened in fear. She witnessed him perspiring and shaking like a person having an epileptic fit. She saw an opportunity with him being defenseless and kicked him hard in the groin. It didn't faze him. He grabbed her, flung her over his shoulders, and raced toward the center of the bridge. With the rhythm of his heartbeat playing tricks on him, he almost fainted at the stress blasting away at his psyche.

"You're history, woman," he ranted several times and tossed her from the railing. He watched the few seconds it took for her to break water before she disappeared. In his excitement, Jamie broke out with some lyrics from an old song he remembered from his youth: ♪♪ "Pack up all your cares and woes. Bye, bye, Katbird.♪♪" He ran back, collected his sack of equipment, and tossed it into the trunk of his car. One more task awaited him.

He drove back to Kat's apartment and found Stryker unconscious on the living from floor. In reality, Jamie had always admired the wild animals that killed prey to sustain life. They were all like him—stalking, brutal, self-serving. Searching her office, he found a wooden ruler and rigged up a splint for the broken wing. He sanitized every surface he thought he'd made contact with. On the way out, he grabbed the baseball bat for a trophy. He left the front door open. It was his concession to Stryker, giving him the opportunity to fly away to the freedom he rightly deserved. He then hopped in his car and sped out of San Francisco.

CHAPTER 36

PARIS

Christmas Eve, 2012

JAMIE DROVE ALL DAY, NIGHT, AND THROUGH THE NEXT DAY. He pulled into the long-term parking lot at O'Hare International Airport. He couldn't bring any of his trusty gear with him on the flight, so he ensured that his car doors and trunk were securely locked. Air France had been booked solid, but he located an empty seat in first class on a United Airlines flight leaving in three hours. After he bought the ticket, he found an Internet kiosk and started his research of Pierre Duvair. A man by the name of Hugues Chaban kept popping up on the screen, perhaps a good friend or even a relative. Gar Underwood had given him everything he had on Duvair but failed to mention anything about Chaban. Underwood even mentioned the spare office with the odd mechanical device that had a small pulley bolted to a supporting ceiling joint. He needed to know more about the specific Montmartre neighborhood where Duvair lived. He'd visited the Pigalle area in the past and was well-aware of its reputation. He decided to call Maria.

"Jamie, you rat! You were supposed to be home for Christmas."

"I'm so sorry, Maria. They postponed the funeral for a few days."

"What?"

"Yes, they had to. The youngest brother is on assignment in Afghanistan, and they decided to wait for him. The military is super good at times like this and will rush him home."

"I feel for the poor family, Jamie dear, and understand the consequences. Please hurry home after the funeral."

"I will. See you before you know it my love."

He hated to keep lying to her. Conflicting thoughts were running rampant through his mind. *How can a lasting and sacred marriage be founded on such deceit, and here I am, running off and doing it again? Maria doesn't deserve a first-class prick like me for a husband. When I get home, I'm going to lay it on the line and tell her she's got the wrong man. At the same time, I really don't want to lose her. She's the first woman I ever fell in love with, and I've been with a ton of women in the past.*

The flight to France went by faster than he expected. The flight attendants constantly joked with him. A short and dumpy attendant gave him her address in Paris and suggested he call her. He wondered what it would be like to fly around the world meeting new and interesting people every day. The big jet circled the airport twice before landing. The pilot had announced that the heavy air traffic was caused by additional planes being diverted to Charles De Gaulle Airport. He hailed a cab and proceeded to his target in Paris.

"Monsieur Richards, you were supposed to call me far in advance of your trip to my city."

"I know, Pierre, but I only had a short window of opportunity to come so I here I am."

"That's fine. You get to spend Christmas with me."

"I can only stay for two days. I have to jump over to Belgium for a reunion of NATO freedom fighters I served with in Iraq." It didn't bother him to fabricate stories of convenience, except for the outright lies he told Maria.

"Where are you now?"

"Standing outside your apartment. Dr. Underwood gave me your address."

"Oh my, I see you now," he said, pulling aside the heavy drapes. "Walk up the stairs, and I'll have the door opened for you."

Duvair kissed him lightly on both cheeks and held both of his hands longer than necessary. Jamie pulled back and checked him out. He looked like a big dog with baggy eyes and drooping jowls. Louie bounced into the room to meet the visitor. The dog backed up and growled.

"Shame on you, Louie. Show some respect for our visitor from America. He's going to be with us for a few days so be kind, okay?" Louie turned around and, in no great hurry, walked to the back room. He was not happy with the arrival of this strange newcomer.

Jamie laughed. He knew about the dog from Duvair's visit to Texas and his constant complaining about his pet not being with him when he was undergoing his miracle treatment. He chuckled to himself. *They look like father and son.*

"How about sharing an aperitif, Jamie Richards? We can celebrate your visit and afterward go to my favorite restaurant near the train station."

"I'll do the aperitif but would like to take a short nap before we break bread."

"Of course, you must still be tired from the long flight. I'll show you to the guest bedroom."

As they walked down the hall, Jamie glanced into the office and noted the pulley suspended a foot from the ceiling. His eyes shifted to the floor underneath the pulley where a chair sat on a small wooden platform. Pierre didn't see Jamie's reaction. He was walking two steps ahead of him. The guest bedroom had two stark paintings done by Pierre's friend Hugues Chaban. One depicted the Eifel Tower at night during a thunderstorm. The second picture was a caricature of Duvair milking a cow in a pasture devoid of greenery.

Jamie was awakened an hour later by a hand gently messaging his thigh. Pierre told him it was time to freshen up and get ready for dinner. Jamie lifted the man's sweaty meat hook off his leg without making any comments. He knew Pierre was gay, but it was difficult to anticipate whether he'd make a run at him. It didn't take long to walk to the nearby restaurant. It wasn't crowded and their order arrived sooner than both of them expected.

"Are you savoring the chicken cordon bleu that I recommended, Jamie? I often order that plate. It's their house specialty. The French words mean blue ribbon when translated to English. The chef here prefers to use a heavy white sauce instead of breading, a minor variation from local tradition."

"It's delicious."

"Hmm, maybe I'll try it the next time."

Jamie glanced at Duvair's plate where parts of a half-finished ham hock swam in a navy bean soup concoction. He knew that pork knuckles were essential ingredients in soul food and other forms of American Southern-country cooking. But in France! He was spooked watching Pierre pick it up with his thick paw-like hand and sucking off the fatty part. Small fat globules dribbled down his bloated cheeks. He spit the meat portion back on the plate. He gnawed loudly at the rounded ends of the bones. It made Jamie sick. Sharing two bottles of a popular *vin de pays* curbed his appetite for the rich dessert that Duvair ordered and ended up eating alone.

"What do you normally do on Christmas Eve, Jamie?" They were back in his apartment.

"Depends."

"What did you say?" Duvair was drunk. He consumed most of the bottle of a premier cognac he opened when they got back from the restaurant.

"It depends on where I'm at and who I'm with."

"If you are with a woman, do you make hot and heavy love?"

"Sometimes."

"Do you want to get it on now?"

"What do you mean by that?"

"Have you ever heard of auto-erotic asphyxiation?"

"Yes, but I don't need to go through that drill to get my rocks off."

"You are a special kind of man, Jamie. With your looks and swagger, you could pick up a beautiful woman every night and bonk her to death. Me? I…ah…have limitations. As you are well-aware from the background checks, your doctor associates made before the procedure to eliminate my cancer. I prefer men."

"No big thing."

"Do you like pornography, Jamie?"

"No, I prefer the real thing."

"Would you have any objection if we watch some DVDs after which you can help me masturbate?"

"You go ahead and view the film. I'll find something to read in the other room. Let's be clear on one thing here. If you mean you want my help to hoist you up to the rafters, I'll do it for you. After that, you're on your own for whatever sexual gratification you dream up."

"Thanks so much. I couldn't think of a greater Christmas present. Please lock Louie in the front closet because he barks at me when I'm nearing orgasm. It spoils the trip."

"Sure, we wouldn't want the slightest inconvenience to interfere with your ride."

Duvair watched three DVDs and signaled for Jamie to come back into the room. Jamie told him he'd help him get started and then take a long walk around the neighborhood. Pierre told him there were many red lights glowing at this time of the night.

No, thanks to that idea. I picked up the clap about two blocks away from here while on leave from my Army unit in Germany.

Duvair wobbled ahead into the office and took out a ligature apparatus, inspected it, and wrapped it in a towel. He instructed Jamie to set up the escape mechanism, a linkage of small chains affixed to the pulley dangling from the ceiling and clipped around his left wrist. He'd used it once in an emergency to prevent a fatal suffocation at the last possible minute.

"How does this contraption work?" Jamie asked.

"It flips you off the platform to the hard floor, a minor discomfort to save your own neck, so to speak." He tried to laugh but gave out a loud belch. "Oops, don't worry about that. Too much food and booze before my auto-seduction." He had a hard time mouthing the words out of his fat mouth. He retched twice until rotten-smelling vomit slithered down his pants pooling at the base of the platform.

"What the fuck!" Jamie scowled as he jumped back. He watched Pierre climb up on the two foot stage and engage the ligature around his neck with the skill of a surgeon. Jamie hoisted him up and watched the action for a few minutes. Duvair hung limp for several minutes as Jamie watched in awe, trying to figure out why intelligent people engage in such stupidity.

"Oh... Ah, my dear Jamie friend, this feels so...so good."

Jamie reeled back in disgust and hurried out the office door. As he reached the front door of the apartment, he opened it and then slammed it shut, having quietly stepped back inside. Pierre would have assumed that he had left the apartment. Then he'd be able to concentrate on his self-abuse in complete solitude. Jamie plunked down on the couch and waited until the moaning and groaning in the other room subsided. It didn't happen soon enough. He overheard his name, Hugues Chaban's name and one other person's name he didn't recognize being thrown in between Pierre's moans He had to cover his ears to block out the overwhelming sick sounds from the other room at the same time suspending the urge of tossing his own cookies. After ten minutes, silence finally creep out from the room. Jamie put on his surgical gloves and was ready for action.

He walked back to the office and kicked the platform out from underneath a comatose body. Duvair had no idea what was happening until his neck snapped like a dried breadstick.

Jamie humored himself and blurted out in song: ♪♪"A-tisket...a-tasket...a Frenchman needs a-casket.♪♪" The jovial assassin danced a jig to the computer, and with his gloved hand, he typed out a suicide note in French script. It read:

> *Forgive me, Hugues, for putting you through this agony. I've not shared with you that my cancer has come back to haunt me. I cannot live anymore with the excruciating pain that I suffered earlier. I have always loved you and will continue to love you to the end of my life. Please find a good home for Louie. Au revoir, mon amour!*

Louie came crashing through the closet door like a Sherman tank taking down a reinforced concrete wall. The snub-nosed dog was stressed out and having a difficult time breathing. He'd been locked up in a hot closet for several hours. He leaped at Jamie with such force that it knocked him off the chair and over the top of the computer. Getting shot by an enemy bullet would have been less subtle. Louie was at his neck by the time he bounced off the nearby wall in a daze. At the last possible second, Jamie forced both arms up to his head in time to halt the dog's teeth from clamping down on his carotid artery.

"Louie, stop! Stop, you bad dog!" he yelled at the top of his lungs.

The dog backed off. Jamie's left wrist spewed blood from the dog's sharp teeth. He saw a metal waste basket on the floor near his shoulders. Grabbing it, he swung at the dog's head but missed. Louie hesitated and then went for Jamie's crotch in one long leap. The dog was about to chomp at the family jewels. Instead of taking another swing, he turned the basket upside down and shoved it on Louie's head. It was a tight fit on the block-headed animal as Jamie pushed it down over the head as far as it would go. Louie yipped and growled, the sound barely heard from underneath the metal helmet.

"Fuck you, you ugly dog!" he shouted as he got back on his feet. Louie tried to push the basket off his head with his short front legs but couldn't budge it. He was completely exhausted and lay motionless on the floor next to the computer desk.

He raced back to the office and shoved the special platform back underneath the body. It had to look like a suicide. Pierre Duvair was hanging from the ceiling pulley like a side of beef in a butcher's cooler. His eyes were opened wide, staring at the opposing wall. His thick tongue extended several inches out of a tightened mouth. He was still hard.

Jamie retrieved the special chemical cloth to rid fingerprints from every object in the apartment he may have come in contact with. He cleaned up the blood caused by the dog's wrist bite. Satisfied that the incriminating evidence evaporated in thin air, he packed his suitcase and headed for the front door. Passing by the computer desk, he stared back at Louie.

I really love dogs. I had one all through my adolescent years growing up. I got to help him even though earlier in self-defense, I tried to snuff out the canine's life. He was only trying to protect his master. That's what good dogs do.

Jamie removed the metal helmet from Louie who stared back aimlessly at him. Jamie decided the dog was no longer a threat and patted him on his broad head. It was time to get out of there. He took off his surgical gloves and shoved them in his back pocket. He turned off all the lights in the apartment and rushed off in the cold night.

CHAPTER 37

CHICAGO

Two days after Christmas, 2012

O'HARE INTERNATIONAL AIRPORT never looked as inviting to Jamie. Two disgusting mutants down the tube and one more genetic anomaly within reach, he reminded himself as the big wheels touched down on the runway. When he boarded the outgoing flight in France, he had no idea how he was going to kill Slade Glick in Chicago. Wrestling with the various options didn't prevent him from stretching out and sleeping on the United return flight. In between the refills of Bombay Sapphire on the rocks and cat-napping, he reviewed the dossier on Glick that Gar Underwood faxed him. He had received the documentation before he left for France, carrying it in his baggage for later review.

Before he walked over to the airport garage, he decided to call Maria from the same kiosk he used a few days ago. He needed to squeeze a few more days out of his return trip home. He knew she would be livid, but then again, she might still be in a jovial Christmas mood. He was wrong.

"What do you mean there was another delay in the funeral? I don't believe a word you're saying, Jamie Richards. I suppose the brother was killed on his way out of Afghanistan, and they're going to have a side-by-side military funeral!"

"No, nothing of the sort."

"What in the hell is causing the delay?"

"I got sick."

"Huh?"

"I'm calling from the San Francisco VA hospital."

"This better be good."

"After the funeral, I had a serious talk with the brother. He was very emotional, out of control. He went into great detail about a raid he was conducting near the outskirts of Kabul. His patrol was ambushed, and he was the sole survivor. I started to break out in cold sweats, began shivering, and then fainted. I had relived some of my own harrowing combat experiences and couldn't handle it, Maria. They are going to discharge me tomorrow. I'll be back in San Antonio before you know it."

There was silence on the other end of the line. She didn't believe a word he told her. This wasn't the first time in their relationship that she questioned some of his so-called exploits.

"Maria, are you still on the line?"

"Yes. I have to think twice about going to Hawaii with you. Call me the moment you get home. You have some bigtime explaining to satisfy me." She slammed the receiver down in disgust.

He knew he had it coming but remained headstrong.

The Bitch, who does she think she is for Christ's sake, Mother Teresa? We're not married yet, and I have to justify every move I make. Screw it. If she wants to live with me the rest of her life, she'll have to make some major adjustments!

After several minutes of cooling off time, he shifted gears and honed in on his assignment. He thought he knew everything about

Glick but was astonished by the detailed report he'd finished reading twenty minutes before landing at O'Hare. With a yellow highlighter, Jamie underlined three unrelated topics which jumped out at him when he first scanned the material. He went back and re-read portions of the document in more detail—the Hawaiian girlfriend, the African rock python pet, and the two cars parked in his rented garage. He was vaguely aware of the first two items on the list but was ecstatic about learning the last one. It would form the blueprint to kill the Chicagoan.

"Oh, hi, Jamie, I didn't know you were going to be in town," Slade said on the phone. "I thought Dr. Biel told me last week he was coming out after Christmas for another brief followup visit."

"He had emergency surgery three days ago and asked me to sub for him." They had ginned up this story in the event Glick tried to verify the switch in plans.

"My goodness, what happened?"

"He got smacked by a car while jaywalking across a busy downtown street near the Alamo."

"How serious?"

"Compound fracture of the right leg but he's recovering well."

"Please give him my regards when you see him on your return."

"I will do that. He should be home from the hospital by that time."

"Where are you staying?"

"At the Drake. I scribbled your address from Dr. Biel's records and decided to stop by in the morning so we can get started. He gave me a simplified protocol to review with you, so it shouldn't take all day. Will that work for you?"

"Of course, I'm just a short cab ride from there. I sure am looking forward to seeing you tomorrow morning. We'll go out to lunch after the session."

"Great, I love the food you folks enjoy in the Windy City. There are so many good restaurants to be found in almost every neighborhood."

Jamie didn't tell him he was driving his own vehicle that had a ding on the right rear fender. He didn't notice the dent in the dim, long-term parking garage at O'Hare when he picked up the car. He was in too much of a hurry to check the trunk to make sure all the tools of his trade were undisturbed. He decided to conduct some reconnoitering before darkness set in. Gar Underwood gave him the address of the building where Slade garaged his two vehicles. He had to see it for himself before he finalized his plan. The building was two blocks west of Glick's condo off Wabash in a fashionable four story building.

"Good evening, sir," the security guard greeted him when he entered the complex. "How can I help you?"

Jamie expected an upscale warehouse to house the vehicles of Chicago's finest. but this place had dollar signs embedded in the well-appointed entrance foyer. He shouldn't have been surprised knowing the kind of rich idiot Glick was with no apparent spending limitations.

"My cousin Slade Glick asked me to pick up an item he left in his car this afternoon."

"He never talked about having a cousin in town. All he jabbers about is the many women that adored him. I think your cousin might be gay."

Jamie sighed. "Whatever."

"I think the dude would misplace his head if it weren't attached to his neck. Excuse my rudeness, but he calls me all the time to get things out of his car and bring them to his condo. I'm not a high-paid delivery boy, but I have to be polite. I did it one time and got my ass chewed by my supervisor on one of his unannounced visits. What did he forget this time?"

"His cell phone."

"Sounds about right. Let me get the keys out of the cabinet for the car. Oh, which one did he leave them in?"

"Um, he wasn't sure. I need to check both of them."

"No problem, but I have to accompany you. You'd think this was Fort Knox the way they've written up the security rules."

The guard took him up one flight on the elevator and led him to the rear of the building. They walked past a Ferrari 458 Italia, three Bentleys, two Mercedes and a fire-engine red Lamborghini. There was a Starbucks coffee vending machine next to a vintage Ford Edsel. Jamie was relieved when he saw several other cars that the average Joe Doe would own. Parked next to the coffee dispenser were Glick's two cars.

"Let's check the Lexus first. He seldom drives the other one." The guard unlocked the F Marquee division flagship model and checked the front seat while Jamie made busy checking the rear seat.

"No dice," the guard muttered. "He must have left it in this jalopy next to the Lexus. I seldom see him drive this antique specimen out of the garage. Why he holds on to this one is beyond me. It had its glory days. I wouldn't be caught dead in it!"

Jamie had the jitters when they opened the door of the popular 1978 Ford compact Pinto. Goose bumps formed on his arms even though he wasn't in any apparent danger in this new-age garage. He had owned one when he was a teenager and kept it until he joined the Army. He lost his virginity to the head cheerleader in the back seat one night after a football game.

His father pooh-poohed the repeated recall letters from the Ford Motor Company. Jamie remembered him talking about the main issue. *The problem encountered was the lack of reinforcement between the Pinto's fuel tank and the bolts in its rear differential. Critics alleged that this design flaw made the gas tank susceptible to becoming pierced by the bolts and catching fire in a rear-end collision. Many suits were filed on behalf of burned owners. Don't you worry about your Pinto, son. Lawyers chase ambulances every day for a chance to sue somebody.*

"Sir, snap out of it. You must be dreaming about the Pinto piece of shit you had when you were a kid."

"You got that right. How'd you know?"

"I could tell by watching you drool."

"I had one too," the guard reported. "Let's check and see if the cell phone is in this car."

They searched haphazardly but only found a McDonald's brown takeout bag with several string French fries glued to the sides by congealed ketchup. Jamie told him to call off the search. He'd seen enough. They retrieved the elevator and returned to the reception area.

"Quite a museum up there, huh?" the guard mocked.

Jamie laughed. "I'd take the ancient Pinto rather than any of the others."

"I couldn't' afford to buy the one I had as a teenybopper," the guard mused as he led Jamie out the front door.

He drove back to the Drake Hotel planning for a good night of sleep. It was dark outside with a lazy snowfall blanketing Michigan Avenue. The time change from Europe was starting to haunt every fiber of his body. Jamie valet-parked his car and took the elevator to the fifth floor and walked the long dark hallway to his room. He fumbled through his pockets for the key and thought he heard a noise coming from inside. He stepped to the side, put his ear to the door jamb, and listened intently. The sound of a cigarette lighter worked its way to the tiny opening under the door.

Who the hell's in my room smoking a cigarette, cigar, or a fucking pipe? I should have brought my Bul M-5 equalizer with me. How damn stupid of me to assume I'd be out of harm's way wherever I went these days. I have no choice. I'll open the door and rush straight at the intruder.

He slid the plastic key down the lock unit. The door unlocked with a loud pop, and he raced in like a blitzing linebacker but stopped short when he saw the woman.

"Who the hell are you?" he snarled at her as she took a long puff of the black stubby cigar.

"Leah Malaka. Slade sent me. *Mele Kalikimaka,* which, in your *haole* language, means Merry Christmas."

Jamie never witnessed a woman as striking as Leah. Her bronzed skin and world class, runway model's body caused him to stop and stare much too long. She wore a tight colorful woolen sweater with a print of two playful dolphins leaping out of the Pacific Ocean. A deserted strand of Waikiki Beach loomed in the distant background. Black leather pants hugged her hips and upper legs but flared out at the bottom. She stood on elevated heels with exposed toes. A silver ring was on both of her big toes.

"So he did, didn't he? It was very considerate of him."

She acknowledged his appraisal with a wide smile. She took his hand and led him to the circular love seat near the window and then kicked off her heels. Leah peered inside his eyes like an optometrist checking for broken blood vessels. Neither spoke a word.

Now what am I supposed to do? I recall from Gar Underwood's assessment of Slade Glick that she wandered in and out of his life. I think he wrote that this woman was either a hustler working without a john or that she was employed by a high-priced escort service.

My Maria is sitting alone in San Antonio during the Christmas Holidays waiting for my return. Should I be faithful to her? That's what she'd expect of me because we're engaged now. What healthy male wouldn't want to bed this beauty sitting next to me? Be patient, you idiot, let's see what she has in mind before you go off half-cocked!

"You're everything Slade promised. Do you like what you see?"

"Er, yes, of course. Did he tell you I'm married with three kids?"

"That's what they all say. Slade told me to make you happy."

"But I'm already happy, just tired from my travels."

"Look, Jamie Richards, you're wasting my time. Do you or do you not want to take advantage of the expensive gift he purchased for you? I don't have time to play around with a deadbeat."

Jamie got off the love seat and went to the door. "Good night, Leah Malaka. For all I care, you can refund the dumb bastard's money when you see him. Get out!"

She walked slowly to the opened door. As she passed him, she gave him a wet kiss on his cheek and slammed the door shut behind her. He undressed and immediately fell into a deep sleep. Slade's call at eleven woke him out of a confusing dream involving his beloved Maria and another man. They were busy fucking on the living room floor of his home, sipping a glass of champagne between each powerful thrust of their moistened bodies.

"Had a thrilling night with her, huh?" Slade laughed when he assessed Jamie's lethargic greeting over the phone. "Welcome to Chicago, my friend. That's what we're all about. Seriously though, she told me you stonewalled her. What the hell kind of fool would turn down that piece of heavenly body? Anyway, it's getting late. Are you coming over here or do you want to conduct the evaluation at the Drake?"

"Sorry I overslept. I'll be right over."

The assessment took longer than Jamie expected. He was alarmed when he massaged Glick's arms and legs feeling for unexplained growths or tumors. His skin consisted of small, smooth scaly deposits. He was surprised at Glick's head, which appeared more triangular-shaped than a normal human's head. When he had him open his mouth he reeled back in shock. There were multiple sharp and backwardly curved teeth.

"What's the fuss, Jamie? Your eyes tell me you don't like my beautiful head."

"I'm trying to be thorough. Dr. Biel told me there might be some slight changes in your appearance, but I don't see anything alarming here."

"Aha! Now you see why the females are always hot after this body."

"So you say," Jamie said.

The rest of the assessment went well until Rocky knocked the door of his serpentarium wide open and slithered into the living from. The snake glared at Jamie and hissed his at him. He rolled, coiled, and thumped up and down. Jamie took a defensive posture as Slade shooed the reptile away, scolding him for his bad manners. The snake retreated to his room, tongue flicking in and out faster than the bolt action of a fully engaged machine gun.

"Sorry about that. He's always trying to protect me. You'd think Rocky feels like you came all the way to Chicago to kill me or something as dreadful."

"That's what faithful pets are all about," Jamie proclaimed, tongue-in-cheek.

"I think he's hungry. I purchased some fruit bats for him. I have them in a special container. He likes them better than the rodents. I'll go in and give him a couple. Maybe it'll shut him up for a while."

He left to handle the feeding, which gave Jamie the few minutes he needed to case the place. He was searching for a second set of keys for the condo and found them in the desk drawer. A metal key ring with "front door #2" penned in left no doubt. He pocketed them and moved on to the kitchen. He found what he was hoping for—a gas-operated range.

Jamie figured he now had two viable options to get rid of Glick. He could return later tonight and kill him and the devil serpent by inhalation of the poisonous gas fumes from the stove. He had the special sleep serum to inject Glick and his Special Forces training taught him how to handle dangerous jungle snakes.

The second option would be chancy and more difficult. He could jerry-rig the Ford Pinto by stripping some of the reinforcing elements that are housed between the fuel tank and the rear differential bolts. This could result in an explosion on the slightest impact the next time Glick embarked on a joy ride in his four-wheeled coffin. But would this happen soon enough? He always wanted the kill action to be more immediate so he could witness firsthand the glorious event and then sign off on its success.

Satisfied with the alternatives to waste Glick, he walked to the bay window and watched the falling snowflakes. He wondered if each flake really had its own DNA as he was led to believe by his grade school teacher. He was also puzzled by the haphazard route each took drifting to the ground. What force of nature engineered the route? Slade's return from the bathroom startled him.

"Sorry it took so long, Jamie. Rocky seems hesitant to feast on the fruit bats, Don't know why, but they were always his favorite meal. Hey, how'd you like to take a spin in my antique auto? We'll cruise the city before we grab some food. I bet you never rode in a Ford Pinto before."

The question threw him for a loop, curious if Glick had been reading his mind while squatting so long on the toilet taking a crap. Bobby had reported that the resultant genetic mutations were "mind expanding" and broadened the scope of each patient's brain capability.

"Wrong, I had one as a kid."

"Great! Even though it's snowing outside, the views along Lake Shore Drive and Lake Michigan are stunning at this time of the year. The traffic is not too bad at this hour. We'll take a ride and catch a late lunch near the McCormick Center at a neat Italian restaurant. It's Leah's favorite eating joint," he snickered, fluttering his thick eyebrows.

Ignoring the remark about Leah, he jumped at the chance to get out and catch some of the interesting sights he'd only read about. Chicago was an attractive tourist and convention city. They walked in no particular hurry to the parking garage, exchanged greetings with the security guard, and climbed into Glick's 1978 Ford Pinto. Slade drove through Grant Park, pointing out the Buckingham Fountain and other interesting sights before entering the Lake Shore Drive on-ramp. The traffic was busier than usual according to Glick as he sped off in front of an oncoming SUV.

"Jesus, Glick, watch what the hell you're doing. You'll get us killed."

Slade laughed. "You are not back in that hick town San Antonio now, my friend. Everybody is in a big hurry here. Relax, enjoy the sights and sounds, and work up an appetite. Look off to your left. That's the world famous Shedd Aquarium and the Field Museum. Hang on, Jamie. We'll be there before you know it."

The snow was falling heavier, and the roadway became slicker. Visibility was severely reduced by the time they passed Soldier Field. All of a sudden, Slade took the Pinto into a spin on the icy thoroughfare. As he was maneuvering out of it, they were rear-ended by a stretch limo barreling along at high speed. Glick bounced his head off the driver side window on impact. He was out cold as the Pinto began whirling like a spinning top. The rear of the car burst into small jabbing flames. Jamie placed two hands on the dashboard and pushed hard as the car bounced off a concrete median embankment.

"Son of a bitch!" Jamie shouted. "This can't be happening!"

The Pinto came to a halt on the opposite side of the road and blew up. Orange flames, black smoke, and searing heat reached the front seat. Slade Glick was pinned in the front seat by a long shank of steel rammed forward by the crash. It had missed Jamie's shoulder by inches. Scrambling as fast as he could, Jamie unlatched the passenger car door and rolled out on the freezing pavement. Glancing back through the opened door, he saw Glick screaming in agonizing pain as he was being fried to a crisp. Jamie crawled toward an exit ramp and after twenty yards, fell flat on his face, and passed out.

Several cars skidded into the stretch limo, ricocheting off the flaming wreck. Drivers and their passengers began exiting their crippled vehicles. They assembled on the pavement and watched in bewilderment the horrible scene unfolding in front of them. Soon, the eerie sound of sirens could be heard off in the distance.

"How are you feeling now?" an EMT with the fire department asked a dazed Jamie. "You were suffering from shock when we arrived, but it appears you escaped the accident with only second-degree burns on the left arm."

"How long have I been unconscious? How's… Did—"

"I am so sorry. Your friend didn't make it."

"Where's the asshole who hit us?"

"He's over there being questioned by the cops," the EMT said, pointing back twenty yards. "We're going to take you to the hospital and have you checked more thoroughly. The police sergeant told me they'd meet us in the emergency room and get a statement from you. Your jacket is scorched. Let's wrap a blanket around you and get moving. Traffic is backed up three or four miles."

"Thanks for your help," Jamie said. "I'm out of here."

"Hey, wait a minute. You need medical attention."

"I'm a tough guy. It'll heal on its own."

"Sir, these burns get infected if left untreated. You could lose an arm."

"So be it. I'll take my chances."

Jamie didn't acknowledge the somber warning and walked up the embankment to flee the inferno below. His head began playing games with him. Two hundred yards from the blazing accident, he gazed back and laughed out loud, mouthing the words, "Ah shucks, I could'a made some yummy S'mores, if only I had my bag of Marshmallows."

He took off the ruined jacket and tossed it in a garbage can when he neared Calumet Avenue. He ripped the shirt sleeve off his right arm, snapped an eight-inch icicle off the underside of a projecting roof, and wrapped the ice tightly around the damaged site. Every nerve in the bad arm that wasn't damaged by the burn sent a shivering pain up his shoulder. As a cab swung around the corner, Jamie flagged it down. He ordered the driver to drop him off at a Walgreen's two blocks from Glick's condo.

"How can I help you?" the pharmacist asked.

"Thanks, but I can find what I need."

He bought a roll of gauze and medicinal ointment for burn treatment. Knowing he'd develop permanent scarring didn't faze him. One additional ugly blotch on his body wasn't going to matter to him or anyone else as far as he was concerned. He was a warrior. They live for the moment. Death always awaits men in arms.

The fickle falling snow had turned heavier and even wetter as he slipped repeatedly on the walk to Slade's condo. A seedy street person slowed him and asked for money to buy a cup of coffee. Jamie spurned the request with a "screw you, buddy" scorn on his face. A young woman walking toward him noticed the arm and stopped him.

"Sir, let me look at that arm. I'm a nurse."

"I'm also a medic, and I'll treat the arm when I get home. Thanks for your offer."

He knew he had to get back to Glick's place and fetch his parked car before the cops arrived. He had planned to kill that monstrous snake and complete the elimination package, but he reconsidered.

Let the slimy devil deal with the loss of his murdering master.

Kat's vicious falcon and Pierre's ugly dog were left to embark on their own destiny after they lost their beloved owners. This situation with the serpent was different. He hated snakes with a passion, having a scare with a boa constrictor during jungle training in Panama years ago.

Jamie climbed into his car, treated the burn scorch marks on his arm, and drove off. As he turned the corner, he glanced at the rear-view window and saw a squad car. It was pulling up in front of Glick's condo. His brain was still in overdrive.

Fate has a funny way of correcting the inequities of life. The Pinto held true to form and didn't disappoint. But I was cheated, denied the pleasure of sending an evil man to plead a lost case with his maker.

His arm hurt like hell as the throbbing pain continued, but he refused to take notice of the discomfort. He was a glorious warrior and protector of mankind but wasn't immune to the nagging after-effects of his violent actions…trauma…pain…depression. He took several deep breaths, turned on his GPS, and found his way to the Stevenson Expressway. Chicago was history. Next up, San Antonio.

CHAPTER 38

SAN ANTONIO

New Year's Eve, 2012

THROUGHOUT THE ENTIRE LENGTH OF ILLINOIS, he constantly rehashed his relationship with Maria Serrano.

Maybe I screwed up, he thought. *I should call her and apologize. I can't go on like this. She deserves better.*

The call was brief, mostly a one-way conversation. He shared his weird dream of the other night and assured her he'd been faithful from the day they began going steady. He told her he'd make it up to her when they got to Hawaii. He thought for a moment that her icy voice began to thaw by the time he hung up.

He couldn't wait to see her again and present the Christmas present he purchased in Paris. He was amazed at the cost of a 24-carat gold cross and necklace. He didn't care. She was his special lady. *I'm engaged to her now, and maybe, just maybe, we'll get hitched real soon. She always talks about having children. I think it's time to make the total commitment. Maybe even next week when we're in Hawaii for Cyclops's wedding.*

After staying overnight in a cheap interstate motel, he got up refreshed and anxious to motor home. Ten miles south of Dallas, he got a speeding ticket. He didn't realize he was pushing ninety when the state trooper signaled him to pull over. Jamie showed him his worn out military ID card trying to soften him up. The cop shared that he was a former Navy SEAL and backed off when Jamie told him about Cyclops and their foray in Somalia. He was relieved that the trunk wasn't searched, or he'd have an awful lot of explaining to do. The trooper had heard about Sweeny's reputation. He sped off with only a warning.

Jamie decided to go straight home when he got to San Antonio. If it wasn't too late, he'd call Maria and have her join up with him. On second thought, she knew he wouldn't be back for a few days. More than likely, she motored up to Killeen and the Fort Hood area to be with her father and cousins. *I'm sure she had a fun time briefing them about our engagement to be married. Maria had told him the family always gathered for a big Christmas shindig and even a bigger New Year's Day watching the bowl games.*

It was dark out by the time he walked through his front door. The house smelled stale. He tossed his suitcase on the couch and elected to leave his other gear in the car trunk overnight. He was glad he didn't have to clean his pistol. He loved to fire the weapon but hated the maintenance such a valuable piece of human destruction demanded of the user. He went to the fridge and opened a can of Bud. Maria was not home when he called her, so he left a message that he had arrived home and was eager to be with her. If she was out of town, he hoped she'd retrieve her messages. Maria was slow to embrace new technology and hated smart phones even though she owned one but seldom used it.

Killing time hoping for a return call from her, Jamie decided to check out the home's sophisticated monitoring system he was proud of. His insurance agent had advised him to set up a simple intrusion device based on his frequent travel and crime in the area. He was able to locate a retired communications sergeant to help install the equipment. The soldier thought it was a bit extravagant and "outside the box" for peacetime surveillance. Nobody in their right mind would imagine what steps he took to protect his interests. Even Maria was left in the dark about it. He slipped the film out of the cameras that were secretly installed in five ceiling vents throughout the house. Three cameras mounted on trees surveyed the outer premises but he decided to wait until morning to view them.

He was getting groggy and about to fall asleep after checking out four of the inside films. The living room film was the final one before he crawled into bed. Yawning and rubbing his tired eyes, he inserted the film. After watching the first few minutes, he nearly fell off the chair. He couldn't believe the scenes that were unfolding.

"Jesus Christ!" he shouted. "It can't be."

Sprawled out on the rug, Bobby was screwing a half-clothed Maria Serrano. Jamie was beyond shocked, hyperventilating profusely, battling dizziness, and almost fainted from the restricted flow of oxygen. His heart was pounding like a jackhammer ready to blast through his rib cage. Finally gaining a measure of control, he envisioned numerous ways to kill both of the no-good bastards. He sprang off the chair and punched a hole in the wall.

He saw them sipping champagne, heard them laughing at each other's jokes and suggesting new positions for the next marathon. It was obvious to him they were stoned beyond belief. After they had returned from San Francisco, he knew Bobby had been experiencing with the drug Ecstasy. When Bobby referred to molly, he wasn't referring to the chimp on the farm but a crystalline form of higher purity. He remembered Bobby telling him not to worry because the sensual overtones of the recreational drug were somewhat like marijuana and not addictive.

His home phone boomed a hissing ring like an incoming mortar round. It was Maria. She sounded excited. "I got your message, Jamie. I'm so happy you're home. I can't get over there right now but will fix you breakfast in the morning. Is that okay with you?"

"Where are you now? It's midnight." He demanded an answer, and it had better be good.

"Um, in Killeen." She hesitated a moment. "You knew I would be celebrating the end of the year with my father and cousins."

"Is that right?"

"Of course, Jamie. Why in the world would you doubt me?"

"Sorry, it's late. It's been a long day, and I'm dead tired," he said without emotion. "I didn't expect to hear from you. See you tomorrow for breakfast." He slammed the phone against the wall two feet above the hole and then set it back in the cradle.

He decided to call his former best friend, Bobby. He didn't care what time it was. He wanted answers and wanted them right now. Bobby better be home celebrating the arrival of a new year. The phone rang several times before the call was answered.

"Welcome home, Jamie. I'd talk to you in more detail, but I'm drunk as a skunnnnk. Hey, good buddy, you won't believe it, but I got the hottest chick in town snuggled up next to me. You may remember her from…ah… Reunion. That gorgeous island in the Indian Ocean. Call me tomorrow, and we'll get together. By the way, I trust your trip was successful. I suppose you want to collect the million bucks we offered you to get rid of our…freaks of nature. Well, the blood money payoff will have to wait until next week. Ta-ta."

Jamie didn't respond and threw the phone against the kitchen wall, shattering it into dozens of pieces. He was certain the hot chick Bobby referred to was his very own fiancée. He elected not to pursue it on the phone. As difficult as it was, he maintained his cool until Bobby hung up and then went ballistic. He needed to think of a way to arrange the demise of both Bobby Biel and Maria Serrano. He didn't give a shit. It would be like planning another punitive raid on two enemies of the state. All the cards had been spread out on the table, and so far, he was the big loser!

AS THE PLANE FLAPS DROPPED OUT FOR LANDING AT HONOLULU INTERNATIONAL, Maria grabbed his arm and held on for fear the jet was ditching the runway. The sudden appearance of strong cross winds challenged the pilots, but they guided the plane expertly to the gate. Deplaning they were greeted by several young and pretty locals wearing the traditional hula getup placing leis around the necks of each incoming passenger. Jamie loved the aroma of plumeria. He recalled the night in Chicago when Leah Malaka tried to seduce him.

The Polynesian beauty was wearing a plumeria-scented perfume that almost caused me to cave but I held out, held out for this cheater sitting next to me. I can't stand her. I hate her. Retaliation is looming. The clock is ticking. It's time for me to stop playing the part of the happy-go-lucky fiancé.

"This place is so beautiful, Jamie. Maybe we should consider getting married here. What do you think?"

"I think we just got off the plane and haven't seen anything in Oahu but this crowded airport. We have five days to take it all in. Let's not rush. We have plenty of time to broach your idea."

"My, my, you are a bit edgy."

They hailed a taxi and arrived at the Hilton Hawaiian Village at the same time three uniformed Navy men were congregating out in front. Jamie assumed they were here for Cyclops's wedding. He liked the location of the hotel on Waikiki, not too far from the Hale Koa Hotel, the Armed Forces Recreation Center resort hotel. He stayed there years ago when he was on active duty and awaiting orders for further deployment.

"Good afternoon, gentlemen. Are you guys with the Denis Sweeny wedding party?"

"Who?" one of them asked.

"My friend who is getting married."

"Nope, we are here on leave. We're gonna have a ball."

They checked into the suite that was reserved in their name and unpacked. Jamie wasn't sure what the dress code was for the event. In his seething state of mind lasting several days before their departure, he forgot to call Dennis and confirm what to wear for the ceremony. Maria brought a leisure outfit and a more formal dress just in case. He didn't have to wait long for the answer.

"Hey, Army man, I was informed that you just checked in."

"For the love of Christ, you CIA sleuths leave nothing to chance, Sweeny."

"You got that right. I'm sending up a bottle of champagne for you two lovebirds. Can't wait to meet her."

"You'll get your chance soon enough. By the way, what do I have to wear tomorrow for the ceremony? Being your best man, I brought along my camouflaged desert fatigues and combat boots. Will that work?"

"I figured as much, Richards, but we are going up one more rung on the formality ladder. Go buy one of those flowery guayaberas, and you'll fit in nicely. I don't want all my male attendants to be color-coded. We're all wearing something different except me. I'm going all white, Richards, purity exemplified. You would be just fine in black. It suits you well."

"What a crock of you-know-what. When do I get to see God's gift to you?"

"At the ceremony and not a minute before then. I don't want her to gander at your beautiful face and check out your sleek body and change her mind about me. She thinks she remembers what you look like. You know me by now. This big guy doesn't like to take chances."

"Are we going to have a walk-through tonight or whatever they call the practice before the main event?"

"We're military. Don't need to waste good drinking time making believe. I'm tied up with some official government business tonight, so won't see you until tomorrow. Just show up, and we'll get it done."

"Before you hang up, refresh my memory. When and where?"

"What the hell, Richards. You want me to send you a fucking strip map?"

"Nah, I can process the info without one. Remember all the terrain I memorized for our Somalia raid?"

"No, did a brain dump on that fiasco. Tomorrow afternoon, three bells, wedding chapel on the inland slope of Diamondhead about half-way to the top. Adequate signage so you won't get lost. It's a fifteen minute cab ride from where we're staying. Don't be late."

Maria wanted to tour the downtown area, which was a huge mistake. Crowds of tourists bucked their way through the casual sidewalk strollers like the running of the bulls in Pamplona. Jamie suggested they stop at the International Center to see Don Ho if he wasn't already sipping a Mai Tai in heaven. She was game but wanted to hire a taxi and check out the pineapple fields. He told her they would do the touring after the wedding. She was upset that night when he fell asleep on the divan. She woke him several times, but he told her to go to bed. She wouldn't talk to him the next morning which was okay with him.

The wedding ceremony was short but beautiful. Cyclops cried through his one good eye when he said "I do" and exchanged rings. The bride had a difficult time slipping his ring over the enlarged knuckle. Jamie was sure it had been broken on at least five occasions that he was aware of. A brief reception was held on the grounds of the wedding chapel overlooking the calm Pacific Ocean and pearly white beaches. Jamie opted out, claiming his stomach was bothering him. Maria stayed and mixed effortlessly with three young sailors crashing the party.

The next morning, he tried to wake her up, but she complained of a headache and rolled over. He got dressed, fixed coffee, and chomped down a stale bagel left over from yesterday. An hour later, she joined him, still in her pajamas. She declined to eat the scrambled eggs room service had delivered, so he finished them off.

"I didn't hear you come in last night, Maria. I trust my good friend Cyclops and the wedding party took good care of you."

"Yes, I had a fun time but drank too much of the so-called Hawaiian punch. Are we going to tour now?"

"Slip on your bikini, grab your flip-flops, and we'll hit the beach first. The maître d' told me of a neat secluded spot on the other end of the island. He arranged for a rental car so we're all set." The maître d' also told him to be extra careful because sharks had been reported in that area. He withheld the warning from her.

I see no need to share that information with her. It would spook her. She worries enough about creatures of the sea. I don't want her to back out on me and demand to go shopping instead. This might be my only chance.

"I guess I can tour later. Maybe a swim in the salty Pacific will clear my head."

She went to the bathroom and changed while he made sure the pocket knife he bought yesterday was still tucked in his swimming trunks. A three-inch blade would suffice. The manager at the specialty knife store became irritated with him every time he told a young clerk to sharpen it more. The manager shot back at him questioning whether he wanted a sporting pocket knife or a surgical scalpel.

They drove to Waialua, parked, and walked the secluded beach past Dillingham Airfield until they found the spot the maître d' had suggested. At least, Jamie thought it was the spot. They tossed their beach towels on the sand, and she was the first to tiptoe across the cool sand to the rolling but gentle waves.

"Last one in is a dirty coward!" she yelled back at him.

He was busy scanning the waters out in front of her. Three hundred yards beyond, he spotted them. He knew their fins were often confused with those of the playful dolphins. He knew better. He was trained by the Navy SEALS to know better. His life depended on it.

Dolphins track the water differently than sharks. Those were genuine gleaming shark fins out ahead of her.

"Slow down!" he shouted. "This coward is hauling ass to catch up with you."

She didn't hear him. A five-foot wave had consumed her. Stroking his arms and legs with Olympic speed, he caught up to her in deeper water. He didn't know she was also a great swimmer.

"This is so scintillating, Jamie! I love it."

"Does it make you feel better now?"

"Yes."

"Is your head cleared up?"

"Yes."

"Are you thinking about Bobby and wishing he were here instead of me?"

She was shocked. "What do you mean by that comment?"

He didn't answer her. Instead, he dug the knife out of the swimming trunk pocket, flipped open the blade, and waved it in front of her eyes. She reversed her direction and started back toward shore.

"I'm going to cut you up and feed you to the hungry sharks that are starting to circle us. You haven't noticed them. Too busy thinking about surfing the waves with Bobby?"

"Jamie, no... No, don't do it!" Her sob turned into an eerie scream. She stopped swimming away from him and began treading water next to him. Her arm shot out to grab the knife. He pulled it sharply away, severing her ring finger. It fell into the water and swirled the dripping blood away from them.

"Scream and holler all you want, you unfaithful bitch. The beach is secluded."

"No, Jamie. I can explain everything."

"Shut the fuck up. You can justify your case to the devil when you meet up with him."

He began a practiced surgical debridement process that took off her cheeks, her breasts, and the top skin of both hands. He felt that would drain enough blood out of her body for the sharks to smell even at their distance. She passed out and began sinking. He grabbed her by the hair, spun her around, and sliced her belly wide open spilling links of slimy intestines. Intermittent waves of muscular contractions caused the bowels to resemble a snake wiggling to the surface of the water.

Jamie was well-schooled. He was taught that sharks have keen olfactory senses, and some species can detect one part per million of blood in seawater. Hammerheads with their widely-spaced nostrils are especially sensitive. At the same time, he doubted these sharks were of that species. He also knew sharks were more attracted to the chemicals found in the intestines. They should make quick work of her. He simply admired these predators sitting at the top of the underwater food chain. *They remind me of Jamie Richards, the blood-licking killer. When they catch up to me and inject the death-induced poisons in my veins, I want to reincarnate as a great white.*

When he saw a group of fins streaking toward her mutilated body, he began to sing: ♪♪"Tiny red bubbles...in the brine...make me feel happy...make me feel fine.♪♪" He swam as fast as possible back to shore. Exhausted, he pulled his body out of the water, strode to secure the beach towels, her clothing, and then walked away. He never looked back at the churning waters behind him. She was history.

Before he reached the car, he spotted a large metal barrel overflowing with beer cans, paper plates, and other trash. He retrieved a book of matches from the car. He was in the habit of carrying an emergency supply of matches on all of his operations. He lit a fire, and soon the burning, foul-smelling refuse spiked orange and red flames.

He slipped the knife out of his swimming trunks, opened the blade, and stared at it. He wanted to examine his favorite instrument of death one more time before disposing of it. A quick caress of the sharp blade with his tongue caused a small gash.

"Ouch! Ouch, you mother—" He loved the taste of blood but never his own.

Looking around the beach area to ensure his isolation from any frolicking beachgoers, he tossed the towels, her clothing, and the knife into the burning container. Satisfied that there was no damaging evidence left behind, he crawled into the car and took off. He drove past several pineapple fields on his return to the hotel, even paused at one to reflect on his good fortune. She was history; the dope-head Bobby Biel was next.

CHAPTER 39

TEXAS

HE DIDN'T GET THE OPPORTUNITY to visit with Denis Sweeny before the Cyclops flew off on official business. However, he did have a chance to catch up with the new bride in the hotel lounge. She was surrounded by well-wishers when she caught sight of him and broke free to join him at the end of the bar.

"Denis thinks the world of you, Jamie. We are both so happy you could help *officiate* our holy union. He wanted to chat with you before leaving, but the boss told him he was already late for an important planning session."

"And you didn't have to accompany him?"

"No, I resigned from the CIA."

"Why?"

"I'm four months pregnant, and we want to start a big family. He wants at least six. I'll settle for three. You knew he came from a big family."

"Yes, I know the Irish. Congratulations."

"Where's Maria?"

"She received an urgent call from home that her mother had a heart attack, so she flew home early this morning. Maria is an only child and needs to be there to support her father."

"I'm sorry to hear that. When are you heading out?"

"Tomorrow morning. I need one more day in paradise before I head home for my final mission."

"Which is?"

"Sorry, I'd have to kill you if I told you." He laughed and ordered two Mai Tais.

"Thank you for the drink. I'll bet you didn't know that the words *Mai Tai* come from the Tahitian word meaning *good*. Everything that has happened here has been very good, Jamie."

"I'm in full agreement," he said with a wicked smile.

They visited with each other for an hour. She told him she had to meet with a group for dinner. He wished her well and went up to his room to pack. He collected Maria's clothing, bagged it, and wrote "contaminated material" in big black letters on the outside of the bag. The hallway was empty, so Jamie walked to the maid's work room and tossed the bag in the garbage bin. He called for room service and began planning for his trip home. He decided to call Bobby and make sure he wasn't out of town.

"Hey, Jamie, how'd the big wedding go?"

"Without a hitch."

"I bet Maria wished you guys were also tying the knot."

Jamie didn't answer.

"When are you coming home?"

"Tomorrow, are you going to be in town?"

"I might drive down to the farm. Roberto called me yesterday, and he's having some problems with the chimps. I'm thinking of selling them while I can still get a good price."

"I want to go down there with you. Wait for me."

"Why?"

"I'll tell you when I get there." *I need to come up with a good reason.*

"Okay, waiting for you is second nature. Gar Underwood is coming to town next week. He asked me to arrange for you to be here. The three of us have to write the concluding chapter of our successful but harrowing experimentation."

"I'll call you when I get home."

Jamie played the mind game on the entire trip home, formulating different scenarios to kill Bobby. The opportunity to erase him on his farm might not happen. Furthermore, he'd have to kill Roberto, an action he would never consider. He could shoot Bobby, poison him, throw him in front of a speeding train, or throw him off the Tower of the Americas. Another option would be to hire the Los Zetas to kidnap him and toss him in the deepest, darkest hole in Mexico. He knew that Underwood also had to go.

I'll take special pleasure in doing them together, a so-called double play hit. Fucking scientist bastards! Jamie thought.

The flight was delayed at LAX due to mechanical problems which developed over the Pacific Ocean an hour out of Los Angeles. He didn't care if he had to stay overnight. He didn't have anybody to go home to. Maria had surfaced in his mind several times as he tried to sleep in the noisy hotel near the airport. He had to foresee contingencies such as friends asking where she was or why she didn't come home with him. People from work would call him because she listed his name and number as an alternate to contact in case of an emergency.

Too bad I never met any of her family, including her father and the mysterious cousin in Killeen. I question whether she really went up there. More than likely, she was squirreled away with the conniving turncoat. Biel, just a few miles down the road from my own home.

The last leg of the journey passed without a hitch. When he got home, he collected the films from his monitoring system and viewed them. Biel was in his house one night, apparently alone. *What the hell was he doing?* Jamie thought and decided to check his security closet and was relieved that the Bul M-5 and his Yarbrough were still on the shelf. He planned to use them very soon. Bobby didn't have the key to get in the house, but he was a genius, and given time, he would find a way.

What was he looking for?

The phone startled him. It was Gar Underwood.

"How'd you know I just walked in the door?"

"Bobby told me you should be home by now. How was the trip?"

"Long and tiring. I heard you'll be in town next week."

"I'm coming sooner. I need a complete debriefing on your Chicago mission. The *Chicago Tribune* covered the sixteen-car pileup and the blazing demise of the shitty Pinto. The paper mentioned that the driver died in the spectacular crash. I couldn't confirm from what I read that the driver was in fact our own Slade Glick. We need confirmation before we move forward to pay you the million we owe you. Will you take care of it before I come to San Antonio?"

"And how do you suggest I do that?"

Underwood didn't have an answer. Jamie was hot, ready to kill the prick with his bare hands if he walked in through the front door right now.

"I was in the same car with Glick and jumped out just in time before I got baked. My left arm is atrophied from the burns I received. There is no way in the world he survived."

"The paper didn't mention a passenger. Find out for sure, Jamie."

He didn't believe it. *Didn't the EMS folks mention that they treated me? How could that piece of information slip through an inquisitive reporter's coverage of a newsworthy catastrophe? Is somebody trying to*

cover up the fact that a passenger in the burned-up car walked away from the scene? Is the Ford Motor Company involved? They suffered enough law suits throughout the years, and I'm sure their past headaches with the Pinto were buried deep in the company's archives. Are they sending a hit man to murder me?

"Jamie…Jamie are you still on the line?"

"Yes, I am. If you want confirmation of Slade Glick's death. Go find out for yourself." He slammed the new telephone down as hard as he could. This time, it didn't break into pieces. He resumed scanning the films but couldn't find an answer for Biel's unannounced visit to his house. He hated him even more and decided to call him but got preempted.

"Hey, Jamie, Bobby here. Underwood just called and said you're pissed. You need to take it easy. You're coming apart at the seams. Maybe that post-traumatic stress symptom is surfacing again."

"Screw you, Biel. You're clueless. Where are you now?"

"About ten miles away from my farmhouse. Roberto is waiting for me."

"I told you to wait for me. I'm driving down there." *Taking orders wasn't in the prick's DNA.*

"No, Jamie. I'll only be here a day or two. Roberto and I have a chore involving the chimps. We'll meet with Underwood when he gets to San Antonio."

"What were you doing in my house while I was in Hawaii?"

Bobby was caught off guard. "How'd you know?"

"My neighbor told me he thought that was your sorry ass sneaking in one night but decided not to call the cops."

"Maria had called me from the Hawaiian Hilton Hotel. She told me you were acting strange and were depressed. She was afraid that you might harm her for some strange reason," Bobby joked.

"It's not funny, Biel. Do you want to know the *strange reason?* You're a fucking Judas, and you betrayed me!"

"Whoa! That's a little high-handed. You asked me the reason I was in your house. Want me to tell you?"

"It better be damn good."

"Maria told me where you hid the extra key for your back door. She told me to check around your house for the expensive gold cross and necklace you brought back for her from France. She thought she had packed it for the Hawaii trip but couldn't find it in her belongings when she got there."

"And did you find it?"

"Yes, it was sitting on the dresser in your bedroom."

CHAPTER 40

SAN ANTONIO

T WO DAYS LATER, UNDERWOOD ARRIVED, and Bobby suggested they have the final wrap-up at Jamie's house. Underwood could sleep there because of the renovations in progress at Bobby's place. They all agreed. Jamie had the refrigerator stacked with six-packs of Samuel Adams. He also removed his weapons of choice from their hiding place and shoved them into a drawer in a table near the front door. He filled two syringes with the sleep serum he used on Kat Kurbell. He was prepared for their trip to the hell.

Bobby wanted to go out for a steak dinner, but Jamie insisted they order food in. He wanted them within reach at all times. Gar was in a good mood. He was able to verify Slade Glick's death by one telephone call to a friend who worked for the Chicago ME.

"You're off the hook now, Jamie. Case closed in Chicago."

"Was never on it, Underwood. Where's my dough?"

"We'll have your payoff ready for you tomorrow."

Jamie had devised a plan to kill both of them the next evening after dinner. He would craft a double murder of the two distraught lovers. The day after he had returned from his trip, he prepared supporting documentation in the form of older letters, bogus taped telephone conversations, and pictures of the two in bed. He had them made by a photographer acquaintance in the porno business. The shrewd magician had helped him in the past on two covert operations.

They were having coffee and donuts early the next morning when they heard a loud knock on the front door. Jamie wasn't expecting company. He opened the door and was greeted by two men in business suits. He didn't like the looks on their faces. They reeked of trouble.

"Are you Jamie Richards?" the shorter, bald-headed man asked.

"Yes. How can I help you?"

"You can call me Pinky. I'm a homicide detective from the San Francisco Police Department."

"What do you want with me?" Jamie demanded.

"You are under arrest for the brutal slaying of two women."

"Go to hell," Jamie stepped back and shouted. Pinky flipped open his wallet with the ID badge and shoved it in Jamie's face as they pushed into his house. "My partner here is with an elite state police task force from Honolulu, Hawaii. Please turn around to be cuffed. He will read your rights to you."

Underwood and Biel remained seated at the kitchen table. Gar stuffed the last chocolate donut into his mouth while Bobby drained his coffee cup. They were stymied by the police intrusion but didn't say a word. Jamie went ballistic after they snapped the cuffs in place, ranting and raving about his innocence.

"Hold on a minute, Officers. You got the wrong man. I didn't kill anybody. Please come meet my friends in the kitchen. They will vouch for my innocence."

He broke out in a cold sweat as they followed him. Jamie introduced the officers to his associates who were still spellbound. Leaving the two detectives standing and talking with Biel and Underwood, Jamie plopped down in a chair next to Bobby.

How in God's creation did they find out about Kat and Maria? There is no way they'll be able to support the arrest and conviction without any evidence. I'll play along and cooperate until my lawyer arrives to straighten this mess out.

Underwood couldn't contain himself any longer. "All right, Officers. Let's all reconvene to the living room, sit down, and relax. Then you can tell us why two detectives from different cities think Jamie committed these crimes." Jamie came out of the kitchen and sat on an easy chair across from the detectives.

"I agree with that. You have the right to know how we caught up with you," Pinky said without blinking, glued to Jamie's eyes. His detective partner was more cautious, not as willing to discuss the circumstances. "For many years, San Francisco and Honolulu law enforcement agencies have shared homicide information on a daily basis. You might say our cities are joined at the hip because of the Pacific Ocean."

"Jamie Richards, don't you utter a single word. Call your lawyer right now," Underwood urged. Biel was silent, a smirk growing on his unshaven face. Jamie reacted and called his lawyer.

"Can you at least fill us in on some of the facts before his attorney gets here," Bobby suggested out of curiosity, not out of concern.

"Okay. As I just mentioned, he should know how this all played out," Pinky said. "You'll have a hard time believing the story, but this is how it unfolded. A great white shark transmitted electronic signals to our precinct after eating parts of the body of a lady found floating under the Golden Gate Bridge. The shark reported that her name was Kat Kurbell and was thrown to her death by a certain Jamie Richards living in San Antonio."

"What the hell!" Jamie screamed. "Impossible!" He tried hard to wiggle the cuffs off. It would have been easier if they weren't clasped behind his back. He had done it before and escaped a "bogus" arrest by a French police officer many years ago.

The Hawaiian officer loosened up and decided to talk. He told the astonished men the same story. A great white off the waters of Waialua Beach devoured the head of a mutilated body. It transmitted her name as one Maria Serrano from San Antonio and made reference to the same Jamie Richards from the same city.

"No way!" Jamie turned white and began to cough and retch. Bobby stoically sat back in his chair, enjoying the tale being woven by the two cops. He was sorry that Maria had to die this way but felt she had deserved it, the two-timing bitch. It was Gar Underwood who stood up and took charge of the conversation.

"I have a good friend by the name of Zach Seltry who is a marine biologist in Florida. He did his PhD dissertation on the great white shark. He concentrated on its behavioral patterns as influenced by advanced brain cognation. I read it on a visit when we had some downtime in the Keys where he is stationed. I was dumbfounded by his conclusions."

"Tell us what he found while we wait for the counselor to show up," Pinky suggested. "Both of our departments are having a hard time sorting this all out."

Jamie was uncomfortable waiting for the lawyer to arrive. The cuffs weren't coming free no matter how hard he worked them. He was ten steps away from his trusted Bul M-5 handgun.

What the hell is holding him up? I hate to be handcuffed like an animal seized in a trap. I'm going out of my mind. I got to do something drastic real soon, manacles or not. Mutt and Jeff are comic cops. I'm not afraid of them. My military training in escape and evasion techniques will prevail.

"Zack found that great whites generally do not take humans because their digestive system is too slow to accommodate the human's high ratio of bone to muscle and fat," Gar said confidently as though he was lecturing to students in the classroom.

"What about the head and brain?" Bobby interjected. Underwood glanced at him and wondered why he decided to jump into the conversation.

"Aha, a different story," Underwood said. Both detectives were in awe at his knowledge of marine life and especially the dreaded shark.

"After dissecting the skull with those sharp teeth and eating the soft brain tissue, the great white assimilates the thought processes of that human. The shark is able to store the entire history in a protected sac located at the base of its dorsal fin."

"So how did they transmit this stored data to us?" Pinky asked.

"Sharks are thought to be more sensitive to electric fields than any other animal. The electric fields produced by oceanic currents influenced by the earth's magnetic field correlate with the electric fields that sharks are capable of sensing."

"All right, Professor Underwood, slow down," Bobby said. "He wants to know how they electronically transmit the information in their special dorsal sac to law enforcement. It's obvious these lawmen haven't figured that out yet."

"Not so fast," Pinky said with a frown. "We've brought in an expert from San Diego, and he's researching the subject jointly with a professor from the University of Hawaii. They should have arrived at a conclusion by now. Maybe we should hire your friend here as a consultant. He seems to have all the answers."

Underwood smiled at the suggestion. He was on a roll. "The information is bundled and transmitted through the dorsal fin which acts like a cell phone tower."

"You got to be kidding me," Pinky exclaimed.

"Please let me continue. A sensitized cartilage spike pushes up and out of the dorsal fin like a submarine periscope. A bundled knob of highly sensitive, thread-like magnetic cells at the tip is spun into motion. An ion thruster, a form of electro-magnetic propulsion then relays voice units through a series of sound impulses. That's it in a nutshell."

Bobby wasn't satisfied. "I'm not trying to dispute your facts here, but why is the information about the murders beamed directly to law enforcement? Why aren't other—"

Biel was interrupted by the loud squeal of car brakes through an opened window. Jamie's lawyer jumped out of the taxi and rushed through the front door interrupting the lecture. He demanded the detectives IDs and called both police departments to confirm their identity. The lawyer laughed and howled after Pinky summarized Garwood's shark thesis. He questioned whether they had enough hard facts at this point in the investigation to arrest Jamie. He decided to play along with them, needed the extra hourly charges to pay for his new sports car.

"Jamie, don't you say another word to these gentlemen. They have valid warrants to take you back to San Francisco. I'll catch a plane later today and meet up with everybody. I want to be there for the hearing."

His words to calm Jamie were an academic afterthought. His client was fuming, mumbling unintelligible words, and shaking out of control.

"It's time to leave," Pinky said. "As a courtesy, we're going downtown to brief the local police department before we take the accused to San Francisco."

"You should have done that before you barged in here and manhandled my client," the lawyer said defiantly. "I'll ride with you downtown."

The two law enforcement officers, Jamie, and his lawyer climbed into the big Lincoln Town car parked in his driveway. Jamie sat in the front passenger seat next to Pinky. His lawyer climbed in the back seat with the other detective. Bobby and Gar decided to follow them downtown and at least lend support to Jamie until they paraded him to the gallows. They followed on the tail of the Lincoln in Bobby's spanking pricy new Lexus convertible.

"What are you thinking about?" Underwood asked his fellow scientist.

"How unbelievable, you are in concocting the great white story. You need to save that one for your grandkids—that is, if you are lucky enough to have any."

Underwood laughed, and the thought of the pregnant Uriel Seltry hit him squarely between the eyes.

As the cars turned the corner, they simultaneously exploded. There was enough C-4, a plastic explosive used extensively by the military, strapped to the lower frame of each vehicle to level a three-story building. The debris, pieces of flesh and bone, car parts, and briefcases were thrown a hundred feet in the air in a fiery mass. The energy of the blast was so powerful, it took down part of one wall and a steel lighting structure at the adjacent Alamo Heights football stadium.

The Lincoln Town car came to rest on the ten-yard line of the football field. Sitting up front, Jamie escaped the main force of the blast which erupted through the back seat. He was knocked unconscious for a short time, but then he was able to crawl out of the blown-away front door. His entire body was numb, his eyesight blurred.

After a few seconds, he focused on his bleeding severed left arm stump sitting on the goal line. He wondered what happened to the handcuffs. They were missing. The rest of his shattered body was five yards into the diagonally chalk-striped end zone. The neatly trimmed grass was soaking up the last liter of his oxygen-starved blood. He began to slip in and out of a consciousness state. In his remaining seconds on earth, thoughts flashed through his mind about little decisions in his life that resulted in big consequences.

If I hadn't slept with that billeting office clerk at Fort Hood, I'd still be alive. And then, there was that geeky character I met as a freshman in high school. What if I didn't stop the burly football player from pounding on Bobby's defenseless body in the school corridor?

Uh-oh, who's that over on the sideline? Is that Louie with my football helmet propped on his head? Is that Rocky crushing my favorite leather football? And up there, sitting on the cross bar of the goal post, that's Stryker flapping his big wings waving good-bye to me. Oh no... No, far above the falcon in the light-blue sky is a silhouette of Father Lawrence. Thank God, he found her, or maybe she found him. He's holding Victoria in his right hand. Blest be Father, for I have sinned, my last confession was...

And soon, there was inky black and then nothing. Dark clouds came rolling in over the stadium. Huge raindrops fell on the lifeless body. A bolt of lightning came crashing through the clouds and struck the limp body. The amassed energy ball bounced the body up and down multiple times like a basketball point guard heading down court. At mid-field what was left of the bloody corpse came to rest on the artificial turf next to the decapitated head of Bobby Biel.

A big black Hummer H1 was parked a block away from the stadium with the windshield wipers waving frantically. Sitting comfortably in the front seat were Maria Serrano's father and her favorite cousin, a demolitions expert in the Army at Fort Hood. The cousin tossed a remote detonator into the backseat, a smile of relief growing on his face. Maria's father still had a death grip on the detonator that blew up the Lincoln.

"Justice is hereby served," the father yelled out in triumphant. He picked up his wooden cane with his other hand and rapped it several times on the dashboard. Freeing his hands, he swirled around and exchanged high fives with the cousin.

With a satisfied look beaming from his face, the cousin said, "I'm sure glad we packed both vehicles with our own military brand of controlled thunder and lightning. We couldn't take a chance on the slimy, no-good bastard being in the wrong car."

"Who were the characters in the Lexus?" the cousin asked.

"Matters not," the father sighed.

The mood suddenly changed in the Hummer. Silence prevailed. They glanced at each other for several seconds and then quietly began to cry.

STAGE FOUR

About the Author

John C. Payne was born in Chicago but moved to Wisconsin as a youth. He played football and basketball at a college prep Catholic high school in Marinette, WI.

He entered the US Army after completing an ROTC Program in college. During the Vietnam War, John served with units in Long Binh, Oui Nhon, and DaNang. He retired from the Army in 1980.

In his post-military career, he owned and successfully operated three small businesses: a retail fruit juice vending operation, a communications company, and a health care consulting group.

He loves to write and teach. John was an adjunct professor in business at several universities, and spent many years in the field of health care administration.

Like the main character of his _Three and Out_ trilogy, he loved to move and change jobs every three years, engaging in new, unrelated, and exciting challenges.

He holds a B.S. degree from St. Norbert College in DePere, WI, and a Masters in Public Health Administration from the University of Michigan, Ann Arbor, MI.

John is married with three adult children. He now resides permanently in San Antonio, Texas.

CPSIA information can be obtained
at www.ICGtesting.com
Printed in the USA
FFOW04n1221170414
4886FF